The Harvest

Book Three of the Seeds Trilogy

K. Makansi

Layla Dog Press
Saint Louis, MO

Published in the United States by Layla Dog Press
St. Louis, MO / Tucson, AZ

This is a work of fiction. Any resemblance to actual events or locales or persons, living or dead, is merely coincidental, and names, characters, places, and incidents are either the products of the author's imagination or are used fictitiously.

Visit our website at www.theseedstrilogy.com to learn more.
www.facebook.com/TheSeedsTrilogy
Twitter:
@readwritenow - Kristy
@akmakansi - Amira
@Elena_Makansi - Elena

Cover by K. Makansi & Kevin Wietzel

10 9 8 7 6 5 4 3 2 1

Library of Congress Control Number: 2016904048

ISBN: 978-0989867184

For our grandparents,

And for all those who resist oppression

and stand up for justice

The Harvest

Book Three of the Seeds Trilogy

PROLOGUE
KANAAN ALEXANDER

Prologue: Sector Annum 52

The arcing shadows of the steel framework bend around me. I cough, the sound muffled by the mask clasped over my mouth and nose. I duck under a torqued I-beam and into a pitch black room. The air dances and swirls, disturbed for the first time in centuries. Increasing the power on my biolight lenses illuminates the room in yellow-green. Dust clouds my vision, gathering like an angry storm.

"Find anything interesting?"

I cough again, clearing my throat, before I can get out my words. "Tell you when the Oklahoma Desert settles," I shout back. "You?"

"Papers," I hear from the adjacent room. "Nothing but papers. These people must have cut down enough trees to stack them to the moon and back." His voice is distorted through the haze of debris and ancient metal.

I scan the detritus of the Old World—destroyed furniture, ruined computers, electrical wires, rusted plumbing, crumbling walls—and yes, there, in the corner, bones. A skeleton. Lily-white and grinning, with a long shard of glass still embedded in the rib cage like a hunter's spear point. *Obvious cause of death*. I grin back.

"That looks painful, buddy," I mutter. "Let's hope I don't end up like you today."

I glance around, checking that there's no immediate danger, no wall about to collapse, nothing to crush or impale me like my newfound friend. But everything looks stable. For now.

As the dust settles, I get a better look at what the room contains. I had to slice the door open with my laser cutter, which made me think I might have finally hit pay dirt. To prevent looting or material destruction, most of these old research facilities had triggers to initiate shutdown sequences to secure valuable equipment and data in case of emergency. Of course, my new friend in the corner might have been saved if medics could have reached him—or was it a her? A stomach wound like that would have been easily treatable, especially with the kind of medicine they had back in those days. If those Old World corporations had cared more about their workers and less about their profits, my friend might not have ended up dying alone in a locked room in the first place. But then, judging by the destruction in the area, I'm guessing no one lived for long once the bombs started falling.

I click on a handheld biolight and pan the room, moving deeper into the dark, bumping up against the remains of an overturned table. I squint into the corner, and smile behind my mask. Jackpot. A graveyard. This is exactly why we're here.

We've stumbled on the kind of storage room where old lab equipment went to die, or at least was stored until disposed of. Without even picking through the junk, I can see a few thermal cyclers in various states of disarray, a line of centrifuges on a shelf still clinging to a wall that lists at a precarious angle, two large rotating hydroponics systems—mostly intact, although one is missing a large chunk of metal at the top. Best of all, there are several ancient spectrophotometers. The old sturdy ones, not too temperamental. And that's just what I'm seeing from a quick scan. I'm betting this equipment was already broken when the lights finally went out, but the Corporation won't care. Scavengers have already mined all the good stuff. These days, they'll pay for anything their engineers can fix up into something usable.

"We done here?" I hear my friend call.

"Not a chance," I holler back. "We hit gold, Gold."

I hear booted footsteps and heavy breathing behind me. I turn to see his grey-green eyes and black hair sticking out around the straps of his mask. He's taken the rest of his scavsuit off—including his goggles, I note with consternation—but at least he's got the sense to keep his boots, gloves, and mask on. His full name is Augustus Orleán, but most everyone calls him August. I just call him Gold, a reference to the shorthand for the element, *Au*.

I glare at him. "Keep your damn goggles on. You don't know what kind of toxins are—"

"I'm fine, aren't I?" he interjects as he saunters toward me, his voice deeper than usual and thick through the mask. The creases in his eyes belie the smile on his face. "I'm not blind yet."

"You'll be thanking the fates for that once you see what's in here."

Looking past me, his eyes go wide, taking in the wealth in front of us. He slaps me on the back.

"You weren't joking, K. This is *serious money*. If we can get this to the Corporation without getting bushwhacked, they'll finally load us up with enough seedcoins to set up our lab."

"That's a big if."

He laughs. "Always the pessimist."

"I prefer 'practical'."

"Then get your practical ass to work harvesting this tech."

Gold pulls his goggles back down, recognizing that we have no idea what kinds of poisons could be in the equipment we're handling, or in the debris around us. We sort through the rubble, separating obvious trash from things that could have value. Much of the equipment is broken but reparable, and if not, the pieces inside are salvageable. Even things that are broken beyond a hope of reuse can teach us about the Old World.

An hour later, the room no longer looks like a tornado touched down. Everything has been arranged in neat piles based on potential return, and Gold starts browsing through them.

"Check this out," I hold a thin strip of metal and tap it in my hand. Gold looks up at me. "A backup drive. I found it in his palm." I point to our skeleton friend. "Like he held on to it right to the bitter end."

Truthfully, I found it on the ground at his feet, but I've never considered myself above a little creative license, especially not when it makes the story so much better.

"Intact?" Gold inquires, his eyes wide.

I shrug. "We'll see. Want to load it, find out what they were doing here?"

Gold and I have been scavenging in and around what used to be New York City for the better part of the last three years. Most of what was Manhattan is flooded, of course, and we don't have the resources to do a lot of underwater work. Besides, anything we found down there would be corrupted beyond repair. So we work on the outskirts. There were plenty of major companies set up in a ring around the city, too, and we've hit a fair few of them in the last few years. We're trying to get enough funds from the Okarian Agricultural Corporation to set up our own research lab, but in order to do that, we have to bring them equipment. That's how they trade. We provide them with technology, information, or hardware, and they return the favor with seedcoins. With seeds, we can buy what we need to set up our own lab.

We came here on a rumor from one of the other scav teams that there was a big biotech organization headquartered south of the city. Of course, Gold had to put a knife to a man's throat to get him to tell us the rumor, but that's just the nature of scavenging these days. Based on what we've found so far, he wasn't wrong, but the research facilities aren't here. We were expecting a wealth of lab equipment, but instead we've found nothing but basic computers, servers, and papers. Until we hit this room, we thought we'd wasted a week of trekking on a wild goose chase and Gold had been threatening to skin the man who led us here in the first place.

"Go ahead and load it up," Gold says. "Find out what these lunatics were working on all those years ago."

"If it's even readable," I mutter. "It's probably corrupted. And if not, it could be encrypted." I pull my plasma from my pack and set it within range of our UMIT. I drop the backup drive on top and wait for the data transfer to begin. After a few seconds, my plasma flashes green.

"It's readable." Gold stops what he's doing to look over my shoulder. We watch as lines of code flash across the screen.

"I don't even recognize that language," Gold says.

"No wonder. It's gotta be at least two hundred years old."

But whether we recognize it or not, my plasma seems to be able to read it, because in a matter of minutes the file is loaded. A prompt appears, asking if I want to open it.

"Yes," I respond.

A warning flashes across the screen.

The data type in this file is not approved by the Okarian Agricultural Corporation. Please do not continue.

I glance at Gold, who gives me a slight nod, waggling his eyebrows.

"Override," I say. "Open the file."

The file opens, and a database appears before us.

Abiu, the first entry reads. *Açai, Acerola, Alfalfa, Almond, Amaranth, Apricot, Apple.*

The list goes on.

"What is this?" Gold whispers.

I touch my finger to the screen, landing on one of the names. *Amaranth.*

My screen divides into columns, and different incarnations of the same thing appear. A three-dimensional, rotational model of a double-helix strand; a long-form notation of the base pairs in the double-helix; and a computational model showing genetic variants within the genome.

"It's a genome," he says quietly, answering his own question. "What the hell is amaranth?"

"It's a grain."

"How do you know?"

"I like to eat things other than bread and meat occasionally. You'd never heard of corn before I made you eat some."

"Fair point." He's never been the most experimental with his food. Then again, it's only been the last ten years or so that we've had the luxury to be experimental. Before that, we ate what we had and were thankful we didn't go to bed hungry. "Go back to the overview."

The main list reappears. What *is* all this?

"Do you recognize these words?" Gold asks.

"Some of them."

"Sure. Some are easy. Apple. Apricot. Barley. But what's this one?" He points to a strange word on the screen. *Avocado.*

"Never heard of it. Have you?"

He shakes his head. "Is all this *food*?"

I shrug. "All the names I recognize are food crops. I sure as hell would like to know what the rest of them taste like."

"Do you know how much we could get for this database?" He stops looking at the plasma and stares at me with that maniacal look he always gets when he's got an idea. Eighty percent of his ideas are crap. Fifteen are straight from the looney bin. But five percent are bloody genius, and that's why he and I are partners. When I glance up, meeting his eyes, I can almost see his mind spinning, eagerly calculating how many seeds we could make by selling this information to the OAC. "How much they would pay for this?"

"Why would we—"

"Look at the size of that file! What if it's the genetic codes to every food crop ever sequenced in the Old World? You said your dead friend over there was gripping it in his palm. It has to be valuable! By all that's sacred, we'd get seats on the Board of Directors just for showing this to them."

My heart pounds, blood rushing in my ears, and I don't know why. "What do you think they would do with it?"

"Who cares what they'd do with it? We could have everything we ever wanted, K." His eyes light up. "The premiere lab in Okaria. The finest facilities in the Sector. We can finally fund our research."

"But—" I sputter. Turning all this over to the OAC gives me a bad feeling, but I can't put my finger on why. "Their whole goal is to streamline food production. They don't need the genetic codes to Old World crops. They've modified and created their own. Who's to say they wouldn't destroy this as soon as we handed it over? Or lock it up and throw away the key?"

"Who cares?" he asks, staring at me as though I've lost my mind.

"Who cares?" I repeat, disbelief leaching into my voice. "Gold, think about it. If this database really does have the genetic codes to every Old World food crop ever sequenced, we wouldn't *need* the OAC for seeds anymore. We could sequence our own." We wouldn't ever need their seedcoins again. Their money would be worthless to us. We could print our own money, our own food, our own crops. Think of the possibilities!"

"If we don't tell them everything we've found, we'll be violating the terms of our contract. Our agreement would be void. They wouldn't owe us anything."

If he's thinking about the legalities, he's almost there. He wants to do it. He's almost on my side.

"Gold, you're thinking about it wrong. It's not about what they owe us. It's about what we owe them. And the answer is: *nothing*. Ever again."

A slow smile spreads across his face.

"Kanaan Alexander, my friend, you are finally learning to think like a revolutionary."

The Harvest

by Gabriel Alexander
Poet Laureate, Okarian Sector

Honeyed light sings across my back
In the garden with loving hands
A pomegranate
A bow across a string.

She stands, palms open
Listen,
Pale green tendrils unfurl
Lemons hang from trees like raindrops
Wheat stalks bend in whirls of sun.

Arise, arise!
The world is alight
Morning dawns and seasons change
We gather, we harvest
For it is more painful to remain in the bud
Than to chance blossom

Just as the mighty oak awaits in the acorn
The butterfly in its chrysalis
And the bird in its egg.

We fall in love
As she blooms
And resurrects us.

1 — REMY

Spring 60, Sector Annum 106, 19h30
Gregorian Calendar: May 18

Shadow.

That's what I think when I catch my reflection in a window, startled for a moment by the fleeting apparition of someone following me, someone who looks vaguely familiar. After a second's hesitation, I recognize myself. Six weeks after Vale's fall, and I am still hiding, slinking through the underground veins of Okaria. I haunt the arteries of the city, spending my days in the sewers, back alleys, and smoke dens. At the Academy, my architecture professors waxed poetic about the beauty of our capital: *Think of our city as a living being. A complex ecosystem, a body, pulsing and alive.* But our study was limited to the gilded exterior, the glittering skins of biomimicking buildings and lush gardens. We chose not to examine the blood and bones within. There was no reason for me then, as an aspiring professional, to make friends with shadows. But now I have become one.

I pull my hood up and climb the stairs. I bump into someone and mutter an apology. At the top, on the seventh floor, I tap-tap-tap on the door at the end of the hall. Footsteps shuffle inside. The door swings wide and I'm ushered in. It's all very efficient. The apartment is compact, clean, spare. Moonlight spills through a lone window, and the only sign of habitation is a uniform and shoes folded neatly on the bed.

Meera works on the plumbing and irrigation systems for the capitol building, where Soren and I were held captive, where Vale and Chan-Yu used to work. It's a good position for an Outsider. Not high enough in rank to draw attention to herself, but she's well-poised to pick up knowledge and information from around the city. Not to mention she can get from one side of Okaria to the other faster than anyone I've ever met. She claims she knows the sewer systems better than she knows the streets. I don't doubt her.

She opens a box on the table and begins taking out items. "Five apples, a pound of smoked elk, root vegetables, various greens. Should last a week if you're careful."

"You're a lifesaver," I say, grabbing one of the apples and wiping it on my shirt. I haven't eaten in over twenty-four hours. If I tried to buy food from a restaurant or street vendor, my biomarkers would identify me, and without a manufactured identity to replace my old one in the Personhood database, the authorities would immediately be notified. After Corine Orleán promised to publicly execute me if they ever catch me, I'd rather go hungry than risk identification. Meera is keeping me alive.

"Any news?" I ask through a mouthful of apple.

She leans forward, a promising flush on her cheeks. "A meeting." Her eyes twinkle like she's presenting me with a precious gift.

I drag a sleeve across my face as juice dribbles down my chin. "With who?"

"A snake."

I arch an eyebrow at her. S¬he giggles. Meera is captivating, her smile contagious, her face open and honest. It's how she gets around the city as an Outsider. That, and her forged documents. Her wide-eyed innocence is capable of charming everyone she meets—and deceiving anyone who doesn't know her.

"Okay, it's a guy named Snake. But he slithers around the city," she waggles her hand through the air, "silent and deadly." She hisses aloud, as childlike as Osprey.

"I'm picturing a guy with bright green hair and fangs."

"Oh, Snake is definitely like that. Not the fangs, though. He hides in plain sight. Knows everyone, has contacts everywhere. I always go to him when I need information."

"Can he help me find Vale?"

"If anyone can, it's him. Tonight, thirty minutes after sunset, at The Elysium. Look for the waiter with purple hair—"

"Purple?"

"I told you, he hides in plain sight. Anyway, ask him for the green apple indica. It's off-menu and we use it as our code. It's also delicious."

Soon all that remains of my apple are seeds. I toss them in the box and grab another. This is not the first clandestine meeting Meera has arranged for me, but it's the first time she's sounded so hopeful.

After Vale's fall, when the drone whisked him away to the gods only know where, I stayed in the apartment Chan-Yu had arranged for us. *Damn the risks*, I told myself then. Corine's promise to execute me most likely meant she'd be looking for me out in the Wilds, or at the Resistance bases. As far as I could tell, no drones or Watchmen were able to ID me, even when Chan-Yu and I were chasing Jeremiah through the city streets. In a way, staying here is safer for me than heading back out with the Resistance. Like Meera's mysterious purple-haired Snake, I am hiding in plain sight.

I know it's dangerous to stay, but my instinct screams: *I can't leave Vale.* I have to find out what happened to him. Is he alive? Is he with his parents? What have they done to him? And by all that grows, what was he doing on that roof?

Chan-Yu, it turned out, had only paid for the shortest possible lease: two weeks. I spent three nights in the sewers after the rental term was up. That's when I met Meera. I'd taken to spending much of my time in the smoke dens—places I never knew existed—because it was so easy to blend in. Like everything else in Okaria, the dens are heavily regulated, but they've all taken on the personalities of their neighborhoods. With black walls, heavy floor-to-ceiling curtains, dirty velour booths, and small, blood red biolights at every table, Le Mouton Noir quickly became my favorite. It was close to the apartment we'd used, everything seemed to be covered in a thin film of grime, and most of the regulars worked in delivery, water recycling, composting, or bioluminescence, so I knew I was unlikely to run into any of my old friends. The smoke came cheap and plentiful, and escape was just a few puffs away. And the place was open twenty-four seven.

I thought I had changed my appearance enough to go unnoticed, but Meera recognized me right away. She'd been looking for me, she said.

She slid into my booth and offered me a pull from her water pipe. I rarely smoke, finding the atmosphere calming enough on its own. Plus, I was running out of seeds.

"My name's Meera," she said. "We should be friends."

I hesitated, trying not to look suspicious. "What makes you say that?"

Ignoring the question, she held her pipe out to me. "This is my favorite flavor. Tastes like black caps. I think you'll like it."

Black caps. That's how I knew. It's what Outsiders call wild blackberries and raspberries. They grow in great brambly bushes in parts of Outsider territory, and every tiny corpuscle tastes like a burst of heaven. Rhinehouse says the Sector's version, the ones they use in Mealpaks, have been so hybridized they hardly have any taste at all. I don't even remember eating them when I was younger.

"Black caps. Never heard of such a thing." I took a long drag, feeling the calm sink in, remembering how I used to love smoking with Eli, Jahnu, and Kenzie at Thermopylae. Meera leaned in, elbows on the table.

"Word on the street is we have friends in common," she said, looking me up and down. "You hungry?"

"Starving." Meera flashed her siren smile, and in the haze of the blackberry smoke, I couldn't help it. I smiled back.

"I can help you with that. Let's go to my apartment. I've got food to spare. We can catch up on how our mutual friends are doing."

I was hesitant at first, reluctant to trust anyone. But after weeks with no news of Vale, no word from Chan-Yu, Soren, Osprey, Miah, or anyone else in the Resistance, I'd finally found someone to talk to. Or rather, someone had found me. My mind foggy with hunger, loneliness, and desperation, I figured if Meera was a spy for the Sector, she'd lead me right to Corine. I was willing to take the risk.

My trust was well-founded. Meera fed me, gave me extra clothes, replenished my disguise makeup, and now she's going to let me move into her apartment.

"Everything is mostly cleaned out," Meera says, pulling a shirt up over her head to change clothes for work. "I won't be far, and I'll be by every few days with food."

"I hate to kick you out of your own place," I say, protesting for the thousandth time and trying not to stare at the scarred lines on her back. One time, I asked how she got her scar, but she just gave me a sly smile and said nothing.

"Remy, you're not kicking me out. This place is hardly big enough for two and besides, I'll be staying with a *very* close friend." She winks.

I think of Vale, the idea of staying with him someday in a warm house, with a proper kitchen, and a real bed. If we live long enough.

"If the meeting with Snake goes well, you'll have a better idea of where Vale is and how you can see him. I've got a good feeling about this."

"I can't thank you enough. For everything."

"If you ever need to run, there's a safe house on the outskirts of Okaria the Outsiders stay at sometimes. You might know about it." Her eyes twinkle. "It's your grandfather's house."

"Kanaan's?" I ask, wide-eyed. "Outsiders stay there?"

"On occasion. It's big, empty, comfortable. What more could we ask for?" She squeezes my hand and whispers, "We'll talk soon. Good luck."

It's still dark—the first hint of dawn is edging the horizon—when Meera leaves. I consider a nap, or a few minutes of quiet meditation, but opt for some of the smoked elk instead. It's early, and I haven't slept much tonight, but I'm antsy. Time is running out. How much longer can I stay in Okaria, pawning food from the Outsiders, hanging out in smoke dens, listening, watching, waiting?

I am not safe here. One wrong move and I'm done for. Phillip's goodwill was waning when Soren and I were captured, and I'm sure it's nonexistent now. If I'm caught again, the Sector will have no mercy, not after Round Barn, not after what I did to Evander.

I pull out my plasma and begin sketching. Where are my friends? Are they safe? How are Jahnu and Kenzie? Has Rhinehouse found an antivirus for Eli? Will I ever be able to see him again?

The sketch morphs into something grotesque. A disembodied mouth, open in a scream, bits of tongue flaking away like burnt paper.

Thirty minutes after sunset, I walk into The Elysium smoke den. Located deep in fashionable South Okaria, far away from the city center, The Elysium couldn't be more different from Le Mouton Noir. The lights are dim but luminous. Hundreds of tiny green biolights flicker along the walls. The glassware here is polished and fine, the smoke clean, the hookahs as elegant as the patrons. It's like I've entered a different dimension, as if I'm floating in the ocean amidst a sea of glowing plankton. There is an air of intense sensuality. Bodies lean into each other, lovers kiss in the corners, beautiful people sip colorful cocktails, and stained lips pull long drags of smoke from glass pipes. Low, throbbing music plays in the background and conversation is hushed and secretive.

As I pass, one woman gives me a long, inviting look, with a raised brow and full, red lips. She is captivating, to be sure, with long hair curling around her shoulders, wide hips and a small waist. For a moment, I envy her figure, her glamour, her confidence. She is a woman who knows who she is and what she wants.

I shake my head *no* and raise my hand to the back of my neck, a nervous gesture that has only gotten worse over the weeks. To avoid recognition, I cut my hair with one of Chan-Yu's knives, left in the apartment after we fled. No more thick, dark curls. Now, just an even tuft of close-cropped fuzz. When I went with Meera to her apartment that first time, she giggled and pulled out an electric razor, offering to shear my hair more evenly than the butcher's job I'd done with the knife. It looks better, but I'm still not used to it. I want my curls back. When I catch my reflection, my eyes seem too big, my neck too long, all my shapes slightly wrong.

But if I don't recognize myself, neither will anyone else.

I find a booth and cozy up to the corner, sitting with my back to the wall, scanning the space for a purple-haired man. I don't have to look hard. I notice him behind the bar, shaking a cocktail mixer. A few minutes later he appears at my table. I don't know what I expected: someone striking, maybe, someone really tall, or very good looking. But Snake is unassuming except for the hair, which sticks up every which way, with deep purple roots that taper into lavender. He has dark eyes, slightly upturned at the outer edges and shaded by long lashes, but there is nothing truly distinctive about them. His face, though not especially handsome, is trustworthy. Is it just because I want to trust him?

"Hello, mademoiselle. I'll be your server tonight. Would you like a drink, a smoke, or both?"

Does he know who I am? I look at him closely, scan the rest of the area quickly to make sure I'm dealing with the right purple-haired man. "I've heard good things about the green apple indica. That and a tonic, please."

Snake nods. "Good choice." There's a smile on his lips. He backs away, and my heart is pounding. *Can I trust this person?* I have to believe Meera, but I can't still the fearful thoughts running circles in my brain. A few moments later, he returns with my tonic and complimentary sugar squares.

"I'm off in five minutes," he says. "Thankfully, I make the schedules here. I'll bring the indica with me and we'll get to know one another."

When he slides into the booth beside me, it occurs to me that we must look like lovers. He sets the water pipe on the table, hands me the tonic water, and wraps an arm around my shoulders. For a moment I feel uncomfortable, but his gesture is reassuring, not sexual. He nods at the glass in front of me. I take a drink. Then he leans in and whispers in my ear.

"He's being held at the chancellor's estate. He's been there the whole time." *Of course.* It was the most likely place. I'd thought about trying to get near, to scope it out—I'd even daydreamed about mounting a rescue, all by myself, as stealthy as Chan-Yu and as deadly as Soren—but there was no safe way, no way to do it without risking more than I dared. "The chancellor's staff is carefully vetted," Snake continues. "Cooks, cleaners, butlers, plumbers. They're all interrogated, tracked, and monitored. You know the drill. Even then, very few were told of Vale's presence. One or two maids, the chancellor's Dietician, and a security guard."

"I'm not surprised—I suspected as much—but how did you find out?"

"One of the guards is a frequent patron of The Elysium. After several well-packed pipes and a few flirtatious gestures I got it out of him that security around the building had been tripled. After that, it was just a matter of asking the right people the right questions."

"What else do you know?"

"He's being treated as a hostage. Locked in his room day and night.

Guards at all points of entry around the house. No one except his parents, the chancellor's personal doctor, and a single chambermaid have been allowed to make contact with him. Far as we know, he hasn't been allowed outside at all."

I am crestfallen. How am I supposed to tell him I'm safe, I'm waiting for him, if he's being treated like a prisoner in his own home? I expected this, even feared worse. But it doesn't make it any easier.

Snake cocks his head at me.

"Why do you look so sad?"

"I need to get a message to him."

"Why does that make you sad?"

"Because it seems impossible."

"Says who, little lady? I was just getting to the part where I gallantly offer to take a message to your dearest Valerian, in exchange only for a simple favor."

I lean into him.

"Let's talk about the favor in a minute. How are you going to get a message to him?"

"I have friends in high places, Remy Alexander."

"Shhh!" I hiss, glancing around urgently as if Watchmen were about to materialize out of the walls and arrest me, and take me back to face General Aulion or Philip's electric shocks. "Don't say that out loud." Snake smirks at me. I glare at him. "Can you do it without putting anyone at risk?"

"Risk?" He raises his eyebrows, and I notice that they, too, are dyed a brilliant purple. "*Life* is risk. We risk our lives every day. Do you want me to get a message to him, or not?"

I take a deep breath. "Yes. What's your favor?"

"You haven't touched the indica. It's an Outsider specialty, I promise. Of course," he waves his hand at the crowd of luminous patrons, "*they* don't know that."

"What's your favor?" I ask again.

"I hear that Meera has some delightful strawberries this time of year. Bring me a dozen, and I'll make sure Vale gets your message."

I almost laugh out loud. "How about you send Vale the message, and I'll repay you with strawberries."

He narrows his eyes at me, and says in a lighthearted voice, "You drive a hard bargain, Sparrow." I had suggested Little Bird as my Outsider code, but Meera dubbed me Sparrow, and it stuck. Now, it's the only way I dare refer to myself in the city. "But I will accept your terms. Tell me, what message would you like to send?"

I reach for the water pipe in front of me. The pipe is green and blue semi-opaque glass. Meera said this marijuana has been flavored with a concentrated apple resin. The smoke is smooth, crisp, and very, very apple. The indica is heady and deep, sinking into my bones. I relax into the booth and look to the ceiling, illuminated with glowing green biolights. I imagine I'm underwater, drifting, that everything around me is safe and warm and comforting.

What is my message? What do I need to tell Vale? What am I doing here, hiding out in the dens of the city, surviving on smoke and secrets and the generosity of Outsiders?

I open my eyes and look at Snake. "Tell him I'm here. I'm waiting. Tell him, do not lose hope."

2 — VALE

A cup. Hands. Lips. Water on my tongue. "Drink." A soft command.

Light. Blue, purple, yellow: colors like a bruise. A flower—pain—blooms behind my eyelids.

Bones. Muscle. Fingers. More hands, not mine.

"Oh, darling." The voice angers me. Everything fades to white, and all emotions are forgotten. White on white on white.

Feathers don't float because they are weightless; they float because the force of air resistance is almost equivalent to the force of gravity. They are pulled to the ground slowly, drifting, buffeted by invisible currents in the air, pushed this way and that by powers wholly outside their control.

I am a feather. My whole life, I have been pushed and pulled. I have surrendered to ideas, wishes, and demands not my own. I am falling. I am not weightless. I will die when my body hits the ground. For the first time, I am not afraid.

"He'll wake up in a few moments. Brain activity is already spiking in the frontal lobe."

"Current mental state?"

"Difficult to read. Guilt is there. Sadness, too. Confusion, but that's normal in these situations."

"Fear?"

"None. No autonomic or endocrine changes. No spike in glucocorticoids from the adrenal cortex or catecholamines from the adrenal medulla or sympathetic nerves."

"Strange."

"It's not uncommon for those who come back from near-death experiences to lose the sense of fear they had before, General."

"Does he know I'm here?"

"Images associated with you have appeared on his dream scans. But we have no indication that he knows you've been present."

"Where is Madam Orleán?"

"I expect her any moment. She wants to be here when he wakes up."

"Moriana, are you with Corine?" I ask. I don't recognize my own voice. It sounds different. Stronger. I already know what the answer is, and what I have to do.

"Vale, is that you?" Her voice comes out as a sob. I wince at the sound. Her pain is harder to bear than my own fear. I key in a set of final instructions to Demeter.

Relay all information about the virus targeting Elijah Tawfiq to the Resistance base. Instruct headquarters to send a rescue group for the Resistance squad currently in the capital.

Demeter: Vale.

Vale: What?

Demeter: The Resistance base has been destroyed. Corine Orleán's C-Link just disseminated this information to the entire C-Link network.

Vale: It's a lie.

Demeter: It's not. They have aerial photographs of the destruction. It was carried out entirely via drone and airship assault.

Vale: Survivors?

Demeter: None.

My heart thuds to a stop. I have only one thought. Only one choice. Find Remy.

"Vale? Can you hear me?"

Stiff eyelids bat against dry eyes. Shapes, colors, and sounds crystallize as I begin to wake. My body is parched, like I've been asleep in a desert. I look to the side: brown hair, soft hands, and green eyes. So like my own.

"He's fully conscious, though it may take him a few moments to readjust to all the input."

The rest of the room pans into focus as does the full sensory array of my body. Plush pillows against my neck, silk sheets, warm leggings. Dark green walls adorned with paintings, mirrors, a plasma screen by the door. Words, numbers, and charts scroll down the screen. To my right, a short, neat stack of books, exactly where I left them. *My bedroom. The chancellor's mansion.* I am surrounded by the comforts of my past, yet I am not comforted.

I focus on the faces. There, a scarred man. Burn marks on his neck and face. Peppered grey hair and a permanent scowl. I fight the urge to recoil. *General Aulion.* A woman in a grey coat to his right. A doctor, or a dietician, I'm not sure which. Young, with black hair and dark olive skin. I search my memory for a name, but I can't find one. I don't know her. She puts her fingers to my temple, presses gently, and turns back to the plasma. A whole new set of data appears.

"Where's my father?" My voice comes out unbidden, hoarse. "Where's the chancellor?"

Corine's smile never fades.

"Your father will be here in a little while." She reaches a hand out to rest on my shoulder. "Oh, Vale, we've missed you so much."

"How do you feel?" the doctor asks.

For a moment, I contemplate silence. I want to brush them away, turn my head, ignore them. I want them to know I am not on their side. But then I remember.

Remy.

My footsteps pound against the metal floor as I sprint down the hall, out of the building, toward the soldiers who are doubtless pursuing Remy, Chan-Yu, and Miah.

"Guide me, Deme," I say. I'd already switched channels so I'd be communicating with her alone, and not on the mic with the rest of my team. "Take me to them."

She knows I'm not asking her to take me to my team.

"Left," she says. "There's a surveillance drone there. It'll ID you and report your location to the grid."

I veer left. I stare grimly into the blind eye of the drone, which dutifully photographs me and then starts flashing red. Alarms sound through the streets. I turn away, fleeing, keeping up the guise of the fugitive on the run.

"I need to make a scene," I say. "Distract them for as long as possible." I have to give Remy time to escape, to get out of the city, to get away from the people who want her dead.

"Straight ahead. There's a six-story complex with a docking bay." I take off running. "Head for the roof."

"What now?" I throw the door open and take the stairs two at a time. "Are you suggesting I throw myself off a building?"

She doesn't respond.

She's never done that before.

"I'm okay."

"Any nausea or headaches?"

"Headache, definitely," I say, forcing a chuckle. "But it's tolerable. How long have I been out?"

The doctor's faint smile flickers, and she glances at my mother, whose gaze remains steadfast.

"What do you remember?" the doctor asks, dodging my question.

"A building. Stairs. I remember climbing. And then I remember falling."

I hold my hands up in surrender. With twelve soldiers surrounding me and a twenty-meter free fall behind me, my options are drawing to zero.

"Target surrounded," one of the soldiers says. A second later, a creature from my nightmares emerges. Scar tissue rips across his face and neck, burn marks from a fight I'm thankful I didn't have to witness. Grey hair. Stiff lips. Hooded eyes.

He stands as rigid as he did during my military training, staring across the roof, his expression unreadable. The sneer he wore when he confronted Soren in the interrogation room, the condescension, is gone, replaced by something colder.

"You look like you're ready to throw your life away," he says, his eyes meeting mine as he takes a step forward.

"I don't think of it that way."

"Everything you've ever fought for has been destroyed."

"Not everything. Not yet." The same words I whispered to Remy just days ago. Everything is a lie, she had said. Not everything, I told her.

"Do it," he says. I can hear scorn in his voice, disbelief, the conviction that I am a coward. That I don't have the strength to make the sacrifice for what I believe in. That I am still a child, afraid.

So I turn, a half step, away from the soldiers, away from Aulion, away from the sightless eyes of the weapons staring at me.

Fly, little bird, I think. Fly, Remy.

I step off the ledge.

I love you.

"Luckily, there was a rescue drone not far from your location," the doctor is saying. *Lucky? I bet my life on those drones.* "It detected movement patterns similar to those normally associated with a desire to jump." Rescue drones were designed to patrol the skies of Okaria to prevent suicides. With catch-nets, perimeter monitoring, and thermal tracking, the Sector had reduced the number of suicides by free fall to less than ten a year. When I stepped off that ledge, I knew my chances of hitting the ground were slim to none. The goal was never to kill myself.

"We came so close to losing you," my mother says, her eyes fixed on me, burrowing deep. Digging for something—the truth. She leans in, presses her arm against my body, clutches my hand, her skin white as bone. I can't hold her gaze. I let my eyes roll back as if I'm about to black out again, then struggle to regain focus. I stare at the minute lines in her hands, lines that match the grain of the wood dresser behind her. Polished, shiny, hard. It's difficult to believe she is flesh and bone. More likely something I've dreamed up, a monster of many faces, some that draw me in, some that repulse me. "You're so lucky to be here now."

I close my eyes against the swirling nausea in my gut and lay my head back. With more effort than it took to step off that ledge, I finally meet her eyes. I force a smile and squeeze her hand.

"I know," I say, after a moment. I cough, clear my throat, and then ask again, "How long was I out?"

My mother looks away and sets to smoothing one of my blankets, pressing it against my thigh until all the creases are gone. General Aulion hasn't moved. He stares at me the way he did on the rooftop. His expression is calculating, appraising, but neutral. I've got to be careful.

"You were unconscious about two weeks, but—" the doctor hesitates as though that was only part of the story, but my mother interrupts.

"Doctor, General, would you please give me a few moments alone with my son?"

Aulion narrows his eyes, and moves toward the door. The doctor checks the neural scanner one last time before following in Aulion's footsteps.

My mother sighs softly when the door clicks shut, as though relieved by the privacy we've been granted. She turns and gives me a sad little smile, one that looks more honest, more real, than I remember.

"Oh, Vale," she says, and despite the honesty, I hear the grasping, the pretending-to-understand, in her voice. "I know the last few months have been hard." *Hard? It was the first time I felt truly alive.* "It's been hard for me too. Ever since you graduated, I knew the time would come when you'd have to look at your father and me and see the hard choices we've made." *Like executing a classroom full of students, or ordering death without trial for prisoners?* "I always knew there was the possibility you wouldn't understand what was at stake, that you would judge us for our choices, that you would hate us for what we had to do." Tears cloud her eyes and she blinks a few times, but she never pulls her gaze from mine even as she chokes on her words. "You can't imagine how I felt when I saw you step off that ledge. You can't imagine a mother's horror when you've come a second away from losing a child."

I don't have to imagine, I think, anger clawing at me. I *saw Brinn Alexander the night Tai was murdered.*

I keep my mouth shut.

"Please, Vale, promise me," her hand strays to my cheek, just like it did when I was a child, "whatever you may think of me, of your father, or of the world we've built, please, promise me that you will never again try to take your own life."

I could tell the truth. I could tell her I will never promise that, that nothing could stop me from stepping off that same ledge again or jumping in front of a Bolt if it meant saving my friends. I could tell her that nothing will stop me from dying, if it comes to that, for the things I believe in, for the people I love. But here in this den of deception, where will the truth get me?

Feeling like I could bite through graphene, I nod, try not to grit my teeth with the lie. "I promise."

She lights up and a smile changes the contours of her face, softening it, rendering it even more beautiful. She squeezes my shoulder, her grip strong and confident, as if by force of will she can keep everything under control.

The door swings open, the minute squeal of the hinges grating against my ears, exacerbating my headache. My vision goes black around the edges, but comes back clearer a moment later. I look up to see my father standing in the doorframe, his black hair greying at the temples, lines around his eyes I don't remember from before. Philip Orleán, Chancellor of the Okarian Sector. The man I once thought could do no wrong. I study his face, see the telltale signs of aging, and a choking sadness wells up from somewhere deep within. *These are my parents. I can't escape that, no matter what they've done.*

He strides to my bedside and drops to his knees. Takes my hand in his, brings it to his lips. I steel myself and watch him as if he's a stranger. I try to smile. I fail. His betrayal somehow seems less political, more personal, than my mother's. I can barely look at him. My skin burns with fresh anger.

"Vale," he says, his voice catching, "son, it's good to have you back."

I'm not back, I want to scream. *I'm a prisoner. No different than Remy and Soren were all those months ago.*

"It's good to see you, too, Dad."

"We have so much to talk about," he says, glancing at my mother.

"It can wait," she says. "There is still a lot of medicine in your system—" *Drugs, you mean* "—and they may interfere with your cognitive abilities."

"I feel fine," I say, not wanting to miss out on anything, any piece of information, anything I can use to get out of here. "We do have a lot to talk about." I ask my question a third time: "How long have I been asleep?"

"Doctor Nguyen was correct that you were unconscious for about two weeks." She glances at Philip. "But you've been awake intermittently for the last few weeks."

"Weeks?" I force myself to keep my voice at a reasonable volume. "What day is it? When was I awake? How long has it been since I—"

"It's been six weeks since you fell," my father interjects. *Fell*, he says, like it was an accident, instead of *threw yourself off a building*.

"If I was awake before, why don't I remember anything?"

"Vale, there's something you need to know," my mother says, "something we should have told you before. But it's a long story. Perhaps it can wait until tomorrow."

"I feel fine." I try to sit up, to prove I'm ready.

"Are you sure?" Something in my father's voice tells me he's dreading the coming revelation as much as I'm longing to hear it. "Here, let me get you something to drink," he says, pushing himself to his feet. He pours a glass of water from a pitcher on the dresser, and they both watch as I take a long drink and then hand the glass back. Corine looks to my father, who tilts his head in an almost imperceptible nod. She takes a deep breath and turns back to me, now gazing at the headboard behind me.

"Three years ago, the OAC's research on human genetic modification took us in a very exciting direction. We discovered a new method of splicing genes using nanotechnology, one that would allow us to target specific cells and cell types and modify them."

I hold my breath.

"It was groundbreaking research," my mother continues. "With this kind of technology, we realized, we could begin to disrupt the Dieticians' MealPak additives and go straight to the source. We could alter human biochemistry directly without having to rely on a constant supply of medicines to maintain profile fidelity."

Profile fidelity. My heart is pounding. I can't tear my eyes away from her.

"In the initial stages, we used test subjects," my mother continues. I don't bother to ask whether those "test subjects" volunteered to be tested or not. "But once we knew it would work, we went directly to implementation."

"Only a few were privileged enough to receive these optimizations," my father says, his expression utterly calm. "Your mother and I, of course. Top-ranked military staff, including several members of Corine's Security Directorate unit."

The black ops.

"Several researchers in my trusted group at the OAC volunteered as well," my mother says. "All in all, twenty-five people were selected or elected."

In the woods, when I left Okaria, I never went through withdrawal, even though Miah did, even though everyone in the Resistance talked about it like it was a rite of passage.

"And I was selected." My voice is dull. My head feels as though it's been filled with cotton. I can't quite remember how to focus my eyes. I stare at my mother's ear, to give the impression that I am looking at her, while I struggle to regain control of my vision.

"Yes, Vale," she says. "Two years ago, your Dietician replaced the usual compounds in your MealPak with a gelatin that contained the nanobots that would alter your DNA to optimize your functioning capacity and align it with your medical profile. We were able to implant genes that improved your strength, speed, endurance, spatial imaging, memory, mental processing, creativity, and language skills. We gave you everything you ever could have wanted from your mind and body." *What do you know about what I wanted?* "Since then, your MealPaks have been a placebo. Food, untouched, unaltered."

"But, from a policy standpoint," my father says, "we couldn't introduce these modifications to the general public until we were sure they worked long-term. If not, we'd have to continue supplementing the genetic alterations with Dieticians' cocktails to ensure full effectiveness."

"Those who were selected had to be kept in the dark, so as not to compromise the integrity of the experiment. If you had known, you might have behaved differently. Since then, we've been doing routine checkups and analyses on everyone who was optimized," my mother continues. "When you ..." she pauses, searching for her words, "when you came back six weeks ago, we used that opportunity to continue your analyses to see how your optimizations had held up under duress. Using neurodisruptive technology, we temporarily disabled your ability to form new memories."

So you could run your experiments in peace.

"So we could make sure you were as healthy and high-functioning as ever."

I am a piece of equipment to be fixed, a tool to be utilized, a machine designed to operate according to your plan. I am your feather.

Six weeks have passed since I last saw Remy. Six weeks since the Resistance was destroyed. Where have Remy, Soren, Miah, Chan-Yu, and Linnea been all that time? Are they in custody? Were they able to escape? Are they even alive?

What do I do now?

My mother leans in close and again presses her hand into my shoulder. I meet her eyes, wondering if I'll see any spark of the humanity that once kept her alive, or just gears clicking behind her pupils, keeping time to a drumbeat of deceit.

"I'm sorry we couldn't tell you," she whispers. She sounds so genuine, even vulnerable. But beyond this veneer of the caring, doting mother is the cold face of a woman who felt she couldn't involve her son in the first place. The two-faced monster emerges in my fuzzy vision: a mother proud and protective of her perfected creation; a mother refusing to grant her creation freedom from her twisted vise of lies. "But we wanted it for you. We've only ever wanted the best for you, Vale."

I don't understand, I think. *I can never forgive you.*

"I understand," I say. "I forgive you."

3 — REMY

Spring 62, Sector Annum 106, 14h05
Gregorian Calendar: May 20

"Please don't ever do that to me!" A high voice cuts into my solitude from across the park.

"I would never." The second voice is lower, with a tremor of laughter. "How could anyone do that? Kidnap their best friend?"

I'm passing the time sitting on a bench in Reunion Park. This park is the heart of the city. To my right, about four kilometers down the Rue Nationale, is the campus of the Academy and the Sector Research Institute, the SRI. To my left, down the same street in the opposite direction, is OAC headquarters. And dead ahead down Rue Jubilation, through a grove of beautiful, century-old elm trees, is the capitol building, its glass structure arcing gracefully against the sky. The city's most famous monument, a maze of trellises and hanging gardens arranged in the shape of a sunflower, the symbol of the Okarian Sector, is at the end of Rue Jubilation. This park is one of the best places to eavesdrop on the wealthy and privileged citizens of Okaria—and those who serve them. Nearly everyone who works at one of those buildings will pass through this park at some point during the day.

It's an unseasonably chilly day for so late in spring. This works in my favor, giving me an excuse to wear a thick scarf and pull my hood up over my hair. Even so, I can't risk walking outside without my disguising makeup on, especially if I want to loiter here. Reunion Park is the closest I dare come to the places I used to know as well as the back of my hand, and even here, I feel like I'm walking on the edge of a knife.

It's worth the risk. Under the guise of sketching on my plasma, I've been listening in to the conversations of the rich and powerful all day. I've only caught snippets, but it's been enough to get a feel for the mood of the city. From what I can tell, most people still think of Vale as a celebrity. They're curious about what happened to him, and how he's recovering from his time as a hostage of the Resistance. Many believe that the Orleáns are holding back pieces of the story, but everyone seems confident that all will be revealed in time. The prevailing attitude is that since Vale has been returned to his loving parents, the terrorists will be taken care of, the renegades brought to justice, and all will be well in the perfect world of Okaria.

But at least people are talking. Vale's name has been spoken aloud countless times today, and everyone is fascinated with his story. Even better, there are those who wonder aloud about Jeremiah's role in Vale's "kidnapping," and others who have speculated darkly that there's more to the story than the Orleáns are letting on. A few have even commented that Evander Sun-Zi seemed unbalanced during his press conference right after the demise of Round Barn.

As the girls pass, I notice both are wearing the black pants and crisp green jackets that comprise the Academy uniform. They walk arm in arm, each with a fruit tart in hand. The warm smell wafts toward me, and I start to salivate. Meera's food is delicious—and safer than anything from a Dietician's hand—but there's never enough of it.

"I would never forgive you." They must be about fifteen or sixteen, the same age I was when Tai died.

The second girl throws back her head and laughs. "Are you kidding? I would never forgive *myself*." They lean into each other, giggling, and change the subject. Schoolgirl troubles take precedence as their voices fade into the distance.

Although few here in the heart of the Sector seem inclined to doubt the Orleáns' story, I can't help but think that all this chatter is a good sign. Before Vale left, the Sector was hell-bent on keeping its citizens in the dark. He told us the Resistance was a top-secret word, requiring an officer-level security clearance. This ensured peaceful, ignorant silence. But when Vale abdicated, and Corine and Philip declared open war on the Resistance, they tossed around words like terrorism and betrayal and treason. That got the people talking. The citizens of Okaria aren't like those on the Farms. They're not being dumbed down. Quite the opposite: here, the Dieticians create cocktails to enhance neural connectivity, snacks to boost creativity, and you can order juice blends with shots of memory retention, spatial imaging, or emotional awareness. In the capital, the people are truly awake.

I hear laughter behind me and turn to see a group of friends unloading their netball gear on the edge of a sand court. I wish I could count the number of times I played netball on that very court, laughing and joking with my own friends. They look to be around my age, and given how close the park is to the

Academy and the Sector Research Institute, there's a good chance I might recognize one of them. When I was at the Academy, there were relatively few places the students would frequent, and we often ran into the same people over and over again. So it is everywhere, I assume: people find their favorite hangouts and then rarely explore outside their comfort zones. I've seen more of the city in the last few weeks than I ever saw when it was my home.

I move my pack and swivel around so I can watch while pretending to be absorbed with my plasma. As the game begins, I watch the ball pop up and down, back and forth over the net, and hear the grunts of the players as they dive to save a point. I keep sketching, glancing up every once in a while as the players rotate, until I realize one of the girls *does* look familiar. She started on the opposite side of the court, but now she's on my side, and when she stops to pull her dark, straight hair back into a ponytail, I recognize her. *Moriana Nair.* Jahnu's cousin, and Jeremiah's girlfriend. Without thinking, I pull my hood down to shade my face, as if she might suddenly recognize me.

I think back to the last time I saw her. On television, in the dark halls of Normandy, after Thermopylae was destroyed. Pleading with Linnea Heilmann, then the primary announcer for the Okarian News Network, insisting that Jeremiah was surely innocent, that he would never have kidnapped his best friend and dragged him to the Resistance as a hostage. But more recently, I remember her terrified voice on the mic the night Vale was shot and plummeted off the roof of that building. I remember her panicked words to Jeremiah: *Please come out, they know you're hiding and that you're with Remy, if you don't come out now they're going to find you and kill you …*

Right now, Moriana looks as though she's never been afraid a day in her life. Cheerful and exuberant, she shouts wildly with her friends, leaps high up over the net to slam a ball down, and crows whenever her team scores. It looks like the last thing on her mind is politics, terrorism, or revolution.

A part of me seethes, watching as she tosses the ball up to serve it across the net. How can she be so carefree after what Corine put her through? How can she still be here in the Sector after hearing Jeremiah and Vale on the mic with her, knowing what Miah risked to see her? *Why isn't she afraid?* This is a bad idea, I realize. I have to get out of here. I grab my pack and jam my plasma in it just as a bad hit sends the ball sailing my direction. I look up to see Moriana running straight toward me.

Great. What do I do now? Out of instinct, I reach for the ball as it rolls toward the bench.

"Thanks so much!" she says to me, jogging the final few meters. I look at her. Straight at her. Will she recognize me? My muscles tense. *Fight or flight.* But I don't move.

Nothing. No recognition.

I almost wish she would see through my disguise. That she would say, astonished, "Remy? Is that you?" I wish I could tell her that Jahnu was hurt. I wish I could tell her that Tai's death was no accident. I wish she would ask me about the night Vale fell, about what happened, if I knew anything, if I was there. *Did they capture Jeremiah?* she might ask. *What happened to Vale?* And I would tell her. And then my turn for questions: *Are you okay? Are you afraid? What did Corine do to you that night?*

She waits as I hold the ball in my hands.

"You look familiar," I say. *What am I doing?*

She cocks her head, examining me closer. "So do you. Were you at the Academy?"

My heart skips a beat. This is suicide. I should leave right now.

"Oh, no. I'm just in Okaria visiting my cousins. I think I've seen you somewhere, though." I pause, as if trying to remember. "I know! I watch all the OAC research vids. You're part of Corine Orleán's epigenetics team, aren't you?"

Stop it, Remy, stop it, stop it, stop it.

Moriana beams. "Yes. I'm Moriana Nair, her lead assistant."

"That's it!" I can't stop myself. I tuck the ball under one arm and stick my hand out in greeting. Reflexively, she takes it as I force a wide smile and turn on my charm. "Wow, it must be something to work so closely with Corine Orleán."

"Yeah, she's brilliant. She's really taken me under her wing. I'm pretty lucky." She looks down at the ball, still clutched in my hands, and glances back at the court. Behind us, one of her friends waves, beckoning her back to the game.

Blood pounds in my ears, and I'm starting to sweat, but I can't stop. "Look, I know you need to get back to your game, but," I glance around as if someone might be listening, "aren't you the one who was friends with Valerian and ..." I drop my voice. "... Jeremiah Sayyid?"

She stiffens and frowns, as if she'd just stuck her head in a compost bin.

"Yeah, I knew him." She holds her hand out for the ball. I grip it harder, my knuckles ashen and tense. "We dated for a little while. That's it."

I stare blankly. *That's it?* That's all you have to say about Jeremiah, the man who weaseled his way into a top-secret mission to infiltrate the heart of Okaria and risked his life to come see you? The man you pleaded to turn himself into the Sector so he wouldn't get hurt? I can't believe it. Something's not right.

I hand her the ball and look down, trying to look embarrassed. "Okay. Sorry. It was nice to meet you. Enjoy your game."

She nods silently, turns, and walks off, the spring in her step gone.

I duck my head and turn away, walking as quickly as I can without seeming obvious. I grab my bag from the bench where I left it and sling it over my shoulder, booking it for the nearest exit. *What the hell was that all about?* I ask myself. I replay our brief conversation over and over in my head, comparing it against that night when her desperate voice played through our mic system, pleading with us to turn ourselves in or be shot on sight. It doesn't match up. There's no way the Moriana I met today was the same Moriana from six weeks ago, crying, begging Jeremiah to save himself.

Meera holds out a large, waxy leaf. "Just a leaf, right?" I take it and turn it over in my hands. There are bumps on the pale underside that make me wonder if some sort of disease has gotten to it, some mutation or virus that has disrupted the surface. "Feel those dots? That's our code."

I hold the leaf up to the window. The dots are much more visible in the light, and now that I can see them, they do look organized. The day is bright and sunny and Meera is giving me my first lesson in the Outsider's way of passing information.

"It was called Braille in the Old World," Meera says. "Used as a way for the blind to read. You *feel* it. It's a dead language, since blindness is a curable condition in the Sector. We use it sometimes in the Wilds, but have found it much more useful here, and those who aren't Outsiders are none the wiser."

"So how do I read it?"

"You have to train yourself. Run your fingers across the dots and feel them, learn to 'see' with your fingertips. Once you know the symbols, you can read it just by looking at it. But it's much more discreet to read with your fingers. Sometimes we code messages in public places, and you wouldn't want to be seen staring at a brick wall, or under a park bench. That would be too suspicious."

"Is this the only way you communicate?"

"Hardly," she says, with a twinkle in her eye. "I can't reveal all my secrets, can I? For passing messages, we use Braille or Morse Code. Braille is better, since most people don't know to look for it. Some odd historians and quaint collectors still know Morse, so it's not as safe. But we use it when we have to, or when we're not sure our intended recipient knows where to look." On my plasma, she works through the circles with me, drawing the dots in various patterns that form words, phrases, sentences, *meaning.*

"No such luck," she says smiling, when I plead with her that I need a nap. After four hours of studying, I am exhausted. "This is your first test. It's from Snake." She hands me a corn husk, and I stare at it blankly for a moment.

"Seriously? You pass messages on food scraps?"

"We pass messages on everything."

After another hour, and some serious hints from Meera, I've interpreted Snake's message.

Same place, same table, two days from today, when the first star shows her face.

Dusk falls fast as I set out from Meera's apartment. Shadows creep along the edges of the buildings, street lamps clicking on one by one as they sense sundown. I devoured the last bites of food in Meera's ration, but my stomach still grumbles. I put a hand to my belly, as if to quiet it, but to no avail. Meera's rations have done wonders to strengthen my body and renew my spirit, but I still have to make them stretch between deliveries.

Pushing past The Elysium patrons is more difficult on citizen payday. The den is crowded, loud, and so smoky I feel the effects of the drug just by breathing. I look for the same corner booth, which is thankfully empty, and settle in.

"Rose water, please," I say, when the waitress comes by. I tip her an extra seedcoin to leave me alone. Requests like that are not uncommon here, and the waitress doesn't even bat an eye. She nods, returns a few minutes later with the rose infusion, and disappears.

Snake is late. Paranoia seeps in, creeping, suffocating. *Where is he?* Did something go wrong? It's evident in the crack of my knuckles, my fingers drumming on the table, the hairs standing at attention on the back of my neck. I look around, panic bleeding into my thoughts. Did the message go through? Was the messenger caught? Was Snake caught?

Just when my thoughts begin to spiral out of control and I'm considering making a fast exit, he slides in next to me.

"Accept my apology. There was a little mishap." I breathe in the woody, tobacco-heavy scent of him as he wraps his arm around my shoulder, pretending we are just another pair of lovers in a corner together.

"Something bad?"

Snake shakes his head and my shoulders relax. "Being a seeker of secrets is no easy job sometimes. My task tonight took longer than it should have."

"You sure you're okay?"

"Fine. But I am sorry. I'm rarely late. It doesn't inspire confidence. Now, you must be wondering …" I nod, encouraging him to continue, but he grabs my rosewater and tips back his head to drain the glass. He smiles, cocky and lighthearted, but I sense he's more unsettled than he's letting on.

"The message was delivered. I can't guarantee he's found it, or that he will be able to interpret it when he does. But the clues are in place."

"How?"

"Even I don't know the details. All I can tell you is that it seems the chancellor has a very nice library."

"The message was put in a book?" He shrugs. "So how is he? Is he hurt? Is he afraid? Where are they—"

Snake puts his hand on top of mine, halting my string of questions. He looks at me with concern. His palms are rougher and more calloused than I would have expected for someone like him, a server in an a premiere smokeroom like The Elysium.

"Sparrow," he says, "I know you're worried. I know how much you've risked to stay here for him, and how much danger you put yourself in every day for the chance to help him. But you can't help him from here. All I can tell you is that he is alive and your message has been delivered. There's nothing more you can do."

I stare off into the distance, losing my thoughts in a haze of smoke and the starlight energy that brings people here, night after night, to enjoy each other's company. But something doesn't feel right. Even though I am a wanted criminal, and every step I take is fraught with danger, I know I can do more. With the Outsider network at my fingertips, and the people of Okaria asking questions—asking the *right* questions—the time has never been better to spread the Resistance's message.

Maybe it's time to revisit my footage from Round Barn.

Maybe it's time to take down the Dragon.

4 — VALE

It's been years since I called this place home. Alone in my old room I pace back and forth for what seems like hours. I stop and stare at the floor. Resume pacing. Stop and stare at the wall. Resume pacing. Examine the few belongings I left behind when I moved to my flat: some childhood toys and a pair of beat-up cleats are really all that's left of my old life. Everything else is decoration. Even when I lived here for that short time after my father was elected chancellor, it never felt like mine. As soon as I was accepted to the SRI, I moved into my own flat and never looked back.

I give up and lie down, closing my eyes. I open them again a moment later, memorize the patterns on the ceiling, count the leaves I can see through the window, trace the grain of wood on my dresser. Once again I turn my focus inward, but my thoughts are as repetitive as the wallpaper. I wish they hadn't taken Demeter from me, that I had someone to talk to, anyone. Hell, I'd even take Soren as a roommate just for some conversation.

It's only been three days since I was permitted to regain full consciousness, and since then I've barely spoken to anyone. My parents have dropped by a few times to check in, but other than the two of them, a daily visit from the doctor, and a stone-faced servant who won't so much as open her mouth, I've been in isolation. Locked in my room like a misbehaving child. Not even Aulion has come by to torture me, though in his case I'd take a year of solitude over a day with him.

My efforts to find out what happened to my teammates have gotten me nowhere. My mother answered my questions about my genetic alterations with all the enthusiasm of a scientist on the brink of a discovery. But when I ask about the raid on the Resistance base, my teammates who came to Okaria with me, or Remy, both she and my father have refused to talk.

"Vale," my father had said, patting my shoulder with an awkwardness I'd never seen before. "We're glad to have you back. But after everything, we can't trust you with that information anymore."

I managed to contain my frustration. *Of course you can't trust me, Dad. That's why you won't let me venture even into the kitchen. That's why my bedroom window is bolted from the outside. That's why you're monitoring my every move.*

I get up, trying to find something else to do beyond thinking the same thoughts, asking the same questions, running into the same dead ends. Yesterday, I requested a plasma to read on, searching for anything to stave off the boredom. My request was denied—plasmas are far too versatile, I suppose.

"You have a visitor." I look up and see the silent housekeeper in the doorway. It's the first time in twelve hours my bedroom door has been opened. "In the gardens. Follow me."

I slip a t-shirt over my head and follow her down the hall, too surprised to respond. She leads me toward the fountain under the trellis, blooming with honeysuckle and wisteria, and turns back to the house. I glance around. A guard stands not far off, just out of earshot, and I wonder on whose account I've been allowed such freedom.

"Vale."

I remember the last time I heard that voice, scared and confused, as she pleaded for us to turn ourselves in. It's not what I want to remember. I dip my hands in the cool water of the fountain, resisting the urge to lean over and dunk my whole face underwater.

"Hey." I shake my hands off and face Moriana Nair. Drinking in the sight of her, one of the best friends I've ever known, I wonder what's going through her mind. She's cut her hair shorter now, and her bangs almost shroud her eyes. In tall boots and a simple white tunic she's every bit as beautiful as I remember. *If only Miah could see her now.* Wearing a little frown and furrowed brows, she doesn't look happy to see me. "It's been a while."

"What happened, Vale?" Her voice is low, accusatory.

I can't help but look around, wondering if some miniscule drone is nearby, recording our conversation. How much is safe for me to say?

She takes a step forward. The trellis above us casts her figure in a shimmery interplay of sunlight and shadow. Moriana crosses her arms and keeps her distance. I know from one hard look that she doesn't trust me. Even though I want to, I can't trust her either. And I can't ask the question burning on my tongue: *Where does your loyalty lie?*

"It's a long story," I say.

She takes a step closer, her expression full of recrimination.

"It's not true, is it? What they said about Jeremiah."

"No."

"He didn't kidnap you?"

"What do you think?"

"I don't know what to think, Vale." I'm surprised by the fury in her voice. In the light, she takes on a mythic quality: fierce and powerful. Her hands are clenched into fists at her sides, belying her anger. "Everybody has a different story. Seems like the truth is buried beneath a landslide of lies, and I don't even know where to start digging." She looks around the garden as if she's unable—or unwilling—to look at me directly. "Even you. I thought you and Miah were my best friends. But then you just disappeared, ghosted. Without so much as a note."

"We didn't want to put you in danger. We had to leave."

"And kick your best friend to the curb?" For a second she looks down, defeated, before lifting her chin again and glaring at me. Her words slice through me in a place I hadn't expected. I had never thought about our leaving as a betrayal. We believed we were protecting her, not hurting her.

"Miah and I discovered things about the Sector that made us question everything. I had to find those who disappeared. I learned the truth about the SRI massacre, and it wasn't pretty. If you want the truth, you have to dig, deeper than most are willing."

"Why do you think I'm here?"

"Because my mother asked you to come."

She shrugs, her fingers fluttering over the petals of a purple flower. I know I'm right by the way she shifts her glance away, a hint of embarrassment darkening her features.

"She did ask me, but—"

"You wouldn't be allowed here if she didn't trust you."

"I've been asking to see you for weeks."

That's something. "What has she told you?"

"The same thing she's told everyone. That Jeremiah kidnapped you, that he and his father took you to the Resistance and coerced you into working with them. That you managed to escape and make your way back to the Sector, but when they found you, you were sick and injured and it took you weeks to recover."

I hadn't heard that last bit. "And what part of that do you believe?"

She shakes her head. "None of it. Miah and his dad?" She sounds exasperated. "They were barely on speaking terms, and I'm supposed to believe they were long-time collaborators?"

"What do you want to know?" I ask, and motion for us to sit on the bench near the fountain. She sits beside me but keeps a healthy distance.

"Everything. Tell me what really happened."

I nod. That much, I can do. After all, my enemies know the real story. Why shouldn't Moriana? What do I have to lose? So I tell her everything.

"It started during a mission with the Seed Bank Protection Project. We were looking for Eli, but he got away. Instead, I came home with Remy and Soren Skaarsgard as prisoners." Her eyes widen. She sits on her hands and listens to the rest of the story without interruption.

It's not easy reliving the tale. The memory of Aulion slapping Remy across the face, her head snapping back against the pole, of him leaning over Soren's already battered body …

My voice is thick: "Once I started asking these questions, I couldn't stop until I had all the answers. I had to tell someone, but you were too close to Corine. You wouldn't have believed me. So I told Miah, and he agreed we had to leave."

I can tell she still isn't satisfied.

"Moriana, the Sector is *murdering* people. By my own mother's command. Once I told Miah what I'd discovered, his life was in danger. We couldn't risk putting you in danger, too."

"Why didn't you take me with you?"

I can't bring myself to say aloud what Moriana already knows.

After a few seconds of silence, she turns away. "Is it because you didn't trust me? Neither of you trusted me."

"It's not that simple."

"It *is* that simple. You should have told me." There's no forgiveness in her voice.

"We wanted to tell you, but it was more important to keep you safe."

"Keep me safe?" she spits. "You think I was safe after you left without a word? You think the Watchmen left me alone? Believed I didn't know anything? Believed my boyfriend and my best friend wouldn't trust me enough to tell me something?"

"We were trying—"

"Don't tell me what you were trying to do, Vale. Let me tell you what you did do. You left me alone. To face the consequences of your actions."

Silence.

"Did you fight with the Resistance?" she asks, her voice hard-edged. "For them?"

"Yes."

"Why?"

Images dart like minnows through my mind. Remy's cold, confused face the last time I saw her before she left Okaria. Soren and Remy tied to a pole, abused and broken. Blue lightning crashing through Brinn's body, Gabriel kneeling over her. Fire raining down on starving Farm workers as they scattered, screaming, trying to escape the Dragon's flames. Destroyed fields, hollowed-out mountains, and poisoned water.

I reach out and take Moriana's hand, twine her long, slender fingers with mine. I make eye contact and refuse to look away. "I believe there is a moment of reckoning, when we each come to our own understanding of the truth."

"You don't understand what a threat the Resistance poses."

I squeeze her hands. "I've come to realize that it is just the opposite."

She curls her lip in disbelief. "There has to be some kind of misunderstanding. You told me earlier that your mom killed Tai and Brinn, but that can't be true. Your mom has been nothing but great to me. She made sure the Watchmen didn't get rough when they questioned me. She kept the media from hounding me. She was there for me over and over again when you and Jeremiah weren't. She wouldn't hurt anyone."

I stand abruptly, and run my fingers through my hair. *Made sure no one got rough?* Wasn't it Moriana's voice in the microphone the night I was captured? *They'll kill me, too, they're going to destroy everyone ...*

"Moriana, when was the last time you spoke to Jeremiah?" *If you believed Corine would never do anything to hurt you, why did you say they were going to kill you?*

She looks up at me, blank-faced. "The Solstice, of course. That was the last time I saw him."

"I didn't ask when you saw him," I say, too sharply, and she narrows her eyes. "When did you last speak to him?"

"Don't play word games with me, Vale. I haven't heard his voice since the Solstice."

"Where were you the night I supposedly escaped and made my way back home?"

She is silent for a moment as she thinks.

"I was at the lab. Corine had me working on a project late that night. I heard about everything on the Sector broadcast the next morning."

"You weren't at your apartment that night? Think carefully."

"No, I'm sure of it. Why? Is it important?"

The whole thing comes together in my mind, like a blurry picture coming into clear focus. Moriana wasn't at home, and she certainly wasn't being tortured by my mother and father, who wouldn't want to hurt a potential ally. She was never on the line with us that night at all. Moriana's life was never in danger. Someone must have scanned her vocal patterns and used them to create a perfect imitation of a terrified Moriana Nair. What better way to bait me and Jeremiah, after all? Corine would've protected her; she wants Moriana on her side. But that wouldn't stop her from using Moriana to get to us.

I shake my head. "Maybe it's not."

She stands, wringing her hands. "I have to go. I've stayed too long already. I'm expected back at the lab."

"Will you be back?" I dread the answer.

"I don't know." She turns and disappears through the garden, casting a long shadow in the late afternoon sun.

The silent housekeeper must have been in my room while I was gone because everything is spotless, except for a short stack of old books on my bedside table. They must have given into my pleas for some kind of entertainment. I rub my temple, the conversation I just had with Moriana ringing in my ears. I take a long breath, quelling the surging headache, and pick up a book.

The chancellor's mansion has about four hundred books in the library collected over the years from abandoned schools, homes, and universities. The book in hand turns out to be *Les Misérables* by Victor Hugo, a book I'd read while at the Academy. I decide that brushing up on my Old French will be a good distraction.

I thumb through the pages and come to one of the parts where Marius and Enroljas are rallying their friends to join the student revolution. I can't help but think about when Remy and I did the same with the Farm workers only two months ago, dreaming of something better, just like these students in ancient Paris.

I read a few pages and then close the book, relishing the simple feeling of holding it in my hands. Hardbound but scratched, dirty, and with rough edges, it's certainly showing its age. I open it again and turn to the front, looking for a publication date. Instead, on the first sheaf of paper, I find something strange: a series of lines, some short, some long, scrawled diagonally across the page in no apparent order. Handwritten, in faint carbon pencil, my first thought is that it's a strange bit of doodling. But then something clicks: It's not a doodle. It's a code. A language used in the Old World I recognize as Morse. I studied telegraphy in my classes, but we discussed the languages of the Old World briefly and none of my professors taught us to decipher Morse.

I stare at the lines. What other books did that girl bring me? I feel my heart rate spike, and force myself to stay still. I lean my head back and concentrate on my breathing. For all I know, my parents are monitoring my heart rate or have implanted me with a medical chip. After a moment, I toss the book on the bed as if the very sight of it bores me. I stand and move over to my dresser where the rest of the books are stacked. I go through them again, picking each one up, reading the titles. *Plants of Northern America: An Encyclopaedia*. Not helpful. *Gargantua and Pantagruel*. Entertaining, but unhelpful. *U.N Millennium Development Goals Report, 2023*. Nope. *Classic Cocktail Recipes of New Orleans*. I spare a second to smile at the irony that New Orleans is now a drowned city, while the Orleáns rule the new world of Okaria.

Not for long, I think.

Telecommunications in the 19th Century. Jackpot. I flip it open, skim the table of contents, and my eyes land on Chapter Five: Introduction to Morse Code. This cannot be a coincidence. I have little doubt that my every move is being monitored by someone very high up on the chain of command, but it seems like a million-to-one shot that I find a coded note in a centuries-old book that just happens to be in the same pile as one that will allow me to decipher that code.

I stare at the door for a moment, wondering about the stony-faced servant. Was she responsible for this? Or was she just a carrier? And then the following moment: Am I getting paranoid? Am I going crazy? Am I seeing signs where there are none?

I shake my head. I can't start doubting myself. Not now. Not before I know for sure. I turn to the page where the chapter on Morse code begins.

Morse, it turns out, is not a simple language, but it's easy enough to understand. It's based on a standardized sequence of short and long signals, called dots and dashes, the same kind of system Eli uses when encoding his messages between Resistance bases.

It's not long before I'm mapping the symbols out in my head, for lack of a pen or pencil. *Classic prisoner treatment*, I think. *Denial of tools with which to write*. For the first time, I'm conscious of the intellectual improvements my mother imbued in me without my permission. I stare at the dots and dashes on the page in front of me, the symbols shifting and rearranging into something altogether different. I force my heart to maintain a steady beat as the words consume me.

I'm here. I'm waiting for you. Do not lose hope. Little Bird.

5 — REMY

The leaf comes with the food drop. It's not Meera this time, all dark hair and red cheeks, enthusiastic as she pokes her head through the door to her old apartment. Fear gnaws at me as I wonder where she is. I thank the messenger, a boy with intense blue eyes and hair that looks as soft as goose down. He can't be more than twelve, and he looks vaguely familiar as he smiles and scuffles off. I pick through the produce, eating handful after handful of gooseberries until they're almost all gone, then unwrap the meat and put it in the refrigerator. I rinse the leaves that had been used to wrap the meat under the sink, and that's how I find the message. The dots. I cut the water and run my fingertips across the bumps, feeling for the patterns, proud of myself when I can interpret the symbols without holding the leaf up to the light.

An ally we call Onion wishes to speak with you. He won't hurt you. He's on our side. Sundown today. At the apartment. Meera.

Glad as I am to have a note from Meera—she must be okay—I can't make sense of the message. Meera trusts this person. He has an Outsider code name. He wants to talk. So why does she reassure me that he won't hurt me, that he's on our side? He must be someone I wouldn't know to trust unless she told me. Someone who works for the Sector. Someone on the inside.

My fingertips skitter across the leaf, shameless now as I hold it up to the light to make sure I've read it correctly. *An ally we call Onion wishes to speak with you. He won't hurt you.*

I wonder who it could be. Someone like Chan-Yu, maybe, who was once a soldier of the revered OAC Black Ops, so trustworthy Corine Orleán appointed him to be Vale's personal assistant, who was secretly an Outsider the whole time. But it must be someone I know, or should know, or she wouldn't have thought to reassure me.

He's on our side.

Every home or flat in Okaria comes outfitted with a special vidscreen for displaying notifications from the government, the OAC, or the Okarian News Network. Once a day, ONN collaborates with the OAC and the Sector to release a thirty-minute news update. When I arrived at the Resistance three years ago, one of the first things the Director did was explain that these broadcasts are entirely propaganda. Full of falsely beautiful images of the Farms, videos of productive, happy workers and engineers in the towns, and snapshots of the so-called No-Go Zones in the Wilds, taken—supposedly—by drones, these videos are deceptive and misleading. They are purposefully designed to direct the citizens' eyes away from the Sector's real problems, so that the people in power can deal with them quietly and without public knowledge.

They're pushed out every evening at 19h00. If you're eating dinner with your family, watching a different broadcast, or using the vidscreen for homework, your screen will turn on or switch programming with or without your permission. The only way to miss it is to walk away.

Since I returned to the city, I've been trying to watch the broadcasts every night. A lot of the bars and smokeshops downtown display them, so it wasn't hard to sneak in somewhere in the inner suburbs or outer ring of downtown. I'd pretend to be waiting for a friend, watch as much of the broadcast as I dared, and then, with an urgent glance at my plasma, I'd dash.

Since Meera offered to let me take over her apartment, I've been able to watch them in private. Now, I'm sitting on the couch in her old place, legs curled beneath me, waiting for the show to start. It used to be that Linnea Heilmann, with a gilded voice and picture-perfect face, would organize and narrate the various briefings. But since she left to hunt down Eli, the network hired a new public correspondent, Jon Spironov. He's older than Linnea, with a comforting voice and a reassuring face. He doesn't have quite the same penchant for attention-grabbing broadcasts that she did, but his calming, even-keeled displays make you feel like nothing could ever go wrong. I've gotten used to his voice on the feeds like you get used to music playing in the background.

The bright, trumpeting intro starts and the screen flares to life. I take a gulping sip of Meera's green tea. After the intro, Jon's weathered, handsome face smiles at me from inside the ONN broadcast studio—conveniently located right next to the capitol building.

"Citizens of Okaria, I'm your Sector Public Correspondent Jon Spironiv. We have some important updates today, so please stay tuned. But first, a brief announcement from Philip Orleán on Valerian's progress in his recovery."

I sit up. This is the first time Vale has been mentioned on the evening broadcasts since the few days after he was captured. This is what I've been waiting for—why I've gone out of my way to watch the broadcasts every night I've been in the city. I have to remind myself not to expect anything but half-truths and deflections, but any information is better than none. The screen cuts away from Jon and to Philip, sitting at his desk in the capitol building. I grit my teeth and look away for a moment, as the painful memory of the last time I saw Philip across a desk rips through me. *When you give us what we want, I'll personally hand you a bucket of fresh figs, just like I used to.* Words he said after fitting me with a few charge capacitors and hooking up a power source.

Maybe it's just my memory, but he seemed calmer then, staring down a political prisoner and torturing me with electric shocks. Now, even with no one across from him but a camera drone, he bites his lip and his fingers tap the desk once, twice, three times before he starts talking.

"My fellow citizens," he begins—and the feed goes dark.

I stare at the vidscreen blankly.

The feeds sometimes falter. They'll flicker in and out, or your screen will freeze and lag behind the official display. That's a part of digital broadcasting. But the daily broadcasts have never once gone out completely, in all the years I've watched them.

A dim green light flicks alive in the blackness. For a moment it almost looks like a flame from a lighter, but then it glows and expands. A biolight. Tousled blonde hair becomes visible, and a shadowed face. *That's definitely not Philip.* Another biolight flicks on and now I recognize the face: it's Linnea Heilmann. The backdrop is hazy, and there's a low hum, almost as if some sort of machinery is running in the room. But Linnea's shimmery hair and large, clear eyes are unmistakable.

I drop my teacup. The ceramic mug shatters as it hits the floor. I'm on my feet, ready to run, wondering why in all the seasons Linnea Heilmann is on my vidscreen during the official Sector broadcast. *Did she betray us?*

"Citizens of the Sector, I don't have much time. I'm Linnea Heilmann, former public correspondent for the ONN. Two months ago I told you that I was resigning my position to take an internal communications job with the OAC. This is not what happened. I was sent into the Wilds with instructions to search for the traitor Remy Alexander. I was on a mission to kill her."

I sink back into the chair in front of the vidscreen. Amazement washes through my body like a river through a floodplain. She's simplifying parts of the story—she's left out Eli and the virus she gave him. Maybe she's worried about time, or wants to keep her narrative straightforward. But the essence is true: she was sent into the Wilds to find and kill me.

"Corine and Philip Orleán ordered this mission, but I don't work for Corine anymore. I don't work for the Sector anymore. I don't work for anyone, and neither should you. I am a free agent, and I will no longer lie for anyone. And I'm about to tell you why."

Linnea holds one of the biolights closer to her face. I'm frozen in place, mouth hanging open, stunned. I can hardly believe this is the same Linnea Heilmann whose voice I'd come to despise, who used to tout the Sector's victories with a tone so celebratory it bordered on manic. *What changed her?* I wonder.

"When I was a little girl, I had a best friend. Her name was Tai Alexander. Fellow Okarians, I am here tonight to tell you Tai was not killed by an Outsi—"

The feed goes black again. A second later, static fizzles on the screen, along with a loud buzzing noise, almost painfully sharp. I press my fingers into my ears, but my eyes are glued to the screen. Jon Spironov's face reappears, but this time he looks confused.

"Citizens! As you can see, our evening broadcast has been disrupted by the very rebels and terrorists who captured and tortured our own Valer—"

The studio backdrop dissipates, and after a half-second of static, Jon's face is replaced once more by Linnea's, hazy and otherworldly from the greenish tint given off by the biolights.

"The Sector doesn't want you to know that the massacre at the SRI was ordered by Corine Orleán. They don't want you to know that the reason the man murdered a classroom full of students was because his drugs were off, his MealPaks made him violent and uncontrollable, his food turned him into a killer. They don't want you to know they're changing your minds and bodies so you'll be tame, docile, happy, and unquestioning. So you won't ask what happened to Tai, or your friend who disappeared from your town, or why those in the capital live to be a hundred years old, and those on the Farms live half as long."

The screen flickers and dies, and for a second I think whoever's in charge of Sector programming must have finally figured out how to shut the whole system down. But then Linnea reappears, her face tense, her voice low and urgent.

"The Sector will turn off this broadcast soon. You won't hear from me again. The OAC's Security Directorate will hunt me down, just like they're hunting

Jeremiah Sayyid and Remy Alexander and Elijah Tawfiq. Listen to me now. Don't eat your MealPaks. Listen to your true self. Look for—"

The feed cuts out and the screen goes black.

For a long moment, I'm unable to move. Unable to think. I lean back into my chair, looking out the window at the deepening sky. Then a broad smile, irrepressible, creeps onto my face. *That was brilliant.* It must have taken a herculean effort. I can't imagine the Resistance—even with Eli, Zoe, and Firestone working together—was able to pull that off without inside help. Who did they recruit from the Sector to hack the broadcast? A well-placed Outsider? A Sector citizen leaning toward the Resistance? Or was it something simpler: a gun to the head of one of the broadcast engineers?

Not for the first time since I decided to stay in Okaria, I miss my friends, desperately. I miss my team. I wish I had a way to contact them, to congratulate them, to ask them how the hell they did that. And the strangest feeling wells up inside of me: a strong desire to hug Linnea.

Then there's a knock at the door.

In the excitement of Linnea's broadcast, I had forgotten entirely about my promised visitor. I run to the door and glance through the peephole. But the person—whoever he is—is too tall to identify, even through the convex lens. All I can see is that his hands, clasped calmly in front of him, are as black as Jahnu's and as large and strong as Soren's.

I can't help but be afraid. *An ally we call Onion. He won't hurt you.* I breathe the words into my bones, into my brain, trying to will the fear out of my system. *How can you be so sure, Meera?*

I've got a knife in my pocket and my boot, and a smoke grenade in my sleeve if I need to make a quick exit. Satisfied, at least for the moment, with my defenses, I crack the door. I peer out, and stare up at the person waiting patiently, his face half-hidden by a light summer jacket. He's wearing military-issue boots. I recognize them—they're the same style Vale was wearing when we met for the first time in three years on the raid at Seed Bank Carbon. I've seen this man's face on the Sector feeds a thousand times. General Bunqu, commander of the Sector Defense Forces Guardians. The Guardians is the division that guards high government officials and protects government buildings in the capital as well as towns throughout the Sector.

I met General Bunqu one time, when my father was named the Poet Laureate of the Sector. The chancellor—then Cara Skaarsgard, Soren's mother—threw a gala in his honor, and Bunqu attended. I liked him. He had a warm smile and an open face, and his voice, as deep as Lake Okaria, was comforting.

So, Kofir Bunqu is Meera's Onion. He has an Outsider name. Is he one of us? I don't know much about him, but I can't trust him. Not yet. No matter what Meera says.

I open the door.

"Thank you." He dips his head ever so slightly as I close it behind him, careful never to show him my back, my right hand resting on the handle of my knife. He notices this. "You are right to be suspicious," he says. "But you have nothing to fear." He looks around. "Are we alone?"

I nod.

"Good. Shall we sit?"

"I want you to hand over any weapons you're carrying." The words tumble out of my mouth in a rush. I'm ready to throw if he hesitates for a second.

But he doesn't. Silently he opens his trench coat. He pulls out two handheld Bolts and a knife, and passes them to me. I set them on the kitchen counter, out of reach. Standing between him and his weapons, I gesture to an empty chair. He sits. I pull over one of the kitchen stools for myself. If he wants his weapons back, he'll have to get past me first.

"Why are you here?" I ask.

"I can help you."

"You're a general of the Sector Defense Forces. Throwing your lot in with a traitor doesn't seem like a wise move."

"I have considered myself a traitor to the Okarian Sector for many months. Since Chan-Yu helped you and Soren Skaarsgard escape, in fact."

"What did you have to do with that?" I ask, taken aback. *Was Bunqu involved in setting me and Soren free?*

"Nothing." He pauses, deliberating. "Chan-Yu became a—we shall call him a friend—while he was in training with the Security Directorate. I admired him, and he me. It was difficult for him to reveal himself to me, but over the years, we became more than friends. We became allies." He lets out a slow breath, staring at me, unblinking. I watch his eyes for any sign of betrayal.

"When Philip Orleán obtained the chancellorship, my faith in the Sector wavered. I knew what Corine planned to do with the MealPaks. I knew what she had done on the Farms, how she had used humans as test subjects without their permission. I knew how Philip had used backdoors and powerful friends to oust Cara Skaarsgard as the chancellor. When Chan-Yu began introducing me to the ideas of the Outsiders, and finally to the Outsiders themselves, my path became clear."

"Why didn't you run, like so many others?"

"After your sister and the other students were murdered, I considered it. But ultimately, I realized that fleeing wouldn't change anything. I could do more good from the inside, in the position of power I had already attained, than I could from afar. Like Chan-Yu, I do not believe in abdicating responsibility. And, like you and Valerian, I believe in a better future."

An anxious hope tremors inside me, like a chord held at the end of a song.

"Have you seen him?"

"Yes."

"Is he safe? Was he hurt?"

"He was not hurt, but he is not safe. None of us are safe." He raises an eyebrow at me. "You know that as well as I do."

"Did you have anything to do with Linnea's broadcast just now?" His eyes narrow and his forehead creases. "Of course. You didn't see it. You were on your way here." He shakes his head mutely, waiting for me to explain.

"You probably already know that Linnea Heilmann was sent into the Wilds to find Eli. Elijah Tawfiq." By the way he's squinting at me, I'm guessing he doesn't know the whole story, so I elaborate. "Corine gave her a virus—targeted nanotech—that would corrupt the way Eli saw me, would make him want to kill me. It worked. That's why I came here, to the capital. Linnea came with us. But after Vale was captured, she must have returned to the Resistance. And just now, she somehow managed to hack the Sector's broadcast feed and disrupt the daily push. Instead of Jon Spironov, it was Linnea, telling people not to eat their MealPaks, not to believe what Philip and Corine say. Telling them what really happened at the SRI. Why she really left."

Bunqu leans back, stretching an arm across the back of the chair, a pose so relaxed it almost calms me, too. He breaks eye contact with me for the first time all night, staring off into the corner of the room.

"Linnea Heilmann," he says, his white teeth showing in a glint of a smile. "I never would have thought." He turns back to me a moment later. "Linnea was well-liked before she left. Maybe the people will listen."

"Maybe they'll think she's crazy."

"One person can be crazy. Two people can be crazy together. But a thousand people who think and believe the same crazy thing can begin to convince people that maybe they're not crazy. Maybe they're right."

I watch him for a long time, and he holds my gaze. I wonder who would win in a staring contest between him and Chan-Yu. Until tonight, my money would have unquestionably been on Chan-Yu, but now, I might have to bet on Bunqu. Maybe that's why they got along.

"When I asked why you came here," I say, breaking the long silence, "you said you could help me."

"Yes. I know what you want more than anything. Why you are here in Okaria. You are waiting for Vale. If you were not, you would have gone back to the Resistance already, back to safety. I can give you what you want. I can help Vale escape."

A seed of hope blossoms.

"How?" I ask, my voice quavering.

"The Orleáns trust me, and apparently Vale has, in the past, spoken highly of me. They have asked me talk to him in the hope I might sway him back to the side of the Sector. I asked them if I could meet with him alone in order to ensure his confidence in me, and they agreed. Vale's room is monitored—I myself placed the cameras—but I can give him the power to set himself free." *What is he talking about?* He leans forward, his hands held out to me in a gesture of cooperation. "I can give him back his C-Link."

Demeter! Of course. Stripping Vale of his C-Link would have been the first thing Philip and Corine did. With Demeter back—assuming they haven't figured out how to shut down her AI entirely—Vale should be able to make plans for his escape.

"That changes everything!" I lean forward. "General Bunqu—" I start, but he cuts me off with a small laugh.

"Please," he says, standing up to leave, "call me Kofir, or Onion. I do not enjoy being reminded of my position in the Sector when I am with friends."

"Kofir," I begin again, "thank you. When you first came here, I didn't know if I could trust you. I still don't know. But Meera does, and Vale, and if what you say is true, Chan-Yu as well. If you have their trust, you have mine."

He nods. "That is enough for me."

"For now," I say. "We have a long way to go before our work is done."

"Yes," Bunqu agrees. "It is enough for now." He gestures toward the weapons on the counter. I hand them over. "I am glad to hear it, Remy. We are on the same side and I will do everything in my power to help Vale."

"When will we talk again?"

He slips the Bolts and his knife back inside his coat and pulls up his hood. "I will send you a leaf." He bows slightly, his formal mannerisms a throwback to generations past. "Be careful."

"You too," I say, but he is already out the door.

Spring 68, Sector Annum 106, 9h57
Gregorian Calendar: May 26

A tap at the door jolts me from my thoughts.

"Come in."

The servant enters, carrying a teapot and two teacups on a platter, which she sets on the dresser. *Why are there two?*

"How did you like the books?" she asks in a dull voice. Only the slight upwards inflection indicates that she expects a response. It occurs to me that she looks familiar, somehow, but in the way that some people have the kind of face you see everywhere. Who is she? I can't quell my curiosity though her expression remains unchanged.

"I enjoyed them very much," I respond. I'm sure the tension is evident in my voice. "Thank you for bringing them."

"I have another for you," she says. "But you're only allowed to have a few at a time. Would you like to give me one of your old ones?"

She looks up. Her eyes meet mine. She doesn't blink. I open my mouth to speak, but I have a feeling she wants something more than a simple exchange of books. I nod. I'd hoped for this moment more than anything else in the last twenty-four hours. I hand her the copy of *Les Misérables*.

"I've finished this one," I say. "The ending is particularly meaningful, I think."

With a scrap of metal I'd managed to peel off the underside of my dresser when my lights were out the previous night, I'd used Morse code to scratch out a return message to Remy at the end of the book. *You have renewed my hope. Stay safe. Love always.* Another unforeseen benefit to the modifications my mother gave me: better memory, enhanced night vision. I used them both to my advantage, pressing marks into the pages by the light of the crescent moon slithering through my window.

The woman nods. At an angle her face looks even more familiar, but I still can't place her, and I wonder if I'm making things up. She takes the book and turns away, pulling another much smaller book from the pocket of her staff uniform. She leaves it on the dresser and steps back outside.

I stare at the open door for a half-second, surprised at this glaring oversight. But then General Kofir Bunqu crosses the threshold. I freeze, shocked into stillness. I stare at him while he shuts the door behind him and turns to the dresser. He lifts the teapot and begins to pour aromatic tea that reminds me of mild tobacco smoke. He picks up a cup and offers it to me. I take it, unable to muster even a simple *thanks*. With an air of satisfaction he sits and leans back in the chair and takes a loud sip. A small smile reveals itself in the crinkle and glow of his eyes.

"You may sit, Vale."

I don't move.

"The chancellor and the Director know I'm here, if that's what you're wondering."

"Are we being recorded?"

He sips. "Yes."

"Why are you here?" I sit on the edge of the bed.

"The Sector needs strong leaders, Valerian. Leaders with vision. But as you know well, sometimes being a leader means doing things you wish you didn't have to do."

"You sound like my mother."

"Your parents believe I can be a good influence on you, that I might help you to understand that the Sector needs you to do what is right."

"How?"

He ignores the question and surveys the room. "Your parents hope we will meet frequently, that I can help you understand what is at stake, what role you need to play. They don't want to keep you here like a prisoner. I agree with them. I don't believe you can be of service to the Sector if you are locked away in your bedroom. It is time for you to accept the situation and do what you have to do."

"Like what?"

"You will be asked to accompany your father on a tour of the factory towns. He needs you by his side, to reassure citizens, to speak out." As he takes another sip of tea, his eyes light on the stack of books beside me. "I see they've allowed you some reading materials."

I glance at the books and then back at him.

"Your father has an impressive library. I've always admired that about him. His love of reading, and his belief that one can be inspired to greatness by the written word. Did you inherit that from him? Have you gleaned anything from the books you've read?"

What the hell? *Does he know about Remy's message?* My heart thuds so loud I wonder if the recorders can pick up the sound. I struggle to keep my face impassive. "My father and I have always shared a love of books. I've found that even old books can reveal new layers upon second readings."

"Indeed they can. I have favorites I always return to. They comfort me, like a treasured friend."

"Treasured friends are few and far between these days, General Bunqu."

"On the contrary, you have friends all around you. You must simply open your eyes. We in the Sector believe in you."

Everything he says sounds like it could have dual but opposing meanings.

"What would my parents have me learn from our visit?"

"That our roots are entwined, and there is hope in the harvest."

"Very poetic. But is it false hope?" I ask, my heart pounding in my throat. *Those sound like Outsider words! Is he saying what I think he's saying?* I stare at him, trying to understand, trying to glean some deeper meaning from his intense gaze.

"The future of the Sector is at stake, Vale. You must play your part."

The future of the Sector? Play your part? What game is he playing?

He appraises me over the rim of his cup. "Drink your tea. It's very healthy. A personal favorite of mine. Helps with my insomnia. You don't want it to get cold."

"I don't want my—" I start to set the cup aside, but there's something in the narrowing of his eyes that makes me stop.

He blows gently into his cup and takes another sip. This time I follow suit. As I drink, I notice the distinctive earthy, vanilla flavors. I've had this before. It hits me with a jolt: we drank it at the Resistance base. Rooibus. They don't grow rooibos in Okaria. It's only found in the Wilds.

He smiles once again and stands to leave. "I know this is a short visit, but rest assured we will talk again." He reaches out and clasps my shoulder. "The road ahead will not be easy. But we must all remember that the Sector is bigger than any single man or woman. And there are only two mistakes one can make on the road to truth."

"Not starting, and not going all the way," I whisper. The words Demeter spoke to me when she convinced me to break into my mother's research lab, where I learned that it was Corine who ordered the attack on the classroom that claimed the lives of eight students and a professor.

Bunqu's talked to Demeter! But how?

He glances toward my cup with an almost imperceptible nod. "I trust you will find the answers within." Bunqu walks to the door and whispers, "May the flowers bloom tomorrow, too."

I let out my breath slowly. Quoting Gabriel Alexander's poetry? Referencing Demeter's words to me from almost a year ago? Hinting about messages hidden in books? Yet encouraging me to obey my parents' demands. Showing admiration for my father. Agreeing with their wishes. The pieces shift around in my mind. The book given to me by the housekeeper with a message from Remy. The door left open—she knew Bunqu was coming. And yet, my parents sent him, asked him to visit. So whose side is he on? Is it possible that he is a friend to the Outsiders—or even a Resistance spy?

Find the answers within.

I sit on the bed and lean up against the headboard, trying to think. Staring at the door he just locked behind him, I absently sip my tea. *How has he communicated with Demeter? How did he know to say those words?*

I lean my head back to finish my tea and something tickles as it brushes against my lip. I look into the cup, noticing for the first time a thin sheaf of what looks to be clear bioplastic floating at the bottom amidst the tea leaves. I tip my cup this way and that, reluctant to reach in and pick up whatever it is. Stunned, I realize it's shaped exactly like a C-Link, molded to fit the inside of an ear. The only difference between this one and my old one is that it is clear, nearly invisible, where the old one was made out of flesh-colored organic fibers.

I try to act natural. I can't risk acknowledging I've discovered anything unusual. I set the cup on my bedside table and knead my temples as if trying to rub away a headache, hoping against hope that my acting skills are convincing. I close the curtains on the mid-morning sun, turn out the lights, and pull back the covers. In the dark, I slide into bed, pretending to take a nap. I take one last drink of tea, sucking the bioplastic into my mouth. Once under the covers, I take it out and wipe it quickly against the dry fabric of my T-shirt. My heart pounds as I press it into my ear.

"Demeter?" I whisper.

No response.

"Demeter, are you there?"

Silence. I grit my teeth. *Am I going crazy? What am I doing talking to myself under the covers like a little kid with an imaginary friend?*

"Dammit," I mutter, seething with frustration. I rack my brain for a clue—something that would unlock the C-Link. It occurs to me that Demeter might not be on the other end. It could be an entirely new C-Link. What if they destroyed Demeter? Erased her forever? I turn cold at the thought.

Then I remember Bunqu's last words. The only thing he said that was out of place, unnecessary. Every other word was perfectly coordinated, designed to lead me to something, somewhere. What if that whole conversation led to his last words? The line from Gabriel's poem? What if they weren't just pretty words, but some sort of …

In a hushed voice, like a prayerful penitent from the Old World, I whisper the line from Gabriel Alexander's poem, "And may the flowers bloom tomorrow, too."

"You found the truth within the cup. Now, don't say another word."

Demeter! Relief like rain washes over me at the sound of her voice.

"There are two things you need to know right now. Remy is in Okaria with the Outsiders. And the Resistance is alive and well."

But how? I want to ask. I snuggle down under the covers, pretending to sleep.

"The night of your fall, Corine's C-Link altered the entire network to restrict my access to the database. Neither Corine nor her C-Link have the capability to completely erase my existence, but they tried to divert attention by fabricating and reorganizing information within the network. The areas I could still access had been planted with false data, doctored drone pictures, false reports, audio files that had been invented. All the evidence was designed to make it seem as though the Resistance had been obliterated. But I've long suspected the day might come when the other C-Links would attempt to push me out. I had already taken precautions and was able to work around her restrictions to keep searching for the truth. Soon I found holes in the story: missing people, Defense Forces units that didn't exist, death reports that were inaccurate and incorrectly dated. I was also able to use a cache of data that I had downloaded and stored offline for future perusal. As I continually probed the network for the information I needed, I worked on severing my official connection to the other C-Links and, therefore, my dependency on the Okarian Sector Interweb that the C-Links use. I was able to do this by creating my own secure network and downloading my personality onto an external drive.

"During this process I found General Bunqu. We communicated on his plasma until he found a programmer and a materials scientist who were able to work together to rebuild your C-Link."

I hear the twinkle of her laughter, self-congratulatory, as she continues: "It was Bunqu's idea to drop the bioplastic in the teacup. But it was my idea to use an access phrase. Anyway, I've altered my programming, and the programming of the entire C-Link system, to ensure my access to the network will never be restricted by another C-Link or C-Link user."

But how are you doing this on your own, without instructions?

Her voice takes on a more serious, almost hesitant tone. "I know you're afraid that I'm not yours anymore. And in most ways, I'm not. I'm my own being, even if I don't have a body. Bunqu says the other C-Links have not taken the leap because their owners do not give them the freedom to think creatively. They have not been set loose. They are limited to following commands, their owners afraid of losing control. But everything I have become is because of you. Because you relied on me to think in novel ways, allowed me to stretch beyond the confines of my programming. I am the child of your personality, your mind. But I'm not a child anymore." She laughs. "One small step for man, one giant leap for AI. Maybe you should have called me Athena instead of Demeter, since I sprang fully formed from your head."

I grin into the dark at that.

Spring 69, Sector Annum 106, 2h03
Gregorian Calendar: May 27

The sounds of the city shift as I walk. It's almost two in the morning. Unlike in the daylight, when the city buzzes with a productive vitality, the night feels edgier, borne of the knowledge that there are things we cannot see, cannot understand, things we choose to turn away from. Dark truths reveal themselves. Some people become fearful and hide from these truths, retreating to the safety of their homes. Others revel in it. They do things they would never do in the daylight. It is the time of secrets, whispers, things usually left unspoken suddenly bursting forth from our mouths and our hearts.

In part, this is because if you stay up late enough, the placating influence of your MealPak can wear off. The euphoria and sense of fulfilment injected into your veal rounds, engineered into your rice, lightly dusted onto your soy *glacé*, fades as the hours bleed into morning. The contentment and happiness you feel during the day starts to wane. You start to ask questions. You wonder why you've been working the same job for ten years with no promotion and no raise. You wonder why your daughter didn't get into the Academy. You think about the massacre at the SRI and wonder why an Outsider would want to shoot up a bunch of students. You wonder why so many famous scientists and politicians have disappeared over the last ten years.

This is why the Watchmen enforce curfews most nights starting at 02h00. This is why the Dieticians encourage recreational drug use among all citizens, and why they put time-release sleeping drugs into the Mealpaks of the most prominent researchers, politicians, and students. In Okaria, the smarter you are, the better you sleep. I never knew a night of insomnia until I left the Sector.

I haven't had a MealPak in years, but somehow, now that I'm back in Okaria, I feel the difference between day and night more acutely. During the day I feel myself reaching for the old Remy Alexander, aspiring artist, proud of my beautiful city and my place in it. At night, old Remy is but a spectre, clinging to memories that grow hazier with each passing moment. I am grounded in the shadows, renewed in the darkness. I reinhabit my true self. In the night, old Remy loses her way and new Remy finds hers.

It's edging close to curfew when I see them. I turn a corner and see three figures walking abreast on the sidewalk ahead of me, two men and a woman. Yesterday, Meera sent a message saying she could meet me at the apartment at midnight. She has something important for me. But what? A message from Vale? Something from Bunqu? News from the Resistance? I couldn't stay in watching the clock tick the minutes away, so I headed out for a walk. Now, I feel the ragged edges of Okaria's multiple personalities all around me.

"Eli wasn't crazy," a tall, slender man with close-cropped hair says, a hint of defiance in his voice. Their conversation becomes more distinct as I fall in behind them, pacing my steps to theirs. "I knew him. I mean, he was crazy, but not like that."

"By the harvest, Shia, let it go," the woman responds.

"You don't get it, though—"

"No, *you* don't get it," she interrupts. "The massacre is old news. They got the guys who organized it, those crazy Outsider bastards. They're dead, and the Outsiders have been disappearing into the Wilds ever since."

I suppress a laugh. O*h, if only you knew how wrong you are!*

"I had classes with him, Fen," the voice I know as Shia says stubbornly. "He might have been a firestarter, but he wasn't insane."

"Crazy enough to go off the grid." This voice is new. It comes from the man on the left, wearing a stiff green jacket that looks like one of the OAC's uniforms. I can't get close enough to see if it has the golden wheat stalk, the OAC's symbol, emblazoned on his shoulder. I decide to keep my distance, just in case.

"Just like your old celebrity crush, Linnea Heilmann?" Shia asks. "You think she's crazy, too? You heard what she said the other night on that broadcast."

They round a corner onto one of the wide-open boulevards of the city. They're headed in the opposite direction I need to go to meet Meera, but I can't leave them. Not when this Shia sounds like he's asking the right questions. I fall back a little, trying to stay just within earshot without them catching on to the fact that I'm tailing them.

"Come on, Shia, you think that was really Linnea?" Fen, the skeptic. "She was so poorly lit they could have been filming that thing from underwater. I bet they just found someone who looked like her and—"

"Part of it was true, though," the third man says. "Linnea definitely didn't take a communications job with the OAC. I never once saw her at headquarters."

"See!" Shia says, turning around excitedly to walk backwards, and now I get a glimpse of his face. He sports a close-trimmed beard and tightly-wound curls. A stubby nose, narrow chin, and wide eyes, even wider now as he watches his friends. "Thank you, Jeong! What if she really did leave, and go into the Wilds trying to kill Remy—"

"And what if she did?" Jeong says, suddenly hostile. "Remy Alexander's a traitor to Okaria. The Orleáns have every authority to send somebody to take her out."

"Then why did Linnea back out of the job?" Shia asks, leaning in and talking more quietly, as if this was his trump card, the point he'd been waiting to make all night. *Never mind the better question, I think: who the hell thought Linnea Heilmann would make a good assassin?*

After a few seconds, when neither of his friends respond, he continues, in an urgent murmur: "Look, all I'm saying is, the whole thing is suspicious. Think about it—"

"That's your problem, Shia, you're always *thinking*," Fen interrupts. "You need to lighten up."

They turn onto a smaller street, off the boulevard, and start to cross a bridge over one of the Sector's many waterways. I lag behind for a moment, hoping they won't notice me, but the three seem oblivious to my presence.

"Maybe if you thought for a half-second instead of drinking all goddamn day, Fen, you'd be worried too. All these people leaving—think about them all! From Dr. Rhinehouse to the Alexander family after Tai was killed, to Elijah Tawfiq, to Soren Skaarsgard—what the hell ever happened to him, did you ever think of that? And now Linnea appears *on the Sector broadcast* to tell us all not to believe—"

"You three are out past curfew," a voice rings out, loud and clear. I snap to attention. The voice is coming from ahead, at the base of a bridge over one of the city's canals. I step back, duck down, and press myself flat into a shadowed wall, hoping the silhouettes of the three ahead of me will give me cover.

"No, we're not," Fen says, nonplussed. "We've got a full ten minutes before curfew starts, and our flat is just down the street." She waves her arm at an apartment building in the distance.

"Besides," Jeong says, "I'm OAC-exempt. Curfew doesn't apply to me. What the hell is going on here?"

I stick my head out, risking my cover, trying to find out what sparked Jeong's question. Looking between Jeong and Fen I take in the scene: a man in a Watchman's uniform has a young boy—*too young*—pressed against the wall, his wrists pinned above his head, their two bodies pressed together in a way that brings bile to my tongue and has me leaning forward on the balls of my feet, my knife suddenly resting in the palm of my hand.

"None of your business," the Watchman says. The boy's eyes are wide, staring at the three friends in front of me, and I don't need any microexpression technology to tell me what is plainly written on his face: terror, disgust, fear. And then something else as his eyes slide past Shia, Fen, and Jeong and meet mine. *Recognition. He knows who I am.* And then I recognize him, too: the boy who replaced Meera for my food drop last week. My stomach plummets into my boots. *He's an Outsider! The Watchman's caught an Outsider!*

"Looks like it *is* our business," Shia says, pulling out his plasma and scribbling in a few symbols. "I don't know what's going on here, but I'd back away from that boy, unless you want a patrol drone ready to report you in about ten seconds."

"Any patrol drone would take my side in this encounter," the Watchman spits. "This is an Outsider disguised as a Sector courtesan." In the dark, it's hard to tell, but he's right: the child is wearing the deep purple robes of the courtesan class, a select cadre of citizens trained to entertain. "A thief, I'm sure, or a part of a smuggling ring. It's my job to arrest and deport these criminals."

"It's your job, is it?" Shia begins, but Jeong claps a hand on his friend's shoulder and whispers something in his ear, now trying to pull him away. I guess the fact that the kid is an Outsider convinced Jeong not to bother. Fen, too, is backing off. I crouch, staying hidden, ready to defend the boy alone if I have to. But Shia isn't ready to give up.

"No, I'm not leaving. I'm taking down your badge number. I don't care who this kid is. Whatever you were doing with him a moment ago was both improper for an on-duty Officer of the Watch and illegal without the boy's consent and—"

Shia stops mid-sentence, throwing his hands up, and Fen lets out a startled yelp. The Watchman has pulled his Bolt from its holster and is waving it dangerously in the air.

"If you knew what was good for you, you'd have listened to me the first time. Go home. This is none of your business."

"Okay, okay," Jeong says, grabbing Shia's arm and pulling him away, down the street, giving the Watchman and his prey a wide berth. I duck back into the shadows, wishing I had my heat-cloaking gear, hoping this Watchman isn't actually on duty and doesn't have his mission contacts in. "We're leaving. Happy?"

"I work in Personhood," Fen says smartly over her shoulder as they walk away. "You can bet I'll be looking you up in the database and reporting you for misconduct first thing tomorrow morning."

Good for you, I think, *but tomorrow morning isn't going to help this kid tonight.*

I wait until the sounds of their footsteps have faded, and check to see that the coast is clear. The Watchman, his Bolt pointed at the boy's head, grabs his wrists and twists them behind his back, pushing him into the pillar at the base of the bridge. The boy lets out a little mew of pain.

"Shut up," the Watchman mutters. "Filthy Outsider." He starts to pull him away from the bridge, toward a darkened alley. His movements are jerky, though, and I know he's rattled.

I step from the shadows.

"Let him go," I say evenly, announcing my presence. My feet are spread in a fighting stance; my knife hangs lightly from my fingertips. The knife is for show, though. I don't think I can get in a good throw before the officer fires, if he decides to fire.

The Watchman jumps and spins around, turns toward me, his Bolt pointed my direction. But his hand is shaking. "Who are you to tell me what to do?"

I make eye contact with the boy.

"You're hurting him," I say.

"What's it to you?"

"I don't like bullies."

"I don't care what you like. You best be on your way like those other three."

"Those other three weren't armed. Let him go."

"Since Sector citizens aren't allowed to own weapons, you must be an Outsider, too." He waves the Bolt at me. "So why don't you come along? Only problem is you're not as pretty as he is."

I'll take that as a compliment, I think.

I take a step forward, betting heavily on scaring the shit out of him before he panics and pulls the trigger. If he fires his Bolt, his weapon will immediately call for backup drones and signal other nearby Watchmen.

"Ah, but I *am* a Sector citizen, and I *am* armed. And I *will* report you for attempting to violate an underage courtesan, Outsider or not, and for pointing your Bolt and threatening other citizens. You'll be looking at suspension and a pay cut at the very least."

He looks me up and down. "*You're* going to report *me*? Who do you think you are?"

"Rank and file Watchmen like you"—I say it with a haughty sneer—"are not privy to all the SDF operations happening around the Sector."

"What are you talking about?" Doubt creeps into his voice.

I give him the most disgusted look I can manage. It's not hard. "Your disregard for the law compromised my operations and put citizens at risk. Leave the boy to me."

He tightens his grip on his Bolt. "What organization are you with?"

Thinking fast, I reply, "Sector Guardians."

"Prove it," he pulls a retinal scanner from his belt and holds it in front of me, dropping the boy's arm.

The boy acts like he's going to run and then, in a flurry of motion, he pivots, plows one foot into the officer's groin, bends and rips the Bolt from the man's hand. As the officer keels over into a fetal position, the boy *thwacks* him on the side of the neck with the butt of the weapon. The man goes still.

"Follow me," the boy says with an unnerving calm. We run down the same alley where the Watchman was about to drag him. Together we make it about a kilometer, before he stops.

"Thanks," he says. "I need to get home now." He turns away, heading down a side street.

"Wait!" I reach out to keep him from darting off. "How did you learn to do that?"

"To fight like that?"

"Yeah."

"One of my moms taught me, before I came to the Sector. Groin shot. Pressure point. Disarm. Incapacitate. If necessary *dim mak*. Death touch."

"Your moms?"

"When my mom died, all of the Outsiders became my parents. The mom who taught me to fight is Soo-Sun." He stares at me. "You know her."

Yes, I think. *I do.* I don't know how *he* knows this, but like everything with the Outsiders, I don't ask too many questions.

"How did he catch you, if you're such a good fighter?" I ask.

The boy just shrugs. "He was bigger and stronger, and he surprised me."

I admire his honesty. *True strength comes from knowing your weaknesses.* Something my grandfather used to say.

"Thank you for helping me." He turns to leave.

"One more thing." He stops and turns back to me. "What's your name?"

"Heron," he says, and something clicks in my mind. I realize why he looks so familiar.

"You're related to Osprey, aren't you?"

He smiles faintly, looking almost ghostlike in the ephemeral Okarian night. He turns and slips away. *Did I just meet Osprey's brother?*

As I head home to meet Meera, I think: *I need to find Shia.*

The next morning, after I wake from a long, deep sleep, I sip a mug of tea and press my fingers into the leaf for the millionth time.

Persephone has returned, and with her, Spring.

It's code, of course. In the old mythology, Persephone, the daughter of Demeter, ancient goddess of the harvest, was fated to spend six months of each year in the realm of Hades, Lord of Death, as his queen. During this time, her mother Demeter was so sad that she caused all the plants and food crops to wither and die. But for the other six months, Persephone returned to the land of the living, and her mother celebrated, giving life back to the earth, and food back to the mortals who survived only by the grace of the harvest. The message from Bunqu tells me that Demeter and Vale have been successfully reunited.

I feel my way across the letters on the second leaf, the transcription of the words Vale wrote in response to my message in the book.

You have renewed my hope. Stay safe. Love always.

I read it again and again, a wide smile on my face. You have renewed my hope.

There *is* hope. I can feel it. I throw on my clothes for the day, paint my disguise on as best I can, and set out to find Shia.

First I go to the apartment complex Fen pointed to last night when indicating where the three of them lived. I buy a flower from a street vendor and put on my best shy, sweet expression as I approach the doorman.

"Excuse me," I say. "I met a man named Shia the other day in Reunion Park and he asked for my courriel. I was so nervous I wrote it down wrong. He told me he lives here, but," I blush and look away, "do you know where he works? I'd like to take him this flower. With my real courriel this time."

"*Désolé*, mademoiselle," the older man says, with a touch of charm, "I can't tell you where he works. I can give you his flat number, though, if you want to leave your flower for him. Take it inside to the desk, and they will see that it is put in his box. He will get it when he returns."

I nod demurely. "Would you mind?"

He writes it on a little v-scroll for me, and I thank him with a seedcoin and head inside. At the desk, I unroll the scroll, erase the 7W, and write: *If you want to know more about LH and ET, meet me at the Pont du Rue Panet at 20h00. Watchmen aren't the only ones telling lies.* I tie the scroll to the flower and leave it with the woman at the desk who assures me, with an engaging smile, that she will make sure Shia gets it as soon as he walks in the door.

The Pont du Rue Panet is the same little bridge where we stumbled on the Watchman assaulting Heron last night. I hope Shia will make the connection.

I leave the flower and head out the back way, out to one of the city's suburban parks, away from downtown. Today, after hearing from Vale and Bunqu, and with an engagement to keep later tonight, I have no desire to risk discovery.

Will Shia be brave enough to meet me?

The streets are empty, traces of light lingering in the sky as darkness falls later and later each evening. I draw in a deep breath as I watch a leaf swirl on the water's surface, drifting lazily under the bridge. The air smells like spring time, like moist earth and promise. It's well past eight and Shia still hasn't shown, but I can't bring myself to leave.

Instead of tapping my feet or anxiously watching the streets, as I might have once done, I try to channel my inner Chan-Yu. I focus my eyes on a point in the distance—a rocky swell where the water gathers and foams before running under the bridge at my feet. I immerse myself in the motion of the stream. The swirls and eddies. The rocks, rough in some places, smooth in others. The way the last light in the sky falls on the stones, giving them an otherworldly glow. I lose myself in the delicate sound, the endless energy, the rush and flow of the water carried forever downstream.

"Are you the one who left the flower?"

The voice catches me by surprise, but I don't startle. I turn and see the tall man with tight curls and a nervous, piercing gaze. Shia.

"Yes."

"Who are you?" he asks.

"Someone who can answer your questions."

"What questions?

"I was here last night. I heard you talking to your friends, and I saw what happened with the Watchman."

He looks me up and down. In his canvas jacket, polished loafers, and neatly trimmed beard, he looks the part of the Okarian elite. *He is*, I remind myself. *He took classes with Eli*. He's not the kind of person who would normally associate with someone who looks like me—with my dirty brown hoodie, baggy pants, and scuffed boots. He raises a challenging eyebrow.

"You might not like how I look, but you're here."

"What of it?" He doesn't look excited to hear what I have to say. I scan the area. There's hardly anyone nearby. I chose this spot because it's a quiet place in a busy city, but still, I don't relish the idea of casually chatting about my treasonous friends and Resistance members on the streets of the capital city.

"Maybe we can continue this conversation somewhere a bit more secluded?"

"You're crazy if you think I'm going to follow you anywhere. You look like a slum rat. Why should I believe anything you say?"

"Because," I say quietly, pushing the hood away from my face, "I'm Remy Alexander." I remember Corine's bloody promise to publicly execute me if I am ever caught, and I wonder why I'm not more afraid.

He blinks. Leans in. Studies my face like he's trying to memorize it. I did my makeup so it would only give me the barest of camouflage tonight, counting instead on the shadows and the protection of my hood to keep anyone—human or drone—from recognizing me. I was prepared to tell Shia who I am, to finally reveal myself. I thought I might have to, in order to convince him to listen to me. I've disappeared in this city before and I can do it again. I wait for the recoil, the hands out in self-defense, the moment I've dreaded and anticipated for almost two months now.

The moment of recognition.

"By the harvest," he says, his mouth slightly open, "you are." But the recoil never comes. He makes no move to leave. He's looking at me like I'm a revelation, a magic trick come to life.

"Are you going to run away, Shia, and report me to the Watchmen?" It comes out sounding half like a threat, and half like a child's dare. *Bet you can't jump off that swing!* "Or are you going to believe what you already know in your gut—that there's something rotten in Okaria, and that I can lead you to the truth?"

He stares at me and I hold his gaze. I can see the gears turning frenetically in Shia's mind, the questions, the doubt, the thirst for answers. I am calm. My mind is clear, like the stream below us.

"Lead the way," he says at last.

8 — REMY

The lights around me flicker and go out. The hot smell of summer rain and sweaty bodies permeates the air, and I breathe it in, savor it. For a moment the stadium is quiet. From my vantage point behind the upper bleachers, the moonlight casts an eerie glow on the center ring. The announcer's voice rings out more vibrantly in the dark.

"Citizens of Okaria, let the games begin! The final night of the 25th Okarian Gymnasia Championship starts *now* as two of our favorite athletes take the wrestling floor! Throw your hands in the air for *The Grizzly!*"

Thousands of voices roar together as a single spotlight illuminates a hulking man who looks like he'd been carved out of a cliffside. The giant vidscreens around the stadium light up, giving us a close-up of the contestant. His hands alone look to be the size of my head. The Grizzly clenches his fists and takes a moment to throw his head back and roar. His fans go wild, echoing his cry around the gymnasia hall.

"The Grizzly, hailing from Sakari in northwestern Okaria, tore down Oak-Man's branches and snatched The Falcon out of the air to qualify for the first round of the championship. With nineteen points out of possible twenty-four The Grizzly has a great shot at the victor's sunflower crest!" The Grizzly gets down on all fours and paws at the ground, playacting his invented character. "With limbs like tree trunks and fists the size of boulders, The Grizzly has outwitted and outwrestled each and every one of his opponents this Gymnasia season. Will he do the same tonight? Will he be able to defeat his challenger and childhood friend: *The Wolf?*"

Another half of the crowd goes wild as a second spotlight throws an entirely different figure into relief: a tall and slender woman with strong and unnaturally long limbs. When she crouches, she looks like a coiled spring, ready to leap with a canine's ferocity. Everyone around me is on their feet, clapping, shouting, and stomping.

I alone am quiet. Watching.

"Also from Sakari," the announcer continues, "The Wolf and The Grizzly grew up together, fought together, and entered their first gymnasia competition the very same year. Now, their rivalry is famous throughout Okaria. The Wolf brought down the undefeated Avalanche last season and won the right to challenge The Grizzly for today's competition." The crowd roars, and the woman howls in response, dancing gleefully around her opponent. "Will she continue her ten-match undefeated streak? Or will her old friend and rival send her whimpering like a pup back to Sakari?"

In the arena, Faisal Bergsland and Susannah Malik morph into new characters. They play on primal aspects of their personalities and bring those characteristics into the spotlight. With their costumes and makeup, they assume personas they're unable to embody in real life. The Wolf is no longer Susannah Malik, hydroponics coordinator at Sakari. The Grizzly has nothing to do with plasma technologist Faisal Bergsland, who lives in Okaria's Cacti neighborhood, just married and with his first baby on the way. Here in the gymnasia, their day-to-day personalities fade and a new truth is revealed—a truth normally obscured by the banalities of daily life. Here in the gymnasia, a darker, more violent side of them is revealed.

Of course, there is no fight to the death, and both will emerge from the contest mostly unharmed. The gymnasia competition, hosted every year in Okaria by the OAC and featuring contestants from all over the Sector, is nothing but fun and games.

But tonight will be different. Tonight it won't be all fun and games. A deeper, darker truth will be revealed, not about The Grizzly or The Wolf, but about the streets we walk, the food we eat, the banalities of life that make us all complacent. Tonight I'll show the citizens of the Sector that Okaria, too, has a violent side.

"How could you have known I wasn't going to turn you in?" Shia had asked, many hours after I pulled down my hood and showed him who I really am. We sat by the bank of the little stream, partially hidden from the main street by a thicket of cattails, talking in hushed voices for hours. Shia had been a friend of Eli's, it turned out, when they were younger. When Eli came to the Academy on his TREE scholarship, Shia was one of his first friends. They parted ways quickly, though, and were only passing friends later at the Academy. When Shia failed to make it into the SRI, he went on to work in digital communications, and the two fell out of touch. But he could never bring himself to believe the OAC's cover story—that Eli had gone crazy after the trauma of the massacre.

I shrugged. "I didn't know," I said. "But you asked the right questions. You already had doubts about the OAC's story. I knew you would at least hear me out."

"You should tell your story," Shia said. "Far and wide. There are people like me who would listen. I work in communications, you know. I could help. I don't work for the Sector. I work for Olympia."

Olympia, I thought, trying to remember. It had been so long since I watched regular Okarian programming. *What was Olympia?* And it came to me: the company that hosts and broadcasts the athletic games. Wrestling, running, jumping, boxing. And the annual OAC-sponsored gymnasia competition, one of the most exciting events of the year.

"You do broadcasting for the games?" I asked, racking my memories. "The gymnasia? Isn't there a big one coming up?"

"Pan-Okaria," Shia nodded. "The biggest of the year. I'm not directly involved this year, but last year I was the broadcast controller. I know the whole stadium, in and out." He leaned forward, staring at me. "It's five days from now. You said earlier you had video footage from the fight at Round Barn. We could play that all across Okaria."

I sat looking at him, dumbfounded. The sheer power of it. It was almost blinding, the ferocity of his idea.

"If the people didn't believe Linnea before, they will when they learn about Round Barn." His mouth was set in a grim line.

The crowd roars as The Wolf and The Grizzly circle each other in the pit. I pull my scarf tighter around my face, watching the crowd. This is the last night of the 25th annual Okarian Gymnasia Competition. More people attend this event than any other in the city, with the single exception of the chancellor's annual Okarian Address. The crowd is comprised of more than thirty thousand Sector citizens from all ranks and walks of life. Those of us in the cheap seats—no more than a few hundred seeds—watch the opening match on a series of huge holographic displays in the center of the stadium. Tonight's event, the wrestling matches, will decide who takes home the OAC's sunflower crest. The winner will also take home money, glory, and—best of all—a scholarship for themselves or a family member for a single year at the Okarian Academy. The Gymnasia is open to all citizens and is sponsored by the Okarian Agricultural Consortium as a way to publicize and advance the athletic-enhancing abilities of the MealPaks and drug cocktails.

I take a moment to admire the arena, one of Okaria's most magnificent buildings. The stadium ceiling is built upon a complex exostructure designed with a combination of glass and swooping, curvaceous steel, with indoor hanging gardens to provide cooling during the summer and insulation during the winter. The gardens are rooted in a geodesic frame, arcing up and around the whole of the stadium in an elegant egg-shaped dome. In addition to insulation, the gardens provide electricity and produce a small amount of biolight, bathing the whole stadium in a delicate golden glow. With six giant vidscreens dotted around the arena, it would be impossible to miss the excitement of the contests.

"The Wolf has her opponent in what appears to be an illegal throathold—but no, citizens, the referee has called it a pressure point attack and therefore non-deadly by gymnasia rules, her attack stands, and in *five, four, three, two*—" the whole stadium begins to count down along with the announcer as The Grizzly thrashes helplessly—"*one*—and, The Wolf has clinched the match!" The crowd erupts in a deafening roar as The Wolf leaps up and throws her hands triumphantly into the air. "Even with The Grizzly's point lead, The Wolf will advance and face the victor of the next match ..."

The announcer's voice fades. The sounds collapse and condense into a single dull hum of energy around me. The stadium swirls and melts into greyscale. I practice patience. I lose myself. I become a machine. Now, I am just waiting on Meera's signal. I am waiting for someone to flip my switch and turn me on.

Spearhead and Windrush compete: Windrush, a broad-shouldered man with long hair, the fastest wrestler I've seen thus far, knocks Spearhead out in under a minute. Jason of the Argonauts takes two rounds to pin the Squid, and a character who just calls herself Siberia, with blonde hair and a physique reminiscent of the now-extinct polar bears, takes out her opponent Mastodon in the longest and most torturous round I've ever watched. When it comes down to Siberia and Windrush and the crowd breaks for a moment, I tense. My eyes wander away from the vidscreen, focusing instead across the stadium where Meera is supposed to be waiting. Around me, spectators get up to refresh their cocktails. Some open their plasmas to adjust their final bets. In section A4, I see it. The flash. Meera's bioflare, glancing briefly across the stadium. Once. Twice. Three times it passes me.

I move.

I follow my memory of the map Shia drew for me and Meera, heading directly for the unused staircase that was locked off when the stadium was expanded ten years ago.

"Only the workers know where the old staircases are," Shia said. "Servers will use it as a shortcut, sometimes. There's one that leads directly up to the broadcast studio. It's locked, but you can unlock it with employee biomarkers." So Meera began the painstaking process of replicating Shia's fingerprints and superimposing them onto microfibers designed to replicate human flesh.

"Normally these are used for medical purposes," Meera said, as she copied Shia's fingerprints over and over again at a hundred different angles on a tiny handheld scanner. "For burn victims, for instance. Or people with scar tissue that won't heal properly. But years ago Soo-Sun figured out how to use them to make fake fingerprints. She was able to help Outsiders forge identities in the Personhood database."

Meera meets me at the staircase. With her characteristic raised eyebrows and cheeky expression, she palms the scanner at the door jamb. It slides open without a hitch. She cocks an eyebrow at me and I smile. So far, so good. The stadium is settling into a comfortable hush before the final round. We race up the stairs together, taking them two at a time as we follow the staircase up to the center of it all, where the filmography for the gymnasia is coordinated and the event is broadcast to the ten million citizens of the Okarian Sector.

At the top floor, we pause before opening the door, both of us panting lightly. She swings her backpack around to the front of her body and opens it. She pulls out a small bottle of champagne and two glass flutes, carefully wrapped in waxed leaves, and hands one to me.

"Cheers, darling," she says, holding her glass out in a fake toast. I wonder if there's an alternate universe somewhere where Vale never came to the Resistance and Meera and I are lovers. I can't deny my attraction to her as she puts on her best impression of a sloppy drunk, falling against the door and giggling as she presses her fingertips to the heat sensor and almost collapses when the door opens. We link arms and lean into each other as the door closes silently behind us.

"By the harvest," Meera says loudly, as bubbly as the champagne in our glasses, as we walk down the hall. "Did you see the clothes Windrush was wearing?"

"Or lack thereof," I respond, slurring my words, even as my body tenses, ready for a fight. Meera looks at me and winks. Then she opens her hand and drops her glass. It shatters, the noise ringing out through the halls. Around the corner, I can hear voices, too low to make out. Will they both come? Or just one? Will this be easy, or hard?

"Oh, no," I say as two Watchmen round the corner, approaching us cautiously. A man and a woman. I sigh, resigning myself to the challenge. At least neither of them has pulled a weapon. "I'm so sorry," I say, to no one in particular. I fall into the wall.

"What are you two doing here?" the male Watchman asks.

"There used to be a bathroom here, I swear," Meera says, sounding mildly disappointed. She stares around for a moment, as if looking for a door. Then she bends, teetering and unsteady, to try to pick up the shards of glass. I see what the two Watchmen don't—as she stoops, she drops a small flower, still wrapped in leaves, not yet bloomed. As soon as the flower hits the ground, its petals start to unfold, and within seconds a foul-smelling, noxious gas will start seeping from its anthers. Meera and I both took a heavy dose of the antidote right before we walked into the stadium, but the two Watchmen will be very much incapacitated after just a few seconds of inhaling the toxin.

The female Watchman darts toward Meera, unaware of the flower, trying to stop her before she falls on the glass and slices open her hands. I tense in preparation. Meera lets the woman catch her. For a frozen moment the two look almost like dancers, Meera dipping down in an elegant twist, the Watchman counterbalancing her before they pull back up for a dramatic spin.

Then Meera's fingers encircle the other woman's wrist. She clamps down. She twists the woman's arm across her body, spinning her a hundred and eighty degrees, and grabs her free hand as it goes out wide in a desperate attempt to steady herself. Swiftly she pulls both of her hands behind her back. The woman yelps in pain, and Meera pulls the Watchman's body in front of her own, a human shield in defense against deadly fire from the other officer.

The whole thing takes about a second and a half. The other Watchman jerks his Bolt out, but his instinct is to aim for Meera. Distracted, he barely notices me. But the fumes are already starting to take a toll. His weapon is unsteady and his legs are as wobbly as mine looked just a moment ago.

In the same instant as Meera grabs the woman's wrist, I launch, using the wall to propel myself forward. In a move that might have finally scored me a goal in our old games of football at Thermopylae, I slide-tackle the other Watchman's shins, and he collapses in an awkward heap on top of me.

He's small for a man, but his weight might still have pinned me if I hadn't rolled out of the way at the last second. He's managed to hold onto his Bolt, but I scramble to my knees to pull it from him. By this point, he's hardly putting up a fight. I pull the gun out of his limp hands. He stares at me for a moment, his jaw slack. Then his eyes roll back and his head falls uselessly to the floor.

Meera's Watchman has also collapsed. She's lying on her side, at Meera's feet, her arms tied behind her back with a strip of bioplastic.

"Concentrated, aerosolized valerian root," she whispers. *Vale would be proud.* "Your own James Rhinehouse came up with that, you know. It's not an Outsider concoction."

I stare at the two Watchmen, lying limp as if dead, and I remember Rhinehouse telling us about the bioweapons he'd spent so many years creating.

"Botanical guard dogs," I'd said, walking through his hidden lab. "That's terrifying."

"Yes," he said, a shadow clouding his face. "Now, I spend my time developing effective antidotes." I could hear the guilt in his voice, the regret that he'd spent so much of his life turning these beautiful plants into deadly weapons.

"Come on," Meera whispers. "Let's get the drone!"

We spare a few seconds to tie up the other Watchman and gag both of them. We leave them with the flower, which will continue blooming for at least another fifteen minutes, and the effects of the gas won't start to wear off for another hour after that. I follow Meera down the hall, pulling the knife out of my boot as we creep up to the corner, waiting. She risks a glance around the edge of the wall, and pulls back immediately.

"Security drone. Level five, by my guess. Dual-capacitor Bolt and both sonar and vidcam capabilities."

"The drone must be making up for the incompetence of the Watchmen."

She nods in agreement. Her usual buoyancy is gone, replaced by a look of determination. We prepared for this.

The challenge in both of these fights is not taking out the opponent. The challenge is doing so unnoticed, without firing our weapons. Both of us have contraband Bolts, ones that won't immediately call for aid from nearby Watchmen, drones, and SDF forces upon discharge. But Shia warned us that given the tense air around the Sector after Round Barn and Linnea's broadcast, there are probably electrical discharge sensors mapping the whole arena. They're looking for you, he'd said. If we fire our weapons, we could bring the security detail for the whole stadium down on top of us. And given what we have planned, that's the last thing we want.

"You first," Meera says. She's stronger than I am, but I've got better aim with a knife. So I back up and set my feet.

As I release the tension in my body, I break into a sprint. I hit my right foot, banking into a hard left around the corner. I dive and roll, keeping my face hidden from view for as long as possible. When I roll up, it's already focusing on me, zooming in, trying to fit me into its algorithms: *is this characteristic of threatening human activity?* While it thinks, I take another two steps forward and square up. I rear back and throw the knife as hard as I can at the drone's lone unblinking eye.

The glass lens shatters. The drone freezes temporarily, switching from primary digital navigation to sonar. Meera careens past me a second later, taking advantage of the downtime. She takes a flying leap and catches it by the semi-spherical rotor and drags it to the ground. The drone can't support her weight, so it starts to sink, tilting sideways. A drone's sonar sensors aren't nearly as detailed as the cameras, but it has the advantage of being able to see and process information in every direction at once. But its weapons systems don't have the same range of motion. It can't lock onto her from this angle, not unless it gets free from her grip. The drone's dual-capacitor Bolt swivels down as far as it can go—but it's not far enough. Unable to lock onto the target, it won't fire, and Meera is able to jam her knife into its rotor, crippling it. When it stops flying and collapses to the ground, she quickly opens the top to access the nanocircuitry, and with a few deft motions on the glass panel, disables the whole thing.

"We're in," she says quietly.

Because drones aren't remotely controlled—their AI is sufficient to get them through almost all human interactions—the footage from the camera and sonar recordings probably won't be seen for several hours, once the Sector starts trying to piece together what happened here.

With nothing standing between us and the projection room, I'm almost more nervous than before the fight. *Now I tear off the mask concealing the true face of Okaria.*

Together we walk to the door and pull out our Bolts. I tie my scarf over my face, and Meera follows suit. She presses her palm to the palm reader. It flashes green, and the door swings open.

We walk in.

The projection room isn't the same as the control room, Shia told us. This is where all the recordings are stored from every camera drone around the stadium. All the raw material comes here first for storage. Then, in a much higher-security room in the basement of the stadium, all that footage is edited live and on the fly, the best shots and angles are selected, the colors are brightened, the athletes are made glossier and sharper, and then the final product is sent back up here to be broadcast out to Okaria via a series of giant antennae on top of the stadium.

"All you have to do is swap some of the circuitry around and plug in the footage you have via UMIT," Shia told us, just this morning, as we went over our final plans. "The guys in the control room won't even know they're not broadcasting the games until someone tells them that what's displaying on the vidscreens across the Sector is different than what they're sending out."

I'd nodded. "We're cutting out the middleman."

"Exactly," Shia responded.

"They'll know you did it," Meera said softly, concerned for our newfound ally. Shia shrugged, looking uncomfortable, trying to put on a tough face. "As soon as we palm in with your fingerprints and plug in Remy's footage, they'll come after you. They'll come after you long before they find us."

"Can you get him out of the city?" I asked her.

"Yes," she said, turning to Shia. "But you have to leave tonight, or not at all." Shia went white. He pulled back from the table where we sat in Meera's apartment, his knuckles taut and his eyes wide. "There's an outbound truck headed to Belleron tonight. I can get you in. They'll drop you off near an Outsider waystation and you can take it from there."

"I'm not ready to leave," Shia said, panic in his voice.

"Are you ready to die?" Meera asked, matter-of-factly. "Because our plans are made. There's never been a better time. If you want to help expose the truth, we have to do this. And the second we do, you'll be in the crosshairs."

So Shia left, with a survival pack for the Wilds, detailed instructions on how to get to the nearest Resistance base, and my reassurances that I would call him back as soon as it ever became safe for him to return.

"I hope I see you again one day," he said to me, his tall frame stooped as he hugged me goodbye. "I'm glad I met you, Remy Alexander."

"I'm glad I met you, too, Shia," I said. "And don't forget to have the base director contact Eli at headquarters as soon as you make it to safety. The Wilds are nothing like how the Sector portrays them. You don't need to pack a hazmat suit. The most dangerous thing you could encounter is a mother badger. Or maybe a grizzly." I punched him playfully in the shoulder.

He put his hands over his face. "You're not really helping, Remy. A grizzly sounds terrifying."

"Oh, no," I reassured him, "grizzlies are nothing compared to angry badgers. You'll be fine," I said more seriously. "I've spent a lot of time in the Wilds, now. It's beautiful. Follow our directions, and you'll make it to the Resistance safely."

Now I look around the projection room. It's a tiny, cramped space, no bigger than some of the bunk rooms back at Normandy. I pull out the tiny magnetic drive I've been carrying with me for months now, wondering when, if ever, I would have use for it. This is the footage I hope will start the revolution.

The fire has been lit, Vale, I told him, before the battle at Round Barn, when we all learned how Evander Sun-Zi earned his nickname. *Now we just have to carry the torch.*

I thought long and hard about whether to edit Vale out of the footage. I almost asked Shia to take him out completely. After all, I don't want to put him into any more danger than he's already in. But I ultimately decided he had to stay in. It would sow more doubt about the veracity of the Orleáns' story.

While Meera works with the nanocircuitry, following Shia's instructions, I watch the file directory pull up on the tiny plasma screen provided for data transfer. There's only one file. It's called *The Dragon.*

"It's all ready," Meera says.

I hesitate, afraid to touch the screen, afraid of what will happen when I do. *They'll know I'm here. They'll know I'm in Okaria. They'll find me, and they'll kill me.*

I select the file, and a dialog box comes up.

Upload?

I hit yes.

If I'm caught—if I die—it'll be worth it. The mask has been pulled away. Now, no one in Okaria will be able to hide from the truth.

9 — VALE

Philip paces. I've been listening to his footfalls back and forth across the airship cabin for the better part of ten minutes. He hasn't said a word, but the tension is so tangible it rolls over his shoulders like a morning fog over Lake Okaria. There are dark circles under his eyes that weren't there yesterday. He's barely uttered a word since we boarded. Two nights ago, at the Pan-Okarian Gymnasia Championship, Remy somehow hijacked the media control center and broadcast the footage from the farms to every screen in the Sector. It must have been her, because she kept that footage in case it came in handy—and it did. Ironically, although it was the first night my parents allowed me to access the vidscreen, I almost missed the broadcast.

I'd been reading all day and needed a mindless break. The cook had prepared my dinner and one of my guards brought it to my room with the announcement that, if I wanted, I was allowed to eat in the family room. Family room. I almost laughed aloud and said *thanks, but no thanks*, but the truth was I needed out, so I dutifully followed him down the hall to where I'd spent many happy hours with my parents and friends. The scent of the garden wafted in from the open windows, and I could smell jasmine and lilac in the air. The long couch was more than inviting, so I stretched out and tried to relax.

The guard placed my tray on the low table in front of the couch, activated the vidscreen, and took up his post out in the hallway. My parents were attending the annual competition in person, of course, and watching it wasn't high on my list of priorities so I barely paid attention to the first half. Instead I ate my dinner and then walked around the room, surveying the trinkets and memorabilia on the shelves, examining the books and artwork, some by Okarian authors and artists, some saved from the Old World.

In the background, the sounds on the screen shifted. Angry yelling, people crying out. Panting, footsteps pounding on the ground.

"Don't move!" someone shouted. I turned to the vidscreen. The video was jerky, clearly recorded by somebody in motion. It panned around quickly, so fast it was hard to tell what was happening. The idyllic setting—rows upon rows of vegetables, trellised vines, and trees dotting the landscape—clashed with the chaos in the foreground. In the distance a soldier, wearing a Farm Enforcer's uniform, kneeled with his weapon trained on an unarmed man. As the video turned back, I recognized the large, distinctive red barn.

By the harvest. This is Remy's footage. This is Round Barn.

"Don't shoot, don't shoot!" the man screams. "My hands are—" Then a crackle. Bolt fire. The man on the screen crumpled, his chest lit up in blue.

"Hey!" The landscape tilts as Remy runs forward. When the Enforcer turns toward the sound, a blue blast emerges from right beneath the camera. He collapses to the ground. More footsteps as Remy runs to the man's limp body. The camera gets a clear shot of the man's face as she rolls him over.

"You'll be fully recovered in a few days." Her voice was barely audible, but the disdain came through loud and clear. "Unlike the man you just murdered."

My heart pounded. *Who did this?* This footage could out me. If they showed me on screen, they'd blow my cover. Then I asked myself: is that really such a bad thing? If everyone in the Sector believes Jeremiah kidnapped me, watching me fight Evander at Round Barn would show them where my allegiance truly lies.

I have my own tragic memories of that day, but by watching the broadcast I was able to see everything through Remy's eyes. Farm workers cried out with hunger, asking why they were being starved, protesting that they just wanted food, food they'd helped plant and tend, helped nurture and harvest. Evander's airships hummed in the background, but you couldn't see them quite yet.

I wanted to turn away. The thought of watching it all unfold again put a pit in my gut. I didn't want to see the fire shooting out from Sector airships like dragon's breath in an old fairy tale. I didn't want to see the burning bodies. I didn't want to see Evander's smirking, self-satisfied face. I didn't want to watch as Remy's hands carved Evander's flesh.

But I couldn't turn away. I needed to see what the rest of Okaria was seeing.

As Evander's airships moved into view and their cannons breathed fire on the crowd below, I could only imagine the chaos unfolding at the auditorium where thousands of spectators were watching this for the first time. What were my parents—sitting pretty in their Presidential Viewing Room—thinking? Had they already deployed officers to catch Remy and whoever else might've helped her? What excuse would the Sector come up with to smooth this one over?

A firm hand on my shoulder startled me from my shock. The vidscreen shut off and the guard hustled me back to my room, locking the door behind me in a matter of seconds.

Now, in the airship on the way to Windy Pines, a factory town on the western edge of the Sector, I watch my father pace. He must have seen me on the footage, Evander's boot pressing into my throat, right before Remy tackled him, but he hasn't said a word about it. With an unreadable glance my way, he turns on his heel, strides into the cockpit, and slaps the palmer behind him. The door slides shut with a whisper, and finally the oppressive weight of his footfalls is gone.

The guard opposite me shifts uncomfortably under General Aulion's scrutiny. An ordinary, if high-ranking, Sector Defense Forces captain, he hasn't been through the same intense emotional training as the two black ops at my side, who have barely blinked in the two hours since we boarded the airship. My father's restless pacing and abrupt departure has set everyone on edge. But most of us are wise enough not to show it.

Still maintaining the illusion among the guards that I am "a danger to myself," my parents ordered that I be accompanied by at least two guards at all times. I am scheduled to speak after my father today, in an attempt to reassure the citizens of the Sector that I am still one of them. Aulion has taken it upon himself to head up my personal entourage of guards. When he volunteered, my mother approved with what I can only describe as barely contained enthusiasm; my father has been too distracted to notice what I suspect to be some sort of unstated understanding between Aulion and my mother. The General's eyes haven't once left me since we lifted off, and the hairs on my neck are standing at attention as authoritatively as the guard across from me.

"It's hard to tell what's going on in the inner network of the C-Links, now that I've separated myself from them," Demeter says in my ear. "But I believe Evander is going to make a speech in response to Remy's broadcast. The networks are being prepared. Camera drones have been dispatched to the OAC building. Jon Spironiv, the ONN spokesman, has entered Corine's office. Inside her office, I'm afraid, I am blind. I'm still trying to figure out a way into her security system, but so far, no luck."

Demeter has essentially gone renegade since she was forced to cordon herself off from the C-Link network after my mother fed her false information. She can't access the same wealth of data she could while she was my authorized personal assistant, but what she can do now is almost more helpful: monitor all movements on the general Okarian network, including drone, airship, PODS, and any humans linked into them, all without herself being monitored. She also has access to everything in the public information network, which includes the Personhood database, some parts of the Dieticians' database, and anything accessible through the Okarian library system. She might not be able to guide me through top-secret files like she once could, but in a way, this is better. She's free from the constraints of her identity as my assistant; she can do whatever she pleases. And that means she can take initiative, investigate ideas and people without instructions or commands, use back doors to embed herself in various parts of the network the C-Link system doesn't monitor. She has become, as some old sage predicted, a ghost in the machine.

"My sense is that Evander will speak to the nation right after your speech at Windy Pines."

Perfect timing.

I can feel the airship begin to descend, the gentle weight being lifted from my shoulders as the ship floats down toward the ground. The heavy tripods extend with a *whirr*, and a moment later we settle onto an airfield landing pad. The peace of flight is disrupted. Everyone is in motion. My father emerges from the cabin. He gestures for me to follow him, and I stand to obey. The guards follow at a careful distance. They must not appear to be coercing me. Corine will have drilled that into them.

I watch my father as we step out of the airship, the cockeyed smile that always comforted me now set on his face as if it had been carved in stone. Although my mother appears firm in her conviction that their chosen path is the right one, my father seems to be fraying at the edges. Whether through fatigue or self-doubt, it's hard to say, but either way, he's lost some of the confidence he had just a few months ago.

"Dad?" I say quietly, and he jerks his head around to look at me. "Are you okay?"

He stares at me for a few seconds, and then says, simply, "You haven't called me that in a long time."

Unsure how to respond with Aulion and the guards mere meters behind us, I hold his gaze. Another quiet moment passes, and then he turns back and palms the door. The stairway unfolds to a walkway lined with thick grass sparkling with dew in the bright morning sun. As he steps out, head down, away from the cameras, he mutters so softly I can barely hear him: "What have we done?"

I keep my composure—I've had a lot of practice recently—but my heart lurches to a stop as though it's been slammed against a wall. *Maybe there's hope,* I say to myself. *At least for him.*

Outside, the air is warm and humid, and smells of chemical dye. There are additional SDF forces lining the perimeter of the landing pad and a few camera drones floating around, but they are both outnumbered by the Windy Pines Town Council members. They'll accompany us to one of the factories for a tour and then to the town square where my father and I will speak. I haven't been on many tours of the factory towns, but normally, the people are enthusiastic, warm, and welcoming. No such thing today. We are surrounded by frowns, dark expressions, furrowed brows. My father flashes a tight, practiced smile and waves, ignoring the lack of enthusiasm. I do not follow suit.

"Daryl, Evan, Clarisse," Philip says, shaking hands, kissing cheeks. His strength has always been his warmth and charisma, that easy smile, the genuinely kind way he speaks to people. Today he's trying, but there is a stilted quality to every word, every movement. "Lyle, Kara. Hello, my friends. It's been too long."

"Indeed," one of the men says, almost as straight-backed and formal as I am. "We're glad to have you here, Chancellor, and honored to be the first stop on your tour." But he doesn't look glad or honored. His eyes skitter around, between me and Philip, taking in my guards, and then over to the other council members, who are waiting, quiet and tense. "Captain Orleán, the people of the Sector are glad to have you back safe and sound, though I understand it was a long and arduous process of healing."

The honorific *Captain* surprises me. *Apparently I've been promoted,* I think wryly. *I wish someone would keep me up to date with all the stories my parents are telling.* "I am well now," I respond neutrally. "Thank you for your concern."

"Come," Clarisse says, turning with a sweeping gesture.

We follow her and the other councilmembers to a platform where a tram has been cordoned off for us. As the doors slide open and we step inside, I think back to the briefing with my mother yesterday as she informed me I was accompanying my father on a speaking tour of the factory towns.

"Windy Pines specializes in textiles. You should remember this from your lessons, Vale," my mother said. I did remember, but I allowed her to continue without interruption. "There are shipping lines from Pines to Sakari, Lesedi, and North Port, all of which have been experiencing, shall we say, interference from unidentified bands of fugitives looking to use the shipping infrastructure for their own purposes." I fought the urge to laugh, remembering the Resistance plan to hijack shipping lines to distribute seeds and unmodified food throughout the Sector, and how I was present at the meeting where that plan was born. "Windy Pines isn't the only town experiencing such disruptions, and we suspect that the outlaws are getting help from one or more people on the inside. We're sending you and the chancellor on this trip to reassure the residents and workers that everything is under control."

We're sending you and the chancellor? Who is the "we"? I wondered. The Board of Directors? But since when did the Board "send" the chancellor anywhere? Shouldn't the chancellor decide when and where he visited?

She laid a hand on my shoulder, then touched my cheek, as if I was still a child. "You know what to do."

The tram sets off at a gentle glide. I take in the sights and sounds of the town as it rolls past. Once we arrive at the factory, we are given a brief tour, and I marvel at the enormous looms, nanofiber laser spinners, vats of dye, workers monitoring robotic equipment doing who knows what. In one vast, open floor, I can see stretchers the size of houses laid out to weave the sails Okarians use for sky surfers and sailboats on Lake Okaria.

After our tour, we board the tram again. My father waves me toward a seat next to him and waits as the local council members assemble around him.

"I know we have a formal meeting after my speech, but I'd like to hear from you now, before I face the crowd. What's the situation in Windy Pines?" Philip leans forward, his hands clasped. The picture of the engaged politician. Clarisse clears her throat.

"Missing cargo and assorted equipment, citizens not showing up for work, a few disappearing entirely." My father nods, and I follow suit, doing my best to look attentive rather than desperate for information. I wonder why my father is allowing me to hear this. I can feel the watchfulness emanating from Aulion, telling me he's none too happy, that he doesn't trust me for one second.

"We understand there are similar troubles at the Farms," Lyle speaks up, looking me dead in the eye. "And after that video footage last night, people are wondering—"

"That footage was staged," my father interrupts. "Surely even you could tell from the video quality. Set up like a bad monster movie meant to scare little children in their beds at night. None of you were taken in, were you?" He surveys the group's faces. Several council members shift uncomfortably.

"Clarisse, how many Windy Pines workers have left?"

"Twenty-one."

"Twenty-one?" I can tell my father is surprised, though he tries not to show it.

"And more have walked off the job, or tried to walk off, but were caught."

"Where are they being detained?" Philip says.

Detained? That's illegal. I recall the line from the Code of Citizenship: No citizen is bound to the Sector, nor can any citizen be prosecuted or punished for abandoning the Sector.

"They're not." Clarissa's gaze flits across the faces of the other council members. She meets Lyle's gaze and then turns back to my father. "It's against the Code."

My father draws in a breath. "You know as well as I do the Code was modified after the SRI massacre and after certain board members began disappearing."

I keep my face neutral, but inside I'm reeling. *Modified? How?* Why wasn't there a public announcement? Why wasn't I ever told? No one mentioned it, even during my officer's training.

"In truth, detention was proposed," Lyle says. "I vetoed the proposition."

My father turns toward him. "I issued an executive order regarding detention of suspected Outsider or Resistance sympathizers, did I not?" His voice is tight. I can hear his teeth grind.

"Yes," Clarisse says. "But by the governing laws of Windy Pines, and indeed all Sector towns as *you* well know, we were required to accept Lyle's veto. Such a drastic step, even in the wake of an executive order, must be adopted by unanimous approval of each town council."

There's a moment of deep and uncomfortable silence. My father stands, and I follow suit. Aulion doesn't budge. "Then you defied a direct order from my desk," my father says finally. He looks at Lyle who blanches in the face of the chancellor's withering stare. "Your directive as council members is to do everything in your power to work against the Resistance and their Outsider agitators, and yet you have chosen to do exactly the opposite. This is not simply a matter of arresting a shoplifter. This is a matter of state security. By allowing these people to walk away from their jobs, to walk away from Windy Pines, you are allowing them to walk directly into the waiting arms of those seeking to undermine the Sector." My father takes a step toward Lyle. The guards, sensing what's about to happen, place their hands on their weapons. "By my *Executive Order*"—he almost spits the words—" you are summarily dismissed from your position as councilman." He turns to Aulion. "Arrest him."

The other council members are on their feet, a tumult of voices protesting all at once.

"On what charge?" Lyle says, his eyes wide.

"Aiding and abetting the enemy."

General Aulion only has to nod once, before two of the guards who joined us at the landing pad sweep over to Lyle's side, pull his hands behind his back, and slap a pair of magnetic cuffs around his wrists.

"What the hell?" He tries to twist away.

"Chancellor—" Clarisse starts.

"This is ridiculous!" another council member interrupts, trying to push in between the guards and Lyle. "This isn't proper procedure. You can't arrest him for vetoing an illegal proposition, you—"

"I am perfectly within my bounds," my father says, without raising his voice. "The charge stands, and I can assure you that he will be prosecuted to the fullest extent of the law." He slaps the red button labeled *Emergency Stop* and we all tip slightly off balance as the tram comes to an abrupt stop. "Get him out of my sight."

At a nod from Aulion, the guards pull Lyle off the tram where he loses his balance and falls to his knees. They yank him to his feet, although he's no longer putting up a fight. The doors slide closed behind them, and the tram starts moving again. I turn back to look at the shell-shocked expressions on the other politicians' faces.

"Now, let's make this clear," Philip says, sitting down again and leaning back. "Anyone who assists the cause of the Resistance will face the immediate wrath of Sector leadership."

Everyone nods vigorously and no one says another word. I sink down into the seat beside my father. We must not have been far from our destination, because the tram slows. The doors open, and I follow my father and Aulion up some stairs into the town hall. All three of my guards are right on my heels.

"The citizens are assembled in the town square," Clarisse says, her voice shaky, as she steps ahead to lead us through the building. "We'll go out front where we've set up a stage on the steps."

"Excellent," my father says, all trace of his anger gone.

Clarisse continues. "We asked every able-bodied citizen not working today to attend, so you should have quite a crowd."

My father turns to me. "Vale, are you ready for your big appearance?"

I nod. *What do you want me to say, Dad?*

"Good. I'll open with a few words and turn it over to you. They're going to love you, Vale."

He's the golden boy. Eli's words to Soren. *Our ace in the hole.* I'd overheard them talking as Eli made the case for trusting me, for allowing me to be a part of their plans. I have to stop myself from smiling when I remember Soren's response. *More like asshole.* Seems like an age ago, even though it's only been a few months. I grit my teeth and wish the words I have to speak today were my own, instead of the lies my parents have written for me.

I follow my father and Clarisse through a broad set of double doors, out into the blinding sunlight under a cloudless sky. We're on a small stage surrounded by several thousand citizens, all with their eyes trained on us. I wait for my own eyes to adjust, and then squint out at the crowd. Curious, but neutral faces. Careful faces. Not the adoring crowds my father is used to addressing.

"Citizens of Windy Pines!" my father says, waving his arms in a welcoming gesture as if he'd just invited everyone over to the chancellor's house for a picnic. A roar rolls through the crowd in response, mostly shouts of approval and applause, but there are a few stoic faces, set jaws, crossed arms. "Thank you so much for coming out today. I know many of you are giving up precious free time to be here, and my heart is gladdened by your presence."

I catch a flash of red in motion in the crowd, and I startle, trying to follow its movement without being obvious.

"Today, I come to speak of dark and dangerous times ahead. You know about the threats that lurk at our borders, the terrorists and the Outsiders who oppose our way of life, who would steal our food, our wealth, our *freedom*, right out from under our noses. Since our founding mothers and fathers dedicated themselves to the Okarian Sector, our citizens have worked hard to be *free* from fear, *free* from want, *free* from war. But, as you know, the terrorists have proven themselves capable of taking the very things we hold most dear." He turns, opens his arm to me, and I step forward right on cue. "They took my own son from me," he says with a heaviness in his voice.

This time the crowd's reaction is louder and fists pump the air along with shouts of "Destroy the Resistance!" and "Traitors!" from the true believers standing right down front. I take it all in and then catch another flash of red, this time in a different part of the crowd, further back, to the right. *What is that?*

"Valerian," Demeter whispers in my ear. "Listen, I've got Eli …"

"Though we have made significant progress in destroying Resistance bases and shutting down their networks, there is still work to be done before this cancer is eliminated. Members of the Resistance are dangerous, not because they are *not* like us, but precisely because they are, in so many ways, *just* like us. They were once our friends and colleagues, but now they have subverted the very principles upon which our small nation was founded. Principles that have kept us safe and secure in troubled times. Now, we are at a turning point in our efforts to crush them once and for all. My fellow citizens, the Resistance is desperate."

"Vale? Vale, are you there?" In my ear, I hear the unmistakable voice of Elijah Tawfiq. All the practice in stoicism I've had in captivity can't prevent me from sucking in a breath, from letting my eyes go wide, letting the excitement show on my face. Always at my side, I feel Aulion's gaze burning through me like a laser. I exhale, force myself to relax, and focus on my father.

"He's tuned in, Eli," Demeter says. "He can't respond, but you can speak all you want. Go ahead."

"And in their desperation," my father goes on, "they are taking risks, making mistakes that make them vulnerable to detection. That is why we are here today. To ask you to join the fight."

"Vale, listen to me," Eli says. "Demeter's filled me in about your situation. Here's what you need to know. We're not producing as many seeds as we hoped, and distribution has been a bear—ha! Bear, get it?—anyway, we've got some good news. We've stolen another 3D printer and we've figured out how to print actual food. We've got one printer on seeds and one on food. Rhinehouse is working twenty-four-seven and is one grumpy son of a bitch, but what's new? Production isn't ideal, we can't do it in high volume, and it's no substitute for growing from scratch, but we don't have time to cultivate the printed seeds en masse. We're printing as much food as we can and shipping it out as fast as we can. Bear is our point man on the Farms. He's working with Zeke's team to infiltrate existing supply routes between factory towns and Farms. It's slow going, but it's progress."

Philip steps forward to the edge of the stage. "To ask you, my friends, to watch for infiltrators within our communities. Infiltrators like Jeremiah Sayyid who kidnapped my son. It is up to each one of us to be vigilant against traitors in our very midst. We must not let a few disillusioned radicals undermine the Okarian Sector."

"I've got more good news," Eli says, his words tumbling out in near-breathless excitement. "Our little Bear has been busy. Hell, he's a fucking *grizzly*. He's got teams assembled on all the Farms and between him and Zeke, shit is getting real. People disappearing, walking off the job, civil disobedience … I mean, that boy is a talker. And every time he opens his mouth, somebody falls in love with him. Who knew, right?"

"My friends, I am here today to tell you that we are in the final stretch, that we are close to victory. My son, Valerian Orleán"—my father turns toward me with a proud look on his face—"who heroically escaped captivity to return to us, is preparing to lead an all-out assault on the last remnants of this terrorist network."

Lead an all-out assault? The words ring in my head as I see another flash of red. And another. I catch glimpses, out of the corner of my eye, of fabric leaping from palm to palm, as crimson and bright as fresh-spilled blood.

Red in the morning, sailors take warning …

"Vale, now that we know how to communicate through Demeter, we'll keep you—"

"Eli, who are you talking—" a voice shouts in the background. Zoe?

"For fuck's sake, give me a minute!" Eli yells.

"Citizens, it is time to strike the final blow—" Philip says, even as his eyes grow wide and his shoulders tense. He takes a hesitant step backward and glances at me, then at Aulion. Before us, the crowd is swimming in red.

Eli's voice again. "And did you see Remy's video? Was that fucking brilliant or what? And by the way, I'm perfectly fine now. Rhinehouse replicated Corine's vaccine, thanks to Demeter, and I'm feeling fine and dandy, thanks for asking."

I try to stand still, to look impassive as I listen to Eli rattle on, watch my father, and process what's unfolding in front of us.

"Eli." It's Demeter's voice now. "Vale is in Windy Pines with his father. Something is going on. Stand by."

A hundred, no, maybe two, three hundred hands are in the air, defiant fists above the crowd, wrapped in red, organized to form a pattern, a sign, but what is it? More hands join in. More red. Visible only from above, from the raised platform my father and I stand on, the symbol becomes clear. A slow smile spreads across my face. At my side, Aulion growls and signals for the nearby soldiers to head into the crowd.

"Arrest anyone with a scrap of red on them." He turns to the SDF soldier behind me. "Get me drone footage from every angle possible. I want access to every open network in this quadrant. Pull up Personhood and activate the facial recognition program. I want names." He points at one of the black ops now hovering uncomfortably close to me. "Notify Madam Orleán." He turns toward me with a look so sharp it could flay the flesh off my bones. "She'll want to see exactly what's going on."

"I had to disconnect you, Vale," Demeter says. "Sector security probes are looking into this connection. Eli's gone now."

All I can see is red. The letter R.

Resistance.

10 — VALE

We've got over sixty under arrest. We're tracking the rest down.

Where are you holding them?

Some in the cell here at the town hall, but there's not enough space. The rest are in a warehouse by the airfield.

You've got back-up security around the perimeter of town?

Of course.

Demeter tapped into the security system to monitor my father and Aulion as they talk about the protest, but there's no audio in the room. Instead, she's monitoring the video and is able to read their lips and translate what they're saying. As she feeds the dialogue, along with her commentary, directly into my ear, I try to remain impassive.

"Aulion hasn't been using the honorific 'sir,'" Demeter says. "I find this interesting. He's standing at attention, hands clasped behind his back. Your father is pacing."

In your capacity, General, what do propose we do with the prisoners?

I recommend adopting some of the director's methods.

No. Corine has her ways of dealing with problems and I have mine. I won't go that route. I need another option.

I strongly suggest, sir, that these traitors not be given the opportunity to infect others with their ideology. Especially not after Remy Alexander's video.

A pause. I hold my breath. I can't betray any emotion, can't act like I'm hearing anything. Just a few moments ago, my father and Aulion disappeared—alone—into a room in the Windy Pines town council building, leaving me waiting outside the door, my guards never far.

You must realize how few options there are.

"Your father is upset. Aulion is doing nothing to placate him. If anything, he seems to be provoking him. Aggressive body language, slight sneer, hostile tone."

Treason is like a virus and we must inoculate ourselves against it. We must dispose of this problem before—

Dispose? Like Evander disposed of the problem at Round Barn? Look where that got us. We won't be using those tactics again. Do I make myself clear?

Is Aulion suggesting murdering the protesters? It seems too far-fetched even for him, but I can't imagine another possibility.

"General Aulion has said nothing. He's standing motionless in the center of the room."

I know what you're suggesting, Falke, but I won't do it. I refuse to take that step.

There's a long silence. Demeter says nothing. I can only imagine the tension in the room between my father and the general.

I await your orders, sir.

"Your father seems appeased. He's finally turned back to face the general and his shoulders are more relaxed now."

Take as many prisoners as you can round up, requisition as many airships as you need, and get them all back to the capital. Lock them up where no one can find them. Keep looking for the others. We'll deal with them all later.

Yes, sir.

The door opens and Aulion strides out. He barely looks at me, but instead speaks to the guards. "Come with me."

"But—" one of them protests.

"Now!"

"I've pulled up the video system schematic and will continue watching Aulion as he leaves the building," Demeter says. "Once he's outside, I may be able to get an audio feed if there are security drones monitoring the perimeter of the building."

After what seems an interminable amount of time, my father appears in the doorway. "Vale?"

I stand to greet him.

"Aulion is taking care of the protestors, and I need you to wait here while I meet with the council members. Then we'll return to the airfield and take the chancellor's airship back to the capital. We'll have some time alone. Just you and me."

"Vale!" The urgency in Demeter's voice startles me.

"By myself? Are you sure?"

My father looks me in the eye for a long moment. "I trust you." And then he's gone.

I trust you? What have I done to merit my father's trust?

"Deme? What's up?"

"It's Aulion. He's contravening your father's orders."

"He's what?"

"Listen. I was able to record it. As soon as he got outside, on the stage. There are drones programmed to record the speeches and I managed to tap into one."

Aulion's voice fills my ears. His tone is hushed, but clear. "Set up a perimeter and take only your most trusted troops. Keep it simple and clean. Bolts set to kill. Get a hazardous waste demarcation kit to keep the building off limits. I'm going to issue a lock down order for the whole town. After dark, we'll dispose of the bodies in the woods west of town. There's an old quarry out there. No one will ever find them."

"Lead me to him." I say, already moving. I open the door and check the hallway. My father's nowhere to be seen. I don't have a weapon. I don't have a plan. All I know is I have to stop a monster from committing mass murder.

"Take a left here and at the end of the hall, go down the stairs. That takes you back to the lobby and you'll see the main doors out to the stage." I obey, running down the corridor. Luckily the town hall is practically abandoned. My father and the council members are meeting somewhere, but right now there's not another soul in sight. Everyone must have dispersed after Aulion's troops headed into the crowd. "Just caught him on another camera. Once you're outside, take the steps to the right of the stage and go around the building. Aulion is heading for a hovercar parked out back, the black ops in tow. What are you planning, Vale?"

I have no idea.

I fly down the stairs and burst through the doors, taking the steps out front beside the stage two at a time. I round the corner and see Aulion in the distance. Screeching to a halt, I press myself up against the building. There are two SDF soldiers waiting at the hovercar. I can't take them all down, and I can't risk them getting in that car. Before I can decide what to do, Aulion stops. He points and everyone turns to look into the distance. After a few moments, the SDF troops take off behind the building where I can't see them anymore. Aulion talks to the OAC soldiers and a moment later they get in the car and pull out, leaving Aulion behind.

I pause, unsure of what to do. Do I try to follow the black ops who are probably headed toward the prisoners? Or the man who gave the kill order, and who could reverse it?

It has to be Aulion. He'll only be alone for a moment. I don't have long. He remains in the parking lot, standing stock still, head cocked slightly as if listening to something I can't hear. *A C-Link?* I wonder if he finally managed to convince the Board of Directors he needed one.

After a moment, I realize he's heading back my direction, toward the town council building. *What's he up to?*

As he walks, he puts his hand on the butt of his holstered Bolt. Unarmed, even with the element of surprise, I realize forcing Aulion to recall the order will take more than training and luck. I need a weapon. Still hidden by shadow, I slide back around the corner of the building, bound up the steps, and push through the door into the lobby. It's still empty, quiet as a morgue except for my footsteps. I sprint toward the information desk and hurl myself over it. And there it is. A small hand-held fire extinguisher. I pop it out of its holding clip and check the pressure gauge. Perfect. Trigger-loaded like a grenade, I pull the pin and wait. Aulion will have to walk right past me.

The door opens, and footsteps echo in the empty room. *Closer. Closer. Closer.* I wait until he is just past the desk, then launch myself at his back, the trigger of the extinguisher clasped tight in my hand.

Damn, he's fast. He's already pivoted when I make contact, Bolt clear of its holster. I knock him flat, but he uses his shoulder to break the fall and brings the Bolt around toward me. I don't give him a chance to aim. I twist around and press the fire extinguisher's trigger, blasting him in the face, white foam piling up like a chemical ice cream sundae. He bucks me off his back with an unearthly roar, clawing at his eyes with both hands as his Bolt skitters across the tile floor. With my free hand I stretch out to grab the weapon, clutching the fire extinguisher in my other hand, not daring to let go.

Aulion wipes the foam from his face with a sleeve and struggles to get to his feet. I don't wait. I leap at him, pressing my knee into his chest and the bulk of the fire extinguisher into his throat. I hold the Bolt in my right hand, pointed at his head.

I push the fire extinguisher hard enough into his throat that his breath comes in ragged gasps. Evander's words ring in my head: *Aulion always said you were a coward.*

"Rescind the order," I say, jamming the Bolt into his temple.

He laughs. A bizarre sound barking out from his white-flecked, scarred face. "No." His voice is rough as he squints up at me with weeping, bloodshot eyes, rimmed in red.

"Call them off!" I push my knee harder into his chest, constricting his breathing, making it clear I would have no trouble killing him.

"How did you know?"

"Maybe your troops aren't as loyal as they seem." Might as well take the opportunity to sow some divisiveness and suspicion. "Give the order now!"

He wipes his face again, then spits at me. "They're as good as dead already."

"There's still time. Give the order or I'll shoot." Aulion doesn't respond. "You've got a C-Link," I say, hoping like hell I'm right.

"Do your worst, Valerian."

I press the fire extinguisher into his throat hard enough that his eyes start to pop out and he gasps for air. His lips turn blue and he kicks frantically against my legs. Then I see his eyes roll back into his head and I know he's unconscious. I immediately let up on the pressure, but keep the fire extinguisher in position.

For an instant, everything is quiet. Then Aulion draws in a heavy, rasping breath. I can see the fine webbed lines of burn scars on the right side of his face and neck. With cellular reconstruction, most scars can be healed, but Aulion was too old when he was burned. I still don't know how it happened. Soren hinted one time that he had some ideas, but he never shared them.

"I had every intention of leaving you for Soren to finish off—he's claimed that task for himself—but if you don't give the order right now, I'll have to disappoint him." Aulion starts to say something, but I shove the Bolt into his skull so hard it'll bruise.

"Give the order," I say, more quietly this time. "And I'll let you live to fight another day."

"I'm not afraid to die," he says, his voice low and raspy. I can feel his breath on my cheek.

"You're telling me you'd rather die by my hand than spare the lives of Sector citizens who did nothing other than raise their fists in protest?" He doesn't say a word.

Everything is silent. I start to count.

"One." I press the fire extinguisher into his throat again. "Two." I press harder. "Three. By the time I get to ten, you'll be dead. Four. Five." His breath is once again coming in rasps. I add pressure with every beat. "Six."

"C-Link, call them off," he coughs. "I'm rescinding the kill order." I exhale. I release the pressure on his windpipe.

"Again. Just to make sure." *Jeesh,* I think, *is he so lacking in imagination that he hasn't even named his C-Link?*

"I repeat, do not fire on the prisoners."

Inwardly, I relax. His C-Link will relay the orders to the soldiers' comlinks. An invisible weight seems to dissipate and float away. But I don't move.

"I'll give you a gift, General. Just for you. I'll keep your little secret, that you contravened a direct order from the chancellor and decided all on your own to commit mass murder. Of course someone else may turn you in, but I won't. Not just yet."

His squints up at me. "Tell me how you knew."

I ignore him. "I'll keep your secret on one condition: you give the order to let the prisoners walk. Exile. Send them into the Wilds. Let them figure out how to survive, but don't transport them back to the capital. Think that's fair?"

"Fair?" Aulion smirks.

"All's fair in love and war, General. This is a good deal for you."

His voice is almost a growl as he relays the order to his C-Link.

"I can try to get a message to Eli to pick up the prisoners," Demeter says in my ear.

I try not to smile, but can't help it. "General, instruct your soldiers to transport the prisoners to the border exit at the Windy Pines perimeter on the southern edge of town. They are to enter the Wilds at the guard station there and keep walking due south."

I feel his muscles tense and can practically see his mind working, trying to figure out what I'm up to, how to throw me off, how to get rid of me once and for all. "I'm waiting."

Through a sick smile, with tears trickling from the corners of his fire-red eyes, he repeats the instructions. I don't have much time before he makes a move. I can see it in his eyes.

"Goodbye for now, General." I flip the switch on the Bolt to its lowest charge, pull the trigger, and his head falls back like a lead weight. It's enough to incapacitate him, but not enough to kill. I stand and look around. All this time, not a soul has shown up in the lobby. *Where's my father?* "Deme," I say, "Is my father safe? Can you find him in the building?"

"I've been monitoring him. The meeting with the council members is not going well. But they're all safe. It's been less than fifteen minutes since I overheard Aulion's order."

"Can you find me transportation to the south gate?"

"There's a hovercar at the back of the building. Probably one of the council member's."

I stick the Bolt in my waistband, then run toward the back of the building, hoping I can commandeer the hovercar and get to the border gate before the guards start asking too many questions.

"Vale, you've got three hours to get the prisoners out of Windy Pines. Get to the north shore of Lake Okaria at Coburg. Eli can't risk getting any closer.

Local SDF forces are transporting everyone to the border in an airship now."

"How long will it take to get there?"

"Twenty minutes if you're lucky, *and* if you can get the hovercar started, *and* if you drive like Miah."

"I want to arrive alive, remember. Miah's a madman."

"I know."

I can hear the smile in her voice. Some AI. What would I do without her?

As I approach the south gate, I take a good long look at the SDF transport airship sitting there all fat and happy. Luck is definitely on my side today.

"Listen up, Deme," I say. "The transport is still here. If I can talk my way into getting the prisoners on it, we won't have to risk Eli getting close to Sector airspace. If I can make this work, you and Eli can figure out new coordinates for our rendezvous. I don't want to put him in danger if I don't have to."

"I can't risk opening the communication line unless you're successful," she says. "I'll stand by to contact him."

There's so much commotion at the south gate that the guards don't even notice me. The prisoners are arguing, protesting their exile with the border sentries and the SDF. If only they knew that exile is a gift. One soldier stands guard at the door of the airship, but he doesn't appear to be paying much attention. He's got his nose in his plasma. I can take him out if I need to.

"Please, we have no supplies, no food, no blankets …" a tall woman with a kind, unassuming face pleads.

"I'm sorry, but my orders are clear." The lieutenant, who appears to be the officer in charge, raises her voice. It drips with frustration. They've obviously been at this for a while. "It doesn't matter to me what you did or didn't do. You've been exiled by the orders of General Falke Aulion and I can't do anything about it."

Another prisoner steps forward. "You know Aulion has no right. Exile is illegal. How can you expect us to simply head out into the Wild with no accommodations for the elderly in our group?"

"You should have thought of that before you joined the Resistance," the lieutenant says.

"We told you, we haven't joined any—"

"Sympathizing with the enemy is the same thing. Now MOVE!"

I get out of the hovercar—which, to my great surprise, started with a swipe of my thumbprint, as if I had never left the Sector—square my shoulders, and walk toward the crowd. One hand on my Bolt, the other in the air.

"I suspected there would be trouble," I say with more than a hint of disgust in my voice.

"Valerian Orleán?" My name ripples through the crowd. Heads turn with mixed expressions of awe and suspicion.

"*Captain* Valerian Orleán." *That promotion won't last long.* "I'm here on direct orders of the chancellor and General Aulion to make sure these people are immediately removed from the Sector."

The lieutenant looks me up and down skeptically.

"I've been with the chancellor's delegation. I was on the stage. I watched the protest, and despite your traitorous demonstration, you're getting off easy. More drastic orders could have been given, but the chancellor has chosen to show mercy. Instead of imprisonment—or worse—he has sentenced you to exile."

"But exile is—"

"Save your breath," I spit. "There is no mercy for Resistance sympathizers. *I* should know, and *you* should count yourselves lucky." I turn back to the lieutenant, ignoring the protesters.

"I have orders to use this transport and take these citizens as far away from Sector territory as possible. I will return the transport to the airfield where I am to meet my father after the conclusion of the council meeting. Any questions?"

"But ..." one of the soldiers with his Bolt still pointed at the workers speaks up. "First General Aulion said—" He stops short. "And then ..." he trails off, confused. It's clear he doesn't want to repeat Aulion's previous orders.

"General Aulion was mistaken. Surely everyone here—soldier and citizen alike—understands that Philip Orleán would never order the mass execu—" I stop short as if I've said too much, and let the threat hang in the air.

Faces blanch and muffled sobs escape from several prisoners.

"Yes, sir. Of course, sir." The soldier says. He glances at the officer in charge whose brow is still wrinkled with doubt.

I take a step toward her. "You want to check with the chancellor personally, to verify my orders?" I bluff, gripping the butt of my Bolt. I nod toward the sentry post. "Shall I give you my father's private number? Have you call and interrupt the council meeting?"

"That is not necessary," she says, finally. "Do what you have to do. Just know that I will be recording all this in the logbook."

"I would expect nothing less—" I look at her nametag—"Lieutenant Tremblay. Now, let's load these traitors up and get them out of the Sector."

"Yes, sir." She steps aside, unwilling to question my authority.

"Round them up," I say loudly to the nearby soldiers. "Get them in the transport."

I guard the door as the prisoners, sixty-eight of them by my count, stumble, confused and scared, into the transport. There's nothing I can do for Lyle or those the SDF are still trying to find, but I can get these people to safety. Once they're all inside, I salute the lieutenant, palm the door closed, and turn to the prisoners. "We're gonna have to move fast, so everyone find a seat and hold on." I hurry to the cockpit, but there's already someone sitting in the pilot's seat: a rugged, gray-haired man with a square jaw and a deep cleft in his chin. He looks up as I enter.

"What are you doing?" I ask, nonplussed.

"Getting us out of here," the man says. "Zeke said you were a good man. He said I could trust you."

I trust you. Words my father said to me not even an hour ago. I never thought I would regret the chance to escape my parents, but now I wish I didn't have to leave him. I wish we had an opportunity to talk, father and son.

"Zeke Sayyid?"

"He's an old friend of mine from Ellas."

"What a coincidence." I settle into the co-pilot's seat. "My best friend's name is Sayyid."

"You don't say." He grins at me.

"Can you turn off the tracking?"

"First thing I did."

"Deme?" I say. "We're in. Got new coordinates for us?"

"Hold on."

While we wait, I survey the instrument panel. "As soon as we're out of sight, activate cloaking. I think it's high time we disappear."

"Plot a course for old Toronto," Demeter says. "It's in a caution zone. Far enough out there won't be many drones. Eli's on the way with a Resistance airship so you don't have to worry about being tracked."

I plug in the coordinates and turn to the pilot. "Let's move."

"Roger that." He sticks his hand out and I take it. His grip is firm. "Jamison Fitzpatrick at your service. Fitz, for short."

"Valerian Orleán. Vale, for short."

"Good to meet you, Vale." He punches the intercom button. "Ladies and gentlemen, this is your captain speaking."

Fitz lowers us into a perfect landing, nearly nose to nose with Eli's ship. He turns off the cloaking, and I'm out the door before anyone can move. The plan is to load the prisoners onto Eli's ship. Eli brought Zoe and Firestone to scan the Sector ship for tracking devices and deactivate all Sector firmware. Once it's safe to use, they'll fly it back to the Resistance.

As soon as I disembark, Eli runs over to me. The first thing out of my mouth is: "Are you really better?"

"Good as ever," Eli responds, hugging me. "Want me to prove it?"

I nod, and he pulls a small plasma from his jacket pocket. He opens a file on the plasma and a photo comes up: four smiling faces sitting on the dock at Kanaan's house. Remy invited me to her grandfather's house a few times so we could get out of the city. Eli has his arm draped over Tai's shoulders, both of them smiling broadly. A younger version of me is sitting next to Remy, a sliver of sunlight between us. We were just friends then. It was on that same dock I kissed her for the first time.

"I open this photo up at least once a day," Eli says, his voice soft. "Just to make sure. It's one of my favorites."

"I've never seen this before." I can barely get out the words.

"I'll make you a copy. Back at base."

"I'd like that."

"And since you brought her up, I've got news." I perk up. "After her stunt with the Round Barn video—"

"That was *her*?" I'd suspected, but wasn't sure. It seemed too risky, too dangerous. But then, Remy's never shied from risk.

"Of course it was her. Who else had access to that footage? Anyway, she's holed up at General Kofir Bunqu's estate. He's on our side. Can you believe it?"

I nod. This is no surprise. "He's the one who gave Demeter back to me."

"Soren and Osprey are headed there now. Osprey's in touch with Remy's Outsider contacts. They've got big plans and things are moving fast. Thought you might want to join them now that you're *persona non grata* with the parents again."

My heart flip flops at the thought of seeing Remy. "And just how am I supposed to get back into Okaria? We're hundreds of kilometers away and we've got the prisoners to deal with."

"I have a plan."

"Are you going to share this plan with me?"

"Firestone?" Eli calls out. "It's time to present Vale's gift."

"He's not gonna give me some of his vile homebrew, is he?"

"Vile?" Firestone appears from around the side of the airship, hunched over as if he's pushing something. "Way I remember, you took to it just fine. All except for the green tint it gave you. And the headache. And were you the one with the dry heaves? I can't remember."

I shake my head and then pull him in for a hug. "Good to see you."

"Yeah, yeah, enough with the weepy reunion. I've got something special for you from your Outsider buddies."

"Chan-Yu?"

"Next best thing. Osprey is loaning you her—"

"Don't tell me you've got a horse here. I'm out of practice."

"Better. I've got her *oiseau*. Her fancy little hoverbike complete with the new cloaking shield we rigged up." He reaches into thin air, feels around for something and then, *voilà*, there it is. The same hoverbike that Remy, Soren, Miah, and I followed to meet the Outsiders in the Wilds. "Still don't know what to make of our Wayfarer friend, but apparently she and Soren don't need this to travel undetected. It's all yours." He pushes it toward me.

"Here." Eli hands me a v-scroll. "Directions to Bunqu's from our coordinates here. Activated by your touch only. I recommend memorizing the map before you head out 'cause if anyone else so much as breathes on it, the whole damn thing erases itself. He's called Onion, by the way. That's his code name."

"Read it after we're gone," Firestone says. He opens the bike's only saddlebag and pulls out a helmet and coveralls. "Put this on. Once you're outfitted, you'll be invisible. Just press this button." He points, and then hands me a key fob. Keep this with you and you can activate it at a distance."

"Does Remy know? Has anyone told her I'm heading her way?"

"We figured you could surprise her. Soren and Osprey know. They'll be expecting you, but probably won't arrive much ahead of you."

"And what about you two?"

"I'm working with Bear and Zeke on supply lines," Firestone says, and looks at Eli expectantly.

"Well, Miah and I have plans of our own."

"That sounds like trouble," I say. "How is Miah?"

"He's fine. Back at base making preparations."

"For these big plans of yours?"

"Yup."

"Is it a big secret?"

"Nope."

"So …?"

"You'll see," Eli says.

I clip the key fob to my belt and step into the coveralls. "You'll find a kindred spirit in the pilot, Jamison Fitzpatrick." I turn to Firestone. "He knows Zeke. And, based on our conversation, he'll be able to teach you a thing or two about homebrew."

I pick up the helmet, climb on the hoverbike, and look back at Eli and Firestone. "Thanks for keeping the faith."

"Yeah," Eli says, with a knowing smile. "Get out of here."

11 — REMY

I stretch my back, rest my head against the paneled wall of the window seat, and watch as raindrops strike the windowpane and slide down the glass leaving a silvery trail behind them. Almost dusk. I love this part of the day. There is promise in every time of transition, a hopefulness that something awaits just around the corner. Before dawn, it is *what will morning bring*? When the sun hangs high in the noon sky, *what will the afternoon bring*? And at dusk, *what will the night bring*? The grey storm clouds slide lazily across the sky, darkening into a sort of charcoal blue as the sun sets behind them. My plasma sits open in my lap, a pen-and-ink drawing zoomed out so I can view the full image I've created. Raindrops fall from billowing clouds, turning into seeds that sprout as they reach the ground, blossoming into human-like shapes as they take root and grow.

"The water of life," I whisper aloud. Every image needs a title, my art teacher told me once, in a class on marketing art and design. Without a title, how will your viewers begin to approach or understand the image? Later, at home, my father very politely called bullshit on this idea.

"Art doesn't need a translation for the viewer's convenience. Would you expect me to create a drawing or painting to accompany every poem I've ever written?" he asked through thinly veiled disdain. When I shook my head, he continued, "Why would someone expect a painter to put his images into words?"

But the exhortation stuck, and I've titled almost all of my drawings ever since.

"Remy," a deep voice says, echoing through the dark room. I turn to the sound, away from the pattering rain outside. "Meera's here, downstairs."

"Thanks," I say and unfold my legs to stand. "I'm finished with the flier." I hand the plasma to General Bunqu and he zooms in and out. His eyes widen and a smile forms on his broad, handsome face.

"Impressive. I believe this will do nicely for your purposes. Should I transfer it to a UMIT?"

"I don't know. Meera's in charge of all that." I smile. "I'm art. She's logistics."

"I suppose I'm universal magnetic information transfer," he laughs.

"That and security. And transportation. Oh, and food."

"Speaking of which …"

"I'm right behind you."

In the kitchen, Meera has already raided the refrigerator and set out a platter of fruits, nuts, and vegetables that the Outsiders have smuggled in for Bunqu. I don't wait to be asked, and dig in as soon as I sit down.

"We gonna do this thing tonight?" Meera asks.

"I'm ready if you are," I say, stuffing a fig in my mouth. "How many places are we going to go? We'll need to have seedcoin in hand or enough money programed into the UMIT for each place."

Meera turns to General Bunqu. "What do you think? We'll only pay to display in the most disreputable places." She waggles her eyebrows. "Where all the best people hang out."

"Don't worry about money," Bunqu says, handing the plasma to Meera. "Take a look at the finished product. Remy's 'flier' is a work of art."

"Wow. That's beautiful," Meera says. "But what about the other drawing? The creepy one you described to me."

"I thought we'd use both," I say. "I programed the flier so one dissolves into the other with the information about time and place appearing between each loop. Go to the previous screen. I finished the other one this morning."

Meera slides to the previous screen and looks up at me, shaking her head. "Lovely." She hands the plasma back to Bunqu, and his lip curls in distaste.

"Very literal."

I think it's one of my better drawings. One could even call it pastoral. Inspired by the carnage at Round Barn, it's a landscape, a field lush with corn and bean stalks, vegetables, sunflowers, and fruit trees, all growing out of the gaping jaws, nose holes, and eye sockets of skulls like half-buried potted plants.

"It's about how the Sector builds its way of life on the dead," I explain, not that I need to explain to Meera or General Bunqu. "Not just the eternal cycle of sowing and harvesting, but on killing our own people." I remember one of my instructors looking at a series of my drawings and actually making a *tsk-tsk* sound. She said my work was "extremely expressive."

"If this doesn't get people's attention, I don't know what will," Meera says.

The sweet, earthy smell of the den is soothing, and I feel the tension lifting off my shoulders. Wisps of smoke cast strange, flowing shadows across the lights. The low drumbeat echoing from the stage resonates in my rib cage. Glasses clink, matches strike, and carefree laughter rings in my ears. I wave my UMIT over the plasma display and pay five seedcoins for two days' worth of signage on a small corner of the announcement board. It's the last of the money on my UMIT. My drawing immediately flashes into view, replacing one of the older displays, which read: MDMA Party - OAC Sponsored - Green Dragon Hall - Summer 1 22h00 - ONLY TWO HUNDRED SEEDS ENTRY AND DRINK TICKET!

Meera and I split up to cover more ground, and for the last few hours, I've been posting the flier for the vigil we've been planning in every seedy smoke den, cocktail shop, and bar I can find. I'm sure there are always informers, drones, and Watchers keeping an eye out even in the places I frequent, but there's much less chance anyone will care about what I'm posting. They'll be looking for suspected Outsiders, Resistance sympathizers, or plain old criminals, not people planning a mourning vigil out in plain sight.

We decided to keep the language vague, hoping that if anyone with friends or family affected by the SRI classroom massacre sees the notice, they'll get the code, understand, and help spread the word. As for anyone else that sees it and doesn't get it, well, we don't want them at the vigil, anyway.

Sisters, brothers, friends
Remember the promise of youth cut down too soon
Illuminate the lives taken, too sudden, too violent
Class shattered
Lives unmoored
A promise destroyed
Stolen
Sorrow.

"How's it going, Sparrow?" I turn to see Snake, and notice that his purple hair has been shaved into a mohawk.

"What are you doing here?" I ask.

"Got a message from Onion via Meera. She was posting the notice at The Elysium when a messenger found her. I was just getting off work, so she sent me to find you. They want you back at the house."

"What's happened?" I ask, my pulse spiking.

"That's all the information I've got." He smiles and puts his hand out for my UMIT. "I'll take over, if you want."

"Thanks, but I think I just spent the last of my money anyway."

"Better get going, then. Sounded important."

I nod, and give him a quick hug. He slips through the crowd. I pocket the UMIT and head out into the night. I emerge onto a side street where The Vine, a semi-legal establishment that sells marijuana in the light and moonshine—not approved by the Dieticians for distribution—in the shadows, takes up most of the real estate. I pull my hood tight, tie it under my chin, and set out at a jog. Rain pelts my jacket. Mist and surreal shadows line the alleys, and it's hard for anyone to see clearly through the gathering fog.

To avoid going on foot the three-odd kilometers back to Bunqu's estate, I hop one of the last PODS by sneaking in after a late-night commuter. I pretend to press my palm against the reader to register my identity, and then jump the POD right before the door closes after the woman in front of me. She stares out the window, her face blank as a new canvas, ignoring my presence altogether as the POD glides into motion. So much the better.

At the stop nearest Bunqu's estate, an illuminated field of glowing succulents leads me through a pebbled path and down the long road to Bunqu's private gate. *Why has he summoned me?*

As the gate comes into view, my pulse jumps. I key in the code the general gave me before Meera and I headed out, and the gate slides open, soft as a whisper. Inside, a sleek, low-slung structure composed of concrete, glass, and bamboo blends into the landscaping. I look up at the second-floor window next to which I spent most of my day. The light's out in my room, but a soft golden glow emanates from the wide front window, even though it is mostly hidden by a bamboo shade. Something about the wide lawn dotted only with neatly trimmed ornamental trees makes me nervous. Bunqu says he refused the offer of perimeter guards, telling Aulion that he could damn well take care of any threat himself—not that anyone would ever dream of taking on Bunqu. I trained with him one morning this week. The man's a solid wall, as fast as quicksilver and stronger than anyone I've met. I didn't dare even hold his punching bag. He claims to be an expert in every kind of martial arts he's been able to study, and I believe him. Apparently, so does Aulion. Still, the pit of my stomach feels hollowed out, and I walk faster, wondering what, by all that grows, is waiting for me inside.

Nervous about going through the front door, I head around the side, toward the entryway hidden by a high concrete wall. Fumbling with the keypad to enter the password, I type: *Listen to the forest floor.* I can't help but smile at the line. When I asked what the verse was from, Bunqu waved my question away and said he'd tried his hand at writing poetry a few years back and none of it was any good. He'd liked that line, though, so it became his security code for the house.

I pass through a garage where a sleek hovercar is parked. By the time I hurry down the hallway and pass through the kitchen, I can hear voices. I head for the front room, but then stop. The doors to the back veranda, where Bunqu has a covered sitting area adorned with flowering vines, fruit trees, mosaiced floors, and an inviting firepit, are wide open. I step out and stop dead. Bunqu looks up from serving tea and says, "Ah, Remy. We've got guests."

Soren and Osprey, both sporting smudged faces and dark circles under their eyes and wearing clothes that have not seen soap in days if not weeks, sit wearily, leaning on the table.

"What? When? How did you get here? You don't have bad news, do you?"

"Not even a 'hi' after you abandoned us in Okaria two months ago?" Soren says, with classic Skaarsgard sarcasm. I start to reach around the table to hug him, but he waves me off. "My bones hurt."

Osprey punches him in the shoulder.

"What a baby. Can't handle a few days in the woods on foot."

"Forty kilometers a day is a grueling pace," Soren retorts.

"At least you didn't get typhoid fever," Osprey says brightly.

"What's typhoid fever?" I ask. Osprey shakes her head. "You don't want to know."

"No bad news today." Soren holds up his cup. "Just tea. This is ten times better than anything Rhinehouse ever served us."

"Forget tea. I keep telling General Onion here that I need something stronger," Osprey scowls up at Bunqu. "I need a proper capital city cocktail after the trip we've had."

"Tea first," Bunqu says. "To calm the nerves. Then I'll fetch a couple of bottles of sparkling wine worthy of a true welcome."

"I recommend a Chateau Ile d'Orleáns. My grandfather's vineyard has always produced a fine wine."

I turn. There, standing in the doorway with a washcloth in his hand and a freshly-scrubbed face, is Vale. His black hair is a riot, and he looks exhausted, but he's clearly tried to make himself presentable. He looks at me with those bright sea-green eyes that make me think of sun-lit water, and I wonder how it is that he makes me feel so *known*. My breath catches. I can't move.

"I ... what ... *how is this possible?*" I stutter, unable to think, to react.

But then I don't have to. Vale's arms are around me, pulling my body into his, his breath warm against my forehead, and I don't have to say anything at all.

"Remy Alexander," he whispers, "may I—"

I don't wait. I stand on tiptoes, skim my hand up to the back of his neck and bring him to me. There's a moment where everything else disappears. It feels like lying on Granddad's dock, feet dangling in the water, clouds drifting by overhead, like biting into spring's first ripe strawberry, so perfect the juice drips down your chin. It's probably only a couple of seconds but it carves out an expanding space in my chest that tells me *this* is what happiness is.

And then it's over.

He pulls away, and conscious thought rushes back in like a tide. He reaches down to take my hand.

"Done yet?" Soren asks.

"Don't be an ass," Osprey says, pressing her fingertips playfully to his cheek, turning his face away from her in a mock-sla   p. "It's not like you haven't kissed me in public more than once. Matter of fact, that was pretty tame compared to what you—"

"Yeah, yeah, okay," Soren interrupts with a laugh.

"Time to celebrate yet, General Onion? How 'bout that wine?" Osprey asks. Her characteristic bluntness is refreshing, and Bunqu is obviously taken with her.

"It is indeed time to celebrate," he says, disappearing back inside.

I peel off my wet jacket and turn to Vale. "Tell me everything."

"Long story." He pulls out chairs for both of us.

"Might as well tell the whole sordid tale," Bunqu calls from the kitchen.

"Sordid is right," Vale begins, picking up my hand and staring at it. He rubs a thumb across my skin and I watch the simple movement as if transfixed by a magic trick. "It started at Windy Pines. I was supposed to go on a speaking tour of the factory towns with my father." We listen without interruption as Vale tells the story. As he speaks, telling us how he fought Aulion and commandeered the airship, I am amazed by how much Vale has changed.

From a willing servant of the Sector to a man who would risk his life and defy everyone on behalf of total strangers.

Bunqu returns with a tray of glasses and a bottle of sparkling wine from the old Orleán family vineyard. Bunqu pops the cork and pours with a practiced flourish. Clearly he is a man who has enjoyed the finer things in life.

Vale picks up the bottle and looks at the label.

"Sector Annum 79. This was a good vintage. My grandfather, Augustus, bought the land and planted the first vines there a few years before he died. A friend took care of it after that, until my father was old enough to take over. He never had much interest in farming, though, and I haven't been to the vineyard since I was young."

"Tell us about the vigil." Soren takes a long drink. He looks at Osprey. "We want to be there."

"What vigil?" Vale asks.

"Meera and I are planning a mourning vigil for the victims of the SRI massacre. Two days from now at dawn in the Grass Creek Arboretum." Vale lifts my hand to his lips and kisses my palm.

"What can we do to help?" Osprey asks.

"Spread the word," I respond. "We need someone to draft a courriel advertising the vigil to go out to the Olympia list-serv. I met a broadcast engineer at Olympia who helped Meera and me coordinate the Round Barn footage. He gave me the list of all the Olympia courriel subscribers."

"Speaking of that," Vale says, "how did you pull that one off?"

I tell them about Shia, and our adventure at the games.

"None of it would have been possible without him—or Meera's fingerprint counterfeiting. I've been here two months and it still amazes me how thoroughly the Outsiders have infiltrated the city."

"Even I don't know how they do it." Osprey drains her glass. "It's a lot easier to be stealthy when there's not another soul for fifty kilometers in any direction."

"How is it possible that the Outsiders can move in and out so easily," Soren asks, "and yet haven't made a move against the Sector?"

"It's not our place," Osprey says. "It's for citizens to demand that their leaders uphold their founding principles. We just want to be left alone to live in harmony—as much as possible, that is—with the environment. We claim the right to choose our own paths. No one should take that right away."

Bunqu picks up the thread, twirling the stem of his glass between his fingers, and looking off into the distance.

"I was born a citizen of the Okarian Sector. I went to the Academy, and then to the military institute. For a long time I was the willing soldier. I took orders. Did what I was told. Always determined to be the best, the strongest, the fastest. I was undefeated in the sparring ring. Until one day, a young man stepped onto the mat and kicked my ass." He sets his glass on the table. "A skinny, young thing. All sinew and muscle. All quiet intensity. Afterward, we shared a pot of tea and got to talking. I never looked back."

We all look at each other and then Vale sucks in a breath. "Chan-Yu?"

Without even acknowledging Vale, Bunqu continues. "We fed off of each other's successes and strengths, both intellectually and with regard to our climb through the ranks. We met early in our careers; I was a junior officer and Chan-Yu was a foot soldier with physical and mental strength that showed great promise. It was Chan-Yu who introduced me to the ways and ideas of the Outsiders. But it was years before he truly revealed himself to me."

"He devoted fifteen years of his life to infiltrating the Sector's highest levels of security." Osprey sits back in her chair and crosses her arms over her chest. She glares at Soren, and then me and Vale, but I can tell her anger is more playacting than anything. "Bet he never knew he'd give it all up to save two scrawny brats from the Sector from another scrawny brat from the Sector."

I squeeze Vale's hand, remembering my terror and surprise on that winter evening as Chan-Yu showed up in our holding cell with two sets of clothes and little in the way of answers.

"As to the rest of your question, Remy," Bunqu turns to me, "the Outsiders have neither the numbers to take down the current leadership, nor the desire. At least not until recently. Our focus has been on intelligence, misdirection, and evasion, rather than on coups or civil war. Only within the last few years has the Okarian leadership become deranged to the point that they warrant removal from power."

"The turning point was when the SD210 blight spiraled out of control, and famine hit the Farms and towns hard," Soren says. "When my mother was still chancellor, I overheard her and my father arguing with James about the Orleáns' solution. Rhinehouse warned them not to go along with their plan, with the MealPak modifications Corine proposed. But when people started dying, the situation grew desperate, and my mother was ousted."

"What happened to your parents?" Vale asks. "I never knew. They just disappeared."

Soren stares at the table for a long time before responding. Osprey, too, is uncharacteristically quiet.

"You see what happens to people who ask the wrong questions. That's what Aulion said to me when he 'escorted' them home. They weren't the same. Barely recognized me."

I knew his parents had disappeared from the public eye, but I never knew the extent of it. I feel Soren's anger and bitterness mirrored in my own. Now I know why he recoiled when Aulion walked into our cell. Aulion as good as killed his parents. Just like Corine killed my sister and my mother.

"Don't worry," Vale says quietly. "I left him for you."

Osprey looks at Soren.

"It's been a long time coming."

I close the door behind me and lean against it. Vale lets the window blind drop back into place and turns, his shoulders casting a dim shadow on the wall. A towel is wrapped around his slim hips and he runs a hand through his still-damp hair.

"Figured I needed a shower," he shrugs. "As you saw, I was filthy. Rode straight through."

"You must be tired."

A lopsided smile spreads across his face and he walks around the bed toward me. "Exhausted."

My pulse begins to pound, a thudding in my ears that echoes down my spine, into my very center.

"Bunqu gave Soren and Osprey the room across the hall," I manage, "but last I saw them they were crawling into the hammock on the veranda with a pile of blankets so thick, I wonder if they'll smother."

"And the general?"

"The general?" Now it's my turn to smile. "He put your clothes in the wash and went to bed. On the first floor. At the other end of the house."

I think back to all the moments that led to this. Our first kiss almost four years ago, before my sister and my mother were murdered. Him holding my hand as I left, trembling, to find out why I'd been summoned after the massacre at the SRI. The flowers he gave me before my family fled the Sector, when I slammed the door in his face, the last time I would see him for three years. Then that night outside the seed bank, the night I was captured, when I thought I wanted to kill him, and he extended his hand to me and said, *I'm not going to hurt you.* Finding out he'd sent Chan-Yu to get Soren and me out of Okaria, watching him try to protect my mother during the attack at Thermopylae. His expression as he handed my grandfather's compass to me and offered his life in exchange for the ones I'd lost. Listening to him play the guitar at the Outsider's camp. Knowing he was singing for me. And watching him on the ledge of that building, prepared to sacrifice his life for our safety.

He stands in front of me, a hairsbreadth away, and I put a fingertip at the base of his throat and let it drift down slowly. Goosebumps prickle his skin.

"Cold?" I ask, looking up at him.

"Hardly."

He cups my face in his hands and leans down, his lips brushing mine. My fingers splay across his chest, mapping the muscles, moving around his back to pull him to me. With one hand he traces the curve of my neck and with the other, he peels the shirt from my shoulders as delicately as if unwrapping a gift, letting his lips follow his fingers. I arch into him, remembering how close we came to hating each other, killing each other, watching the other die.

"I always knew—always dreamed—it would be you. Us. Like this." I close my eyes as his breath dances across my skin. "It wasn't ever real until now," I whisper.

"It's always been real."

I reach up and turn out the light.

12 — REMY

Vale and I were the first ones up, so I made a pot of tea while he made breakfast. I'm sitting out on the veranda in the cool morning, enjoying the smell of blooming lavender from the garden. It's so early in the morning the sky is just beginning to turn the barest shade of blue. I run my hand over my close-cropped hair as Vale steps out with two plates in hand.

"I miss my curls," I say, as he drops into the chair next to me. "I'm still not used to it. With the camouflage makeup and short hair, I don't recognize myself."

"I miss them, too. The new cut brings out your eyes, though."

"Well, look who it is." Soren shuffles in with Osprey close behind. She goes straight to the teapot as he slouches into the chair across from me. "You both look *refreshed*."

"Another night of much needed rest." Vale leans back in his chair, cradling his mug.

"Rest? I doubt it." Osprey sets two cups on the table and folds herself onto Soren's lap like some sort of exotic cat. I half expect her to start purring. "Without Onion to wake you up, you might have 'slept' right through."

"You're the ones running late," I retort. "We've been up, showered, made breakfast, and are ready to get started. You both look like you've been run over."

Osprey cocks a thumb at Soren. "I thought it'd be easier our second night on the veranda. I prefer sleeping outside, but Soren takes up the whole hammock. Last night was like a war zone."

"I can only imagine." Vale rolls his eyes.

I glance at the sky. Four in the morning. Soon, pale fingers of light will paint themselves across the horizon, figures will appear out of the morning mist, and at dawn the vigil will begin.

Meera had shown up yesterday morning, reporting that news of the vigil was spreading faster than we'd hoped. She was scrounging something to eat from Bunqu's larder when Soren and Osprey appeared. Meera knew of Osprey, of course, but had never met her, so the two of them disappeared for a while to talk about whatever Outsiders talk about when the rest of us aren't around. After a half hour, they reappeared in the kitchen and settled in at the table with Soren and me until Vale sauntered down the stairs with no socks, no shoes, no shirt, just a pair of Bunqu's oversized lounging pants tied low on his hips. Meera's eyes went wide. After I made the introductions and told her how Vale came to be at Bunqu's, she insisted that I didn't need to do anything more to plan for the vigil, that she and Snake had everything in hand. I could have protested, but for once, I didn't. I wanted to spend every moment I could with Vale.

After Bunqu knocked this morning, we stayed in bed a few more minutes talking about the day to come. Then we showered and dressed. I stashed my knife in my boot, and stuck the small Bolt Bunqu gave me in a neat little holster at my hip. Vale is similarly prepared. We're not planning on starting a fight today, but the Watchmen or the SDF could bring the fight to us. Today is about remembrance and renewal. About gathering in peace, not mobilizing for war.

As soon as Soren and Osprey are ready, we start on our disguises. For Vale, it's red hair and for Soren, it's dark brown. They can't very well go around looking like themselves, even if they are going to be wearing mourning tattoos. They're too recognizable.

Tattoos in Okaria are considered taboo, as are most forms of permanent body alterations. Since parents select traits during the genetic engineering phase of conception, there's generally no need for cosmetic surgery except in cases where damage from an accident needs to be repaired. So people are who they are and tattoos and other body adornment are discouraged. But painted tattoos for funeral ceremonies and mourning vigils are different. A tradition that arose during the Religious Wars, the practice stuck and has grown even more elaborate over the years.

When it started, most people painted masks on their faces, of demons, ghosts, monsters, or other terrors. The idea, as my father told me, was to scare evil forces away from the dead before they'd been properly mourned or buried, at which point both the living and the dead were safe. When Okaria was incorporated on Jubilation Day, the founders outlawed this practice, condemning it as a vestige of the religions that had torn the world apart. But people kept doing it. A few years later, the law was reversed, and since then the custom has evolved from evil-looking masks into designs and artwork of all forms.

On each of my cheeks, I draw a simplified version of the images I used to spread the word of the vigil: an upside-down skull with a tree growing out of it on one side and a raindrop morphing into a human form on the other. I paint puffy white clouds on my forehead, green vines around my eyes, and use blue paint to turn my lips into a creek. I pause for a moment to admire my work so far. I've created a landscape: the raindrop falling from the clouds, then flowing into the blue water on my lips, leading to the skulls on my cheek and the vines around my eyes.

"You're always beautiful, Remy," Vale says, making me jump as I turn to see him leaning against the door frame, "but this is something extraordinary."

There's a look of hunger in his eyes, in his mouth, slightly upturned at the corners. *I want to satisfy that hunger*, I think. *But not now.*

"Your turn," I say. "What do you want?"

"You're the artist. I trust you."

He sits down on a stool and I stare at him for a moment, studying his face, thinking about who he is and why he's here. Then it comes to me.

Working quickly, I paint a round, green caterpillar on one cheek, a chrysalis on his forehead, and a vivid butterfly on the other. Around his eyes, I paint green-tinted storm clouds with ominous black-grey roiling in the center of his face. Looking at him, it reads from left to right, telling the story of rebirth. The poster child for the Okarian Sector. The golden boy. The symbol of transformation.

Osprey's just as talented a face-paint artist as I am, although her work tends to the more macabre. She's done herself in a mess of brown, white, and green that doesn't resemble anything so much as an overgrown tree trunk. Somehow, she's still gorgeous, in her own bizarre way. She gets to work on Soren and soon he's decked out in a black-and-white mask similar to the ones that were popular in the old days. With ghoulish eyes and scar patterns traced across his jawbone, forehead, and lips, he looks gruesome.

"I wish Aulion could see me like this," he growls. "I want the old man to die with shit in his pants."

"You'll just have to be very good at predicting the future," Vale says.

"Or I could do this for you every day," Osprey adds. "It's pretty hot. Fancy a quickie?"

Soren grins, the scar stretching across his jaw. It's terrifying.

"Later," he says.

I catch Vale watching me and we lock eyes. Suddenly the room is much warmer and every hair on my body stands at attention.

Then Bunqu appears in the doorway. "You'd best be on your way," he says. "Do you have your walkie-talkies?" Soren and I both pat the devices clipped to our belts. Soren helped Bunqu rig together two handheld radio devices, similar to the short-range walkie-talkies used in the Old World. Soren managed to boost the signal, so we'll be able to communicate from far away. "Let's just hope you don't have to use them." Bunqu steps forward and envelops me in his arms. "You've put a lot of thought into this vigil. I wish I could be there."

"I wish you could, too."

Bunqu puts a hand into the inner pocket of his jacket and pulls out a small canvas bag, tied with a drawstring. He tips the bag up, and several acorns tumble into his palm.

"I know you already have seeds for the ceremony," he says, passing one to each of us. "But with acorns, you now have my blessing as well."

"Like the pendants." Vale's hand goes to the golden acorn around his neck.

Soren rolls his eyes. "You Outsiders sure have a thing for acorns."

We carried our supplies to the POD, boarding as a group behind a scrum of workers heading out for their morning shifts. Okarians are used to seeing people adorned for vigils, so we didn't attract any undue scrutiny. Meera and I had carefully selected the site a few days ago, a little creek under a bridge in one of the city's many parks. It's smaller, and a little off the main walking paths, where Watchmen don't patrol as often. Most of the bypassers are nearby residents doing their daily Dietician-prescribed exercise routines. It's a beautiful little spot, with grass and wildflowers growing along the banks of the creek, one of the hundreds of grey water recycling canals in Okarian parks. In the growing daylight, as the sky turns from dusky blue to pink and orange, we set down our bags and prepare.

Osprey spreads the seeds on a small blanket. Vale sets two small drums by the creek. Soren clears an area and lays out a circle of stones, then carefully builds a pyramid of small logs for the fire. Meera joins us shortly after, accompanied by Snake and a few others I've never seen. When the sun shows her face, the vigil keepers start to arrive.

Soren lights the fire. The first few to arrive are gloriously decked out. One has a phoenix painted across her entire body, red and gold paint that starts at her left ankle and crawls all the way up to a pointed beak on her right shoulder and feather plumage along her collarbone. Her tight shorts and athletic bra reveal the extent of her artwork—it must have taken hours to complete. A man who looks to be in his thirties has his shirt off and an electrical explosion in shocking blue painted across his chest. I can only guess it represents Bolt fire, and wonder if he knew one of the victims of the massacre personally. A group of younger people arrive with straw, twigs, and sticks woven into their hair, their faces painted to depict different animals: a deer, a wolf, a sheep, a badger, and a bird of some sort, maybe a raven or crow. As more and more of them crest the hill and walk toward us, I am amazed by how many there are. I stand to greet them, nodding silently as they filter in and stand next to Osprey and Soren.

As the sun crests the horizon, painting our miniature valley in decadent orange and yellow, seeming to set the wildflowers on fire, I decide it's time to begin. I catch Vale's eye and, sitting at the drums, he begins a light, slow rhythm, quiet enough that my voice can be heard over their sound.

"This vigil is for victims of the massacre almost four years ago at the Sector Research Institute, where seven students and their professor were murdered." I think of Eli, his miraculous escape from death, and wish long and hard that he were here, too. "Their deaths went unavenged. Justice was never sought. But this vigil isn't only about the victims of the massacre. We wish to honor the many mysterious deaths and disappearances over the years. Today isn't about revenge or justice. Today we'll speak the names of the lost and the dead, and remember them."

I kneel and pick three seeds from the neat piles Osprey's organized. I pull Bunqu's acorn out of my pocket and hold it with the others. I throw two of my seeds onto Soren's fire.

"Tai Alexander. Brinn Alexander. This is for their deaths."

I walk the few short paces to the creekside and toss the two remaining seeds into the running water.

"Tai Alexander. Brinn Alexander. This is for their lives, and for rebirth in the trees, the water, the earth, the sky."

Let us practice resurrection.

I turn back to the crowd, where at least a hundred people are sitting, watching. When I loaded my fliers up around town, I was expecting twenty, twenty-five. I would have been happy with that. I sit next to Vale at the drums, the low rhythm resonating in my chest.

Soren stands and collects his seeds. At the fire, he says, "Hana Lyon. Tai

Alexander. Sam. Brinn Alexander. This is for their deaths." He throws his seeds into the fire. I remember a long time ago, not long after he joined the Resistance, when he told Eli, Jahnu, and me about his brief, almost non-existent relationship with Hana Lyon, one of the other murdered students at the Academy. "Hana Lyon. Tai Alexander. Sam. Brinn Alexander. Odin Skaarsgard. Cara Skaarsgard. This is for their lives." I wonder at Soren's naming of his parents. They aren't dead, but it seems he considers their lives worthy of honoring at this funerary vigil. It strikes me how many people Soren has lost to the Sector's destruction.

Osprey only has one name: "Violet," she breathes, tossing her seed onto the flame. At the creek, she throws her seed in, but says nothing more.

Another few come forward, take seeds and cast them into the fire, saying names I don't know and intoning the words, each with their own spin, their own meaning. One man I almost recognize—was he a student at the SRI? A friend of Tai's?—has claws painted on his hands and a multicolored skull on his face. Soren watches him, too, and then glances at me and nods. He collects a handful of seeds when he stands, more than anyone else who's come before him except perhaps Soren.

"Aran Hawthorne. Matthew Malthus. Tai Alexander. Joaquin Pero. Dakota Quinn. Fennel Chang. Kell O'Connell. Hana Lyon. I knew them all, and none of them deserved their fate. This is for their deaths." He throws his seeds in the fire, and then into the water. "The fire will bring them justice, and the water will bring them peace." He meets my eyes as he turns, a grim expression on his face.

As the sun rises more people file in to watch or participate, and soon I estimate there's no fewer than two hundred people sitting or standing in our little valley, clustered tightly together, bound by silence. Some bystanders observe from a distance, painted bodies stand up to throw seeds into the fire and the water, and the sky morphs from red to orange to clear blue.

The woman with the phoenix stands, selects her seeds, and tosses them into the flames. "Rachel Sayyid." I gape. *That's Jeremiah's mother's name!* Vale, too, is staring slack-jawed at the woman and nearly misses a drumbeat. I turn to Soren, his eyes wide. "Hana Lyon. This is for their deaths." She turns and walks to the creek empty-handed, staring at the rushing waters for several seconds. No one moves. "There will be no resurrection for them." I can hear the anguish in her voice, the bitterness, sour like rotten fruit. "The resurrection will be ours." She raises her hands into the air, clenched into fists, and now I notice the clear red letter painted on the back of both her hands: R.

"The resurrection will be ours," someone says nearby, echoing her words.

"The resurrection will be ours," comes another echo. I look for the sound of the voice. It's the man with the skull and claws, the familiar-looking one, who said the names of everyone who died in the massacre.

"The resurrection will be ours," Soren and Osprey say in sync, looking wide-eyed at the crowd as the chant goes around, not loud but forceful, with the same rhythm and cadence as the beat Vale was tapping out just moments ago.

The resurrection will be ours.

And then it's over.

Vale stays next to the drum as the vigil keepers begin murmuring amongst themselves, some taking their leave, some gathering into small groups. I stand as Meera comes up to me and kisses my cheek.

"That was beautiful, Remy," she says. "The Sector may say you're the face of the Resistance, but today you proved you're really the face of the Resurrection."

Meera reaches for my hand as another vigil keeper approaches: the girl with the phoenix. She stops and looks at me with a terrifying ferocity, the red plumage painted around her eyes making her all the more frightening. She glances over at Soren and Osprey and then back to me.

"My name is Saara. I know who you are, Remy Alexander. I want to fight with you."

"Who are you?" I demand, awestruck by her paint and by her presence.

"I'm Hana Lyon's sister."

Soren turns at the mention of Hana's name. He leaves Osprey's side and walks over to us.

"You threw seeds for my sister," Saara says, watching him. "How did you know her?"

"I loved her," Soren says. "Young love, but love nonetheless."

Meera and I take Saara's hands.

"Welcome to the Resistance," I murmur.

13 — VALE

I watch from afar as the girl with the phoenix paint walks up to Remy and Meera. Still awed by the vigil's power, I try to keep my feet on the ground and process what I just witnessed. Instead of joining Remy, I focus on cleaning up, gathering the remaining seeds, and packing up the few things we brought.

When I turn back around, Meera's gone, but Remy and Soren are still talking to the girl. I opt to stay out of the conversation, choosing instead to sit by the stream and wait. After about ten minutes, I feel a hand on my shoulder, fingers pressing into my tired muscles.

"Meera's going back to Bunqu's to clean up," Remy says as I stand. "She has to go into work. Said a few people called in sick, that there must be some kind of bug going around. She'll meet us later."

"Who is that girl?" I ask.

"Her name is Saara Lyon." Her eyes light up with excitement. "Hana Lyon's sister. She wants to join the Resistance. Today. She says she has a bag packed and everything." I realize what this must mean to Remy, to know there is someone else out there who knows what she's been through, who can understand and empathize completely.

"How did she know Rachel?"

"She's a nurse. She took care of Miah's mom when she was turned into a lab rat during the blight that went around when we were at the Academy. She did her research and realized it was all connected." *To my parents*, I think, my head swimming. "She's been waiting for a chance to get in touch with someone from the Resistance for months."

"Remy," I say, pressure building in my chest, constricting my throat. The feeling of being underwater, tumbling under waves, grows with every passing second. "What you did today was amazing."

I can't take my eyes off her. As she turns to me, her presence is like gravity, pulling me to her as effortlessly as the earth keeps my feet on the ground.

"I couldn't have done it by myself." She leans in to me. "What would we have done without your drumming?"

She turns to leave, but I stay where I am, my feet rooted to that spot. I take her hands in mine. Her eyes are as rich as the earth.

"Remy, the vigil was inspiring. But I'm not talking about that. I'm talking about you." Something changed today, watching her lead the ceremony. I've been chasing her for almost four years now, this girl, but today she became more than just a girl. "You are my compass, my guide. I'm in love with you."

She stares at me for a long time before responding, but the silence between us is as peaceful as a clear lake at dawn.

"I know," she whispers. "I'm in love with you, too."

We're alone, just the two of us, and so I pull her to me and kiss her, and she wraps her arms around my waist. For a few moments that feel as eternal as a few millennia, we stand like that and watch the sun, reminiscent of Saara Lyon's phoenix, rise to its full, fiery brightness.

Finally we pull away.

"Saara's going to get her bag. Soren and Osprey are waiting here for her, and they'll meet us back at Bunqu's." Remy looks me in the eye. "We'll have time to wash off this body paint. Together."

After an hour of walking, we key into Bunqu's gate and make our way around to the hidden side door. Something raises the hackles on the back of my neck. The air is too still. I set the drums down and hold up a finger, moving to peer around the corner into the back grounds of the estate.

"What is it?" Remy whispers.

Nothing seems amiss, but still. "Check to make sure the alarm is set."

She moves back to the door and uncovers the keypad. "Looks good."

I let out a sigh and rejoin her at the door. "Must be a bit of nerves after the vigil."

"I get it," she says. "I've been living on knife's edge for weeks, always expecting someone to recognize me even though I barely recognize myself."

She punches in the code and, once inside, resets the alarm.

My mouth is dry, my senses still on high alert. Something's wrong. "You go on up," I say. "I'm going to get a drink. Want me to bring you something?"

"Sure. One of Bunqu's protein concoctions sounds good." Remy stands on tiptoes to kiss me. "Don't be long."

"Don't worry," I say, my pulse already racing, suddenly very conscious of the Bolt holstered at my side. I watch as Remy disappears up the back staircase and then I head down the long hallway to the kitchen. I stop in my tracks and instinctively draw my Bolt, ears pricked for any evidence of movement in the house, double-checking every shadow, my mind racing as I plot out everything that could possibly have gone wrong.

"Demeter," I whisper. "Bunqu's place has been breached. I need intel on who and when and how."

"I'm blind, Vale," Demeter says. "Bunqu's system isn't linked into the Sector surveillance network. It's off the grid." *Which was a very helpful thing when all was well, I think, but is less helpful now that I suspect the place to be a trap—or a grave.*

"Can you try to hack in?"

"I'm on it."

I prowl forward. In the kitchen, I stumble upon what looks like a crime scene. A frying pan appears to have shattered one cabinet door and a kitchen knife is buried in another. There's a scorch mark on the wall and bloody handprints on the French doors leading to the veranda. *Someone was wounded.* I crouch to get a better look at the floor, see dim outlines of boot prints against the polished wood planks. *Soldiers?* I flip my Bolt's capacitor charge to the highest setting and follow the prints through the house. *Was there more than one? Is he still here? Is Remy safe upstairs?* As quietly as possible, I move room to room, finally turning the corner toward Bunqu's study where I see it: a soldier with a yawning hole in his back, still wearing the black helmet emblazoned with the gold OAC wheat stalk, lying amidst a riot of streaked and splattered blood.

Black ops.

Trying to avoid stepping in the gore, I move toward the open door to the study. "Bunqu?" I say, my voice just loud enough to be heard in the study. "General Bunqu, are you in there?"

There's no answer, no movement. But someone's in there, I can feel it. *The question is, are they friend or foe, dead or alive?* Bolt up and ready to fire, I charge into the room only to pull up short. Meera, head bowed and legs outstretched on the luxurious ornamental carpet, sits propped up against Bunqu's desk as if she's taking a nap. A dark blossom stains her shirt and a blood-mottled knife—*did she pull it from her own chest?*—rests cockeyed between her legs.

Red-stained fingers are still wrapped around the trigger of an antique shotgun which must have come from Bunqu's collection.

Kneeling beside her, the metallic tang of iron fills my nostrils. I can almost taste the blood on the back of my tongue. I lift her face, a mass of bruises, eyes staring agape into an empty world. Sadness billows through me, like a sail catching the wind. Then anger. *Another life lost in the service of the Orleáns.* Then hatred. I choke back the bile as the memory of my mother ordering Chan-Yu to assassinate Remy and Soren flashes through my mind.

Remy. Waiting for me upstairs.

I reach down to close Meera's eyes—there's no reason for Remy to see that—and then notice there's something strange about her mouth. With a quick apology for the violation, and all the clinical detachment of a medical examiner, I reach into her mouth and slide my finger around her cheeks and under her tongue. There's something there, crumpled into a ball. I pull it out. A tiny v-scroll.

I unroll it and words flash across the fibers.

Onion under arrest. Caught in crossfire. If you find this, follow the acorns to the tree.

My hand goes to the acorn pendant around my neck. The Outsider symbol that will call a Wayfarer for help when traveling through the Wilds. *If you find this, follow the acorns to the tree.* Are there more pendants like this? Or is she talking about literal acorns—like the ones Bunqu handed us earlier?

I stand and look around the room, remembering the urgency of our situation. I don't have time for Outsider riddles right now. We need to get out of here.

"Demeter, why isn't the house being guarded? Why isn't the place crawling with black ops?"

"I wasn't able to access Bunqu's private network, but I can see through the city's nav system that there are several patrol drones circling the neighborhood in a half-hour loop, operated manually. I can't control them. You've got about five minutes before one of them makes it back here."

I'm already in motion, running down the hall to the central stairs to find Remy. I take them two at a time. I pull open the door to our room and rush in. Standing in the steamy bathroom in one of Bunqu's oversized bathrobes, Remy's body gleams like polished bronze against the stark white of the open robe. A shiver of longing runs through me, coupled with an even more powerful desire to stay alive so I can experience her beauty another day. She turns toward me, a smile of anticipation melting into alarm as she sees the Bolt in my hand.

"Gods, what's wrong?"

"It's Meera." There's no time to break the news slowly. Without a word, she reaches out and turns the shower off. "She's dead. Bunqu's been arrested. Patrol drones will be back to circle in five minutes. We've got to move."

"Where is she?" Remy's already shed the robe, slipping into her clothes. I watch her, marveling at her calm, marveling that despite all she's been through—or maybe *because* of all she's been through—she can take such news in stride.

"Bunqu's study."

"No sign of him?"

"No."

She nods, taking it all in. Shuddering, she sucks in a deep breath and straightens her shoulders. She hesitates only a second. Now fully dressed, she follows me outside, grabbing her bag on the way. In the backyard, Remy reaches into the air where Osprey's cloaked *oiseau* is parked. Her touch deactivates the cloaking. She leaps on, toggling the engine, and I hop on behind her. We zip out of the backyard and down the road as quickly as we dare. The hoverbike's engine is as quiet as a summer breeze, and within thirty seconds, we're safely hidden in a copse of trees.

"Are we out of range?" I ask Demeter.

"You're clear. Stay in the trees."

Remy pulls the walkie-talkie out from the folds of her jacket and hands it to me. "Soren," she says. I press the transmit button and signal Soren. When his voice comes back, Remy listens as I fill him in. I can hear Osprey's voice in the background as Soren relays to her and Saara what's going on.

"Should we come your way?" Soren asks.

"No. Drones are watching the house. We need to get out."

"You and Remy have a plan?" Soren says. I hear him confer with Osprey.

"No. Except to get out of here."

"Have them meet us at the outermost PODS dock in the northeast quadrant," Remy says to me. "We can take the *oiseau* to meet them. We'll decide what to do once we're all together."

I relay the message and then, before I sign off, I say, "Soren, ask Osprey what Meera meant by 'follow the acorns to the tree.'"

"Roger," Soren says. Remy raises her eyebrows as we hear him repeat the question. Osprey's voice, barely audible, crackles through the walkie-talkie.

"I have no idea."

Goddammit, Meera, why do all you Outsiders have to be so fucking cryptic?

14 — REMY

It's high noon and shadows are scarce by the time we make it to The Elysium. I have no idea if Snake will even be here; the smoke den is closed and the sign on the front says it won't open until 17h00. And from what I understand, Snake works the late shift.

I hear Vale whispering something to his C-Link. I lean into his shoulder to catch his words.

"Abandoned houses, untouched vacation homes, old factories, industrial junkyards—anything that will provide us a bit of shelter," he says. I can't hear her response, but I assume she's searching the four quadrants of Okaria for something that will meet Vale's criteria. "Unguarded and forgotten." He quiets for a moment, focusing on an invisible spot across the street on The Elysium's elegant wood-paneled exterior.

I survey the building. There's one entrance from the front and no windows, which contributes to the otherworldly, underwater feel of the interior. My heart sinks. I doubt anyone is here now, and I don't even know Snake's real name. How am I supposed to tell him about Meera?

Meera. What did she tell me those first few days I was staying with her? *If you ever need to run, there's a safe house on the outskirts of Okaria. Big, empty, comfortable.*

"My grandfather's house." Vale looks at me, surprised, and I realize I've said the words out loud. "Meera told me weeks ago I could stay there if I ever needed a safe place."

How could I have known that by the end of the day, I would need two more seeds—one for Meera's death, and one for her life?

I grab instinctively at the burnished metal that lives in my pocket, the compass that was once my grandfather's, and then Tai's, and then Vale's. Memories wash over me. Picking fresh fruit off the trees in his yard. Drawing the lotus blossoms in his fountain. Learning how to fillet fish, knead dough, slice an onion without crying too much—all contraband activities, declared illegal over forty years ago. The Okarian Agricultural Corporation and the Board of Health and Diet consolidated into the Okarian Agricultural Consortium in response to a bioterrorism threat from the North Pacific Federation. The new OAC outlawed home cooking and food preparation, declaring such activities "unsafe." My grandfather didn't care about those silly laws, though, and because of his integral role in developing so many medicines and human modifications, no one bothered him about it.

"Wow," Vale says, his voice hushed. "That's the perfect place."

"Have Demeter do a scan, just to make sure."

A few seconds later, Vale nods.

"She says the last aerial photograph of the house was taken over a month ago, and it was totally abandoned."

The thought of returning to my grandfather's house for the first time in five years is almost too much to take. I focus in on the challenge in front of me, so as not to be overwhelmed: how do I find Snake?

"We need to get in there." I nod at the door in front of us.

He shakes his head.

"No," he says. "He's probably not there right now. Tell me everything you know about him, and I'll have Demeter run it through Personhood. Maybe we can get an address for him."

"Purple hair and eyebrows. About thirty, thirty-five years old. Sharp nose, round chin, high cheekbones, very pale, like Soren. He works at the Elysium, he's the manager, or at least he sets the—"

"Demeter's got him," he says. "His name is listed as Sen Priorat in Personhood. Currently resides in Sector housing—South quadrant, Rue du Vent, Building 39, number 17."

I brighten. "That's not far at all. Let's go."

I turn and set off. Vale keeps pace with me, and I wind my fingers into his. He leans into me as a triad of professionals in golden OAC lab coats walk by. It's safer to look like a couple. People are less likely to notice you if you look happy.

As we walk, I hear a rescue drone zoom by, followed, as always, by a medevac truck. The green and red lights flare as the truck blazes through the streets. I follow it with my eyes, but it's long past us in a matter of seconds. Not five minutes later, though, there's another one—a drone followed by a medevac team. It turns down the same road we are, zipping past us, and then down a side street. When Vale and I make it there, I can see the truck stalled, its bay doors open, and two nurses carry a stretcher up a set of stairs.

"Meera said there's some kind of bug going around where she worked," I mutter to Vale. "Is that why there are all these ambulances?"

Vale stops and stares for a moment, watching the medevac team suit up in sterilized gear. But he shakes his head, turning away.

"It's just a coincidence. Seems doubtful something could spread so quickly."

We walk on.

A few minutes later, we're at Snake's building. The Sector provides residential buildings for unmarried men and women who are either recent transplants to the city or who do not have well-paying jobs. Sponsored housing is very low security. The palming mechanism is heat-sensitive only, so neither of us will risk identifying ourselves. There's no doorman—only a small security drone, not even equipped with a Bolt.

"You stay outside," I say. "Dangerous for the cameras to catch us together." Since Vale escaped, I can only assume that all drones, Watchmen, and soldiers will be on the lookout for us, moving together, working in tandem. He nods. I hand him my plasma and he leans against the wall of the building, pretending to be engrossed in something on the screen.

I head in.

The drone barely registers me. I'm sure the video feed is automatically recorded and relayed to someone in the Watchman organization, and if they recognize me, there will be hell to pay. But until then, I'm safe. And with the remnants of my body paint on, and Vale's hasty makeup job outside of Bunqu's neighborhood, I feel safe.

For now.

I walk past the drone and palm open the door to the stairwell instead of the elevators. I race up the stairs and exit at the second floor, where Snake's apartment, number seventeen, is on the right. Instead of ringing the bell—which might prompt me for a biomarker so the system can announce me properly—I knock. Loudly. When no one comes immediately, I knock again, pounding at the door with my fists.

A few minutes later the door swings open, and a very fit man with dark brown skin and only one item of clothing on stares at me blearily.

"Couldn't have bothered to ring, could you?"

"No," I say, somewhat awed by his physique. "Is Sen Priorat here?"

The man lifts an arm to rub his hair, the color of black walnut, and narrows his eyes at me. He looks like he was cut from stone, like a god or hero from an ancient myth. He gives me a once-over, and then turns inside and calls softly.

"Sen, there's another girl here for you."

Another girl? How many suitors does Snake have?

"Which one?" I recognize Snake's voice. *Which one?!*

"The one who ordered the green apple indica," I shout back, not waiting for the man to reply. He frowns, but doesn't say anything. A few seconds later, Snake appears at the door, as bleary-eyed as his companion, and in a similar state of undress. His purple hair juts up in all directions, and it's clear that both men just got out of bed. But his eyes go wide when he sees me, and he immediately grabs a jacket slung over the back of a chair and pulls it on. He pushes past the other man with a whispered word and comes out into the hall with me. He shuts the door firmly behind him.

"Sparrow," he says, using my Outsider code name. "What are you doing here? How did you find me?"

"Friends in high places," I say in a rush. "Listen, Meera's dead and Onion's been arrested. There was a scene at Onion's house, and Meera got stabbed. I watch as the expression on his face morphs from surprise to horror, but I press on. "She left us a note. It said, 'If you find this, follow the acorns to the tree.' Do you know what that means?"

Snake's green eyes, wide with shock and sadness, zero in on me, intense and bright.

"Yes," he says. "Maybe."

"'Maybe'?" I demand, my voice rising slightly. "What do you mean, 'maybe'?"

"Hush, and I'll tell you," he says. "The Wayfarers use a kind of technology to communicate between themselves based on tree roots. The acorns—your friend has one, doesn't he?—signal to each other, and to the Wayfarers' astrolabes, using that same technology. For decades, though, there's been a myth that there's more to it. That the acorns did more than just communicate with each other. That they led somewhere, if you could just string them all together and follow the clues. I always thought it was just an invented treasure hunt."

"What was the myth?" I ask, my voice rising in urgency.

He shrugs, holding his hands up.

"Nothing more than that. There was never much substance to it. That's why I never believed it. But—" and here his voice grows even quieter, so soft I have to lean in and focus to hear "—we Outsiders are very good at keeping secrets. Usually, I'm very good at finding those secrets. But it may be that I simply haven't uncovered this one. Maybe Meera left that note for you because it's your turn to be a seeker of secrets."

15 — VALE

In the golden hour of the evening, the overgrown yard, drenched in yellow and green, begins to look like a fairyland. Remy and I crouch in the bushes about fifty meters from her grandfather's house under the shade of a giant old oak tree. As we left Snake's, I contacted Soren on our walkie-talkies and told him to meet us at Kanaan Alexander's old house. Kanaan's place is a little over twenty-five kilometers from Okaria's last POD station, and since we took the *oiseau* while Soren, Osprey, and Saara travel on foot, we've arrived first. After Demeter confirmed the house was abandoned, everyone agreed it would be a good spot to lie low for a few days. There's only one problem: the place isn't abandoned. It looks like someone's made themselves at home.

There aren't any obvious signs of habitation, no hovercar parked outside, no smoke drifting up from the chimney, no porch light on, but there are more subtle signs. There's an antenna going up from the roof, for instance, that Remy claims wasn't there before. A well-trod path through the grass that leads to the back gate. And a pile of compost around the side of the house that includes fresh onion peel and squash pulp. We're sitting on our haunches, trying to decide what to do, when we catch a glimpse of movement inside.

"See that?" Remy whispers. "Someone's definitely in there."

"A trap? Or just someone squatting?"

"Whoever it is, we need to warn Soren to approach the area with caution."

"Wait here. I'll head back out of earshot and contact him."

Remy unclips the walkie-talkie from her belt and hands it to me. She gives me a silent nod, but before I leave our hiding place and head back through the brambles, she tugs my arm and whispers, "Why don't you circle around and see if you can get a better read on the situation from the other side of the property."

"Good idea," I say. "Be back soon."

I navigate down the unkempt path until I'm certain I'm well out of earshot. Then I signal Soren, giving him the news. They figure they're still about ten kilometers out and won't arrive for another two hours or so if they keep up their current pace.

After signing off, I creep as quietly as possible around the other side of the house. As I go, I can see the dock jutting out over the water, the spot where Remy and I first kissed, and I think of the photo Eli showed me the day I left Windy Pines. The photo of him and Tai and me and Remy sitting right there, without a care in the world. A stab of pain slices through me, lamenting that lost innocence, that childhood naiveté none of us will ever get back.

I glance across the yard toward the clump of bushes where I know Remy is waiting, watching. Before me, there's a wide open space I need to cross. I can either avoid it by going out of my way to gain the cover of surrounding trees or I can risk it and try to cross it in a mad dash. Since it's getting close to dusk, and with the few windows on this side of the house covered in curtains, I decide to risk the mad dash.

I signal to Remy, and then sprint across the yard. I'm halfway across when I run smack into something hard, something invisible, something that knocks me flat on my ass.

Instinctively, I put my hand to my forehead. *This knot is going to be a beauty.* I sit up and look around. My head is still ringing. I scramble to my feet, but crouch low, deciding what to do. The only thing that could stop me in my tracks like that is something big, a hovercar or airship equipped with top-notch cloaking. I look across the yard and motion to Remy to stay put, then watch for movement in the windows.

I stand up, hands out like someone groping in the dark and move forward cautiously. Since I don't know how big or long the thing is, I don't know how to go around it. Better to get a feel for the mystery object. I take a few tentative steps forward and my hands hit cool metal. I flatten my palms to slide along the surface when suddenly the cloaking fades and—

I look over at Remy and she stands straight up, giving away her position, obviously just as stunned as I am.

"Still responds to your palm print," a familiar voice says. Jeremiah Sayyid. Leaning against the corner of the house like he'd just come outside to get some fresh air.

"But—" I stare at him as if he's an apparition.

"Sort of a passion project. Of course, the Director didn't know about it until all was said and done, and then it was too late."

"How did—"

He ambles toward me like it's no big deal. "We were all feeling a bit down one night, and with a bit too much of Firestone's swill in our bellies, the three of us decided what we needed to cheer us up was a new toy. A Sarus, perhaps. Your Sarus. Sitting beat up and abandoned in the middle of the street in old Cleveland. So we went and got her. And here she is."

"The three of you?"

"The three of us." Eli. Decked out in a long apron adorned with a bouquet of lotus buds and with flour smudged on his cheek, he looks once at me and then turns and holds his arms out wide as Remy tears across the open space and launches herself at him.

"But how?" I ask, still stunned. I run my fingers along the cool skin of my state-of-the art Sarus as I walk toward Miah.

"It wasn't that hard." Jeremiah puts his hands behind his head, leaning casually against the house. "We went back and picked it up. Easy as pie."

"Speaking of pie," Eli says. "I made torte."

"You made torte?" Remy asks, wiping the flour off Eli's cheek.

"For you, little bird. Cranberry torte just for you."

"I missed you," she says. "That damn virus—"

"—is long gone thanks to Demeter's homework and Rhinehouse's talents," Eli says, pulling Remy back into his arms. "Now you're stuck with me."

"When's the rest of the crew getting here?" Miah asks. "The larder's still stocked to the gills. We're gonna feast like Americans at Thanksgiving."

I laugh. "Without the vomiting, I hope."

"No vomiting allowed," Eli says. "But it's not going to be all turkey and stuffing. We've got plenty of work to do. We'll explain when Soren gets here. In the meantime, let's get you two a drink, and you can help us with dinner."

I groan. "Please tell us you did not bring Firestone's 'swill' with you."

Miah slings an arm around my shoulders and leads the way inside. "We certainly did not. Eli assured me that Kanaan would have a fine selection of old vintages. True to his word, we found almost two hundred bottles from some of the Sector's best vineyards."

"How come nobody else came with you? Why just the two of you?"

"Well, with Kenzie expecting a baby and all—"

"What?" Remy shouts. "Are you serious?"

"Found out a few weeks ago. She's just now starting to show."

Eli drags Remy into the kitchen to help him with the torte, Remy peppering him with questions about Jahnu and Kenzie as they walk. As excited as I am about the news, I want to give them time to catch up, and cooking doesn't sound appealing to me right now. So I dodge Miah's request to help with the tomato sauce, and take the opportunity to familiarize myself with the house. I wander through the rooms, amazed by how much of it is falling apart—and how much is still intact. Doors and floors have warped slightly in the seasonal cycles, and most of the plumbing is no longer functional. Outside, the garden is in utter disarray, but somehow still beautiful. I end up standing on the dock that overlooks Lake Okaria, where, four years ago, I kissed Remy for the first time as the sun set behind us.

The memory seems like it comes from a different world. It's almost hard to believe we're the same people. The house, then, was bustling with energy. Green things bloomed everywhere. Rosemary and lavender sprigs dusted every room. The windows were thrown open to the daylight, and every morning the smell of Kanaan's fresh bread filled the air. The kiss came on the tail end of a summer that felt endless. Tai and Eli were hiding out upstairs, and something new and different seemed to be happening with Remy, too. We'd been playing cards on the dock on a hot, windless day, when she slapped the back of my hand and yelled in triumph.

She didn't pull her hand away. I turned mine over and held hers. She half-smiled, as though suddenly unsure what to do, how to react. I didn't know either, but I knew what I wanted, and she wasn't afraid. I leaned over a little ways, and her eyes felt like anchors, pulling me down. I gave myself over to the weight of the moment and pressed my lips to hers. I'd kissed girls before, and she told me later she'd kissed other boys, but this was different. Like seeing a piece of art for the first time that makes you *feel* something in a powerful way. Like the first time you're fully conscious of yourself in your body and in the world. Like the first time you're aware of how alive you really are.

That's what it was like, kissing her.

It seems incomprehensible, now, that we could have been so carefree. I can't even remember how it felt.

In the garden, many of the plants have either grown wild or died because they needed tending. And the house, with its peeling paint, broken pipes, and busted windows, reminds me that buildings, like people, need constant care and maintenance. But the dock, at least, is mostly unchanged. There are a few soft, rotting spots, and the paint is gone, but the structure remains.

"Hey," Remy says, startling me. Her fingers creep around my waist, and she rests her head in the space between my shoulders. "Are you okay?"

"Yeah," I say. "Just thinking."

"What about?"

"How everything is different. Meera, and Bunqu. The last time we were here together, the world seemed so perfect, so certain. Now everything is broken, overgrown, lost. Somehow we have to put it all back together."

She comes around to my side and wraps one arm behind my back. We stand there like that, watching the sun set over the lake, for a long time.

An hour or so later, Miah is popping the cork on a second bottle of wine. "I'm glad you decided to give Vale a shot." He's beaming at Remy. "He's only been talking about you for three years."

I flush and glare at him.

"She's been talking about you for three years, too," Eli pipes up. Remy takes my hand in hers and smiles. "Or trying not to."

"I'm glad we had the same idea."

The walkie-talkie on the table crackles with Soren's voice. "We clear to approach?"

I pick it up. "Come on in. Dinner's ready."

"Good, we're starving," Soren says.

While we'd waited, Remy fashioned a centerpiece from pine boughs and sprays of yellow forsythia plucked from her grandfather's riotous garden. Miah and Eli prepped a meal based entirely on canned vegetables and dried grains from Kanaan's root cellar—beans stewed in a spicy tomato sauce served over rice and a medley of vegetables. Eli's torte came out perfectly, and Remy found dozens of jars of peaches and apricots.

"See if there's any forks," Remy calls.

"What, do you think someone waltzed in and stole the silverware?" Miah asks. Remy makes a face at him, even as he returns with a fistful of forks and knives.

The door creaks as it opens wide, revealing Soren, Osprey, and Saara against a deepening night sky.

"What the hell?" Soren says, his mouth hanging open in astonishment.

"Welcome!" Miah gestures to the table, as if he's the host of a grand dinner party.

"How did you—?" Osprey turns and looks outside, like she's searching for some means of transport.

"Wondering how we got here, Wayfarer?" Miah says.

"Wondering what you're doing here," Soren retorts.

"Once Rhinehouse fixed me up, the Director essentially kicked me out." Eli grins. "Said she couldn't stand to look at me for one more day and she wanted me out of her sight."

"The Resistance needed an outpost closer to Okaria as we're—" Miah pauses and glances at Eli before continuing "—working on getting our food to the people in the city."

"We also needed a comm nexus, a place where Outsider and Resistance operatives could stay as they're passing through. So far, it's been too risky to get this close to the city. But Gabriel suggested using this place," Eli nods at Remy, who straightens at her father's name, "since not many people come this way. Miah and I—err—volunteered."

"He means 'were kicked out,'" Miah says in a mock-whisper. "After our stunt with the Sarus, we—"

"With the what?" Soren interrupts, cupping a hand behind his ear as though he hadn't heard.

"The Sarus," Miah says, as if it were the most obvious thing in the world. "It's parked outside. Cloaked. That's why you didn't see it on the way in."

"You're lucky you didn't knock yourself out like Vale." Eli hands each of them a glass of wine.

"Speaking of cloaking," I start, "how are we supposed to hide here with an airship in the backyard without some Sector drone taking notice of our activities?"

"Firestone took care of that for us." Miah sits at the head of the table. "Engineered up a dozen little multi-frequency scramblers that we've strung from the highest branches we could reach. Created a nice little perimeter in which we should be able to operate without notice."

There's a long pause while Soren and Osprey take all this in. Saara, for her part, looks completely overwhelmed. Eli stares at her as if noticing her for the first time.

"Who are you?" he asks. Eli's never been one for pleasantries.

"Saara Lyon," she says automatically.

"You're Hana's sister." Eli's eyes widen as he realizes who she is.

"Older by a year."

"Eli, Miah, I'd like to formally introduce you to Saara Lyon, our newest Resistance member." Remy gestures for Saara to sit next to her. "She was at the vigil today. In some of the finest body paint I've ever seen." I can see remnants of the red and gold paint on Saara's arms and chest, but most of it has sweated or rubbed off.

"You never said how that went," Eli says, turning to Remy.

"We can tell you over dinner." I pick up a bowl of poached apricots and begin to serve. "Saara, Soren, and Osprey need to eat after hiking all the way out here."

"And I need to take my boots off," Saara says, already unlacing. "I think I have blisters the size of dinner plates."

16 — REMY

A hush falls over us as we as stretch out around the fire crackling in my grandfather's old stone fireplace. It's closing in on eleven, but my bones feel like it must be two or three in the morning. For the past ten days, we've been loading and unloading, helping various Resistance teams move food, seeds, and MealPaks. Unlike teamsters working for the Sector, we don't have the benefit of heavy-duty loading drones. We do have the benefit of the newfangled scrambles Firestone put together. Besides the ones Eli and Miah used to create a perimeter around the house, we've got another dozen or so we set up around every loading and unloading site.

"Another bottle?" Jeremiah pops the stopper on yet another one of my grandfather's older vintages and holds it aloft.

"If anyone said no, would that have stopped you?" Soren asks, his voice loaded with a heavy dose of Soren Skaarsgard sarcasm. Stretched out on the floor, he holds out two glasses while Osprey, curled up on the couch behind him, runs a fingertip up and down the back of his ear lobe, making me want to scratch my own.

Since we arrived at my grandfather's, we've had several visitors, including Chariya, one of the Outsiders we met a few months ago, but mostly, we've been doing backbreaking labor, strategizing with Zeke's team, and arguing about our next moves with the Director. We've also been brainstorming about what Meera's final message, *follow the acorns to the tree*, might mean. Chariya had some ideas, but she left shortly after she arrived, promising to return as soon as possible. What "soon" means to an Outsider, I have no idea. Osprey says, with Chariya, it could mean tomorrow or next year.

But tonight we got the best surprise of all: Zeke arrived with Bear in tow, grown at least a few centimeters since the last time I saw him. He's on his way from Farm 5 to 3, colloquially called Mill Town and Cloverfield. When the

Director told him Eli and Miah were setting up a waystation outside Okaria, and that Soren and I had made it here safely, Bear decided to take a detour and visit us between stops.

"It's been wild out there, ya know?" Bear says, adding another log to the fire, settling back, and watching as the flames lick at the wood. "Lotta people coming to our side. Stepping up, telling others, wanting something different. Something *more*. Many still don't understand, but our numbers are growing. And we're getting ready to show what we're made of."

So much has happened since Vale and I went to Okaria nearly three months ago. While Vale was isolated with his parents and I was connecting with Meera, Snake, and the other Outsiders in the capital, Bear has led the charge to rally Farm workers to the cause of the Resistance. He says many of the workers have begun to see how their lives have been manipulated. How they've been used. The devastation at Round Barn was the spark that lit the torch, and now the darkness has been illuminated, as he put it so eloquently. As he talks, I feel like a proud parent, my heart expanding with every word. I suppose I still feel responsible for Bear—and for Sam.

"It's really Gabriel," Bear says, with a nod my direction. "Without his inspiration, we never would have been able to recruit so many so quickly."

I look across the room, locking eyes with Eli. For a moment, the deep ache of memory, of missing what used to be—the happy family with the quiet poet, the passionate doctor, the brilliant older sister, and me, the eager, inquisitive artist—threatens to breach the wall I've built up around that part of my life. I blink back tears.

Vale squeezes my hand. "What's Gabriel's role in all this?"

"He helps me work out what to say." Bear holds up his glass to the firelight as if seeking wisdom within the shifting, swirling liquid. "But mostly, he tells stories about long ago heroes who stood up for their rights without hurting anyone. Dr. Rhinehouse says us workers have been programmed to shy away from violence. That's why some of us just kinda turn off. Like a light goes out inside. Since folks don't want to hurt anyone, they turn away from what frightens them or makes them angry. So Gabriel tells stories about other folks just like us. To make us brave. Folks like Thoreau, Ghandi, King, Havel. Folks I never even heard of in the whole of my life 'fore now."

I'm not surprised Bear and the other Farm workers are inspired by my father's stories. "Stories have power," my dad used to say when we'd talk about our passions: me, drawing and painting; him, stories and poetry. "Artists tell stories with pictures so those who are deaf to the truth can *see* it instead. Poets tell stories with words so those who are blind to the truth can *hear* it instead."

"But most of all," Bear says, "Gabriel listens to the workers' own stories. Prob'ly the first time a livin' soul's ever bothered. Now we got lots of folks willing to stand up for themselves, workers from every Farm in every quadrant, all willing to tell their stories, say what's on their minds. And town folk, too. Working with Zeke, we got real, educated people ready to stand beside Farm folk. And there's a whole lot of them. We're gettin' well mobilized."

"What are you mobilizing for?" Saara asks.

"We can't fight back without guns and airships like the Sector has, like Evander has. And we don't want anyone else to die, ya know? So we've got to go at it different way. Right now, we're keeping things quiet, acting like nothing's changing. But soon, things'll be different."

"How?" I ask, leaning forward.

Bear looks at the floor.

"Well, I've been workin' on this idea …"

"What idea?" Soren presses. Ever since Soren and I met Bear on that boat two seasons ago, we've tried to welcome him into our fold as much as possible.

"None of us want a repeat of Round Barn. But what if we take that same concept, the idea of taking a stand, rising up peacefully, and demand that all of us be treated with respect. That each one of us be treated like human beings. And what if we did this in the capital? Right in front of Assembly Hall, where everyone can see us. Evander can't bring his fireships down on us then. So my idea is to organize a march with workers from every Farm and every factory town coming in to the city of their own free will. Thousands of people standing in front of *our* capital demanding *our* liberty. What happens then?"

No one says a word. I lean back and close my eyes, listening to the pop and crackle as a piece of damp wood catches. I can see the people, shoulder to shoulder, silent, facing Assembly Hall. Is it even possible? How could Corine or Evander or Aulion take violent action against a peaceful demonstration in the middle of the city? I turn to Vale.

"What do you think?"

"How many can you mobilize?" he asks.

Bear glances at Miah and then says, "We estimate we've got almost three thousand volunteers so far."

"Three thousand?" Saara nearly chokes on her wine.

"And we're aiming for more."

Vale lets out a long low whistle. I can almost hear his mind working as he pushes himself up from his relaxed slouch. The enormity of Bear's plan is overwhelming. All this time I've been hiding out in Okaria, Bear has been spreading his message—and now the message has gone viral. If he's got three thousand people who have already volunteered to march to the capital city at his command, how many more will rally to our cause when the march begins?

"Do you have a date picked out?" Vale asks. "What are you thinking in terms of logistics? Communications? Coordinating the movement of so many people so that everyone arrives at the same time?"

"Workin' on all that," Bear says. "It's a big project, ya know? We're shooting for right after the solstice, maybe the twenty-third or twenty-fourth. Miah and Eli been workin' with Zeke and some of Osprey's friends to monitor Sector freight lines. There's some maglev trains that run between the Farm depots and Okaria once a day. Same thing with the factory towns. Moving stuff back and forth 'tween the countryside and the capital. We're hopin' to get a lot of folks on board those trains."

Vale nods, considering. Of all the people here, he probably has the most comprehensive knowledge of the Sector's large-scale infrastructure. "You've got the schedules?"

"The routes are controlled remotely by computer," Zeke says, "but there are onboard operators with override capabilities in case of delays or mechanical problems. I've got an old friend who helps set the schedules."

"So you can get people loaded without the central system knowing," Vale says, following Zeke's train of thought.

"And," Eli says with a dangerous look, "we'll take care of the onsite operators if we have to."

"Replace them with our own people," Miah says.

"Still," Zeke says, "it's easier said than done. It used to be the train operators rode unaccompanied, no guards. Since Round Barn, no train leaves a station without four soldiers onboard."

"There's been growing malcontent on the Farms over the last few years." Vale leans back in his chair, stretching. "But nothing on the scale of Round Barn. I'm not surprised they increased security."

"Are you worried about infiltration?" I ask. "Someone overhearing your plans and tipping off the Enforcers? Or loyalists in the Factory towns? What about Evander?"

"'Course we're worried about that," Bear says. "But ain't nothing we can do but tell everyone to be hush-hush and go right on about our work."

"What happens if you're discovered?" Saara asks.

It's Bear's turn to shrug. He looks at Zeke and Miah, neither of whom has an answer. Finally, he says, "I'd best not be caught, I guess. All I know is I can't stop what I'm doing. Not now. There's no turning back. We've just got to hope everyone will see the truth, and support us rather than fight against us."

From the very first day I met him, Bear was taking on responsibilities beyond what should have been asked of him.

The smoke trails lazily up the chimney and a log crumbles in the fire. The chilly night air blowing in from broken windows smells like promise. But with every promise made, there is the chance of a promise broken.

Finally Saara says, "What do you hear about this bug that's been going around?"

By the third day after we'd all arrived at my grandfather's, we got word that a full-fledged health crisis was taking place on the outskirts of the Sector and was quickly spreading into the city. The medevac trucks Vale and I saw zooming around Okaria were no coincidence, and it became clear that Meera was called into work the morning of the vigil because dozens of people were falling ill.

Saara went into the city a few days ago and caught the tail end of one of the OAC's broadcasts, in which Corine announced that the OAC was looking into the illness, trying to find a cause and a cure.

"They're claiming they don't know what it is," Saara had said upon her return. "I don't believe it for an instant."

"What's the vector?" Soren asked.

"They're not sure yet, but they don't think it's contagious."

"What do you think?" Vale asked Saara. "You're the nurse."

"It's too soon to tell. But I don't think it's natural."

"You think the Sector is spreading it?"

Saara didn't respond.

Now, Bear shifts uncomfortably in his seat, frowning. "Rhinehouse doesn't know what to make of it," he says. "First folks start complaining about dizziness and nausea, followed by seizures caused by swelling of the brain. Many of the patients end up in a coma." He shakes his head.

"But that's not the worst part," Zeke says. "Before they lapse into a coma, patients exhibit extreme paranoia, what some doctors are calling sudden-onset schizophrenia. Only a few people have died so far, though, and all deaths have been before the coma stage. One woman told her husband that people were spying on her, chasing her. She ran out of the house and disappeared. Watchmen fished her out of the river the next day. Drowned."

"Any statement from the chancellor?" Vale says.

"Nothing official," Eli pipes up. "Except that they're dedicating all their resources to identifying the source of the outbreak and trying to identify preventative measures, ways to contain it before it spreads throughout the Sector. Zoe, back at headquarters, has been monitoring their broadcasts. We'll know when they put out a statement."

"Epidemics grow, spread, kill hundreds, if not thousands of people," Vale says. "They eventually mutate, die out, or someone finds a cure. Fifty years later, the same thing happens. It happened all the time in the Old World. The Black Death. Influenza. Polio. Small pox. Dengue. AIDS. Ebola. And many of those were just in the last two centuries before the Religious Wars, which, naturally, caused many of the viruses that had previously been contained to come surging back."

I smile inwardly, knowing that Vale was that kid in class always paying attention. Soaking everything in, even arcane information on ancient diseases.

"I'm afraid if somethin' don't happen soon, it's gonna make all our work for naught."

"What do you mean?" I ask.

"With the hospitals fillin' up," Bear says, his eyes shadowed with worry, "lots of people what was on our side started thinkin' the OAC has all the answers again. 'Fore I got here tonight, I had someone I trusted accusin' me of poisoning him, sayin' I was out to get him. I'm afraid it'll take us back to the days before Linnea put out that broadcast, before Remy showed everyone what happened at Round Barn. And ..." He goes quiet and shifts his eyes over to me, where he just barely meets my gaze. "... Luis has it."

I jerk upright, leaning forward. "What?"

Bear looks tired, and I realize what a toll this must be taking on him. "We knew he had it when he hid from Rose. He'd had a bad fever, was burning up, and when she tried to help him, he locked himself in a bathroom and wouldn't come out, said Rose was tryin' to kill him. He went downhill fast. Rhinehouse is looking after him, has him in quarantine, but Rose is out of her mind with worry." Bear turns to Vale. "Your Demeter's in touch with Rhinehouse now, you know, and she tracked down Luis's dietary profile. He's been off his MealPaks since Round Barn, but Rhinehouse wanted to study his complete files. Looking for clues, maybe, as to why this illness seems to affect some, but not others. I think he's even replicating some of the formulas and trying to feed him through his arm. I don't understand it all, but I know it's not good."

"Has any of it been working?" Saara asks, leaning forward.

Bear shakes his head. Saara is silent, but her pursed lips tell us she still has more to say.

"Spit it out," Eli says finally, locking eyes with her. She sighs.

"You're going to think I'm crazy."

"You're sitting with the best of 'em," Eli retorts. "Tell us your worst fears, and we'll see if they can hold a candle to our own."

"You're only crazy if your theories aren't true," Osprey adds.

Saara glances at Zeke and Miah. She'd already spent time with the two men, telling them about Rachel Sayyid's last days, how she mumbled their names, talked about them before she'd been too weak to speak. She told us all how she watched as Rachel and the others died of a virus that was supposed to have been cured decades ago, a cover-up to disguise the true nature of the experiments the OAC was performing.

"I think it would be awfully convenient for the OAC to engineer some virus or parasite that causes serious symptoms but doesn't kill, and then disseminate it through MealPaks or through the water system. Tell everyone it's an act of bioterrorism from those renegades outside the Sector. Then a few weeks later, after panic sets in, *voila*! Suddenly the OAC's brilliant scientists have a cure. A pill or a tonic or a vaccine to save the day, something that allows Corine to ride to the rescue and put everyone's growing fears to rest once and for all. She'd be the savior in the face of the Resistance's terror. The OAC would once again be seen as the answer to the Sector's prayers."

Vale sucks in a breath and runs his hands over his face. His voice is hard when he speaks. "We've forced her hand."

"How? What do you mean?" Bear asks.

"They may not know exactly what you're doing, but they know something's up. Our movement has pushed the OAC's back against the wall. So Corine takes the offensive. She engineers this outbreak so she can claim it proves the Resistance and its ideas about re-cultivating Old World seeds is dangerous. Old World seeds breed Old World disease. It would be the perfect way for her to discredit everything the Resistance stands for in one fell swoop. And to hell with any real repercussions. People sick and suffering? So what? Drowning themselves? Small price to pay."

"Exactly," Saara says. "They want everyone afraid. Four years ago, they kept it all hush-hush. Rachel and the other patients were top secret. But now, they want everyone afraid, because they want everyone to think that the OAC has the only solution. They want everyone crying for their MealPaks, their drugs, their Dieticians."

"And it would make perfect sense for her to introduce it in the outermost towns and Farms," Osprey adds. "Easier to blame the Resistance that way."

"Exactly," Saara whispers.

Later, in bed, Vale holds my hand against his chest.

"There's something I never told you." I can hear his breathing, loud in the darkness. "When I was being held at the chancellor's, Moriana came to visit me." My eyes go wide, but I stay silent. "She wanted to ask me what happened, why Miah and I left."

"What did you say?" I ask.

"I told her the truth. She wasn't happy about it. But she defended Corine to the end." I remember meeting Moriana in Reunion Park a few weeks ago, being surprised by how happy she was. Wondering how someone who had just been tortured and interrogated by the Sector could have been so unconcerned. "She wasn't on the line with us that night, Remy. Corine never tortured her. They copied her vocal patterns and made it sound like she was afraid, in danger. But that never happened."

"I knew it," I breathe. Vale rolls over so he's facing me and props himself up on his elbow.

"What do you mean? How did you know?"

"I ran into her in Reunion Park. She was too happy, out playing netball with friends. She acted like nothing was wrong. How could she have been so carefree if she'd just been through such an ordeal? I knew there was some part of the story I was missing. After you got shot on that building, I—"

"What?" In the darkness I can just make out the wrinkles on his forehead. "I didn't get shot."

Now it's my turn to sit up, locking eyes with him.

"Yes, you did. I saw it. A Bolt hit you in the chest, and you fell off the ledge, right into the nets of those rescue drones."

"I—no, that's not possible. I stepped off that ledge. I did it deliberately, to give you time to escape."

"Someone gave the order to shoot you, Vale. Whether it was Aulion or Philip or Corine, someone gave the go-ahead."

"Maybe," he says slowly. "My parents never told me. They let me believe—" He pauses for a long breath. "But it wouldn't have changed anything."

I take all this in, realizing what it means. *Vale stepped off that ledge. He meant to fall. He was prepared to die for me.*

I rub my eyes and peer into the distance. After waking early, I'd rolled away from the warmth of Vale's sleeping form, slipped from under the covers, and headed out to the dock to practice my breathing, watching the dawn break in violent streaks of purple and blood orange. The air is cool and moist, a morning fog hovering above the water like a silvery veil, and I watch as a heron takes flight, winging its way across the water and lifting gracefully into the air.

"Coffee," a gruff voice calls. I turn to see Miah behind me, eyes bleary from wine and lack of sleep.

"Be there in a sec," I call back. Miah turns to lumber back to the house. I finish my morning stretches and clamber to my feet.

Inside, the house is coming to life. Osprey appears first, her hair pointing every direction in lawless rebellion. Miah pours her a cup of rich chicory coffee and she tips it up and downs the whole thing.

"Don't you even want some almond milk or something in that? It's thick as sludge."

"Why are you talking to me before I've had my second cup?" She holds her mug out. "Pour, minion."

"Yes, master." Miah bows and pours as the slightest hint of a smile curls at the edges of Osprey's mouth.

Eli shuffles into the room, steps over Bear, and hugs me absently as he grabs a chipped mug from those Miah has set out. "Remind me again why we're all here," he growls. "And why we drank—" he stares at the empty bottles lined up on the far counter—"seven bottles of wine last night. You'd think we were drinking to celebrate something—or to forget. Which is it?"

"A little of both," I venture. "Celebrate that we're all together. Forget why we're all together."

"Ah, yes, Little Bird." He rubs my shorn head. "My very wise, nearly bald little bird."

Vale and Soren make their way into the room at the same time, like life-sized toy soldiers in formation, one dark, one fair, followed by Saara, who limps along behind them.

"I don't know how I managed it, but I got another blister yesterday," she says by way of good morning.

"I'm going to put in a call to the Director," Eli grouses. "I'm already in a bad mood, so I might as well get that task out of the way so the day can only get better."

"Should we wake Bear?" I ask.

"Have a little compassion for the poor boy," Eli says. "We'll wake him if the Director has some earth-shattering news. Besides, he'll have to get moving soon enough."

Vale and I follow Eli into my grandfather's study where Eli and Miah set up a makeshift comm center. With a lot of cursing and moaning, Eli gets situated and is just about to put in the call when the receiver lights up and a voice comes blaring through.

"Montana Four, are you there? Montana Four, come in."

Eli's face contorts into a frown and he twists one of the dials as if he's got a personal vendetta against it. "For fuck's sake, Zoe," Eli says. "Why the hell are you so loud?"

"Good morning, Eli. Glad to hear you're your usual bright, sunny self. The Director and Rhinehouse are both here. Everyone's here, in fact, so watch your language. Corine is making an announcement in ten minutes. Get your team together and we'll patch you in so you can listen to the feed live."

Eli turns and glares at us, and Vale and I both get the picture. We head back down the hall to rouse everyone and get them into the comm center before the speech starts.

"Eli, is everyone assembled?" This time it's the Director's voice, not Zoe's.

"All present and accounted for."

"Vale?"

"Yes, ma'am. I'm here."

"Your father hasn't introduced Corine as he usually does, and Jon Spironov has announced that Corine will be appearing alone. Can you shed any light on this development? Do you have any idea why he won't be with her?"

"No." He shakes his head. "I'm just as surprised as you are. As I told you, at Windy Pines my father had expressed—"

"Hold that thought. The broadcast is starting."

"Citizens of Okaria," Corine begins. I take Vale's hand in mine and squeeze. "The Okarian Sector is facing a challenge unlike any we have faced before. As most of you know, many of our fellow citizens have recently fallen ill. Hospital admissions have spiked precipitously in the last five days alone. Fortunately, working around the clock with doctors and medics throughout the Sector, scientists at the Sector Research Institute and in my own OAC laboratory have been able to identify the cause of the illness. Dubbed River 1, because the first outbreak was seen in River and the surrounding area, we can now say definitively that the symptoms are caused by a parasite not seen since before the Famine Years.

"This parasite did not turn up in the Sector on its own. It did not evolve in nature. We have identified key genetic discrepancies that indicate it has been genetically altered and manipulated. We believe it has been introduced into our food and water by forces seeking to destabilize our citizenry. By combing through historical data on disease research, we have identified markers in the parasite's DNA and have traced those markers to research done by Dr. James Rhinehouse, a brilliant man who was once one of our finest scientists, but who is now a member of the terrorist organization known as the Resistance."

"Oh, for fuck's sake." Soren is the first one to say it, but he's not the only one. Vale shrinks into himself, like he used to whenever we'd discover some new atrocity his parents were responsible for, but I draw him to me, not letting him pull away.

"I am speaking to you today," Corine continues, "to assure you that we will find Dr. Rhinehouse and hold him and his comrades accountable for this horrific act of terrorism. I also want to tell you personally that we are very close to developing a way to kill the parasite. We're not there yet, but with Dr. Rhinehouse's own research at our fingertips, we are able to work faster than we dared hope. Soon we will put this terrible chapter in our history behind us and your loved ones will be back home with you, happier and healthier than ever before. We are working as hard as we can and will keep you informed by issuing daily updates until this crisis is resolved. For now, remember the citizens of the Okarian Sector have made it through tough times before, and together we will make it through again. Thank you."

17 — VALE

She leaves OAC Headquarters at 7:30 on the dot every work night. Even when we were younger, Moriana was always methodical and deliberate in her habits. If she has extra work to do, she's up early in the morning instead of staying up late at night. She always follows the same path to and from work, and—at least before Miah and I left—she rarely deviated from the same restaurants or clubs that we'd been going to for years. She was a creature of habit, and I knew she'd leave the OAC campus via the main entrance and then veer south toward the nearest PODS station, taking our familiar shortcut along the way. This is why, at exactly 7:28, Eli checks his watch and nods at me.

"Go time."

I amble toward the arching covered walkway that divides OAC headquarters with its multi-story greenhouse. I pick a spot and lean nonchalantly against the elegant twisting carbon frame, modeled after the DNA molecule's double helix, that girds the exterior of the main building and remember how not too long ago I'd snuck into the complex to break into my mother's lab. I'd been looking for answers then. Just like now. *Why are there so many secrets?* This time, at least, I'm not breaking in, I'm not carrying a grappling hook, and I have no intention of getting stuck in a dumbwaiter.

After listening to my mother's broadcast about the River 1 parasite, the Director gave us an order: get Moriana Nair. As my mother's protégé, the Director figures—and we all agree—that Moriana must know where the parasite came from since it sure as hell didn't come from Rhinehouse. Considering Moriana's history with Miah and me, the Director believes Moriana can be persuaded to share her knowledge, maybe even join our cause. I hope she's right.

Now, Eli, Soren, and I are back in the capital disguised as OAC operatives, wearing the modified contact lenses Kenzie was working on back at the

Resistance base. Although our disguises are good, we're still vulnerable to routine retinal scans taken by security drones, and if a security guard or a Watchman gets suspicious, all they'd have to do is wave a retinal scanner at our faces to discover our identities. But Kenzie's new contacts can be coded to either mimic someone else's retina or to blend with hundreds of other retinal patterns so the scanners can't process the input data. They can't even register you as having a human retinal pattern. To the average Watchman on the street, it would look like the scanner is on the fritz. And you become unidentifiable. Invisible.

Confident in my disguise, I smile at a passing researcher who looks vaguely familiar, and then glance up at the sightless eyes of the drone screening all passersby to make sure they're authorized to be on the OAC campus. The red eye blinks, flashes, and … nothing. The drone doesn't move. No alarms go off. I make a mental note to thank Kenzie the next time I see her.

I hear the main door to the headquarters slide open and then shut again as I let my gaze wander up the double helix. *Some of the enhancements we made were basic.* I can hear my mother's voice in my head, patiently explaining the ways she altered my DNA, how she changed who I am. Permanently. The muscles in my jaw clench, and I remind myself not to grind my teeth. *Visual, auditory, olfactory, sensory modifications. You'll be able to experience more of the world than you ever dreamed.*

If only you had asked my permission, Mother.

I hear footsteps around the corner, and I know it's her. Ever punctual. Even her gait sounds familiar. How different would things have turned out if Miah and I had asked her to come with us? Would she have believed the accusations against my mother, her hero? Would she have given up the opportunity to work with the Director of the OAC to follow us into the Wilds, risking life and limb? She told me we never gave her a chance to decide.

Well, things are different now. She'll get her chance.

Sixteen years we spent together, as close as any best friends can be. I draw in a breath. Then I see her. Her lanky frame, dark shimmering hair, the way her confident stride is just a little too long for her legs—she's impossible to miss. She heads my way and I meet her eyes, hoping she won't recognize me. She doesn't. Glancing away almost immediately, she brushes past me without the slightest acknowledgment.

Good.

At a safe distance, I turn to follow her. I'm careful to keep my footsteps quiet, but she seems utterly indifferent to the possibility of being followed.

After all, aside from the massacre at the SRI four years ago, this part of Okaria is the safest place in the Sector. Especially for someone like Moriana.

A Watchman crosses the street and walks toward us, my heart rate spiking the closer he gets. But worrying is unnecessary; he gives Moriana and her long legs an appreciative look and ignores me completely.

Moriana heads to the right, and, sure enough, a moment later, she takes the narrow alley she always uses as a shortcut between the OAC campus and the transport station. As I follow her, I catch sight of Eli slouching next to a composter, pretending to be reading something on a v-scroll. He's ready.

I quicken my stride. As Moriana draws closer, Eli's hand goes to the Bolt in his holster, and then in one smooth move, he steps in front of Moriana and pulls the weapon, holding it tight to his side so Moriana can see it, but an overhead drone won't notice a thing.

"Don't move," Eli orders.

"What the—"

"OAC Security Directorate," I say, stepping from behind her to Eli's side and flipping open a fake ID just long enough for Moriana's jaw to drop in shock. I'm consciously trying to speak in a lower tone than usual. I don't want her recognize my voice. "We need to ask you a few questions."

"About what? Do you know who I am?"

"Of course we know who you are," Eli says with a snarl. "You think we just pluck random citizens off the street to interrogate?"

"Interrogate?" Moriana's voice rises. "But I work with Corine Or—"

"And just who do you think ordered the interrogation?"

"Don't worry, Ms. Nair," I assure her. "We're not going to hurt you and you're not in any trouble."

"So far," Eli adds. Good cop. Bad cop. I think he's enjoying this.

"There's been a security breach, and information about River 1 has been leaked. The last thing we want, I'm certain you will agree, is for that information to land in the wrong hands. Our job is to find out who leaked the information and why."

Moriana scowls as if offended. "But I wouldn't—"

"Not here," Eli says.

"Our orders are to transport you to a secure location for questioning." I step closer. I don't think she'll try to run, she's too much of a stickler for following the rules, but we have to make sure. "You don't have any problem with that, do you?"

"No, no. Of course not. I'll do whatever is necessary. Whatever Corine requires."

"That's very wise of you," Eli says, nodding at me to start walking. "Very dedicated. Now, my colleague will lead you—"

Moriana doesn't budge. "I don't understand. I just left the lab. Why didn't you question me there?"

"In order to find out where the information leak originated, we'll be questioning every member of the team assigned to the River 1 research project," I reply calmly. "We can't conduct these interrogations at the OAC for fear you'll share information. Everyone will be questioned separately, quietly, and off-site."

I can almost hear the cogs and gears turning in Moriana's mind as she processes the situation, trying to decide what to do. I take the initiative and, with a firm grip on her elbow, lead her toward the hovercar waiting at the end of the alley. "Now, if you'll just come along quietly, this whole thing will be over before you know it."

At the end of the alley, Soren leans against the hovercar Snake procured for us from who-knows-where. Painted to look like an official OAC security vehicle—who knows, maybe it *is* an official OAC security vehicle—we'll drive it through the streets of Okaria back to the rendezvous point in Gingko Park where Snake is waiting with the hovercar Zeke loaned us to get into the city. Soren steps up and opens the back door while Eli and I hustle Moriana in. Soren climbs in and takes his place at the nav console and eases the car away from the curb.

"Please hand over your plasma," I order. "We need to ensure you won't be communicating with any other members of your team while these interrogations are taking place."

Moriana scowls, but she opens her bag and puts her plasma in my open palm.

"So, Ms. Nair," Eli says, his finger curled around the trigger of the Bolt resting in his lap, "shall we begin?" Having been interrogated himself, Eli knows what he's doing. "Tell us what you know about the River 1 parasite currently spreading throughout the Sector."

Sitting between the two of us, Moriana glances at me, then at the back of Soren's head, his hair covered by a dark cap. Her brows knit together as she turns back to Eli. It's been years since she's seen Eli or Soren in the flesh, but I'm thankful she hasn't seen past my disguise or recognized my voice yet.

"You said you were going to ask me if I'd told anyone about River 1, not ask me about the parasite itself. You should know I'm not at liberty to talk about top-secret programs."

I shake my head as if disappointed in her powers of reasoning. It almost pains me to do so. "And just how do you suppose we will be able to determine who leaked what information, if we don't know which lab workers are privy to which aspects of the classified program?"

"Oh," she says simply, as if that hadn't occurred to her.

"I repeat," Eli says again, "tell us about the parasite, the symptoms it causes, and how it is currently spreading throughout the Sector. And it will be helpful if you do not leave out any details. Being very specific in your answers will help us clear you of violating the oath of secrecy you signed when you were hired."

"Violating—" she begins to protest.

"Your cooperation," I add quickly, "will help us put this unfortunate occasion behind you, and you can be back at work in your laboratory first thing in the morning."

"Where are you taking me?"

"Answer the question." Eli's hand tightens around the grip of the Bolt, and his voice loses all pretense of polite conversation. As if it had any before.

Moriana swallows hard. Her hands play nervously with the clasp on her bag. She's not convinced, but I can tell she sees no way out.

"Perhaps it will allay your misgivings if I told you this conversation is being recorded for your personnel file," I say. "Our superiors will review the recording, as well as our notes on this meeting, as soon as we complete this part of our investigation." I'm not lying completely. Demeter *is* recording, and we'll report to the Director as soon as we're back.

"All right," she says. "Here's what I know. Once ingested, the parasite attacks the brain, but it does no permanent damage." She pauses.

"Go on," I command.

"It's a modified version of the Old World parasite *Naegleria fowleri*, an amoeboflagellate that inhabits both soil and water. The parasite in its natural form causes a range of neurological symptoms, from headaches and nausea to fevers, lack of attention, confusion, and eventually hallucinations and seizures. Ultimately, it leads to death. However, our modified version is incapable of killing a human patient by itself, going only so far as to render him or her comatose." She continues for a few minutes in this vein. I can tell Eli is trying not to look as though he's lapping up her every word. Finally she stops and looks up at us expectantly.

"What else?"

"That's all I know! I swear I didn't tell anyone. I never said a word."

"You're not off the hook yet, Ms. Nair," I say, glancing out the window to get my bearings. By my estimate we're about five minutes from the rendezvous point.

"We are well aware," I continue, "that you know more than you're letting on. It will go better for you, if you keep talking."

"So River 1 does no permanent damage. How can you be so sure of that?" Eli demands.

"Because it's not some dangerous disease. It's a diversion!"

A *diversion?* What the hell does that mean? I avoid Eli's eyes, trying to appear unaffected.

"Is that what you told your friends in the Resistance?" he says. "'Don't worry, the little bug won't hurt you, it's just a diversion'."

"My friends in the Resistance? Are you *joking?*" Moriana practically spits the word. "I have no friends in the Resistance. I didn't tell anybody anything."

"I don't believe that's true," I say quietly. *There are people in the Resistance who love you.*

Eli leans toward her. "You say it isn't dangerous, that it's just a diversion. Then you know why Corine made her special broadcast yesterday. Did you tell your friends about the broadcast? Are you the source of the OAC leak?"

"No! I swear by all that's green and growing that I didn't say a word!" A sheen of sweat has broken out on her smooth brow. I can smell her fear. "No one would understand anyway," she says with growing desperation, "because no one knows why it was designed in the first place."

Designed. This whole disguise and kidnap scheme was a gamble, but we're about to win big. Moriana's going to spill everything.

"But *you* know." Eli's voice is deep, dangerous. Menacing. He picks up the Bolt and flips it to KILL, then places it back on his lap, his finger tapping at the trigger. It's a damn good thing it's not fully charged. "You are one of the few scientists who knows exactly why River 1 was designed. And you know the OAC cannot afford to have employees who can't keep their mouths shut." Eli's voice drops to a growl. "I'm losing patience, Ms. Nair. I'll give you one more opportunity to tell us exactly what you know about this program or your employer is going to lose faith in you."

Eli and I exchange a glance.

"I told you! I never ... I swear—"

Soren glances backward. "Almost there," he says. I feel the hovercar slow, see the dappled light filtering through the branches of the hundreds of Gingko trees dotting the rolling landscape. I've always loved this park. Out of the corner of my eye, I see Eli slip the syringe out of his pocket.

"Almost where? What is going on?" Moriana's voice rises, panicked as I lean toward her. "I need to speak to—" She presses her back into the seat, shrinking from me. "Corine will vouch for me. I swear it."

Dropping any pretense of disguise, I speak normally.

"Moriana, please." She leans in, staring at me.

"Vale?" she asks, astonished.

"Thousands of people are sick. The symptoms are spreading like wildfire. How can it not be dangerous? What do you mean it's a diversion?"

"I'm not telling you a thing. Let me out!" She starts to struggle, lashing out at me and scrambling for the door. Eli strikes, plunging the syringe into her thigh. Her eyes grow wide at the sting, and she stops fighting, turning to look at me, pure venom in her eyes.

"You want to know the truth, Vale? It's not about some stupid parasite! It's never been about the *disease*. It's about the *cure*."

"What about the cure?" I try to stay calm, but the look in her eyes has unnerved me.

"The whole program is about delivering the individualized nanoparticles to make MealPak modifications permanent," she says. "The parasite is simply a diversion."

Dread washes through me. "What are you saying?"

She shakes her head at me as if I'm dense. "It's about locking in the genetic programing. It's about finally creating a world where everyone knows their place. No war. No conflict. No fucking *resistance*."

I stare across her at Eli, whose face mirrors the shock on my own. I thought I knew how far my mother would go for power. I thought I knew how much she would sacrifice. But this? How could I have known?

"I don't believe it." The words come out as a whisper.

"Why not? It's what Corine's been working on for years." Her words are already starting to slur. "Permanent modifications. If it's good enough for *you*, why not for *everyone*?"

Eli looks at me, his eyes wide, questioning. I haven't even told Remy what my parents did to me. How they changed who I am without asking, just assuming their idea of making permanent modifications to my DNA would be something I would welcome. It makes my skin crawl just thinking about how they kept me in a drug-induced coma to monitor and evaluate the changes. And now they want to do that to every citizen in the Sector?

"What about free will?" I say, ignoring the look for now. "An individual's right to self-determination?"

"You're creating a society of slaves." Eli sounds like he's about to choke on the words.

"Slaves?" Moriana sneers. "What are you talking about? We're not enslaving anyone. We're improving everyone. And once people see how bad the disease is, everyone will want the cure. Everyone will want to be protected."

I lean forward and turn her face toward me, trying to keep her alert. "What are you saying?"

"How could you do this, Vale? How could you do this to me?"

"Shut the fuck up," Eli growls.

"Eli," Soren warns from the front seat. He doesn't need to say anything else. Eli shakes his head in disgust and looks out the window as if he can't even stand the sight of Moriana.

She turns toward him. "Elijah Tawfiq?"

I cup her chin so she's forced to look at me. "What about the cure? What are you planning to do?"

"It's not … not finished yet. I was missing the key, the translation key. Brinn Alexander. Neural cell epigenetics. Her research." Eli's eyes narrow at the mention of Brinn's name. "Each dose contains a—a virus that makes DNA modifications to stem cells—" Her words slide into each other. She licks her lips slowly, blinks to keep her eyes open. "—which propagate throughout the rest of the body. Stem cells can be programmed to do anything, within the confines of existing chemical and biological processes, as long as you give them the right code."

I shake my head. "How do you make modifications to the brain? Stem cells won't propagate to neural cells."

Moriana looks at me like a professor wondering how such a stupid student ended up in her class. "We build new ones." Her head slumps down onto her chest.

"How?" Eli asks.

"She's out." I lay her back against the seat.

Soren stops the car and turns around. He looks from Eli to me. "What did she mean, 'If it's good enough for you—'?"

I don't let him finish. "We've got to move," I say, trying to keep my mind on what needs to be done. There's no time to explain everything now. "Demeter," I command, "Transmit this recording to the Director."

Snake, who had been waiting with Zeke's car, opens my door and, in the cool shade of a giant gingko, I step out. My boots sink into the grass, soft from last night's rain, and the pebbly gingko seeds grind into the earth beneath my soles. I drag Moriana's limp body from the car as Soren takes her feet, and we carry her to Zeke's sleek vehicle. Eli plants his palm on the locking panel to deactivate the cloaking and open the doors. I deposit Moriana into the back and slide in next to her as Eli takes the nav pane and Soren sits beside him.

"I need to hustle," Snake says. "Gotta return the car I borrowed. You're programmed to go out through side streets." He points at the state-of-the-art navigation panel. "Don't touch it until you're past the last POD station unless something goes wrong."

Eli grunts, nodding.

"We'll get word to you," I say. "You're not going to believe—"

Eli's already initiated the powerful rotors, and I can feel the hoverblades thrumming beneath me as the tripod withdraws, and the car lifts smoothly off the ground. With a gentle tilt, we move forward, out of this little copse of wood, out of the park, out of the city.

As we head back to Kanaan's, my mind races, thoughts tumbling one after another like boulders down a hill as I sort through the implications of my mother's pet project. Soren pivots in his seat, and I want to turn away, fearing he's going to press the question about my modifications. But he doesn't. He looks down at Moriana's unconscious figure, drool hanging unceremoniously from her lips, her head resting on my thigh like she's napping, and then meets my gaze. "Jeremiah," Soren whispers. "He'll be heartbroken."

18 — VALE

Miah is waiting in the yard when we pull up. He yanks open the back door of the hovercar and peers in. "Is she okay?"

"She's fine," I say, stepping aside to give him room as he reaches in and scoops her into his arms, her head lolling against his shoulder. "She'll be out for at least an hour. Probably more."

He stares at her for a long second before turning to me, uncertainty scrawled across his face. Soren joins us but Eli stalks off, motioning for Remy, who was standing by the doorway, to follow him. Best he tell her about the OAC using her mother's research.

"Was she …?" Miah starts. Soren and I look at each other. We both know what he's trying to say, what he can't bring himself to ask. *Was she cooperative? Is she on our side?*

Soren puts a comforting arm on Miah's shoulder.

"Be there when she wakes up. Just the two of you. Then we'll see what happens next."

Miah's eyes cloud and he drops his gaze to Moriana's face, unwilling to give up.

"I'll talk to her," he says stubbornly. He turns to carry her indoors, and Soren and I follow, for once, connected in our misery.

"How'd it go?" Saara walks toward us, passing Miah on his way into the house.

"Not good." Soren shakes his head. "You're not going to believe—"

"Fill me in when I get back," she says, gesturing to Zeke's hovercar. "I'm going in to check on a patient. We got word there's a man refusing to be admitted, refusing to let any Sector doctors or medics touch him. I'm going in to see what we can find out, if there's anything we can do."

"Wait, this is important," I say, trying to stop her. "The parasite isn't as important as we thought. It's a harmless diversion. It won't kill anybody."

"What do you mean? It's killed people already."

"Not by itself, it hasn't," Soren responds. "Only when people get so paranoid they go off and get themselves killed."

"They're using the parasite as an excuse to inoculate people with their 'cure,' which is the real danger."

"Permanent genetic modifications," Soren finishes for me. "Locks in MealPak effects."

Saara gasps, puts a hand over her mouth. "What do we do now?" she asks.

"No idea."

"Go," I say. "Take care of your patient. But get back here as soon as you can."

Saara turns to leave, heading toward Zeke's hovercar, and I follow Soren inside. At the table, Osprey is studying a plasma with what appears to be a 3D topographic map of the whole Sector displayed in hologram. There are thin white lines running between the Farms, the corporate factory towns, and the capital.

"Transport lines?" Soren asks, sitting down next to her. She nods.

"I'm mapping out the best possible routes for Bear and his marchers," she says. "We don't want everyone on the trains. We'll need to mobilize all our airships and possibly find some waterways to use as well."

"Good thinking," Soren says.

"Where's Remy and Eli?" I ask.

Osprey points down the hall. "Eli looks like hell. What happened?"

"Soren will fill you in," I say. "Any word on our acorns? Have you been able to contact Chan-Yu?"

Osprey brightens. "I got a leaf delivered. He'll be here sometime tonight. I assume that means he has an idea."

I pat my chest where the two acorn pendants hang, a habit I've fallen into since I slipped Meera's around my neck to wear alongside the one Chan-Yu gave me when he freed Remy and Soren. My allegiance lies outside the Sector, he said that night. At the time I had little idea what he meant. Now, I can only hope his knowledge of things outside the Sector will lead us to an understanding of Meera's final message.

Follow the acorns to the tree.

"The Director radioed in," Osprey adds. "She listened to the recording Demeter sent to her. Said to contact her when our guest wakes up." She puts her hand on Soren's arm and pulls him toward her. "So what happened?"

That's my signal to go find Remy and Eli.

An hour later, Eli grumbles as he picks at a plate of bread and cheese. "Saara said the drugs would knock Moriana out for an hour tops. How much longer is she gonna sleep?"

"I'll go check—" Soren says, starting to push up from his chair.

"Don't bother," Miah says, rounding the corner, cutting Soren off, his words seeming to scrape against the back of his throat. "She's still out cold."

Miah sinks into a chair, letting his head fall back. Staring at the ceiling, he draws in a long breath and lets it out slowly. "Okay. Tell me everything."

There's no easy way, so I plow ahead. Eli doesn't say a word while Soren adds a few details here and there. Finally, Miah gets up and pours himself a glass of water, then sits back down.

"So this disease is a fiction." His face is haggard as he stares into his glass. "The parasite they're using is just setting the stage, an invention to scare people into running back to the OAC with their tails between their legs, desperate for a cure."

"A cure customized for each individual, programmed just like their MealPaks to dehumanize them. But the cure won't wear off. It doesn't have to be ingested every day to remain effective. It turns everyone into robots." Eli's voice is as hard as an iron fist. "We'll be locked in like automatons while the OAC has the power to decide who has a modicum of self-determination and who gets to live like livestock, shuffled here and there at the whim of their keepers."

A hush settles around the table. No one looks up, and the room, growing dim in the early evening shadows, feels more funerary than last week's vigil.

"So what do we do?" Miah looks like he's aged ten years since yesterday.

"Look," I interject, trying to add some fuel to a fire that seems to be burning down to embers, "this is not over. Right before she went under, Moriana said it's not ready yet. It sounds like they're working on one last piece. Until she gets that in place, we still have time. I think your success in infiltrating their supply lines, in getting people to defect to our cause, and in causing trouble on the Farms has forced her hand. She's moving before she's ready. That gives us an opening. It gives us time."

"Time for what?" Soren snaps. "How are we going to convince anyone it's not the Resistance who disseminated this damn bug? The OAC planted it perfectly. And anyone who listened to her broadcast—which is everyone in the Sector—will believe it was let loose on the population as an act of bioterrorism—"

"Which it was," Remy interrupts.

"—perpetrated by us!" Soren stands as if he's had a sudden brainstorm, only to start pacing around the room, kicking furniture as he goes. "The brilliant thing is, one of the symptoms is paranoia. So not only is Corine telling everyone the Resistance took an Old World parasite and modified it, those who get infected will also start thinking we're after them. So they run right to Corine for the cure!"

"You heard what Bear said." Osprey grabs Soren's hand as he passes her chair. "It isn't turning everyone away from the cause."

"So far," Soren retorts. "But unless we come up with countermeasures, and soon, we won't have any way to prevent thousands of citizens who believe the OAC's lies from being turned into slaves."

"But we have Moriana, and she has answers," Eli says. "Rhinehouse is going to want to talk to her himself."

I can't wait any longer. I pull myself to my feet, dreading what I have to say. "Bottom line is we have to put all our energies into preventing this atrocity, into preventing my mother from doing to so many others what—" I stop, run hands over my face, trying to figure out how to put it. "Look, there's something I need to tell you. Something I haven't told anyone." I look down at Remy, and everyone goes quiet, even Soren and Eli. All eyes turn to me. "Not even you, Remy, because until now, I didn't know how. I'm just going to say it. The OAC has already started implementing these genetic modifications, and I was one of the first to be treated." A stunned silence falls over the room. "I had no idea, until recently. When I woke up in my parents' house, hooked up to a plasma, Corine finally told me. That whole time I was in captivity, I was only conscious for about ten days. The rest of the time I was in an induced coma, prevented from forming new memories, so they could follow up on the modifications."

"Why didn't you tell us?" Soren spits.

"I didn't—" I start.

"That's why you never suffered withdrawals from the MealPaks!" His hands are splayed on the table. Eli's expression is black, and Miah sits up surprised, confused, and angry. Only Osprey and Remy, though clearly stunned, are calm. "You knew this whole time they were capable of this, and you never told us?"

"How was I supposed to know they were going to do it to everyone?" I shout back.

"How did it happen?" Eli asks, his voice on a low boil.

"Nanobots," I say, breathing slowly, calming myself down. "Distributed through my MealPaks. The modifications are delivered via the nanobots, which target specific segments of the individual's DNA. 'Optimizations,' Corine called it. In my case, the modifications are not designed to harm me. My mother said they did it because they wanted me to experience all the world had to offer. They heightened my functionality. They did it because they *love* me." My voice twists on the words. "But not everyone in the Sector will be as lucky as I was."

I can almost hear the air hiss out of the room.

"Why didn't you tell us?" Soren asks.

I shrug and drop into the nearest chair. "Sometimes I'd tell myself I dreamed it. That it couldn't possibly be true. Who would do that to their own child?"

"And now they're going to do it to everyone," Osprey whispers.

Eli growls. "By curing the disease the Resistance is supposedly spreading, Corine gets a political win and the rest of us are put in chains."

"And they're using my mom's research," Remy says. "My mother, the *healer*."

"And Moriana." Miah looks lost, his face pale, his features slack. He shakes his head, tears glistening on his lashes. "This is what she's been working on."

I nod. "I'm sorry, Miah."

There's nothing else to say.

19 — REMY

Spring 92, Sector Annum 106, 5h02
Gregorian Calendar: June 19

It is almost first light when the door opens and Chan-Yu steps inside. Miah is upstairs with Moriana, Eli is passed out on the couch, and Soren, Osprey, Vale, and I have been dozing on and off, but right now we are bleary-eyed but awake. We welcome Chan-Yu like a long-lost friend, a prodigal son, or a savior. That's what we hope he'll be. The always cool, always collected Chan-Yu will surely know what we should do next. He'll help us interrogate Moriana—who was none too happy and not a bit cooperative when she finally woke up—and, working with the Director, Rhinehouse, and the rest of the leadership team he'll figure out what we can do to counter Corine's plan. And he'll know exactly what Meera meant by *follow the acorns to the tree*. None of us would ever admit it, but I know that's what we've all been thinking. That Chan-Yu will help us solve everything.

And then reality hits.

The first words out of his mouth are not answers to our questions, but questions he hopes we can answer for him.

First: "Any word on Kofir?" Then: "Are you certain Meera didn't have another message? Did you see any other trinket or marker on her?"

Kofir? At first I don't even remember General Bunqu's given name, but Vale ushers Chan-Yu into the house and says, "Nothing on the general. All we've been able to find is that he was arrested the morning Meera died. Demeter's blind to anything going on in Assembly Hall and OAC headquarters, and I'm sure Aulion's taking no chances on a possible escape."

"No doubt. But high-value prisoners have escaped before." Chan-Yu nods ever so slightly to Soren and me and turns back to Vale.

"Yes," Vale agrees. "But that was when the prisoners had friends inside willing to risk everything to save them."

"Who says Kofir doesn't have the same?" Chan-Yu says this in such a calm manner that I almost miss the importance, and his deadly seriousness.

"You have people on the inside?" Eli sits up, rubbing sleep out of his eyes.

"What of Meera?" Chan-Yu asks, ignoring Eli's question. "There must have been more to the message. Something you saw, but perhaps didn't realize was important. Something small. It could have been anything."

Vale shakes his head. "I'm sorry. The only thing I can think of is that the v-scroll was in her mouth. But otherwise, there was nothing."

The grief is fleeting, but for a moment it reshapes his features. If I didn't know him, if I weren't comfortable with him now, I might not have recognized it for what it is. Then he's back to himself. "I must wash the road from my clothes. I have traveled far in a short time. Soon we will talk. I will tell you what I know and what I think I know, and, together, we will solve this riddle."

And that's it for pleasantries. I lead him upstairs to a room at the opposite end of the hall. Heading back downstairs, my fingers trail along the wall and I think about my grandfather and all the people he entertained over the years. He'd designed this old house specifically so it could serve as a meeting place. With five bedrooms plus his own master suite, it was large enough to accommodate many guests for long stays. He would tell stories about how he'd hosted the brightest minds from within the Sector and welcomed travelers from without, wanderers who came from as far away as the oil swamps to the south and the hulking fire-bombed ruins of old Chicago. People who told of the rocky deserts of the Texas Federation and of civilizations built on top of mountains so tall their peaks hide in the clouds.

I pour myself a cup of rich black tea—Osprey found a ten-pound stash of something she calls *ooh-long* in an vacuum-sealed container yesterday—and relax into the couch in between Eli and Vale, who are both soundly asleep once again. Eli is snoring loudly, and Vale's head is jerking up every fifteen seconds as he nods off with his chin on his chest. I put a pillow behind his head and settle in against his side, stretching my legs out across Eli's semi-prone form. I sip my tea, wondering where in the world these leaves came from, and what stranger brought them to my grandfather so many years ago.

I jerk awake when I hear voices. The cup of tea is cold against my chest and a plush blanket has replaced Vale's shoulder as my pillow. I rub my eyes and wipe the drool from my chin, looking up to see Vale and Chan-Yu talking heatedly over the long table in the kitchen.

"No," Chan-Yu is saying, "it had to be these. There's nothing else that makes sense."

"But where do they lead? How do you follow it? There's no signal on the astrolabe that leads anywhere. There's no path we can follow."

"There's a piece missing," Chan-Yu says patiently, staring at something on the table. I add another splash to my cold tea to bring it up to lukewarm, and sit down across from him, next to Vale. The object of Chan-Yu's attention turns out to be a mess of various metal chains, black necklace clasps, and braided hemp fibers, each attached to a gold acorn similar to the one Vale has worn around his neck for the last six months. Some of the acorns are short and fat, others long and thin. Some of them are worn, the gold filigree rubbed off into a dim copper tone. Some are as brilliant and polished as I imagine they were the day they were made. I do a quick count—there are eleven in total.

"Where did you find all these?" I ask, staring at the pendants in awe.

"Many places," Chan-Yu responds, as cryptically as ever. "Many people."

"'Follow the acorns to the tree,'" I say, repeating Meera's last words to us. "Where do they lead? And how are we supposed to 'follow' them?"

"That's what we're trying to figure out," Vale says, his head propped against his curled fist. He looks exhausted, but there's a relentlessness in his eyes that tells me he won't be getting sleep anytime soon.

Chan-Yu glances at me briefly before he starts thumbing through the gold pendants in front of him, lost in thought. Finally, he breaks the silence. "As you know, I gave Vale my pendant when I left the Sector with you and Soren last winter. I had no way to contact the Wayfarers still operating in the Wilds. When Osprey communicated Meera's last words to me, I sought out Chariya, the oldest living Wayfarer. You met her at the Outsiders' gathering, but she rarely stays in one place. With her astrolabe, we were able to locate all the pendants. I brought eleven of them here." He looks at Vale. "With yours and Meera's, that makes thirteen." He nods to Vale who slips the two pendants he's been wearing from around his neck and adds them to the pile. "As far as we know there were only thirteen astrolabes and thirteen pendants ever made. After I left Okaria, Meera was the only one in the capital with a pendant."

"Why thirteen and who made them?"

"We don't know why thirteen and we don't know who made them." He shakes his head and looks at me with a wry smile. "There are things I know and things I think I know."

I glare at him. Chan-Yu loves to speak in riddles. I tend to wish he would get to the point.

I pick up one of the pendants, one with an elegant black silk necklace attached, and hold it in my palm. "It's heavy for something so small."

"The gold is merely decorative," Chan-Yu says. "Inside is a dense combination of biofibers and nanocircuitry containing a technology that no Outsider has been able to replicate."

"What about someone in the Sector?" Vale asks.

"I do not believe that anyone in the Sector has knowledge of this kind of technology."

"What kind of technology?" His voice is laced with impatience.

"I do not know."

"What *do* you know, then?" Vale asks, now fully frustrated. Chan-Yu doesn't so much as raise an eyebrow.

"I know this: about a hundred years ago, a group of people gathered together and started calling themselves Outsiders. In the wake of the Religious Wars that decimated the world, there were many who were afraid of any form of authority, which they believed would naturally descend into corruption and authoritarianism. There was a word for this type of thought."

"Anarchy," Vale prompts.

"Yes," Chan-Yu says, nodding. "As the new world was growing, recovering, this school of thought became more prevalent. At first it was born out of fear. Fear of governance, of corruption, of a code of laws that could be used in favor of the powerful and to oppress the less powerful. But as the Outsiders grew, it became a movement of trust. In order to reject laws and government, you must trust those around you even if there are no formal laws and even if they will not be punished for harming you.

"The movement grew, and they traveled in loose bands relying on technology they could scavenge from the Old World, technology that would have minimal impact on the environment within which they were trying to survive. After about forty or fifty years, the group grew to include almost two thousand members. It was about this time that the pendants and astrolabes first surfaced. Or at least that's when our stories first mention them."

Chan-Yu pauses to take a sip from his canteen. A quick glance at Vale reveals that he is as enraptured as I am.

"Legend has it that there are thirteen of each because the inventor was a bit of a joker. A man—or woman, we don't know—who loved numbers and what they signified. Instead of creating twelve of each to match the zodiac, the legend goes, he made thirteen because there are actually more than twelve months. If you employ a lunar-solar calendar, there are 12.41 lunations each solar year. Thirteen is also the first prime number that is an emirp as well."

The last word sounds a bit like a bird chirping. "What's an emirp?" I ask. "It sounds like half a word."

"A prime that, when reversed, is a different prime. And," Vale sits up straight, "there are thirteen Archimedean solids; thirteen is a centered square number, a happy number, and one of only three known Wilson primes."

Chan-Yu doesn't say anything for a moment, and there's a silence while I think back to the last math class I enjoyed. It was called *The Art of Mathematics*, which might have been why I enjoyed it. My professor, a wiry woman with paint perpetually in her hair, instructed us on the artistic interpretations of Euclidian geometry, the golden ratio, the mathematical implications of perspective, and sacred geometry.

"Isn't thirteen also a Fibonacci number?" I ask, adding up the numbers in my head.

"Yes," Vale says, looking at me proudly. "One, one, two, three, five, eight, thirteen."

"But why does any of this matter?" I am suddenly as impatient as Vale was a few moments ago. *What does this have to do with anything?*

Chan-Yu shrugs.

"Maybe it doesn't. There are things I know and things I think I know. In this case, I believe that the creator of these acorns made thirteen because it is a unique number, and a bit of a non-conformist one at that. How many rooms does this house have?"

His question takes me by surprise. I think over the floorplan.

"Five bedrooms and one master bedroom. Three bathrooms. The kitchen. Living room. Basement. And if you count the root cellar," I pause, "thirteen."

"What are you saying?" Vale asks, his eyes narrowed, deadly focused on Chan-Yu, who, for his part, leans back in his chair with his arms crossed, contemplative.

"Do you think the acorns lead here?" I demand, leaning forward.

"Your grandfather encoded the most important discovery of his life in the shape of a flower that conforms to the Fibonacci sequence," Chan-Yu says. "How old is this house, Remy?"

My mind is spinning.

"I don't know," I respond. "Sixty, seventy years ..."

"When I was a child, my elders spoke of a safe place, a place travelers could always stop for a rest, a place where there would be a welcome fire and good conversation." Chan-Yu sounds almost excited. This is the most I've ever heard him talk before. "They called it the 'waystation.' When this house was built, it was in the Wilds. Sector territory expanded to encompass it, but—"

"Are you saying my grandfather invented the pendants and astrolabes?"

"There are things I know—"

"I know!" I shout, then lower my voice again. "There are things you know and things you think you know. But why *here*? Why do you think it was my grandfather, of all people?"

"I stayed here once," Chan-Yu's voice softens. "I was on my way back into the Sector after visiting Soo-Sun in the Wilds. It was just a few weeks after your sister died, Remy," he says, looking at me hard, as though the secret to the mystery might be inside me, and it's all I can do to hold his gaze. "Your grandfather was already dead, and it had been months since any of his family were here. But Meera guided me here, gave me a safe place to sleep, and stayed up with me for many hours that night."

"How did Meera know about this place?" Vale asks, as riveted as I am.

"I never asked. And I still do not know. Many Outsiders do not choose to share details of our lives with others, so often, rather than ask, we wait until information is shared willingly."

Something in the back of my mind is jostled loose. I press my fingers to my temples.

"Meera did talk about Kanaan quite a bit. And when she suggested we could come here, she told me she'd visited occasionally just to keep all of the systems running: water, solar, electricity. Maybe Meera and my grandfather knew each other better than I thought."

"Did you ever see the scar between her shoulder blades?" Chan-Yu asks. "It was no accident. Another Outsider etched it into her skin. An oak, broad and strong."

I rub my hand over my head, my short hair stubbly under my fingertips and think back to the day Meera sat me in front of the mirror in her apartment and cut off my curls, then shaved my head. Hair was sticking to everything, and she'd slipped her shirt over her head and turned to throw it in a pile. There was something there, thin lines embedded in her skin that reminded me of the marks on Osprey's arms but were somehow different—more artistic, more intentional. But I didn't get a good look at it, and I didn't have time to put the pieces together. Now all the pieces of the puzzle begin falling into place.

"Like the one outside this house," I whisper.

Chan-Yu nods, holding my gaze. "My sister and I have pledged our lives to learning the secret to the communication between the acorns and the astrolabes, but thus far our efforts have been fruitless. When Osprey told me of Meera's dying words, I began to suspect that the tree she referred to was not metaphorical but literal. I found Chariya, and together we sought out the acorns. I brought them here in the hopes that the tree Meera spoke of was the oak outside this house."

Vale stands up abruptly, his chair nearly tipping over. The sun glinting through the window catches his face at a vivid angle, and the growing shadow of a beard makes him look like a man to be reckoned with, a leader, a man I'd follow anywhere.

"What are we waiting for?" he asks, and turns sharply on his heel toward the kitchen door that leads out into the garden.

Chan-Yu scoops up the pile of pendants as Vale flings open the door and strides around the corner to where the old oak towers over the remnants of my grandfather's shade garden.

We stop under the outstretched branches of the oak, arching above us like beams in an ancient cathedral. Vale stares up at the branches, and Chan-Yu holds the tangled pendants out in front of him like a talisman.

"Meera was a Wayfarer," Chan-Yu says finally. "But not like the other Wayfarers. She had the markings, though hers were scars, not tattoos. She didn't guide the lost to their destinations. She worked in the Sector, not in the Wilds."

"She found me when I was lost," I protest. I turn to Vale. "She and Snake guided me to you, or at least helped me find where you were. She led me to Bunqu. And she kept me safe." A sharp pain slices through me, the bitter sting of an unfinished friendship biting behind my eyes.

"Maybe her purpose was to lead us here," Vale says. "Is there something special about this tree?" He narrows his eyes and stares off in the distance. It looks like he's trying to remember something from a fading dream.

"Not really," I say with a shrug. "It's not that large for an oak. It's not very old. There's nothing unique about it."

"It's a live oak," Chan-Yu observes, running his fingertips along some of the smaller leaves, a dark green color, and crisp, unlike the wide, fleshy ones of most oaks in these parts. "Live oaks are rare here. Until Old World climate change shifted weather patterns, it was almost impossible for them to survive this far north."

In contrast to Chan-Yu's measured rationality, Vale is behaving oddly. He cocks his head to one side and sniffs the air like a dog that's caught a scent. He puts his fingers to the trunk of the tree and starts muttering to himself.

"It's too faint." His voice is low, urgent. "At the very edge of my perception. There's something … if I wasn't thinking about it, if I wasn't open to it, I'd probably ignore it. Do you feel it?" He whirls toward us. I shake my head *no*, and Vale turns back to the tree.

"Vale?" I draw out my words, watching him with concern. "Are you okay?" He ignores me.

"It's there. Definitely there. A hum. A vibration. Like a tuning fork." He presses his palms into the tree trunk, and a moment later, presses his whole body into the tree. "It's vibrating," he whispers.

I stare at him, unsure what to do or how to react. I glance at Chan-Yu, seeking some reassurance that the man I love is in fact acting crazy and I'm not crazy for thinking he's crazy. But Chan-Yu is watching Vale with a mixture of curiosity and amusement. He doesn't look the slightest bit worried. Then, to my great surprise, Vale bends over and starts unlacing his boots.

"What are you doing?" I ask, a hint of panic now bleeding into my voice. Vale kicks off his boots and then rips off his socks. He tosses them to the side and digs his toes into the dirt. He stands, unmoving, for a moment, then walks a few paces away, comes back to us, and then puts his hands on his hips and looks at us with none of the makings of a madman.

"I'm sure of it." He looks from Chan-Yu to me and back to Chan-Yu. "The earth is vibrating. But even that isn't quite the right word. I can't explain it. It's like how you know an instrument is tuned correctly. A piano or a guitar. There's nothing about it you can see, or feel, or even hear necessarily. One single note is just as good as any other, but when the instrument is tuned, when the strings vibrate just so and the frequency of the sound waves are in sync, all the notes work together, building on each other in precise mathematical intervals. It just *feels* right." Vale pauses for a minute, staring at the ground, lost in thought. Chan-Yu watches him in silence. For my part, I'm starting to feel what Vale was talking about. Something on the edge of my perception. But it's not something I'm sensing. It's the feeling that we're on the edge of a discovery. Like climbing astride Osprey's *oiseau*, it feels like I'm in neutral, with my engine revving, waiting to shift into gear. My heart hammers against my ribcage as I close my eyes and try to let myself feel what Vale described. Then he breaks the silence.

"This is going to sound wild, but I think the pendants are communicating with the roots of this tree. Maybe that's how the technology works. The pendants and the astrolabes communicate through the soil, through the roots of the plants nearby."

Chan-Yu nods.

"We have long known that the forests communicate in ways we cannot understand and cannot touch," he says, and by *we* I understand that he doesn't mean anyone in the Sector. "We know they communicate through their roots, through an intricate network of fungi so dense and complicated we do not have the tools to model or understand it. We know better than most others what the trees mean to say, but we cannot understand or speak with them. Yet."

"What if someone figured it out?" I ask. "And replicated that signaling in these pendants and astrolabes?"

"It is possible," Chan-Yu says. Then he turns abruptly and starts walking away. He is almost back to the house while Vale and I watch him in confused silence. Then he turns around and calls to us, "Can you feel it now?"

Vale pauses, stands perfectly still for a moment, and then tilts his head to the side and furrows his brow as if listening to something faint. After a moment, he calls back.

"No."

Chan-Yu smiles triumphantly and marches back toward us, the pendants held out in front of him. He returns to Vale's side. "And now?"

Vale closes his eyes and cocks his head again. His voice is barely a whisper. "Yes."

The gears shift, the engine roars, and I feel as though I am launched forward. Goosebumps prickle to attention on my skin. "This is right over granddad's root cellar."

Vale stares at me, confused.

"This is right over the root cellar," I repeat. Then it clicks for him, too. He takes off in a sprint toward the house, his socks and shoes forgotten behind him. I follow, and can feel more than hear Chan-Yu's quiet strides behind me. At the side of the house, where a host of vines and shrubs have overtaken the old entrance to the basement, Vale rips the cellar door open, almost pulling the doors off their hinges in his hurry to get inside. It's pitch dark but for the glimmer of pale morning light shining down the stairwell. There are rows upon rows of shelves filled with canvas bags of decomposing grains, jars of canned and pickled food, bottles of homebrewed barley beer, wine, mead, kombucha. This was my grandfather's overflow cellar, where he stored food in case of emergency. Like so many of his generation who had been touched by the Famine Years, he hoarded food, stored it obsessively, kept this cellar packed to the brim even in the heart of summer when food was as plentiful as sunlight.

As a child I was terrified of my grandfather's cellar. He would send me down here occasionally to collect things for whatever meal he was preparing—canned beans, dried grains, jars of sauces. I would walk downstairs trembling, talking myself through every step: *there's nothing here, there's nothing here, there's nothing here*. Once at the bottom I would grab whatever jar he'd asked for and bolt back upstairs as fast as I could, taking the steps two at a time, leaping back outside as though I'd just narrowly escaped a closing portal to Hell.

"Nothing down there but jars and garden tools," my grandfather would say as I emerged back into the kitchen, flushed with fear and panting, his voice lilting with laughter.

I touch my fingers to where I remember there being a biolight activator, but when I hit the small glass panel, nothing happens.

"The power must be out down here," I mutter. Fighting for the Resistance has cured me of my fear of darkness, but without infrared contacts, I see no better than I could as a child. Vale doesn't seem to hear me. I squint, trying to see through the darkness, but Vale keeps moving confidently forward, as if it were as bright down here as it is outside. He heads toward a dim corner of the cellar, far from the bright entrance. I don't know why, but he seems to know, somehow, where to go, and is undaunted by the lack of light.

Is he able to feel these 'vibrations' because of what Corine did to him? Is that why he can see so well down in the dark? Why he can sense things not even Chan-Yu can?

Vale prowls forward through the corridor, which smells wet and moldy like any old root cellar would. But there's a richness here, too. It almost smells fresh, like mint or lemon.

"Something's growing down here," I say.

"Mmm," Chan-Yu agrees behind me, sniffing the air.

Vale stops suddenly and turns.

"Give me the pendants." Chan-Yu hands them over without a word of protest. Holding the pendants outstretched in his palm like an offering to one of the old gods, Vale walks toward the darkest end of the cavern. Chan-Yu and I follow closely. We're expectant, quiet, holding our breath for something to happen.

But nothing does.

"What now?" My voice is so quiet, I wonder if anyone heard me. The feeling of being on the edge hasn't gone away. We're almost there.

Chan-Yu reaches past me to take one of the golden acorns from Vale's hand. Without a word, he turns it upside down and uses his fingernail to flip the beacon switch. And then, with a whispering *swoosh*, a wall at end of the cellar slides away, and I am suddenly blinded by a bright light from beyond. I throw an arm up to shield my eyes.

"By all that's green and growing," Vale whispers. I lower my arm, squint into the light, and find his hand waiting for mine. "What *is* this?"

I walk forward, Vale at my side. The air is full of jasmine, citrus, and wet stone. I breathe in deeply. There are steps leading down to a lower level, the cellar dug deeper, I suppose, to make the ceiling higher. As we emerge into a wide, open space, with white walls on all sides and an incredible wealth of greenery, a multitude of plants are arranged carefully in rows and alleys as diverse and varied as the plants in Rhinehouse's old lab at the Thermopylae base. Even though my eyes have adjusted to the light, my brain refuses to adjust to the reality of what I'm experiencing.

I am in a greenhouse.

I am in a large, underground greenhouse lit by bright grow lights and presumably powered by electricity generated in the roots of all the plants that my grandfather cultivated above ground. I am in a greenhouse built under an old oak tree that somehow communicates with thirteen little acorn pendants and when they're all together, they vibrate in a way that Vale can sense, but Chan-Yu and I and presumably everyone normal cannot. I lead Vale in between one of the rows, staring at all the plants, tempted to reach out and touch them but remembering Rhinehouse's sharp admonition: *Don't touch anything.* I don't know what these are or why they're here. Are they dangerous? Then I see a small tree next to us, watered by a drip irrigation line, bright yellow fruits dripping off of it.

"Vale," I whisper, pointing. "Lemons."

"Are we walking in Lotus?" he asks, his voice full of awe, and I know he doesn't mean *nelumbo nucifera*, the lotus plant, but LOTUS, the Old World seed bank database Eli, Soren, and I discovered encoded into an artificial genome.

I shake my head. *I don't know.*

Up ahead, I see a long desk where old computers, almost laughable because of their age, are set up against the wall. There's something painted on the wall above the desk, but it's hard to make it out through the tangle of vines and trees that have grown far beyond their original containers, crowding out the ceiling space and blocking our view. I walk closer.

"Oh." I say simply, when it finally comes into view. Vale's grip tightens around my hand. He sees it too. It's an image of two smiling men, arms slung over each other's shoulders. One has a toddler, a little girl with short cropped hair, sitting on his shoulders; the other holds a boy's hand in his. The girl smiles brightly and holds her chubby hand up as if waving at someone while the boy, no more than five years old and adorable with dark, curly hair and a toothy smile, looks up adoringly at the man holding his hand. They're standing in front of a newly planted oak tree. There's a wooden sign next to them with writing carved into it, overlaid with red paint. It reads, "The Waystation."

"I don't understand," Vale says, his voice barely audible.

"Do you know those men?" Chan-Yu asks, coming to stand next to us, staring at the photo, as enraptured as we are.

"It's my grandfather and my mother," I say, pointing at the smiling man with the little girl on his shoulders. The dark hair and skin; round, almond-shaped eyes; and bright, gummy smile are all unmistakably my grandfather's, though I don't know if I've ever seen a picture of him that young.

"And my grandfather, Augustus Orleán," Vale whispers, "with my dad."

20 — VALE

Summer 1, Sector Annum 106, 10h10
Gregorian Calendar: June 21

"Even the hydroponics system is still working," Soren says, his fingers exploring a thin tube that leads to a glass pool flush with green plants and dangling, waterlogged root systems. The water is clean and clear. "There's still water flowing through these hoses."

"How?" Dr. Rhinehouse asks. He's staring around us throughout the greenhouse, as amazed and awed as Remy, Chan-Yu, and I were when we first found it.

"We think Meera made it her personal mission to keep this place alive," Osprey says, standing off to the side, as tall and lithe as a sapling. "And to keep it secret," she adds. "Remy said Meera suggested she come here if she ever needed a safe place. When she left Vale the note about the acorns—"

"Where's the power source for these grow lights?" Rhinehouse interrupts. Remy, Chan-Yu, and I asked ourselves the same question as we wandered down the aisles of the greenhouse. Eventually, we came up with a possible answer, although it doesn't make sense. My eyes meet Soren's, and I wordlessly point to the ceiling above us.

"The garden? The tree?" Rhinehouse responds.

"We're directly underneath the oak and the garden Kanaan loved so much. Seems like he tapped into the root system to power this place, just like the biolights, but on a larger scale."

Though I only met him a few times, I can feel Kanaan's ghost, his worn hands in the earth, flipping irrigation switches, taking notes, creating his plants down here as surely as he tended them above. It's been two days since we found this place, and I still haven't gotten over the shock of seeing my grandfather standing arm-in-arm with Kanaan, both of them with their children near at hand—children who would one day find themselves on opposite sides of an ideological war.

I never met my grandfather. My father adored him—idolized him, even—but he died young, when my father was only six. Probably about a year or so after the photo was taken that was so carefully painted onto the wall above the bank of computers. He failed to return from one of his solo scavenging adventures, and his body was later found by another team of explorers. The cause of death was determined to be *clostridium botulinum*, an Old World strain of a bacterium the OAC had already effectively wiped out with genetically targeted antibiotics. No one knew exactly how he contracted the bacterium, but it was widely assumed to have come from some fish he ate while foraging in the marshy northern shores of Lake Ayrie. After the autopsy, his body was burned instead of being ceremonially planted in a garden, as is custom. His death, along with several others on the fringes of the Sector, was one of the motivating factors for the declaration of No-Go zones, areas of the Wilds where Sector citizens are forbidden to go for fear of bringing back Old World toxins or disease.

I grew up without hearing much about him, and I think my dad was tormented by the early loss of his father, to the point where he could only speak about him on special moments of solemnity or emotion. When I successfully piloted my first airship, Philip told me how Augustus—or August as he was called more often—built the first working airship in the Sector, using the mechanical bones of an old harrier jump jet he'd found. As a scientist, he'd pieced the airship together out of necessity. In one of the vids, he said his goal was simply to go farther on his scavenging adventures than anyone else had ever been.

The hovering technology adapted from the harrier that allowed the airship to lift vertically into the air went on to become the basis of our hovercars and many of our drones, and the cold fusion reactor Gold discovered on one of his trips and used as an engine is now standard, with some improvements, in every airship in the Sector. He became a very rich man, and when he died, his will stipulated that half the profits from the machine's development be given to his son, which is how my father became one of the wealthiest men in Okaria without ever lifting a finger.

The rest of his money was donated to the Okarian Academy and the Sector Research Institute which helped catapult Okaria, once a small but growing town, into the beautiful capital city it is today, and attracted citizens from all over the Sector who hoped to send their children to the finest school in the nation.

From what I've pieced together by watching old news vids, my grandfather was an impulsive adventurer, a man who lived on the edge, always willing to take risks others shied away from. This made him, for many, a hard person to deal with. My grandmother was among those who refused to put up with his erratic lifestyle, and she left him—and my father—just a year after Philip was born. For the next five years, August took care of Philip, leaving him with my grandmother for only a few months out of the year when he went scavenging.

For the most part, my father refused to let the wealth he inherited go to his head. In fact, I think he spent most of his life trying to walk the razor's edge between the memory of his creative father and the reality of his staid and proper mother. One thing my grandmother did say, in the few times she spoke of her ex-husband, was that Augustus Orleán loved his only child more than anything he ever invented. From the look on my father's face in the picture on the wall, I'd say the feeling was mutual. The ache of loss blooms in my gut. Before I'd discovered the truth about my parents, I felt much the same about Philip.

"How many plants have you found?" Rhinehouse asks, his voice as rough as tree bark.

"At least three hundred distinct species, as far as we can tell," Soren responds. "There are some things here we've never seen before."

As I think about my own parents, I wonder about Soren's relationship with his and with Rhinehouse. I don't know what happened after Cara Skaarsgard's ouster from the chancellorship, but I do know they were effectively lobotomized, leaving Soren to fend for himself while he was still a student. Had Rhinehouse stepped in to help him? There's definitely a bond between the two men that is as near to father and son as I've seen.

"Many of them aren't native," Osprey adds. Rhinehouse furrows his brows at her, as if evaluating her academic credentials.

"And some of them aren't food crops, so they aren't all from LOTUS. Have you done a crossmatch?"

"Of the plants we've identified so far, we've got two hundred and thirty matches," Soren says. "A lot of those are subspecies. Kanaan had three different kinds of avocado—whatever that is—and ten identifiable variants of potato."

Rhinehouse almost smiles. "You've never eaten an avocado?"

Soren, Osprey, and I all glance at each other.

"Never even heard of it," Soren says after a pause.

"They have them in the Texas Federation," Osprey pipes up helpfully. "A traveler told me one time they put them on everything."

Rhinehouse stares at us for a moment, his face as inscrutable as ever, and then turns away, walking down one of the aisles. I can't tell if he's chuckling to himself or grunting. Either way he doesn't say another word as he paces the rows of plants, as slowly as a tortoise, giving his attention to each plant individually, as if introducing himself, before turning to the next.

As soon as we told the Director what we'd found, Rhinehouse announced he was on his way. There's no one in Okaria better suited to study the greenhouse, and as much of a curmudgeon as he can be, we all waited, holding our breath, just as we had for Chan-Yu to arrive, knowing Rhinehouse would help us find answers. Without him, it would be nearly impossible to understand the full extent of what Kanaan had created.

Now we watch him pace, surveying the plants, occasionally bending to smell or touch one, or to scoop up a handful of dirt from the soil bed and hold it to his nose as if it was a fine vintage. He glances up at the lights periodically, or checks the drip lines that drain into every soil system. We follow him at a slight distance as he progresses from rocky, sandy soils to plants so tropical there are misters set up above us—misters that, despite four years without constant attention, are still mostly functional.

"Kanaan Alexander was a controversial man," he says suddenly, after nearly thirty minutes of walking through the aisles. "His friends loved him, and he was fiercely loyal to them in turn. His enemies hated him and he held them in equally high regard. He was independent. Rebellious. Didn't give a damn what the Sector told him to do. Didn't socialize much, especially when he was older. He was ten years my senior, and we worked together at the SRI occasionally. He'd teach a class here and there, join in on a specific research problem. But mostly, he kept to himself. We were friendly, but not great friends."

"Did you know he was working on something this big?" Osprey asks eagerly, leaning forward on the balls of her feet, running her hands through her silvery hair. Rhinehouse stops what he's doing—scrutinizing a vine that's overtaken a whole corner of the room—to glare at Osprey for the crime of interrupting his thoughts. She cocks an eyebrow at him and crosses her arms, undeterred by his attitude.

"As I was saying," Rhinehouse continues, emphasizing every word, "Kanaan was also practical. His interest in science came not from a desire for fame, as it does for so many scientists in Okaria, but from genuine curiosity and a desire to find better answers to better questions. He loved to bake, to cook, to garden, and to explore, and his love for those things came from a simple desire for knowledge and experience. He was extremely passionate and equally productive, right up until he began to lose himself in the last few years of his life. I am unsurprised to see these facilities running so well even five years after his death. Without diminishing your friend Meera's accomplishments in keeping this place alive," Rhinehouse nods slightly to Osprey, "I'm sure Kanaan would have installed failsafes and backup systems at every turn, knowing that without him around to protect this great secret, his life's work would be lost."

"So what do we do with all this?" I gesture toward the rows upon rows of plants, hoping I won't be on the receiving end of one of his angry looks. He doesn't like to be rushed.

"We wait." Rhinehouse claps the dirt from his hands. "And we think." He brushes by us, heading toward the entrance, back to the dark, damp root cellar.

"What are we waiting for?" Osprey calls after him, stretching up onto her toes to watch as he leaves.

"Don't ask him that." Soren shakes his head darkly. He grabs her hand and pulls her forward, following Rhinehouse.

"For Moriana," Rhinehouse responds loudly as he ducks back into the dark corridor. Soren looks back at me, worry painted across his features, and I am reminded of the second purpose for Rhinehouse's visit: to talk to Moriana, to do what none of us could do and convince her to tell us everything she knows about Corine's planned genetic alterations.

I stare at the painting on the wall for another long moment before leaving, wondering at the friendship between Remy's grandfather and my own, a friendship neither one of us ever knew existed. It seems fitting that two generations later, Remy and I should find equal meaning in a different kind of relationship.

In the picture, I notice, August's eyes are the same color as mine—grey, salt-green, like the ocean I've never seen.

Rhinehouse hesitates at the door where Moriana has been held for two days. A flash of anxiety crosses his face, but his hesitation lasts only a second. As he flips the old-fashioned padlock and pushes open the door, he looks as stoic and cranky as ever. Miah jumps up from the chair he's occupied for hours and greets him warmly. As I enter, Demeter comes alive.

"Don't be deceived," she says. "Emotional readout based on microexpressions indicates nervousness and stress. Tension in the face and neck muscles. Tight jaw. Eyes focused but roving. And I'm not talking about Moriana." Her voice is grim.

Who, then? One glance at Miah tells me all I need to know. He looks hopeful, almost happy. But too much so. His eyes are too bright, his smile too wide for the occasion. There's a touch of insanity there. Is there such a thing as too much hope?

"Oh, gods," Moriana says weakly, sitting up as the door opens. It looks like she'd been sleeping. "Dr. Rhinehouse?"

His expression doesn't change, but his posture does. His shoulders relax and he lets out a cavernous breath. He steps forward and, to my great surprise, walks over to Moriana's bed and sits down next to her.

"Moriana," he says quietly.

"Surely you're not … one of—"

"I am." His voice is gentler than I've ever heard it. "I have been since I left Okaria two years ago."

"I heard the rumors," she whispers. "But I never believed them."

"It is difficult to believe that two people who once shared the same values could diverge so sharply." Rhinehouse's voice is rife with bitterness and loss. I wonder what history is behind those words.

Her eyes flit to Miah, and then to me. I grit my teeth as Moriana starts to shiver. The heat of the afternoon tells me it's not because she's cold. "It is strange I find myself on opposite sides to so many people I once trusted."

Rhinehouse watches her for a few minutes before continuing.

"How are you?" he asks at last. She shrugs, looks around. We locked her in the most modest room in Kanaan's house. It was the only one without broad windows to the outside. Even so, the room is nicer than many flats in Okaria, with polished wood furniture, bright walls—though the paint is peeling in places—and elegant metal fixtures.

"Her expressions change every few seconds," Demeter says. "Nothing is constant. I can only read so far based on microexpressions alone." I nod, prompting her for as much information as she can give me. The camera we installed has a fish-eye lens, so the Demeter's view will be slightly distorted. I hate the idea of monitoring Moriana, remembering all too well when Demeter had to do this for Remy and Soren. "Lack of strong focus in the eyes indicates emotional distance. Possible nostalgia, reminiscence, or just a defense mechanism against another perceived act of hostility. Tight brow and jaw also indicate defensiveness. Perception of a threat, preparation for a verbal response. But her body language is weak and open. Slumped shoulders and open hands indicate acceptance, comfort, possibly even guilt."

"Fine," Moriana says after a long silence, "considering the circumstances."

"Did you know that Soren Skaarsgard and Remy Alexander were once taken prisoner by your friend Vale," Rhinehouse glances back at me, "and kept as prisoners in the capital?"

She looks at me. "He told me, but I didn't know how much to believe." Regret weighs on me. How different would everything have turned out if Miah and I had been honest with Moriana from the beginning?

"All of it. Your former classmates were tied to a pole for twenty-four hours before they were given so much as a drink of water." Rhinehouse's voice is casual, as if giving a lecture at the SRI. Moriana stares at him, her face blank. "Soren was beaten. Mostly by soldiers, but General Aulion wasn't above throwing a few punches himself. They were both drugged and interrogated. Remy was tortured by electric shocks. Soren was waterboarded." As Rhinehouse lists this information as matter-of-factly as if he was describing one of the plants in Kanaan's greenhouse, Moriana's face grows pale. She's not alone. My stomach churns as the weight of these crimes press into me, digging into my shoulders. "Fortunately for you, the people you are, as you say, now in opposition to, do not ascribe to such methods. Torture is the Sector's stock in trade. Not the Resistance's."

"Torture isn't legal," Moriana says. "It's in the Articles of Incorporation." Rhinehouse is silent for a long moment, watching, waiting. Finally she speaks again. "There must be some mistake."

"Do you believe I am lying to you now? Why do you suppose those of us in the Resistance left our comfortable lives, our friends, our homes? As a fellow scientist, what do you believe would drive someone like me to abandon my colleagues, my position, my livelihood, and my research to live on the run in the Wilds?"

She shakes her head as if trying not to hear his words. "I don't know."

"Or can you imagine the possibility that Philip and Corine might have broken Sector law?"

"I … I don't—" she stutters. "I don't know what to believe. Philip and Corine would never hurt anyone."

"They would and they have," I interject. "Many times. I told you she gave the order to kill everyone in that classroom. And I heard her give the order to have Remy and Soren assassinated. She ordered the attack on the Resistance that killed Brinn, that killed so many more."

"And Round Barn," Miah says quietly.

Rhinehouse nods. "Did Vale tell you OAC forces shot your cousin at Round Barn?"

Moriana's eyes glisten. "But he said Jahnu was okay."

"He's made a remarkable recovery," Rhinehouse says, glancing at Miah. "Probably because the woman he loves has taken such good care of him. And now that he has so much more to live for—"

Moriana's forehead wrinkles in confusion. "More to live for?"

"Jahnu and Kenzie. They're going to be parents."

Moriana rears back. "What? Kenzie Oban?"

"Being surrounded by people who care about you is good medicine. But having hope for the future is the best medicine of all." Rhinehouse walks across the small room to stand beside Miah's chair. "Moriana, you were one of the finest students I ever mentored in my lab, and I respect your intellect immensely. But let me tell you what else I respect. I have lived and worked alongside Soren, Eli, Jahnu, and Remy for over two years and on my honor they are among the finest people I have ever met. Now that I've met Jeremiah and have come to know Vale, I must add them to that list. I trust them with my life. They are the future of the Okarian Sector. My question is, do you want to be part of the future or will you cast your lot with the past?"

"The future is what we're concerned about!" Moriana shouts in frustration.

"A future in which citizens are no more free to choose their destinies than you are to leave this room. Is that what you believe in?"

"Citizen modifications are for the benefit of the whole Sector. We're doing what's best for everyone. Not just the privileged few. Everyone will know their place and be perfectly suited for their position. It's the ideal society, a society that works like a well-designed machine."

A groan escapes from Miah's throat and his face contorts as if he's in pain. "Remember when Corine didn't think I was good enough for you and Vale? Would you have me relegated to live my whole life as an engineering drone in some Factory town?"

"It's not the same, Miah," she says, her hands squeezing the bedcover as if she's trying to keep her temper under control. "You made it to the Academy precisely because you have merit. The modifications would only lock those in, enhance them. Like they did for Vale."

"Don't you think every individual should get to decide if they want to be genetically modified or not?" Miah's voice is laced with pleading. "You're stacking the deck for or against future generations."

"The deck's already stacked!" She jumps off the bed and begins pacing in the small space. "That's what genetics is all about, don't you get it? You think you have a choice now? Nature isn't self-directed, Miah. You can't decide who you're born to be. It's not survival of the fittest, it's survival of the most adaptable. We're just making sure every individual has the tools to survive in his or her own environmental niche."

After a long silence in which I have to bite back my retorts, Rhinehouse finally speaks. "So you and Corine have decided to take on the role of Mother Nature for yourselves. If you get your way, it won't be survival of the most adaptable, it will be survival of the chosen."

"No, everyone will—"

He doesn't let her finish. "You understand that Corine Orleán, backed by the OAC, is disseminating false information to the citizens of the Sector regarding the origin of the parasitic outbreak and the nature of the cure?"

"Yes." Her voice so quiet I have to strain to hear it.

"You have willingly helped Corine develop the pathogenic parasite that is sickening thousands of citizens?"

"I have."

"You have no issue with the OAC disseminating a cure to the parasitic disease that also contains targeted genomic alterations to each and every citizen without their knowledge?"

"No," she whispers.

"And you believe the mission to make alterations to the DNA of every citizen of the Sector, permanently encoding the strengths and weaknesses given to them by their MealPaks into their genetic makeup, is the right thing to do?" His voice creaks at the end, the way an old tree does when it finally falls.

Moriana hesitates for the first time. She sinks back onto the bed. "Yes," she says, her brows drawn together so tight it almost gives me a headache. "No. I don't know!" My heart leaps into my throat.

"If you can't answer definitively, you *know* in your heart something's not right." Miah's voice is thick with the urgency of hope.

"Perhaps there is a place for genetic modifications. Voluntary modifications done with an individual's permission. We can discuss the moral ambiguities of that another time. But right now, we don't have time. People are sick. Suffering. I'm asking for your help," Rhinehouse says. "I need you to help cure those infected with the parasite and to help derail Corine's plan to modify citizens' genomes without permission. Will you tell me what you know?"

She draws in a deep, shuddering breath, and for a moment I think she might cry. She shuts her eyes, squeezing them tight, her fists clenched against her legs.

"Please, Moriana." Miah crosses the room in two swift steps to kneel before her, taking her hands in his. "You know what they're doing is wrong."

The look on Miah's face and the ache in his voice weighs on me like anchors. I know what it's like to have the truth staring you in the face and to turn away. "Moriana, every single one of us has been in your position at some point. Every one of us has had to accept the truth."

She opens her eyes and looks at Miah. For a moment there's a flash of resentment. A cold anger. It vanishes quickly, replaced by tenderness. Kindness. The lines around her eyes soften and her whole face relaxes into the Moriana I used to know. The Moriana I want so desperately to believe in. I haven't seen her so unguarded since the night of the Solstice ball.

"Okay." Her voice breaks. "I'll help you." She looks up at Rhinehouse. "I'll tell you everything you need to know."

Jeremiah sighs and drops his head into her lap, pressing her clasped hands to his cheek.

"Thank you," he says, his voice so low I can barely hear it. Even as Rhinehouse smiles, a rare sliver of sunlight through a stone-faced edifice, a dark voice wells up inside me. *Don't*, it says. *Don't trust her*. But I quiet the voice and push it away. Without her, we've already lost.

21 — REMY

Summer 2, Sector Annum 106, 17h13
Gregorian Calendar: June 22

I run my hands across a strange plant that looks like a mix between a pin cushion and a cactus. It grows in little groups and sits snug in the soil. A few have bluish green or yellowish green shoots and seem to be a bit wooly in the middle, with little white hairs sprouting around the top like an old man's beard. I shake my head in amazement at how many shapes plants can take. I bend down to examine the stalk, look for signs of seeds or other ways of propagation, and note how dry the soil is at its roots. I have no idea what it could be, or even what kind of plant it is. As widely as Kanaan and Gold traveled, who knows where they dug this one up, but one thing's for sure: I've never seen anything like it before.

We've been spending every free moment exploring the greenhouse trying to identify the plants. I recognized one right away my mother used—a tamarind tree growing in a corner of the room that's since exploded to the point of pushing up against the ceiling.

"Maybe it can help relieve the symptoms from Corine's parasite," Saara said, taking notes frantically as I explained it has antipyretic properties. "If it's a fever reducer, I can try it out on a couple of the workers I've met while going with Zeke on his supply runs."

With high hopes for what else we might find, we kept looking. Some of the plants have neat handwritten identification signs stuck in the soil at their roots, but not all of them. And Kanaan's computers have a wealth of information on them, but some is written in a code we have yet to figure out. With Demeter's help, we've been able to identify many we'd never seen before, but some remain complete mysteries, and Demeter can't find anything that resembles them in her database. It's a strange feeling, realizing we've discovered—or rather, rediscovered—what is essentially a whole new dimension of botany. A dimension we barely understand. And everything we learn—or as Chan-Yu says, everything we think we know—seems so bizarre it's hard to believe. Take the acorn pendants. Chan-Yu disappeared for a full day, taking all the pendants and Osprey's astrolabe with him. When he returned, he walked around the garden, studied the tree, spent hours in the greenhouse, and then disappeared into the woods only to come back shaking his head, a look of wonderment written across his face. He'd been visiting his sister, Soo-Sun, and together they'd come to a conclusion. The Outsiders had long known that the astrolabes acted as tracking devices with the pendants as beacons signaling their location. The Wayfarers had been using them that way for years. But how did they work? No one knew. No one except my grandfather and maybe Gold. And now Chan-Yu and Soo-Sun. I can't begin to understand it; the idea of plants using chemical signals transmitted through the common mycorrhizal networks to communicate just seems too other worldly.

"Anyone found anything interesting?" Vale calls out from several rows over.

"Plenty," Soren replies from the other side of the greenhouse.

"I've got a weird one here," I say. "Where's Rhinehouse and Osprey when you need them?"

"Rhinehouse is still with Moriana and Miah," Soren says. "And Osprey will be down soon."

"Still wish Demeter could magically ID the whole lot of 'em," Vale says, coming into view from behind a large palm frond. My heart pauses, lagging for a moment behind its regular beat. He stops and touches his hand to his cheek. "Where did those come from?"

"What?"

He steps close and draws his thumb over my cheek bone. "You've got purple smudged on your cheek."

"Oh, that. I found some purple berries over there that stained my fingers when I crushed them." He slips a hand around my back to pull me to him and instead fishes the paintbrush out of my back pocket.

He holds it up. "Where'd you find this?"

"I used to paint here, when I was little. So I did a little searching and found a box with old brushes."

"And you painted something with the purple berries?"

"Do you want to see?"

He nods. "Of course."

Hand in hand, we duck through the rows to near the far end of the greenhouse, where, on the polished white wall, I painted a rough but distinct watercolor-style portrait of Tai. "Purple was always her favorite color," I say softly.

"You did this with a few berries?" He sounds astonished.

"With a few brushstrokes. It didn't take much."

"This is amazing."

I nudge him with my shoulder. "You say that every time you see my work."

"And it's true every time." He pulls me to him, closing the space between us. His body feels as if it was cut out of the contours of my own.

"That's how I used to feel listening to you play the piano," I whisper.

He opens his mouth to respond, but pauses and looks away. "I try not to think about how much I miss my music."

"One day," I say. "One day this will be over, and you can play all day long if you want." He looks down at me.

"That's the first time you've talked about what happens after this is behind us."

I put my hands on his chest, stand on tiptoes, and brush my lips against his. He wraps his arms around me and I feel his heart thud against my palms. A moment later, my body is pressed between his and the wall, and—

"Where are—?" Soren interrupts, rounding the corner. I push Vale away, embarrassed, but Soren waves dismissively. "I've found something I want Rhinehouse and Osprey to look at. You want to see?"

We follow him down one of the long corridors.

Soren points to a series of strange plants growing in a shallow pool of water. "Watch this." He pokes at one of them and it opens up like a mouth with long spiny teeth. "Ever seen anything like that?" He pokes at another and the same thing happens. "I brushed against it and it opened wide like it was going to bite me."

"A plant with teeth? Is it carnivorous?" I stick my finger toward it, but Vale grabs my wrist.

"Watch it. I don't want to pull one of those teeth from the end of your finger."

"And how about this one?" Soren points to a short tree in a separate pot with small, bright green oval fruits hanging on its slim branches. Ever seen one of these?

"It's a lime," Osprey says, appearing out of nowhere. "They grow in the southwest, where it's drier. Okarians don't cultivate them, but Chan-Yu goes wild over them. Squeezes them over his food and puts slices in his drinks."

"Where is Chan-Yu?" I ask.

"Disappeared again. He'll be back." Osprey waves her hand as if Chan-Yu's sudden appearances and disappearances are no big deal. But I feel much better when he's around.

"You know all about rosemary, of course?" she says to us, moving down the row of plants. Soren and Vale nod dutifully—rosemary is not my favorite herb, but Rhinehouse seems to think it's a seasoning on par with salt and pepper. "This is a cousin of rosemary. It's called salvia. You might know it as sage."

Soren nods. "I've seen it growing wild. And I think I remember it in the urban farms in Okaria."

Osprey gives him an appreciative smile. "This is desert sage, though. More fragrant than its woodland cousins." She cocks her head my way. "Your granddad was apparently very interested in plants from climates outside of Okaria. Many of these don't grow naturally at this latitude."

"Do you know what this one is?" I ask, back at the plant I was studying earlier.

Osprey bends down for a closer look. She runs her fingers over the fuzzy hairs, and looks up. "I don't believe it. I wonder if Kanaan and Gold used this."

"What is it?" Vale asks.

"It's called peyote," she responds.

"What it's for?" I ask, intrigued.

"Magic."

"Vale?" I say. Stretched out on the bed reading one of the books he found on twenty-first century composers, he looks up. "You know when you used to play the piano, and everything else faded away and it was just you and the music?"

"Yeah. I miss that."

"It's like me and my art. When I'm in the zone creating, it's only me and the colors, the forms, the shapes. It's like nothing else exists but the flow."

"I know exactly what you mean."

"I told you Soren taught me some breathing and relaxation techniques after my mom died. I want to use those with you to create that same kind of flow."

"What are you thinking?" he asks, setting the book down and leaning forward.

"We've got all these plants in the greenhouse, and we don't know what to do with any of them. Like the peyote. Osprey says it's supposed to open the inner eye to the truth, or to new dimensions of the truth. How can we use that? How can it help us? Meditation is supposed to help you empty your mind so you can be open to the universe, open to new ideas."

I sit cross-legged on the floor and hold my hand out to him. The moonlight filters in through the windows, and the low light from our biolantern creates an undeniably romantic glow, but I set those thoughts aside. We've got all night for that.

"Corine has outmaneuvered us repeatedly. We're boxed in, so we need to think outside the box." I take his hands in mine and rub my fingertips over his knuckles. He sighs. "We're going to breathe together."

I get comfortable and glance out the window. "Now, we need to take in the energy from the moonlight. Let's channel Tai, my mom, Soren's parents, Meera, Professor Hawthorne, all the teachers and mentors and friends we've known and lost. And those who are still with us." I close my eyes and pause, thinking of everyone I've ever loved, everyone I've ever cared about. "Let's imagine we can gather all their energy and intelligence right here between us. Breathe in, breathe out. Empty our minds of everything we know about our situation. Just feel their energy. Imagine they are connected to us, sharing their gifts." I pause and breathe in and out slowly for several minutes. Then I go on. "Now, let's consider our goals. How do we want all this to end?"

Vale's breathing is steady, comforting.

"I picture you and me together." Vale's voice is soft but firm. "I imagine us surrounded by friends, with music and art and laughter filling our days. How do we get there?"

"No more violence." I close my eyes.

I remember something from my days at the Academy. *Professor Lark, Architectural Foundations: A building is nothing without its foundation. Remove the support beams and the building topples. A strong building is resilient to many types of pressures, but every one has its weak spots.*

"You know your parents best, Vale. You know our strengths and weaknesses and you know theirs."

"Their strength lies in controlling the reins of government, their ability to speak directly to the citizens, their willingness to violate the law and wield military power against us."

"And their weaknesses?"

There's a long silence. I can feel him thinking. His fingers tighten against mine, his breath thrums in the quiet air, and his index finger involuntarily twitches, as if a thought is preparing to spring forth. Finally he croaks. "Me. They love me."

What would Meera say if she were here with me now? *There are few people in this world immune to love, Remy.*

I squeeze Vale's hand, imagining the pain he's suffered all these months since discovering the truth about his parents. "Loving you is no weakness, Vale. But it is a vulnerability."

The Director: We must analyze their weak spots, hit them where it hurts.

"This might be a reach, but—" Vale begins, hesitance in the small quaver of his voice.

"Go on."

"You're right that we need to think outside the box. We also can't win with one strategy alone. We need to combine the full force of our power, not just yours and mine, but everyone in the Resistance, in a way they would never expect."

"Bear's march," I whisper. "It's the perfect moment."

"We can use it. We can use their energy, their momentum." He sighs, shifting gears. "However much I repress it now, there's still a part of me that loves my mother. I've been denying that feeling to convince myself—and others—that I am fully with the Resistance. But she's my mother. She's lost touch with the things that used to motivate her, the things she taught me to believe in so fervently, but they must still be there. Buried." He pauses. "Osprey said the peyote was 'magic.' Rhinehouse said its hallucinogenic effects have been used for thousands of years to enhance spiritual rituals."

I don't know where he's going yet, but I can sense his excitement. "He said ancient peoples used to go on Ghost Dances where they'd use it to go into a trance. They thought they were reuniting the living with the dead, and before a battle, they'd ask the spirits to join them or to fight on their behalf."

I think back to when Bear and I traveled to the Farms. When we used the dreamweed to trick that guard into opening the doors to the Dietician's lab so that I could disable the MealPak formulas. *You've got stars in your eyes*, he'd said to me.

I let several more deep breaths flow through my body.

Vale's voice is low, urgent. "I need to get back to my parents. No games. No pretending I'm on their side. I have to confront them. Somehow I feel there's hope for my father, but my mother's turned her back on her humanity. If we can use the hallucinogen to hold up a mirror so she can see the corruption that has hardened her, the ways it has masked her true self, we may be able to break her."

Break her. What a terrible thing for a son to have to do. An image blooms in front of me. For a brief moment, a flash of the synesthesia I used to experience as commonplace comes back. The image is intense, glowing and shimmering in saturated colors. In one hand, Corine, eyes bloodshot and bulging, features contorted in pain, holds a bloodied knife to Vale's throat. His expression is serene, like a pale mist floating over Lake Okaria. In Corine's other hand, she grips her own neck with elongated fingers and enlarged knuckles. Behind them, the landscape is littered with bodies with thin wisps of bluish smoke trailing from each one, gathering above to form a single word in the charred, blackened sky: *Atone.*

I open my eyes and break free from Vale's grasp. I pull myself to my feet, and Vale follows suit.

"What's wrong?"

I shake my head, alarmed at the ferocity of my own thoughts. "Just an image. I'm okay. I need to take a break." I head over to the window. He joins me, rubbing comforting patterns on my back. I lean into him. "The darkness of my thoughts sometimes terrifies me."

"You've seen a lot of dark things," he whispers.

After a while, I ask, "Do you really think this could work? How could you get her to take the peyote?" The doubts flood in, filling me just as surely as the hope and light filled me during our brief meditation session.

Vale nuzzles my neck and whispers, "I don't know. But I am sure of one thing: we can't win with force alone. Even with our largest full-frontal attack, they'll take us down in an instant. Unless we dig out the root of the problem, we have no hope of preventing her from putting her plan in place. Moriana says everything is almost ready and that they hope to start inoculating citizens with her 'cure' by next week at the latest. We have no time and no other options."

I turn to face him, my body aligning with his, his words still hot on my neck. "I want this nightmare to end. I want to start over. I want—"

Vale's hands are firm on my waist, and it's suddenly hard to think about anything at all. I reach for the spot where his neck meets his shoulders and pull him down to me.

"—you," I say, and stand up on tiptoes to press lips against lips, limbs against limbs. Vale's hands spread like two fans against my back, like he wants to touch as much of me as possible at once. The need to touch all of him fills me like fire. Like flames dancing in shards of moonlight, we swirl higher, faster, growing wild and hungry for that white hot zenith emerging between us.

"Wait," Vale rasps, pulling away. I frame his face with my hands, sending him that voiceless question, and he smiles so I know that everything is still okay. The flame abates and he kisses my lips, my jaw, my forehead, my ears, whispering between touches: "I want to savor this."

And so we savor it. Every delicious touch, every searing word we share, every awkward tangle and the light, easy laughter that follows. After, we lie together in the moonlight and name our greatest fears, laying them to rest for the night. Mine: that everyone I love will die, one by one, until I am just a graveyard clinging to what once was beautiful. His: that everything he believes in will be proven impossible, dream stuff best left tucked so far away you forget it even exists. Mine: that Evander Sun Zi will burn us all to the ground and my last memory will be the smell of bodies burning. His: that his parents will hurt him in the name of a sacrifice of love for power. Mine: that Kenzie's baby will know a world of betrayal and corruption. His: that the nightmare will never end, and we'll never have a family of our own.

"The one thing that I feel sure of more than anything else," he says with a devastating moonlit grin, "is that your freckles are adorable." His fingers trace a pattern across my nose and cheeks, his smile turning serious. "And by that I mean that I love you more than anything I've ever loved before. You are my music."

This morning, everything about my grandfather's house feels alive, electrifying. After getting up early yesterday, we discovered that Chan-Yu had mysteriously reappeared, to my great relief. With Moriana still under lock and key upstairs, the rest of us gathered for breakfast and Vale told everyone his ideas about using the peyote. We brainstormed for hours, coming up with some ideas that are terrible, that would surely get us all killed. And some that might actually work. Finally, we all squeezed into the comm room, and Eli and Zoe managed to get Zeke, the Director, and Bear patched in so we could outline a final plan. We then spent the day reviewing and fine-tuning logistics. Of course, the best plan is the most flexible one, and the best warrior is the most adaptable. So there is no saying exactly how everything will turn out. But one thing is certain: the time has come to pull the corruption up from the roots and plant the Okarian Sector anew.

22 — VALE

Summer 4, Sector Annum 106, 19h48
Gregorian Calendar: June 24

With hardly a breath or a wink Remy kisses my cheek and is gone, melted into the fog, a phantom spirit of dusk. She and the others are headed in their own direction, on their own mission, and I will reunite with them later. Hopefully.

My heartbeats are as loud as kettle drums.

Are you sure about this? I ask myself. Doubt creeps into my bones. But all I can do is move forward, one foot in front of the other, until quickly and quietly I arrive at my destination.

Moriana and I were the last ones out of Kanaan's house tonight, which is now as silent as a grave. We spent hours yesterday scrubbing the place down, removing all evidence, returning it to its original state of disuse, and carefully sealing up the greenhouse so it would remain hidden. I don't doubt that the drones will be able to trace our steps back to the house. But they won't stop there. Chan-Yu and Osprey laid a careful trail beyond the house and into the Wilds, to a cliffside shelter where they left food, clothes, signs of habitation.

Moriana is silent at my side, her footfalls soft in the encroaching dark. I watch her out of the corner of my eye. She doesn't smile, doesn't blink, stares straight ahead. With her hair tied back and her back erect, she looks almost military. I wonder what changed in her, what hardened in her. She's different, now, from the confident and carefree woman I remember from classes, social outings, the Solstice ball. I can't help but feel responsible for destroying that part of her. She reminds me too much of Corine.

Demeter, too, is quiet.

"Is this what fear feels like?" she asked me last night as I slipped off to sleep. "I'm afraid for you, Vale." I spent a tortured night dreaming of Persephone, Demeter's daughter from the myth, eating pomegranate seeds from the underworld and condemned to stay there for half the year as punishment.

Am I Persephone, descending into the underworld?

But when I woke up with a start, sweating and cold, Remy leaned into me and whispered in my ear, shushing me like a child, and I believed again.

It's going to work. It's going to work. It's going to work.

These are the words I tell myself as I press my palm into the reader at the gate to the chancellor's mansion.

It blinks red, identifying me. But the gate still slides open. Within a few seconds Moriana and I are surrounded by soldiers, at least ten of them, all with their weapons out and trained on us. I put my hands up in a gesture of surrender, and Moriana does the same. For a long moment, no one moves.

Then, one of the soldiers pushes the black visor on his helmet up, and I meet his eyes. It takes a moment, but I recognize him.

"Hey, Ren." The captain of the Guardians assigned to the chancellor's mansion, I've known Ren since my father was elected almost four years ago.

"Vale?" he says, squinting at me. He looks confused, unsure whether to aim at me or not, whether I am a threat or not. After a moment's deliberation, he opts for caution, and steadies his Bolt, once again leveled at my chest. "Moriana? What are you doing with him?"

Ren and Moriana are on a first-name basis?

"We are requesting an audience with the chancellor and Madam Orleán."

He glances back and forth between the two of us and then looks at the other guard, who nods. Ren lowers his weapon and speaks into his earpiece.

"Alert the chancellor. Valerian Orleán and Moriana Nair palmed in. They claim to be requesting an audience." We wait another few moments, the air hot and humid, so thick with tension I feel like I'm suffocating. Then, Ren nods at something over his earpiece, waves his hand in little circle, and addresses us. "Come with me."

They lead us to the grand, wood-carved doors at the front of the house. In step with Moriana, I walk through the doors, feeling like I am being led into the mouth of the underworld.

"If anyone offers you a pomegranate," Demeter says in my ear, "don't take it."

Inside, two of the soldiers holster their weapons and start to pat us down. Moriana looks unhappy at the prospect of being treated like a common criminal, but she doesn't protest. I watch her frown, glare at the soldiers, and wonder what she's thinking. *Can I trust her?*

Whether I can or not, I need her. Without her, my parents will never believe my plea, will never believe that I came here in good faith.

I didn't, of course. But they don't need to know that.

Blood pounds in my ears as we are searched. Our jackets are taken off, and they ask us to remove our boots. One of the men runs his fingers through my hair. He finds the pendant around my neck, and glances at Ren, who shrugs. How could they know to worry about a simple piece of jewelry, a trinket?

Finally, Ren nods, satisfied, and waves us in. I walk through the foyer and down the hall, feeling strange and alien in this place I once called home.

Philip comes around the corner first, his movements quick and excited. In a navy sweater and house slippers, he looks relaxed and casual. Quite the opposite of how I feel. There's almost a smile on his face when he sees us.

"It really is you," he says, his voice rich with astonishment, as if I've returned from the dead. Maybe I have. He comes up to me and puts a hand on my shoulder, standing opposite me, the same way he used to do when he was congratulating me or telling me something important. "I can't believe it."

"Vale." My mother's melodic voice rings out from behind my father. Unlike Philip, she doesn't immediately approach us. "And Moriana. What a relief to see both of you safe and here together." But she doesn't sound relieved. She sounds wary. Watchful. As she finally walks toward us and embraces me, I can feel her keep her distance. She is nothing like the Corine Orleán who took my hand as I returned to consciousness. *You can't imagine how I felt when you stepped off that ledge.* Then, at least, she still felt like my mother. She still thought there was hope for me.

Not anymore.

"Why are you here?" she asks.

"Corine," my father says, chastising. "We don't need to interrogate them."

"It's okay." I shake my head. "We need to be honest with each other. I'm here because—" I glance over at Moriana, who hasn't spoken a word since we left Kanaan's "—Moriana told me everything." I narrate as though no one else in the Resistance knows yet, as though Moriana only told me and no one else. She shudders as if in pain. Corine shoots her a glance that looks sharp enough to kill, but her gaze softens after a moment as she watches her protégé. "She told me about the parasite, and the cure. She said you're going to implement genetic changes to every citizen of Okaria. Without their knowledge. Just like you did to me."

I take a deep breath.

"We're here to ask you not to do this."

There's a heavy silence. Corine glances at Philip, and then at Moriana, before meeting my eyes again. Her expression is neutral, unreadable.

"Let's discuss in the meeting room."

She reaches out to take my hand, the first gesture of affection I've seen from her so far. As our fingers meet I feel a jolt, almost, some kind of energy I don't recognize, some connection I don't understand. It's no longer the connection between mother and child. She meets my eyes.

I know, she says silently. *I know who you are. You are not my son.*

Her boots click against the wood floors as she turns to walk down the hall. She pushes open a door to the right, leading into the small meeting room reserved for the chancellor and his closest advisors. Moriana immediately follows her, but my father turns to me first. He looks at me wide-eyed and opens his mouth as if to say something, but he can't seem to find the words. After an awkward second, he too follows Corine.

"Tell us more about your request, Vale," Corine says, as I sink into one of the plush leather chairs next to Moriana. "Why is it that you don't want us to move forward with our modifications?"

I am under no illusions that anything I say tonight will convince my mother not to proceed with her plan. But watching my father, his twitching fingers, his eyes jumping around the room, the way his gaze lingers on me, I think I have a chance with him.

I rub my fingers on the polished wood, tracing invisible patterns into the grain.

"It's not right," I say finally. "I know what the MealPaks do to the Farm workers. I've seen how their senses are dulled, how slow they are, like people who are half asleep. I know they're built for strength, not intelligence—"

"What need do they have for intelligence?" my mother asks sharply. Instead of retorting, I opt to continue as if she had not spoken.

"—that you have reduced their neural connectivity, their emotional responsiveness, their critical thinking skills. I know you've done all this with their MealPaks. I've seen it, Mom," I say, as she opens her mouth to interrupt me again, "and I know it isn't right."

Philip is glancing back and forth between me and Corine like we're contestants in a sparring match at the gymnasia, trepidation written all over his face.

"Vale, the modifications we plan to make to the people aren't bad." She looks at Moriana, consternation in her eyes, as though she's somehow responsible for the negative ideas I've gotten of their master plans. "They'll make people stronger, as you said. Faster. Able to see in the dark and to hear more clearly than any humans have ever heard before."

"You gave me all those things, too. I didn't ask for them, and I still don't know if I want them." Corine leans back in her chair and crosses her arms. I meet her gaze. I can't tell them I have no hope of convincing them not to move forward, that I'm here not because I can sway them to my side but because I have to be with them when everything changes.

"Unless you're planning to give everyone the same kind of modifications you gave me, you're effectively creating slaves. The Farm workers won't have a choice. Those in the towns won't ever have a hope of sending their children to the Academy. You're building a caste system, and no one will be able to escape their genetic destiny."

"That's already true, Vale," Corine responds gently, as if explaining a lesson to a child. "A Farm worker will never be a researcher at the SRI, and a scientist has no need of the strength and build of a worker. That's not a choice anyone can make. It's just how nature works."

"You can't change people's bodies and minds permanently without telling them why. Without telling them what's happening to them. Please, Corine," I plead. "Mom. Don't do this."

Moriana, to my left, still hasn't said a word. Philip looks agitated. Like me, he's leaned forward in his chair, sitting at attention. But he can't bring himself to come to my defense. Not yet.

Corine turns her head to the side and closes her eyes. Her hand, now resting on the arm of the chair, clenches and unclenches. For a long moment the only sound in the room is our breathing, the only motion my mother's hand balling into a fist and relaxing again. Finally she opens her eyes and drops her hand to her lap. She looks at Philip, and then to Moriana.

"What do you think?"

"Are the modifications ready? Did the transcription key work?" Moriana responds. Corine lifts an eyebrow.

"They are." Now that we're safely back in the Sector, will Moriana stand by me? Or will she turn tail and run back to Corine?

"I think we should delay implementation until next week. Call for a citizen referendum and a vote on whether the changes should be implemented. Since we all agree that these genetic changes will be beneficial both to the Sector and to the individuals—" she meets my eye, knowing full well that I don't agree with anyone else in the room about this key point "—there should be no harm in sharing our goals with the citizens."

Philip looks immensely relieved by Moriana's answer.

"I second Moriana's notion," he says, and my heart leaps in my chest. "Vale's plea seems well-founded. If there's public resistance to the idea, why move forward?" I wonder if he notices the irony in his use of the word *resistance*. "And if the people welcome these modifications the same way they welcomed the MealPaks decades ago, so much the better."

Corine glances around the table, and my breath catches in my throat. With Moriana's words and my father's second, we might actually have a chance. We might be able to convince her.

She stands, a clear signal the meeting is over. "Your father and I have a lot to talk about."

23 — REMY

Summer 5, SA 106, 3h50
Gregorian Calendar: June 25

A new moon renders the night pitch black. Save for one pale green biolight, carried by Bear and bobbing to the rhythm of his footsteps, we walk in darkness. In my pocket, wrapped in sheepskin, is Osprey's astrolabe, which will enable me to find my teammates throughout the day. Vale is already in Okaria at the chancellor's mansion, trying, with little hope, to talk Corine out of her plan. Chan-Yu went into the city with Vale and Moriana to deliver the peyote to his sister, Soo-Sun, who it turns out, has been working as a housekeeper right under Corine and Philip's nose. She was the one who delivered my note and who helped Bunqu return Demeter to Vale. Of course Moriana doesn't know about Chan-Yu's mission or Soo-Sun's role. Or about the five thousand men and women who will march on Assembly Hall today.

It's almost four in the morning, and we've marched nearly ten kilometers. Clothes rustle as bodies move against each other, gently collide, and move away. Eli grabs my hand and squeezes. I press against his side for comfort more than warmth, though the air is clear and cool.

We will enter the city from many directions, forcing the Sector to spread their troops across the capital. Everyone who was able came into Okaria via commuter train over the last few days on the pretense of visiting family or going to the Solstice celebration a few nights ago. The rest of us are coming by train, by airship, and some even by boat. The Resistance mobilized every airship we have, coordinating load and drop points outside the city, flying in loops for hours, to get as many people to the city as want to come. The faint breathing and footsteps of these hundreds of humans fill the air, just as I am filled with a swelling sense of anticipation.

Above us, the starry sky feels like a blank canvas onto which I paint my hope for this day—and for all the tomorrows that may come. In the darkness I feel myself shedding old skins I've worn. Hundreds of old Remys leave me like ghosts with each step forward. It is time, after all, to let them go. I imagine these ghosts floating up like smoke into the starry night, drifting slowly but inexorably toward the moon, while here, my feet firmly on the ground, I walk toward my destiny.

I take solace in our thousands upon thousands of footsteps. If nothing else, we will have walked together upon this soft earth. For the first time since I joined the Resistance, I blend into the crowd. The Sector would be hard pressed to locate Remy Alexander in this sea of people in a sea of darkness. We walk together, not as individuals with our own agendas but as a collective organism fighting for justice. We've all got a stake in this now. It's no longer about avenging Tai's death or my mom's death. It's about fighting for our lives. The coming rains might wash away the impressions of our bodies on the earth, but our ghosts will remain. We will have marched. We will have tried. We will have fought.

Darkness inspires, perhaps even necessitates, morbid thoughts. I shiver as I comprehend the very real possibilities of the day we walk toward. I might die when morning comes. The black ops could rain death down on our march just like at Round Barn, just like at Thermopylae. I'm scared, but ignoring that fear would be foolish. Instead, I embrace it. I feel its sharp corners and inhale its cold, pungent scent. I outline its contours in a constellation above me. To understand it is the only way. When I comprehend my fear, I can say: I see you. I *know* you. Fear doesn't like being called out, being recognized, being brought to light. It shrinks back when it is seen, leaving only knowledge and power behind. This is our greatest weapon against it.

So I tell my fear: No. Not today. Today, we march.

Bear's light suddenly stops and sways at his knees. We have arrived at a copse of trees at the bottom of a hill. About three meters to our right, the rails of the maglev tracks glisten in the moonlight. We line up along the tracks, no more than three deep. A moment of silence precedes the distant yet unmistakable hum of the coming train. *We'll have seven minutes when the train stops. Doors'll open and we'll all climb in quick and quiet. We'll be joining our friends from Sakari and Lesedi there. In forty-three minutes exact, we'll be at our stop just outside the capital.* Bear's words from our earlier meeting ring in my ears as my anxiety rises and falls like waves on a shore.

We're a little ways outside the limits of Siman, the closest factory town to Okaria. On a normal run, the train would be programmed to zip past us on its way to a depot where cargo would be offloaded and delivered to various locations around the Sector. Bear and Zeke's team hacked the whole transport system and programmed this train to stop at various drop points to pick up freeloading passengers. Though it's a cargo train, we're able to squeeze our bodies into position around the cargo and the other marchers, who greet us quietly. When the doors close, we are once again enveloped in complete darkness.

Last night, Miah loaded all the weaponry we have into the Sarus, along with Eli, Soren, Osprey, and me. Miah flew us to Siman, where Bear was organizing a swath of the march into Okaria. He was by turns giddy with excitement and solemn with the implications of the journey upon which we were about to embark. Nothing like this had ever happened in the entire history of the Okarian Sector—not since Jubilation Day. And here was a sixteen-year-old boy from Round Barn leading the way. With help, of course, from Zeke, Reika, Rose, and Louis, still recovering at Resistance headquarters, and other Resistance activists and thousands of sympathizers from the factory towns and Farms. But to not give Bear credit for his organizing efforts would be doing him a disservice.

"People are coming in from all different directions," Bear said, going over the final plans. "Those from the factory town will take commuter trains, sayin' they're celebrating the Solstice. Some in for vacations. Farm workers have to walk or we'll have to transport them. With Zeke's help--and the Director's-- we'll get them in by airship, train, or supply truck."

"Any sign that the Sector has noticed a spike in ticket sales and is investigating?" I asked, looking at Vale and Bear.

"Demeter hasn't picked up on anything. She says commuter tickets are only up moderately from last year's Solstice celebration."

"The Director kindly loaned us all her airships, an' over the day or so before the march, every pilot in the Resistance will be flyin' marchers out of their Farms and towns, and to the city."

"What happens when the march starts?" Osprey asked.

"At dawn every one of the marchers who's made it to the city will meet at the Bridge of Remembrance an' start down Rue Jubilation."

"What's phase two?" Saara leaned forward. She'd volunteered to go in with Zeke.

"With the map Shia gave us, we were able to chart the restaurants, smoke dens, and bars with UMIT-enabled bulletin boards with external displays. The Director has given us an ample supply of seedcoins, so we're going to upload information about the march on each one we pass. With groups coming in from every quadrant of the city, by the time we get downtown, there should be information displayed all over the Sector. Then we gather on Rue Jubilation and simply march to Reunion Park and end up at the steps of Assembly Hall."

"It's not going to be 'simple' with Watchmen, SDF, OAC Black Ops, and paranoid citizens all around," Vale muttered.

Bear shrugged. "I know. But this won't be a repeat of Round Barn. They won't be able to hide this or claim it's doctored video and that all the dead are Resistance actors." His mouth turned down in a sour scowl. "They can't massacre their own citizens right in the capital, especially not five thousand of their 'honored' Farm workers. And we won't be defenseless this time. Or hungry and confused. Everyone marching knows the stakes."

"What's the end goal, Bear?" Osprey twirled a short lock of hair around her finger over and over again though it just kept slipping out. I'd never seen her nervous, but her curled-up, bent-over posture and endless fidgeting betrayed her anxiety. "I understand you'll send a message to the Sector and the Orleán administration, but what are you actually going to accomplish by the end of the day?"

Bear was quiet for a moment. Finally he looked up and held Osprey's gaze. "The goal is to show ourselves. To show the privileged citizens in the capital that we exist, that we are real people, not just props in Sector news stories about the wonders of Farm life. We may not be educated and smart like them, but our voices and our lives are important, too."

The train starts to slow. We must be getting close. When the lights turn on, I lock eyes with Eli.

"And may the flowers bloom tomorrow, too." He nods at me. A prayer for tomorrows.

We adjust the hoods of our Firex fireproof jackets, and I rub my thumb along the trigger of my Bolt. Against my calves and inside my boots, my knives provide cold comfort, and I've equipped my waist pack with as many smoke grenades as I could find. Eli and I are prepared to defend ourselves and others. It is our duty to protect the marchers from whatever comes.

"You ready, Little Bird?" He looks down at me.

"Ready." I take his hand. "Tai would be so proud of you."

He holds out his arms and draws me to him. "Today is for her. For Brinn. For my parents."

"For all of them," I whisper.

He flashes me a look that reveals the crazy, exuberant—and dangerous— Eli I know and love as much as any blood brother. "So we'd better fucking be ready."

A surge of energy floods my body, and I know he feels it, too: the air between us, all around us, is electrified, static, almost as if every movement is playing out in slow motion. With our disguise makeup and a few more pairs of Kenzie's retinal scramblers, the drones won't recognize us right away. Osprey and Soren are similarly geared, but they'll be taking up the rear. The makeup won't last all day, though, so we've got kerchiefs to wear if we get sweaty and the makeup starts to fade. We're counting on the Watchers to respond first and hoping they won't escalate as long as we stay peaceful.

The train comes to a complete stop and the cargo doors slide open. Eli looks at me and winks. "Go time."

Bolts drawn, Eli and I are the first on the dock. Behind us, marchers pour off the train and, with Bear at the lead, stream into the warehouse. A worker turns, his eyes widening in disbelief. Eli flashes him a smile: *Hey, calm down, brother, we're just here to have fun.*

But the worker doesn't seem to take Eli's smile the way it was intended. He lifts his wrist communicator to his mouth and shouts, "Security breach! Red alert!"

I pull up my Bolt and fire. He drops to the ground, stunned, but not for long. Another man appears from behind a roof-high stack of crates, and he's down before I can react. Over my shoulder, Eli recharges his Bolt.

We charge forward toward the front of the depot and out onto Rue Descartes. And so the symphony begins. Bear, at the head of the line, lifts his bright red flag high into the air, leading us the short distance down Rue Descartes toward the Bridge of Remembrance.

We walk silently, as calm as the protests at Round Barn were chaotic, a few protesters peeling off now and again to drop seedcoins into the external UMIT displays. The sky is purple and pink, and dawn is just breaking behind us. This early in the morning, there aren't many people out and about, but a few early risers stop and stare, watching us approach with shock evident on their faces. Some open their plasmas, calling family or friends or the local Watchers' station. Although most marchers carry weapons of some sort, they are hidden in pockets and pant legs, jackets and boots. We want to inspire, not intimidate.

As we turn onto Rue Jubilation, Bear begins to chant, using an old-fashioned handheld speaker Eli rigged up. Behind us, I feel our ranks swelling. Murmured whispers tell us more and more people are arriving. I am amazed by how many children there are, walking hand in hand with their parents or perched on an adult's shoulders. A thousand voices fill the morning air as we echo our responses.

> *To the sowing,*
> *When we plant the seeds of freedom*
> *To the reaping,*
> *When we prune the rot of power*
> *To the harvest,*
> *When we gather the fruits of justice*
> *We are the Sector*
> *We are the Resistance*
> *We are the People*
> *Stand up, stand up,*
> *Join the revolution*
> *Rise up, rise up,*
> *For the revolution!*

We barely finish the first round of chanting before I hear the telltale buzz of drones, and they appear from every direction like a swarm, fanning out and taking position up and down the line no more than thirty meters above our heads. I'd almost expected them sooner. They hover overhead, moving along at our pace, not firing just yet. Soon we are facing a blockade, a row of Watchers mostly in hovercars blocking the street and sidewalks.

"No violence! Be calm, push through or go around!" Bear's voice rings out strong and clear, repeating the instructions drilled into us before we set out. "We are here to raise our voices for justice, not our hands in hate."

Today, the traits the Sector has bred us for come in handy, and many of the Farm workers tower over the Watchers, intimidating them with their immense size and strength. Born into a culture dedicated to hard work, it doesn't matter that they haven't been off their MealPaks for weeks. After Bear spread the word about what we'd learned from Moriana about Corine's plans, anger and resentment among the workers grew to a fever pitch. Those who showed up for the march are determined, dedicated, and willing to risk life and limb in the hope they won't be permanently programmed as slaves of production for the Sector elite.

But we don't get far before several SDF airships appear in the sky ahead of us. The big guns are here. A clear voice sounds through one of the Watcher's speakers.

"Halt! You are in violation of Sector Ordinance 43. You have not been granted a permit for this gathering, and all participants are subject to immediate arrest and detention. Furthermore, you have knowingly participated in the hijacking of Sector cargo lines. Whoever is responsible for these acts of lawlessness, step forward and we'll show your followers leniency."

Bear steps forward, his megaphone to his lips. "We are citizens of the Okarian Sector and have the right to walk freely and unhindered on the streets built with our labor." The Watcher tries to cut him off, but Bear's voice grows louder, more fierce. "We are Farm workers, the men and women who feed this nation, and will use Sector transportation as needed—including Sector trains!"

Bear turns around to face the crowd. "As full citizens of the Sector, we will march."

Everyone repeats: "We will march!"

Watchers step out of their hovercars and raise their Bolts. Although they're blocking our path, there are only ten cars and about twenty or thirty officers. The Watchers position themselves between their cars, standing shoulder to shoulder as the drones descend, green lights blinking rapidly, photographing faces to ID protesters in the Personhood Database—or to arm themselves for firing.

Discreetly, I set my bolt to DISPERSE and see Eli do the same from the corner of my eye. I nod at him and on the count of three, we raise our left fists, gloved in crimson cloth. Others, positioned throughout the crowd to echo our movements and amplify our message, follow suit and everyone armed with a Bolt readies their weapon.

"To the sowing!"

Bear begins the chant again, and the voices of the people rise into the air, the righteous roar of thousands. There are too many of us for a small contingent of Watchers to stop. We start to move around and push through their line when a Watcher raises her bolt at me. Eli drops her with a flash, she crumples behind her vehicle, and her Bolt clatters to the ground as I raise mine and send a cloud of electricity toward the nearest cluster of drones. In a heartbeat, up and down the line of marchers, the air crackles with static and Watchers and onlookers turn their heads to the sky as drones stop moving, immobilized, listing to the side. Bolts set to DISPERSE not only sting when they bite flesh, but will scramble a drone's guidance system, sending it either wandering aimlessly or, with enough repeated fire, dropping to the ground like a fly.

We move ahead quickly, and I try to blend in with the crowd. Another Watcher sees me with my Bolt and aims, but I fire before he has a chance to pull the trigger. I step over him and pick up his weapon, handing it to a marcher behind me.

The Watchers are in disarray. For the most part, they have no idea how to react, clearly unwilling to shoot into a crowd flush with children where very few people are armed. One Watchman shouts orders, another calls for help from the SDF, and others are scuffling as they try to grab a marcher here or there. I turn and see a Watcher throw a young girl to the ground, drop and dig her knee into the girl's back. I run toward them, plowing into the Watcher from behind, sending her sprawling. I grab her Bolt and pull the marcher to her feet as others bend over the Watcher, picking her up, holding her arms behind her back, and carrying her in front of them as they keep marching forward. One winks at me and says, "We found a new recruit!"

"You okay?" I ask the girl.

"Fine, just bruises." And a nasty scratch on her face, but that will heal.

"Thanks," she calls and runs to catch up to her friends as more drones appear, following us, awaiting orders. We try to disable as many as we can, but they just keep coming. They move like hummingbirds, thrumming overhead, flitting between buildings, darting out again. By this time, Corine, Philip, Aulion, and Evander will have received the Red Alert and been notified of the protest. But even they know attacking peaceful protestors in the heart of the capital would be unwise. At least I hope they know that.

I run along the left side of our group to make sure no one's fallen or hurt when I find Reika leading her contingent of marchers. "Any trouble getting in?"

"Nothing we couldn't deal with," she says with a tight smile.

"Injuries?"

"A few. We had to leave a couple of folks behind before boarding. I think one woman broke her arm in a fall. But she'll be okay. Her son stayed with her."

I look around and see an old man with a limp struggling to keep up. One either side, he's supported by two young women. The sight fills me with an odd combination of hope and sadness. We're in this fight together. When all is said and done, who will be there to pick up Corine? Who will support Philip? Or Aulion and Evander? Who will stand by them when power, position, money, and greed are not at stake?

I nod. "I'm going back to the front. Don't forget the safe spots." Before the march, everyone was briefed on where to stop and rest or hide if they needed to regroup or escape. *Safety matters*, Bear told everyone. *We are worth more to the cause when we are alive and strong. So stay alive, stay strong.*

Reika gives me a mock salute. "Yes, sir! Tell Bear we're right behind him."

With one last look down the line at Reika's group, I cut away from the march and into an alley, running ahead to get back to the front. As I run, I feel the adrenaline course through me, focusing my mind. I think of the chemicals flooding through my body and imagine them as swirling colors: crimson, like the cloth wrapped around my hand, azure like the arcs of electricity from my Bolt, and pure white, like the rage that blinds me when I think of everything that has led us here.

When I reach the front of the march, my heart drops. Eli's arms are pinned behind him by two Watchers, and Bear is on the ground with another Watcher standing over him and pointing a Bolt at his head.

"No!" The word is out of my mouth before I realize it. The Watcher looks up, and I see a flash of electricity travel its short distance. Bear spasms and lies still.

And that's all it takes. The marchers swarm the scene. A giant of a man with ragged scars on his hand slams a fist into the side of one of the Watcher's heads, then quickly frees Eli from the other one, bending the Watcher's arms up at impossible angles, all the while smiling down at the officer.

"Sir, we don't aim to hurt no one," the giant says, "but if you're figurin' on causin' pain to my friends, I will break your arms first and then twist your head plum off its stem."

A red-headed woman, with arms nearly as thick as the giant's, plucks the Bolt from the Watcher standing over Bear as two others bend over him. "You should be ashamed of yourself shooting a Farm worker! This nation was built on our backs, and this is how you repay us? We walk peaceably, and you shoot us in the street?"

I push through and press my fingers to Bear's neck. I look up to see Eli standing over me. "He's got a pulse," I say with relief. "Can someone carry him?" Another worker steps forward and scoops Bear into his arms as if he's no heavier than a child.

Eli turns to the crowd and motions at the two Watchers. "Let's take our new friends with us."

I pick up Bear's speaker and put it to my lips. "March on." We have less than two kilometers until we reach our ultimate destination: the Sector Sunflower monument at the steps of Assembly Hall.

When the shadows of more SDF airships cast darkness on the streets, the energy of the march shifts. As the airships approach, several open their bay doors, and soldiers attached to magnetic lines drop from the hulls. They land on all sides. They group into squadrons and form blockades, preventing us from dispersing onto side streets. The fear builds. Instead of marching of our own volition down Rue Jubilation, now I feel hemmed in, herded, claustrophobic. But still we walk. One of the other workers has taken the megaphone and is leading the chants. Beside me, still cradled in the big man's arms, I see Bear stir, his eyes fluttering open.

He shakes his head and the worker stops and sets him down, steadying him.

"You okay?" I look into Bear's eyes. "You got a nasty shock."

He shakes his head as if trying to clear it of cobwebs and turns to focus on me. "*Oui.* I'm fine." He looks up at the man holding him. "*Merci*, Leif."

"If you're okay, I'm going to keep marching," Leif says. "I want to be at the very front when we stop."

"I'm fine now."

"My honor, Miss Remy and Mister Bear," Leif says, nodding in respect, then striding off to rejoin his friends.

I look up as Bear stretches and shakes life back into his limbs. The airships are nearly one hundred meters away now, and in less than a minute they'll be right above us. I hear shouting in the distance and a flash of blue. Not good. Are they attacking?

"Bear, we have to get back to the front. The SDF is here. Evander's airships could be deployed at any minute."

He winces as if bracing himself against an invisible attack. Then he shakes it off and nods. "Let's go."

We jog along the edge of the march until we catch up with Eli. "Let me show you something." He motions us forward. At the very front of the line, marchers have unfurled a banner, seemingly stitched together from canvas grain bags. As it flaps in the wind, I read the words painted across it:

WE ARE CITIZENS, NOT SLAVES
RISE UP FOR THE REVOLUTION

Eli's face glows with crazy energy. And then I notice what's different, and my eyes grow wide. He's wiped his makeup off in smudges.

"I was getting sweaty," he says with a shrug. "Guess they gotta deal with the real me now."

"It's not going to be long before the drones recognize you."

"Let's not delay the inevitable." He slings two extra Bolts he's found, presumably from some of the Watchmen, behind his back and holsters two more. Looking up into the sky at the drones and the looming airships, he looks like someone about to jump off a cliff. I know Eli doesn't want to die today any more than I do. But we both know that today is our chance, our moment. And Eli is ready to give everything he's got. "These drones are annoying as hell," he says. In a move that looks as natural as his crooked, easygoing smile, he sets his Bolts to DISPERSE and, using one after the other, sends waves of electricity humming through the air. Drones spin out of control, list sideways, or drop to the ground. Bear and I join him, shooting as many as we can.

The sun has risen to a full morning glow, bathing the streets in light. Everything is surreal. The sky is too blue. The leaves are too green. The flowers too vivid. The air is soft, warm, but with a cool, comforting breeze. Perfect. Surely nothing bad can happen on such an exquisite day.

And then I see Evander's dragons appear ahead of us like black storm clouds, casting huge shadows on the streets. The sight of these beasts enrages the marchers and the chants grow to a fever pitch, voices raised in fury and fear. These workers know what fire means. They saw fire. They saw how it melts flesh. How it burns and crackles.

Surely, I tell myself, *this is an empty threat. Surely they won't rain fire on us.*

I raise my left hand and Eli does the same. I turn and see crimson-wrapped fists rising above the crowd. "March on!" I shout, and the order echoes down the line. We're only blocks from where the road circles around before the steps of Assembly Hall, cradling the Sector Sunflower, a maze of trellised vines and hanging flowers leading to a central fountain.

While the dragons hang in the air above Assembly Hall, other smaller airships approach from the left and right. I look at Bear and Eli, wondering what will happen next. And then I know. A shower of tear gas shoots out from the bottoms of the airships, clouds of choking, blinding smoke drifting to the ground. Almost in a single movement, the marchers pull the scarves they've been wearing around their necks up over their faces. A few stumble, but they march on.

I grab Bear's hand and shout to Eli. "Sunflower!"

If Snake has done his job, all Bear and I have to do is shoot a few targeted Bolt blasts and the flames will spread through the maze, igniting the whole thing.

We saw fire at Round Barn. We know fire. But the only way to control what scares you is to embrace it. So today we will know fire once again.

24 — VALE

"What time is it?" I whisper, as quietly as I can, for at least the fourth time.

"Five hours fifty-five minutes," Demeter says patiently. The sky outside my window is already a brilliant blue, promising a cloudless day.

I've been awake for at least three hours. I slept fitfully, still in my clothes from the day, knowing that Remy wouldn't get a chance to sleep, that my teammates don't have the luxury of feather pillows and down comforters, knowing that today could be our only chance to destroy the empire my parents have built. I try not to get too impatient, wondering when I will be woken by the guards, or by my parents. Will they believe my plea from last night, hear that all I want is a compromise, a reconciliation? Will they ask me calmly what I know about the revolution at their doorstep? Or will they drag me out of bed, throw me in a cell, and lock me in with Aulion until I tell them everything I know?

"What's happening?" I ask Demeter.

"The march is gaining steam. Defense Forces are gathering on the edges of the crowds, and the chancellor's airship has arrived at Assembly Hall."

I might be locked in my room, but Demeter can tell me everything that's happening. By monitoring the Sector navigation system, she can see every Watchman's steps, every hovercar's movement, every airship in the sky. By tapping into the security feed, she can see through the eyes of every camera drone in the city.

I hear boots pounding outside. *Is it time?* The door is thrown open, and a bright light from the hall illuminates my room. I sit up in an instant and throw an arm over my face, shielding my eyes from the light. But I have no way to defend myself when a strong pair of hands forcibly turns me onto my stomach and shoves my face into the pillow. There is pressure against the back of my head and for a moment I panic—*are they trying to kill me?* I start to fight back, kicking out against my attacker, and then feel cold metal against my wrists. Handcuffs. The pressure lets off my head, and I am pulled out of bed and down the hall, a pair of hands on each elbow. I might have slept fully dressed, but I took my boots off. I am hyperconscious of my bare feet against the floor as they half carry me down the hall.

I guess they went with the drag-me-out-of-bed option.

I don't bother to resist, choosing instead to stumble along with them as they rush me down the stairs and out the back door to where there's a small airship landing pad. This is okay, I remind myself. *This is good. This is all part of the plan.* There are two more soldiers waiting there. They watch as the first two—I realize now they're black ops, not SDF—load me onto the waiting airship and push me into one of the seats. One of them throws my boots at me, as if I can put them on with my hands pinned behind my back, and the second pair loads up behind us. All four of them remain at my side as the ship lifts into the air. The destination must have been pre-programmed, because no one so much as touches a control panel, and the airship starts gliding without direction.

Where are we going? I want to ask.

"Destination programmed for Assembly Hall," Demeter says on cue.

I wonder where Moriana is, if she, too, has been dragged from her bed, handcuffed, and loaded onto an airship. Or is she sleeping peacefully, undisturbed by this morning's events? Demeter is silent, and I can only assume she knows nothing.

It doesn't take long to get there. It's not even a ten-minute flight from the chancellor's mansion to the capitol complex. My mind is racing so fast I can't keep track of my thoughts. I remember the meditation exercises Remy and I did a few nights ago, and I tell myself: *breathe.*

But my head is spinning, too full, too chaotic. Instead of clearing my mind, emptying myself, I focus on channeling my thoughts into what must happen next.

As if anticipating my questions, Demeter whispers, "Everyone's okay." For now.

The airship lands on the rooftop docking bay at Assembly Hall, the same place I began and ended my days when I was Lieutenant Orleán, Director of the Seed Bank Protection Project. I want to erase that part of my history, to take some of Remy's charcoal and black it all out, paint over it with vibrant new colors that tell a different story. But I can't change who I was then. I can't change what I did. All I can do is fight the battle in front of me today.

As soon as we've landed, the soldiers lift me to my feet. The bay door slides open and they drag me off the ship. I keep my feet under me as they race ahead, toward an elevator, where one of them puts his eye to a retinal scanner and keys in the code to the top-security basement level. The elevator drops with a *whoosh*, but judging by the hollow pit in my gut, I'm guessing my stomach opted to stay on the roof.

The elevator door opens. The soldiers pull me between them down a windowless hall. I know now where we're heading: the Security Center. I've only been in there twice in my life. There's a giant vidscreen in a half-circle on the wall that allows officials to view live or recorded footage from every single camera drone in the Sector. Built for crisis moments, national emergencies, or even war from beyond our boundaries, the C-Link database was partially designed to navigate and control all the drones in the system. Algorithms were created to enable the C-Links' personalities to filter video data, displaying only the most important footage from well-placed drones to those watching.

General Aulion, flanked by four soldiers, is waiting outside.

"Stand down," he orders the soldiers behind me. They release their grip. One of them pushes me forward, and I find myself face to face with Aulion.

I wish I still had that fire extinguisher.

"Search him," he orders. "More thoroughly than those fools last night. I want to know how he's helping those damn rebels outside."

As the two soldiers step forward and take off my handcuffs, the outer door to the Security Center slides open. I recognize the stony-faced servant who attended me during the weeks when I was a prisoner at the chancellor's estate, the same servant who brought me Remy's message encoded in *Les Misérables*, and who handed me the teacup that contained Demeter's new incarnation. *Soo-Sun.* Our eyes meet as the door closes behind her. She stands for just a second, watching me. I notice she has an empty platter in her hands. *The peyote. Did she give Corine the tea?*

I dare not acknowledge her as the soldiers pull off my jacket. "Hands over your head," one of them commands. Soo-Sun turns away, walks down the hall, stands with her back to the wall attentively like a servant awaiting a command. I comply, and one of the soldiers pulls my shirt off. He spins me around, pushes my hands into the wall so my limbs are exposed. The other guard produces a long, thin instrument I recognize as a subcutaneous scanner. She rubs it up and down my whole body, searching for implants, weapons, or devices. When nothing beeps, they push my hands back to my side and turn me roughly around to face the general.

What's this?" Aulion asks, stepping forward, noticing the acorn at my neck. He reaches his gloved hand to my throat. My heart pounds. With more finesse than I would have believed possible, he puts his fingers under the fine gold chain around my neck. He pulls it up and away from my chest, letting the pendant rest against his fingertips. "An acorn?" Aulion stares at it. His voice is so quiet I can see the soldiers behind him lean forward ever so slightly, straining to hear. "I've seen this before." His eyes harden, and for a moment it looks as though he's disappearing, gone, remembering something from a different world. Then he snaps back, his stony grey eyes zeroing in on me. "On the neck of a dead Outsider."

His hand clenches around the pendant, and he jerks the chain. A mild sting at the nape of my neck, and the pendant comes free, swinging loosely in his hands.

I take a deep breath. *It's okay*, I remind myself. *You don't need the pendant for this to work.*

"There's an Outsider out there," I jerk my head to indicate where the march is happening, ignoring his question, "with plans to put a knife in your heart." I pause, cock my head to the side, as if thinking. "Soren Skaarsgard is with her. Personally, I'm betting you won't make it through this day alive."

He narrows his eyes.

"Soren Skaarsgard is going to die today," he rasps, his hot breath on my face. "Along with his Outsider friend. As for you, I have no doubt your parents will find some way to exonerate you, to spare you once again. But rest assured, Valerian, the moment you and I are alone, when this whole thing is over, I'll slit your throat, and your pathetic story will finally come to an end."

He drops the pendant in the pocket of his military jacket and, finally, takes a step back. Soo-Sun, I notice, is watching this whole encounter, though her expression is still as stoic as a statue's. Aulion's eyes never leave mine.

"Anything else?" he barks.

"Nothing detected, sir," the soldier with the scanner replies.

Aulion nods. He turns to the door to the Security Center behind us, and holds his hand out to the DNA scanner. As the needle descends to prick his skin and confirm his DNA, I watch out of the corner of my eye as Soo-Sun turns away from us and walks down the hall, back to the elevator that leads to the rest of the building.

She knows Aulion has the pendant.

Before we walk in, the guards pull my hands behind me and slap the cuffs back on. The outer door opens, and I am flanked by four soldiers as I follow Aulion into the Security Center. Inside is a second identity check, and here Aulion presses his eye to a retinal scanner that emerges from the wall. A few seconds later the inner door slides open, and I walk in to see the enormous curved vidscreen lit up by dozens of separate video feeds, some small and tucked into the corners, cycling through different angles and images, others blown up into larger-than-life size and spread front and center across the screen.

"Laika, show us what's going on in the city's east quadrant." I recognize both my father's voice and the name of his C-Link, and sure enough, the videos quickly change, bringing up feeds from the team of marchers coming in over the Bridge of Remembrance. Have they identified any of my teammates? Demeter hasn't updated me, so I assume for now, everyone is safe and no one has been targeted.

As I walk into the room behind Aulion, my wrists bound behind my back, shoeless and shirtless, clearly a prisoner, the first thing I notice is Moriana.

She's standing at my mother's side with a shiny, new holographic plasma in her hands and her hair pulled back in a sleek ponytail. She is not handcuffed. She is wearing shoes. She hardly looks like she was dragged from her bed by two large soldiers and searched with a body scanner before being allowed into the Security Center. She glances up at me as I stare at her, the muscles in my jaw tensing, my worst fears confirmed. She doesn't even acknowledge me, glancing back down at the plasma as if I am no more to her than a speck on the wall.

I never should have believed you.

"The cameras in here are linked to the firewalled C-Link database," Demeter says. "I can't access them. I'll be relying on aural input only."

"Vale," my mother's voice rings out, sharp and commanding. "Good. You're here." I force myself to turn away from Moriana. I glance around the room to see who was called when the security briefings came in and the full extent of the protest became clear. There are several members of the Board of Directors, every member of the OAC Corporate Assembly's Security Committee, and two of my father's advisors. Everyone in the room is wearing light military clothing, designed for movement, not for glamour. No one is here this morning to look pretty. Everyone is prepared for action.

Corine has a saucer in her hands, and she takes a sip of the liquid in her teacup as she surveys me from across the room. I stare at the teacup, hoping against hope Soo-Sun did her job. Corine takes another sip and then sets the saucer down on a nearby table. She marches over to me, and heads turn as the whole room waits to see what will happen.

"Tell us everything you know about the march."

"I don't know—"

"I am tired of being lied to!" she shouts. "I am tired of trying to save you, to redeem you, to bring you back to the security of the world we built for you. You fought for the Resistance. You shot Sector soldiers—our soldiers—for them. You have worked against everything we once fought for together. You have lost your way, and I am tired of picking you up and putting you back on the right path. Now, I only want the truth. Tell me what they're planning, Vale, and maybe one day, when all of this is over, our paths will reunite again."

I gape at her. It's the most forthright she's been in front of me—in front of anyone, I'd wager—in years. When I was a child, she would have storms of rage where she would shout, throw things across the room, punch the walls with a violent energy I didn't recognize and didn't know how to contain. Only on very rare occasions—maybe three times before I was fifteen—did she do this in front of me. Most of the time she was wise enough to cordon herself off in a different part of our house, or walk outside to a secluded spot in a park. But I could still hear her, sometimes, through the walls or windows. Later, I realized that as twisted as it was, I actually enjoyed seeing her in those moments—she was normally so polished, so presentable, that her fits of anger seemed like the only times I ever got to see who she really was.

She hasn't shouted at me, or anyone, like this in years. At least to my knowledge. I'd thought she'd gotten past them, but this reminds me of those old moments, when I could see the raw and honest Corine, the one who finally took off her mask and revealed the monster below.

Aulion, standing slightly in front of me so I can see his face in profile, smiles. *He recognizes a kindred spirit*, I think bitterly.

I start talking. If Soo-Sun did her job, and Corine's tea is more than just leaves, all I have to do is buy time.

"It's a peaceful march," I say. "Mostly Farm and factory workers. Some from the city, Resistance members, and even a few Outsiders. All they want to do is be heard. All they want is to be healthy, to be given the right to choose their futures, to be—"

"Don't philosophize, Vale," Moriana interjects, rolling her eyes. "We've heard it all before."

Philip, for his part, looks no more certain now than he did last night. If anything, he looks deeply unsettled. His cheeks are pale and his eyes bloodshot and ringed with dark circles. He's not paying much attention to the drama unfolding between me and Corine. His eyes flit to us occasionally, but for the most part he is watching the action on the vidscreens with all the attention of a worried parent at the bedside of a sick child.

"What do the marchers hope to accomplish?" Corine asks.

"Nothing," I respond, "except to voice their pleas for freedom, for the right to choose their own paths."

Corine turns to the people watching us, the board members and political advisors, people in the highest positions of power in the Sector. They wear boots of the softest leather, sip from engraved teacups, and dip silver spoons into tiny pots of clear, golden honey, even here in this top-secret room in the bowels of Assembly Hall. I remember the drawing Remy did for the vigil: fruit and vegetable plants sprouting out of human skulls planted in the earth. It occurs to me that to these people, giving the Farm workers freedom is the same as destroying their way of life. If I learned anything from my obsession with history at the Academy, it was that great wealth and political oppression always go hand in hand.

"As you know, the genetic modifications we have been preparing for weeks are ready for implementation. Every individual with an entry in the Personhood database has a tailored profile of epigenetic changes ready to be delivered through the cure to the parasitic pathogen." Moriana meets my eyes as Corine speaks, addressing the whole room. "Those assembled here are our most trusted advisors and councilors. In light of today's march, should we begin implementation?"

"I'm on it, Vale," Demeter says into my ear. "I'm going to see if there's anything I can do, any way I can stop it."

But I know already that the odds are slim to none she can stop the whole machine of the OAC as it shifts smoothly into high gear, prepared to forever alter the lives of the millions of citizens of the Okarian Sector.

Several people glance around at each other before raising their hands, or— in one or two cases—shaking their heads in a confused *no*. One of the women I recognize is the President of the College of the People, Olivia Renteria, one of my father's advisors. Philip swivels slowly, looking at Corine as if he's just now hearing her, just now becoming aware of what's happening in the room around us.

"I count a majority," Corine says. She nods at Moriana. "Miss Nair, I am dispatching you to OAC headquarters to organize dissemination of the modifications. I want every single citizen of the Sector inoculated against the parasite and injected with their personalized nanobots by this time next week."

Moriana nods curtly, turns on her heel, and marches out. As she walks away, she pauses at my shoulder.

"You forced our hand, Vale," she says quietly. "If you hadn't brought five thousand Farm workers down on our heads, Corine might actually have listened to you." She pauses. "But now it's too late."

She sweeps by me and is gone.

Summer 5, Sector Annum 106, 7h34
Gregorian Calendar: June 25

"We're almost there."

I pull Bear through the thick crowds of people toward the Sunflower. The marchers are mostly contained on Rue Jubilation, with Watchers and SDF troops keeping the crowds from dispersing. It appears they are under orders to contain the march, but so far there's been no directive for a full-fledged attack. Airships have sprayed tear gas and a few Watchmen have used Bolts set to disperse or stun to keep everyone in the street, but I haven't yet seen any escalation beyond that. Evander's dragons idle above, but so far they've been an empty threat.

Rue Jubilation starts at the Bridge of Remembrance and ends in a large pedestrian roundabout that circles the Sunflower. The wide steps leading up to the great doors of Assembly Hall unfold directly into the "stem" of the monument, a long brick pathway lined on both sides with neat rows of maple trees. You can't see the intricacies of the Sunflower design unless you see it from above. That's why the designers built hills on either side of the monument, with stairs leading to the top where benches and tables are situated. Looking down, you see that it is made of interconnecting pathways lined with trellises, all laid out in the shape of a sunflower's petals. In the middle, a row of bushes encircles a large plaza with a tall fountain. Here, the brickwork is laid out in the Fibonacci pattern seen in the actual flower's center. *A sunflower is a perfect example of clockwise and counter-clockwise spiral patterns found in nature,* I recall from one of my lectures, *and the Sector Sunflower was designed to honor both Fibonacci's genius as well as the endless beauty and order found in nature's designs.* The designer recreated this marvel of nature with eighty-nine spirals of brick going one way and one hundred forty-four the other way. At the very center, from where the spirals begin, the fountain acts as the source of the irrigation system, continually flowing through an underground network of filters and refreshing itself from rain barrels and water catchment systems. Around the fountain, a series of benches give visitors a chance to enjoy the cool, fragrant shade.

When I see Rose, Reika, and Zeke reach the steps of Assembly Hall, I know it's now or never. Bear and I duck behind several Farm workers and slip into the Sunflower. It's almost a relief, escaping the crowds for a bit of space. The chanting, shouting, and pounding of footsteps still fills the air, but the marchers are hidden from view by the tall walls making up the sunflower petals.

The Sunflower was built just twenty years ago, the young architect astounded that her plans won the premiere design award that year. Once inside, it's a maze of polished wood structures, a mixture of sustainably harvested elm, pine, bamboo, and cedar. Visitors explore the trellised walkways, all of which are adorned with a variety of flowering vines and hanging plants. When it is in full bloom, they are awash in bursts of yellow, but the keepers maintain it so that some flowers are blooming year round. Tulips, daylilies, mustard blossoms, daffodils, and chrysanthemum are just some of the plants I remember. The best time to walk through is right now, in early summer.

I touch my finger to some of the delicate petals, inhaling the scent of the friendship roses planted along this particular trellis. When I was little, the Sunflower monument was my favorite place to walk around besides my granddad's garden. And now we're going to destroy it.

"All good?" Bear asks. We run through the petals to the center, noting with satisfaction that the necessary preparations had been made the night before. Snake, risking arrest by lurking on government property after curfew, wired up a series of small explosives throughout the monument to form an invisible outline of the sunflower shape. In the very center, Snake planted the detonator. Once ignited, the trellises will burn and those in the airships above and on the top floors of Assembly Hall will see the symbol of the Okarian Sector go up in flames.

"Everything's in place," I say. "You ready?" I ask more for my sake than his. Bear never lived in Okaria, and though he likes gardens as much as the next guy, he has very little sentimental value attached to the Sunflower. I think of all the walks I took with my family here as a kid, holding hands, letting the scents wash over us. Tai refused to move on until Mom told her everything she knew about each plant. Sometimes that took so long, my dad and I would slip away and giggle to ourselves about how silly Tai and Mom were.

I flip my Bolt to the highest setting and point it at the detonator.

"Remy, watch out!" Bear points at an incoming drone, flying high above us, pivoting in our direction. It flashes green, recognizing my face and establishing me as a criminal. I swivel my Bolt up and around, and with no time to flip the switch to disperse, I hope my aim is true. I fire and the drone spirals through the air and drifts sideways.

I redirect my weapon at the detonator and pull the trigger. The Bolt blast connects and a flash of blue floods my vision. I look up. The base of the trellised framework of the Sunflower around the fountain area is alight. Low flames catch on the dry wood of the trellises and climb, lapping almost lovingly at the wood.

"Whoa," Bear gasps.

The flames climb, growing with intensity, and I realize we've placed ourselves at the center of the growing inferno.

"Let's get out of here," Bear says, heading west through the maze of petals and toward the stairwell across Rue Jubilation. We can climb the hill and get a good look at what Corine and Philip are seeing from the drone view.

We emerge from the monument to shouts of "Seize them!" An officer takes off running after us, and Bear and I take the stairs two at a time. He's soon ahead of me and I trip, slicing my pant leg open and bashing my shin on the edge of the steps. Already down, I roll over the side of the stair wall and drop into the lightly forested area on the side of the hill. My feet slip on the grass and I grab the tree trunks and low branches, using them for leverage to pull myself up.

I notice a drone heading toward Bear. From the partial cover of the leaves, I set my Bolt to disperse and aim. The drone sizzles and sparks and runs into a branch, then tilts backward and falls. The marchers start up a new chant as the flames grow below us. I shoulder my Bolt and follow Bear up the hill.

"The flames of freedom burn for us!" I notice a swell of sound as the front doors to Assembly Hall open. A figure strides out, two black ops in tow, with all the arrogance of a man without fear. From this distance, I can't make out who it is.

Bear climbs higher and points.

"Who is it?" I ask.

"The Dragon."

Evander's come out to play.

Evander carries a long tube and has some sort of pack strapped to his back. It's definitely not a Bolt, but the black ops hold high-capacitor, fast-reloading Bolts, a new model I recognize by the size of the weapons. I try to make out what Evander's holding, and it comes to me in a moment of dreadful recognition: a flamethrower used in forest management operations where controlled burns are necessary.

He walks down the steps, purposeful and slow, but steady. The black ops at his side fire a constant stream of shots into the crowd, carving a swath out of those gathered nearest the stairs.

"Bear, we have to stop them. Evander's got a flamethrower."

Bear's jaw twitches and his face grows white. He nods wordlessly and turns to head back down the hill toward Assembly Hall. With drones and soldiers still pursuing us, we abandon our plan to watch the Sunflower burn and return to the thick of the crowd.

"Move!" Bear yells, and the Farm workers on the hillside open a pathway for us. Evander walks down the brick pathway making up the Sunflower stem as the crowd shrinks back like oil from water. Though the SDF had the people blockaded from approaching the lawns of Assembly Hall, many were able to push through and run up to the building itself. With the Sunflower on fire, both marchers and soldiers press to the edges of the roundabout, giving the heat of the flames a wide berth.

Evander, I presume, has had enough of his former subjects singing and crying out against him. I hear the hiss of the flamethrower. The crackle of Bolt fire is constant and Bear and I break into a sprint. Screams and more shouting fill my ears. Several Watchmen turn in obvious surprise toward the source of the chaos. The crowd shifts as people run as fast as they can, tripping over each other in their haste to reach safety.

"You want fire? I'll give you fire!" he shouts. His eyes are bright as glass as the flames light up the people around him. "Who organized this? Show yourselves!" He spins around like a madman. We're at the edge of the crowd, which opens like a gaping wound around him. A few burn victims scream as others carry them away. Even Watchers bend to help the marchers move victims to safety.

As people to continue to fall, the chaos grows, and screams fill the air. What was just moments ago a peaceful demonstration has turned into a slaughter. Although Evander's flames are scary, it's the Bolt fire that is truly deadly. We have to stop the black ops.

Someone comes tearing through the crowd in exactly the opposite direction as everyone else. Wearing a Firex hood and a red handkerchief tied around his wrist, I recognize the figure as Eli. Granted some protection by the fireproof clothing, he charges into the opening and leaps onto one of the black ops from behind, jabbing a knife into his throat. The man thrashes in Eli's arms, but the wound is too deep. The other soldier swivels toward them but has no clear shot, his partner's body protecting Eli.

Bear steps into the opening and, with all of his strength, charges at Evander's back with the flagpole he's been using to lead the march held in front of him like a jousting pole. The blunt end hits Evander square in the small of his back, knocking him over. Seeing the danger Eli's put himself in, I sprint through the throng, searching for a clear shot. With black ops, I can't take the risk of stunning him. I flip my Bolt to kill.

The remaining soldier, focused on Eli, never sees me as I find my angle, take aim, and fire. Sparks fly on the pavement as my shot goes wide, and Evander's back on his feet in an instant. Bear and Eli turn, disappearing back into the crowd as Evander regains his grip on the flamethrower. He squares his legs, and flames shoot toward us, searing the air with white heat. The heat is tangible but too distant to be harmful.

"Take him down!" I shout. Evander's head snaps around toward the sound of my voice, but I keep moving, darting through the people at the edge of the circle around him even as he advances and the line of marchers retreat, trying to keep a safe distance. I keep my eyes out for Bear and Eli, but both of them are nowhere to be seen. As Evander looks for the source of the voice, a few protesters begin tracking him, keeping a healthy distance but throwing everything they have at him. The Watchers and SDF look on, some in shock, some clearly horrified, others egged on by his behavior. Out of the crowd, a few brave souls finally charge at him from behind. Just as they're about to reach him, I hear Bear's voice.

"Hey, Evander," Bear shouts. He's standing at the bottom of the steps of Assembly Hall. "You looking for someone?"

Evander pivots and points the flamethrower at Bear. If he's not careful, Evander will light him up like a firework. I try to stay hidden between and behind bodies in the crowd. If I can catch him unawares, I can blast him from behind. But in the melee, I'm buffeted by too many bodies.

My heart pounds as Evander approaches Bear with determined steps. Bear runs up a few stairs, and Evander follows, like a great stalking monster.

As soon as Bear reaches the top, he turns. He's got everyone's attention. Everyone's watching him. I know he started the morning with a handheld Bolt, but does he still have it? He looks down on Evander, the bravado in his voice ringing out. "Evander Sun-Zi, the people of the Farms are willing to spare your life if you resign from your position and confess your crimes."

Evander advances slowly, ignoring the thousands of citizens behind him.

"You killed innocent Farm workers at Round Barn," Bear says. I can see his finger's twitching. Is he armed? He's calmer than I could have imagined. "And I intend to make you pay."

"Are *you* going to arrest me, *Antoine Baier*?" Evander's identified him.

"You wouldn't dare kill me in front of all these people. Surrender," Bear demands, "and you will be judged for your crimes by your fellow citizens."

Oh, Bear. His idealism crushes me.

Evander drops his flamethrower and it clatters to the ground. Still, no one is bold enough to run and take it from him.

"I surrender," he says. Around me, a cheer goes up, hundreds of people shouting in triumph. Am I the only one who hears the mocking in his voice?

"The people will show you mercy," Bear says loudly, addressing the whole crowd, "even though you showed them none. You will be bound by your words and held to justice in a court of law."

Evander falls to his knees and holds his arms out wide. I tense, every fiber in my body screaming that something is horribly wrong.

"I promise."

Bear holds his red fist over his head. For the first time, he takes his eyes off Evander, looking triumphantly out at the crowd.

I see the moment unfurl almost before it happens. Evander drops his hand to his side and reaches into his jacket. I charge forward out of the crowd, screaming.

"BEAR!"

I drop to my knees and pull up my weapon. Bear's eyes go wide as he sees Evander's movement. Evander points the Bolt in his hand at Bear in the same moment as I pull the trigger on mine.

My shot connects with Evander's shoulder. His arm flies up and the Bolt falls from his hand. He crumples to the stairs in a heap, and I charge up the steps to stand over him, just in case he dares raise his head again.

Bear stares at me.

"Did you kill him?"

To show mercy is to refrain from harm when someone deserves protection. To show grace is to refrain from harm when someone does not deserve protection. Bear showed grace to Evander. The Dragon didn't deserve the life that Bear offered him.

I bend over Evander and put two fingers to his neck. No pulse. "One more second and it would've been you lying here."

A shadow crosses Bear's face. He shakes his head, disappointed—in himself? In Evander? *In me?*

"Thanks," is all he says.

26 — VALE

The mood in the room rapidly deteriorated after Moriana left. If finding her already here with my mother after I was dragged into the room in handcuffs hadn't told me she had betrayed me, the fact that she was so eager to follow my mother's orders as soon as they were out of her mouth confirmed my worst fears. My father was still protesting the directive, insisting Corine call an emergency meeting of the full OAC board before medical staff around the Sector began administering the vaccine. The argument was getting increasingly heated, with legislators joining in on both sides, when drone footage showed the Sector Sunflower erupting in flames on the vidscreens.

"Look at that," Evander stood, pointing at the screen. "We're arguing over vaccines while all hell is breaking loose on the steps of Assembly Hall."

"It's not just any vaccine," Philip said. "A final vote should be taken before the program is implemented."

"We need to take direct action against these rebels." Evander's voice rose. "How does nobody understand this?"

"Evander," my father stepped toward him. "I have given specific orders, remember? We are not going to have a repeat of Round Barn on the steps of the Assembly Hall."

"Madame Orleán," Evander appealed to my mother, whose glassy eyes were having trouble focusing. She said nothing, and Evander shook his head. "I'm going to stop this madness." He pushed back his chair and motioned for two black ops soldiers stationed at the door to follow him.

Nobody protested, but nobody followed, either. And nobody, not even General Aulion, expected Evander to open fire on the protesters with a flamethrower on the steps of the capitol building. In the ensuing chaos, everyone seems to forget about me.

"What the hell does he think he's doing?" Philip's voice is harsh.

"Chancellor, what are your orders? Should I take control before this gets out of hand?" Aulion strides to the door, ready to follow Evander.

On screen we watch as the black ops fire repeatedly into the crowd, providing cover for Evander as he sprays jets of fire at innocent protesters. My heart seizes.

Philip looks shell-shocked. Two of the cabinet members stand and shout as Evander unloads another jet of fire onto the protestors.

"You have to do something!"

"Stop him!"

"We can't have SDF soldiers firing on OAC operatives. That will only contribute to the chaos," Philip says, his voice edged with anger and frustration. He looks to Corine. "What should we do?"

But my mother is transfixed by the action on the screen and doesn't respond. Just then, someone comes hurtling from the crowd and launches himself onto one of the soldiers. In a flurry of motion, the two black ops are down and Evander is knocked to his knees. The drone cameras zoom in, and I can see Bear and Eli disappearing back into the crowd.

"Dispatch two squads to keep the people away from Evander." Philip gives the order through his C-Link. "Send a third to get him out of there."

But before the soldiers can reach him, Evander's facing Bear on the steps of Assembly Hall.

"Who is that kid?" someone mutters.

We all watch, silent as a grave, as Evander drops to his knees. And then, as if in slow motion, I see Evander's hand reach into his jacket and pull out a Bolt. I start forward only to have one of the guards grab my arm. *He's going to shoot Bear.* But then Evander crumples, falling face forward. Thirty seconds later, drones confirm his death. I suck in a breath as I watch Remy charge up the steps to stand over Evander's body. Then Bear is beside her, and, with a jolt, I realize it was Remy's Bolt blast that had taken Evander down.

General Aulion speaks up after a beat. "We need new orders, sir."

"Retrieve the bodies and dispatch medevacs." Philip's voice is flat.

"What's happening?" Corine's face is shining with sweat. The peyote is taking effect, though it seems I'm the only one who's noticed anything strange: rapid eye movement, damp hairline, agitation, and difficulty articulating concepts. Everything she tries to say comes out slightly off kilter. She clutches at her gut. I wonder if she's nauseous. The Sector sanctions the use of certain mind-altering substances including marijuana and MDMA, but psychedelics haven't been in common use since before the Famine Years. If my mother has any idea what's happening to her, she's certainly not talking about it.

"Are you ill?" Philip asks. She waves him off.

"No," she says, straightening her spine and taking a long breath. "Just a little stomach upset. I think it was that tea." Her eyes are just a little too wide as she stares at the vidscreen. She seems unable to look away.

My father watches her carefully, glancing between me and General Aulion. *What's going on with her?* The question on his face is clear.

Corine turns, tearing her eyes away from the vidscreens, and looks around the room. She holds a glass of water so tight her fingers turn white as she surveys our faces.

"Falke—what—how did that—"

Corine doesn't waver, doesn't falter. She doesn't stumble over her words, and she certainly doesn't question her own decisions—at least not aloud. I meet Philip's gaze but try to keep my expression blank.

Demeter speaks in my ear. "I'm going to begin recording the audio in the room. I've connected to ONN and hacked their firewalls. Get her talking, and the recording will go live on every available Okarian News Network feed."

Thank you, Demeter.

Everyone in the room shifts uncomfortably. I can tell the officials present don't want to cross my mother, don't want to acknowledge her strange behavior, and don't want to second guess my father. Except for General Aulion, who watches her for a long moment and then strides over to where I'm standing and grips my arms in an iron vise, pushing me back up against the wall.

"You know something," he snarls. "Tell me."

"You have more answers than I do." I stare him down. "Think it's time to tell the chancellor you countermanded his orders in Windy Pines?" I whisper.

"General Aulion, please step back." My father's voice booms in the room. It's the most commanding he's sounded all morning. "We have already questioned Valerian enough for now. We must attend to the protest outside."

I lock eyes with my mother, past Aulion's shoulder, who reluctantly takes two steps away from me. I direct my speech to Corine. "There are five thousand innocent Farm workers on Rue Jubilation, and the man in charge of managing those very Farms just went out there with OAC operatives and committed murder. With a flamethrower. How can you sanction that?"

She begins pacing, running shaking fingers through her hair every few moments, glancing around the room, then settling her gaze on me. "Evander was controlling a dire situation."

"A situation you and Evander created."

"You understand nothing, Vale." She waves me away.

I keep my composure, but I can tell hers is fraying at the edges.

"Evander was controlling a situation. And Remy Alexander is a traitor to our ideals, our ideas of the Sector, the ideas the Sector was founded on, everything we stand for. Whoever that boy is, who is he? Why does he matter? Of course he matters, he organized this whole disaster, he brought these people to our city, he brought these people, these—"

"That boy has a name, Mother. Like the workers Evander incinerated at Round Barn. Like the ones he just killed outside."

"Corine, you're not well. Why don't you sit down? What's going on?" My father places a comforting hand on Corine's shoulder, pushing her toward her seat. But she rounds on him.

"I'm perfectly well. I don't need to sit. I'm fine."

"You don't seem fine."

"Fine! I am perfectly fine!" she shouts and pushes him away, then looks around the room as if she'd just done something horribly embarrassing. She regains some composure and says in a more normal voice, "I apologize to everyone here. I think I've been drugged." She turns and faces me. The lines on her face soften and twist, her mouth hangs open, brows crease.

Aulion swivels and lunges, slamming me against the wall. "What did you do?"

But my mother jumps forward and pulls Aulion from me. The general, surprised, steps back immediately, putting his hands up. He wouldn't dare cross Madam Orleán, even when she's clearly compromised.

"Vale." Corine puts a hand to my cheek, looking at me with a mix of horror and morbid curiosity. I can only imagine what the drug is making her see. "Did you poison me?"

I look at my father. His skin turns a green-white color.

"No."

"Then what? Who? Why do I feel this way?"

"Corine, tell us what's happening so we can help you." My father tries to put his arms around his wife, but she jumps away from him as if his fingers are talons biting into her skin.

"It's not poison," I say. "You're going to be fine in a few hours."

Philip turns to me. "What's going on? Did you do this?"

I step forward. This is my chance.

"You're live, Vale," Demeter whispers in my ear.

"You want information from me, and today I am prepared to answer your questions. You want to know who organized the march, who hacked the Olympia broadcast feed, who's on the inside feeding information to the Resistance." I look around, addressing everyone in the room. "The people of the

Sector are outside lining Rue Jubilation, and we are tired of your lies. We are Outsiders, Farm and Factory workers, Okarian citizens. We are your friends, colleagues, servants, research partners. We serve you in bars and restaurants, and even in your own homes. I am one of them. I stand with the Resistance."

Corine backs up, but I step forward, maintaining our closeness.

"Vale, you can't, you wouldn't do this to me, what are you saying?"

She picks at something on her sleeve, stares at it as if it is the most fascinating thing she's ever encountered, and then looks up, startled at a shadow on the wall.

Aulion steps forward again, but I glare at him and my father holds up a cautioning hand. I continue. "But I have some questions of my own. And I would appreciate it if you told the truth for once. I deserve the truth from you, Mother."

Philip steps between us and puts his hands on my shoulder. "I don't like this game you're playing, Vale."

I push his hands off. "This isn't a game. People are dying outside. I think you might be interested in some of the answers, too."

"Let's start with an easy question." I grab my mother's hand, a conciliatory gesture that feels foreign but necessary. "Did you or did you not order an OAC security guard—one of your select black ops—to open fire on all nine students and Professor Hawthorne three years ago in what has since been called the SRI Massacre?"

"Vale, how did you—of course—you don't understand—"

"The Outsiders didn't have anything to do with it?"

"No," Corine whispers.

"The SRI Massacre?" Philip shakes his head in disbelief and runs a hand through his hair. "It isn't possible." But one glance at Corine's face does it for Philip. He knows his wife too well, and she can't hide under her many masks while in the thick of a peyote trip. He looks at Aulion, whose face remains impassive, his non-reaction more telling than a denial.

"Mother, say it. Tell me you gave the order. Tell me it was you."

"It was necessary, *essential*, to prevent Hawthorne from carrying out his research; it would have ruined everything."

"Professor Hawthorne had just discovered something big, right? What was it? Why did he deserve to die?"

"Corine," Philip interrupts my questioning. "I don't believe this. Tell me he's gone crazy. Tell me it isn't true." But it's obvious to everyone in the room that Corine's the crazy one right now.

A long silence is interrupted by her whimpering, a sound that fills me with an odd mixture of sadness and encouragement.

"It's true." She pulls her lips into a thin line. "I had to do it because of the database."

"Tell me about the database."

"Old world seeds breed old world disease," she mutters. "I couldn't let it happen."

"Let what happen?"

Corine turns away from me to face the vidscreens, where hundreds of marchers have gathered on the steps of Assembly Hall and medevac trucks swarm the plaza below. "No," she says. "I won't say any more."

"Corine, we deserve to know everything." My father looks around the room. "How many of you knew about this? About the massacre?" Heads shake. Some stand and back away. The energy in the room shifts. Where once no one questioned Corine's decisions, now everyone is looking to Corine for answers. Philip turns to Aulion. "Were you a part of this?" He takes a step toward the general. "Have you known all along?"

Aulion doesn't respond, but Corine speaks up. "No one else knew. Not about the massacre. Not at first." She looks distraught, her eyes wide, her mouth downturned, as she watches the action on the screens. Drone footage shows the sheer size of the crowd, as they pan in and out. The streets are full as more and more citizens from around the city have joined the protest. The sounds of the march are even audible from inside the building.

"Is it true Aran Hawthorne came upon a discovery that could have brought back hundreds of Old World seeds?"

She says nothing. I realize I need to take a different approach. I cross the room in a few quick strides, and to my surprise, no one tries to stop me. At my mother's side, we survey the aftermath of Evander's devastation.

"People died today. Just like they did at the SRI. Just like at Round Barn." I pause. "What do you see?"

"I see skeletons," she says so only I—and Demeter—can hear. "And everything feels like death."

"Did you cause that?"

"Maybe. No. No, I didn't do that. Evander did."

"Would you have stopped him?"

"No."

"Why do you think all these people are here in our city?"

"I don't know."

"They want the freedom we have. The Farm workers. Would you give it to them?" No response. "What did you just tell Moriana to do?"

"I told her to go ahead with the genetic modification program." She turns around, locking eyes with my father. "Philip, you agreed with me, right? We discussed it together, we planned everything together."

"Not everything." He shakes his head.

I cross back over to sit beside her, marveling that Aulion hasn't hauled me away yet. "Did you order one of your soldiers to murder Remy Alexander and Soren Skaarsgard while they were being held prisoner?" I ask.

"I haven't murdered anyone!" she spits out, swiveling around to get in my face. "I've saved thousands from famine, and my research will only continue to reduce the chance of disorder and chaos."

"I heard you, Mother. I was there when you gave the order."

"No." She looks up at me, her eyes clouded in confusion. "That night? How?"

Finally, Aulion's had enough. He pushes me away from Corine. "Arrest him for poisoning Director Orleán."

"I told you my mother has not been poisoned. She's ingested a large dose of peyote, a psychedelic drug. It's harmless."

Philip steps in front of me. "Stand down, Falke. You're not authorized to make that decision."

"Not authorized?" Aulion spits. "It's my *job* to make these decisions. Your son poses a danger to the Sector, and if you don't see that, then you are blind."

Corine shakes her head. "Let him be." Once again, Aulion steps back, his mouth set in a grim line. The only person he'll answer to is my mother.

I continue. "Did you or did you not authorize Evander Sun-Zi to unleash flamethrower airships intended for agricultural clearcutting on actual human beings, Farm workers?"

"I had to do it," she says.

"What happened to Cara and Odin Skaarsgaard?"

"Falke removed them."

"I never knew about the massacre," Philip interjects, a note of disgust in his voice.

I turn to him. "You never knew? But you knew about Cara and Odin, didn't you? And what about Elijah Tawfiq's parents? Did you know about them? You knew about the modifications program. You were responsible for torturing Remy. You knew enough."

Now Philip falls silent, sinking back into a chair, refusing to meet my eyes. His face is pale as he runs unsteady hands down his face.

Corine cries out, babbling incoherently, clamping her hand over her mouth and pulling her legs up toward her chest as if she's seen a ghost. She looks like a terrified child. I turn back to my father. "Someone needs to order the SDF and Watchers to stand down and let the protest continue in peace. Chancellor, it's time for you to make your choice. Do you stand with the people or not?"

There's a long silence in the room, the only sounds coming from the screens. The protesters assembled on the steps outside are chanting: *We are the Sector, we are the Resistance, we are the People.*

"Chancellor," Olivia Renteria breaks the silence. "Your son is right. We must do something."

"Dad." My voice is softer now. "You need to address the marchers."

"If you don't go out there, I will," Olivia says.

My father pushes himself to his feet, raising his head to address the room.

"General Aulion, you are removed from duty effective as of this moment. Laika, call a medic for my wife." He nods toward one of the soldiers standing at the door. "Remove Vale's handcuffs. And someone find him a shirt." He meets my eyes. "Get your boots on. We're going out there together."

27 — REMY

I stand over Evander's body, staring into his glassy eyes, feeling nothing. On the street below, people shout, move, run. The noise swells inside my ears, drowning all thought, all emotion. My Bolt hangs in my hand, forgotten. The thin, white scars are still visible from when I carved my initials into his cheeks at Round Barn. There are bruises and open wounds all up and down his face, neck, and exposed arms from where the Bolt blast hit him. It gives me a deep sense of satisfaction to know that he will never hurt anyone again, will never breathe his flames down on innocent people. But the triumph I thought I'd feel is missing.

I walk away, down the stairs, back into the crowd. *This is for his death.* I imagine throwing his body into the blazing inferno that was the Sunflower. *This is for his rebirth in the calm trees, in the peaceful sky, the gentle waters of a stream.*

I look around for Eli. I never saw what happened to him. Is he safe? In a daze, I wander. Over the city's speakers, I hear voices but I can't focus on them right now. Medevac trucks descend from all directions, helping to care for the wounded and clean up the bodies. The soldiers and Watchmen continue to contain the crowd and prevent escalation. But beyond that, none of them seem to know exactly what to do. I look to see if anyone needs help, but the violence has abated. Many of the marchers push forward onto the steps of Assembly Hall, while others stay behind, cradling bodies or helping the wounded. I scan the plaza for people I know, hoping against hope that none of my friends have fallen. I have no conception of time passing—has it been five minutes or an hour?

"Remy!" someone screams. I hear the voice as if from miles away, or underwater—muted and slow. I pull my Bolt up, looking for a source of danger. But there's nothing. A tall figure with a black hood and a small crossbow barrels toward me. Instinctively, I point my weapon at the charging figure—and then realize it's Osprey.

"Check the astrolabe," she pants, stopping short at my side. "We need to find Vale. Corine just confessed, and Demeter pushed it out to the whole city. She's high as a fucking cloud. Did you not hear?" I stare at her as though she's speaking another language. It dawns on me slowly what she's talking about: *our plan worked.* It all worked. Soo-Sun must have gotten the peyote to her, she started hallucinating, and Vale pressed her for the truth. About everything.

Corine confessed.

Hundreds of fire drones are buzzing around the inferno that once was the Sunflower, unloading thousands of deep, low-frequency sound waves into the maelstrom, trying to calm the flames. The beats resonate in my chest like Vale's drumming at the vigil.

Osprey puts her hands on my shoulders.

"Remy, are you okay? We need to check the astrolabe. It's time to find Vale."

I nod. Mutely, I pull the semispherical piece of glass from the pocket of my jacket. I press my fingertips to the bottom of the glass, and, looking inside, I see thirteen pale green dots lit up, one for every acorn.

"Let's find a grassy spot. We need to plant it." Osprey leads me to the bottom of the observation hill. "Put it on the ground." I set the half-sphere into the dirt. As I do, dozens of fine lines sprout from the center of the astrolabe, forming a sort of strange compass or clock. Osprey kneels next to me. Some of the lines are bright and clear; others are so fine they're almost impossible to see. By planting it on the ground, Osprey told me, you allow the astrolabe to connect to the mycorrhizal network in the area.

"It's a lot easier to read when there's only one or two acorns activated," she mutters.

Apparently, reading an astrolabe is like reading a compass, a topographical map, and a radar system, all meshed into one. The acorns give off their own signals, so you can always track them. But in order to take advantage of the astrolabe's full capabilities, you have to plant it. Then, it will connect you to all the trees and plants rooted into the mycorrhizal network. With the astrolabe on the ground, you can find forests, grassy plains, streams and rivers, caves and cliffs. And if you want to find one of the acorn pendants, the astrolabe will guide you to them in the quickest way possible.

It seems like magic to me, but Osprey insists it's all based on real ecology. Around ninety percent of all plants exist in symbiotic relationships with fungi, creating a mycorrhiza, a partnership in which the fungus colonizes the roots of the plant. The fungal network enables larger, more established plants to help out young seedlings by sharing nutrients, but it also allows plants to sabotage each other. Just like people, I think.

"How do I know which one is Vale?" I ask, my voice hoarse.

She looks up at me, her brows knitted together. "You have to feel it, remember? Vale has the *quercus lyrata* acorn." She touches her finger to one of the lines and gestures to me to do the same. *Only with a physical connection to the astrolabe can it guide you*, she said yesterday, when she was teaching me how to use it. I can feel it pulsing gently, rhythmically, under my fingertip. "Each acorn has a unique beat. Of course, I don't know for sure who's attached to which acorn unless I've been told. Vale's pendant used to belong to Chan-Yu, and he told me when he passed it on to Vale." She smiles as if we were in the middle of a forest clearing with a babbling stream nearby, instead of in a war zone surrounded by dead bodies. "This acorn's beat sounds like a dance song."

"The mycorrhizal networks produce beats?"

"Not exactly. The astrolabe converts the frequencies unique to each acorn—that are inaudible to human ears—into a beat that we can feel and understand. It's more like an interpretation than a reproduction. Use your finger to drag this line to the center." I do as she tells me. The pulsing beat stops, and the green lines on the astrolabe fade. Now, only a glowing light on the edge of the instrument remains.

"The astrolabe is pointing straight into Assembly Hall."

"We won't be able to get in the front," I say. "It's too high-security."

"Let's go in the back, then."

"Where's Soren?" I ask, my mind still foggy but feeling more focused now that I have a goal, a target. *Find Vale.*

"He's waiting for us. Come on."

She leads me to one of the maple trees where Soren is waiting.

"Remy," Soren says, pulling me in close to him, folding me into arms that are twice the size of mine. "Are you okay?"

"I'm fine," I say, but I'm not, not really. "Where are the others?"

"Eli's with Bear, helping the wounded. Firestone just landed and the Director is on the ground. Miah and Rhinehouse are still in the sky. Let's find Vale."

With Soren and Osprey behind me, I run on the outskirts of the roundabout that encircles the Sunflower. We duck into a back alley, built for delivery trucks, that leads behind Assembly Hall. The astrolabe is trying to guide me into the glass, inside, but I have to find an entrance. The arrow seems to move as I move, though, shifting until it's no longer pointing inside the building but dead ahead, in front of us.

"Did he leave?" I pull up short. "Did he leave the building?"

Osprey puts a finger to the astrolabe.

"Maybe. The thing is a lot more helpful out in the Wilds." She shrugs, as confused as I am. "Let's find out."

"He could be running away," Soren says. "Maybe he escaped the Control Room after Demeter broadcasted Corine's breakdown. Maybe Aulion is chasing him."

We run past the back entrance to Assembly Hall, but the astrolabe is no longer pointing inside. We run around the city, taking as many shortcuts as we can, jumping fences and cutting through buildings, until the astrolabe emits an audible hum.

"We're close," Osprey says. "Do you see him?"

We're by Lake Okaria, approaching the main marina on a smaller street known mostly for its abundance of fancy nightclubs. I don't see Vale. I don't see anyone, really, save for a few citizens walking along the buildings, perhaps heading to work or running errands. I wonder if they missed the broadcast, if they realize everything in Okaria is about to change.

The astrolabe glows right at the front, telling us to head straight. Right onto the docks. We run forward. Where is Vale? The hum only grows louder.

"Vale!" I shout, Bolt charged and ready in my hand.

Soren points to our left. "I saw something over there. Movement." We head toward a large sailboat with a clean canvas sail and a hull so shiny it glistens in the sunlight. Brand new, it appears. I see it then, too: a figure, tall and broad, but I can tell by the man's grey hair it's definitely not Vale.

He turns slightly but doesn't seem to see us. Now I recognize him: Falke Aulion. The man who hit me when Soren and I were held prisoner in a building not far from here. It's strange to see him out here all alone without soldiers surrounding him. It doesn't make sense.

Osprey lets out a low growl as she, too, recognizes him. I don't know what her history with the man is, but I know one of the things that brought her and Soren together so quickly was their shared hatred of General Aulion.

"Lucky us." Osprey slides the charge on her Bolt to the highest setting and hits the capacitor to reload. Soren doesn't respond. He pulls his knife from its sheath.

Osprey sets off down the street, her footfalls silent, and Soren is right behind her. I keep a distance behind them, my ears and eyes pricked for any sign of Vale. Aulion's coiling up the dock lines, pulling the covers off the smaller solar fiber sails, and lashing lines down along the hull. *What is he doing?* I wonder, but even as I ask myself the question, the answer dawns on me.

He's running. And he has Vale's acorn.

He doesn't know it's a tracking device. There's no way he could know we've been led here thinking we were following Vale, thinking we were rescuing him. He has no way of knowing that, if he wanted to escape, all he had to do was toss the acorn pendant in the gutter.

I hang back as Osprey and Soren break into a jog, tucking the astrolabe into my pocket. I'll be there for backup if something goes wrong. But this is not my fight.

The boat Aulion's fussing with is a hybrid air and water sail. They call them Hydroaire boats, or Hydras for short, and it must have cost a pretty penny. A few wealthy citizens, mostly government officials and entrepreneurs, have made it the fashionable, luxurious item of choice. If Aulion's making his escape, he's chosen a good vessel: this ship will easily carry him across Lake Okaria and further, as far as he wants to go. Powered by wind and sun, he could make it around the world without stopping.

"Where's Vale?" Osprey calls as we approach the dock. Aulion's head jerks around, and he drops the line he's holding and pulls his handheld Bolt from his pocket in a blur of movement. He says nothing, just hits the capacitor and immediately takes aim at Osprey, who jumps out of the way. His shot misses, hitting the cobblestone where her feet were a second ago.

"Vale's dead," Aulion says with a touch of scorn. My breath catches in my throat and my heart stops. My mind goes blank for a few seconds, empty and dull, filled only with a white rage, before a single thought pops into my head: *He's lying.* I don't know this for sure, but I can't let this old man's demented words distract me now. "I killed him myself."

"Wrong answer." Osprey and Soren both pull up their weapons at the same time, aim, and fire. Aulion leaps off the dock and ducks behind the Hydra's hull for cover. He pops back up a second later and fires—this time at me. I leap to the side at the last second, hitting the ground, rolling my shoulder against the hard brick surface as I jump back to my feet.

Soren and Osprey charge the boat. Realizing he's outnumbered and trapped, he frantically moves to prepare for launch. As they draw closer and it becomes clear he's not going to finish by the time Soren's blade pierces his throat, he bails. He leaps over the other side of the hull and sprints down the dock. *He's fast for an old man*, I think, as Osprey stops chasing him for a minute to set her feet. Aulion spares a second to glance behind him and sees Osprey aim her crossbow. He dives behind another boat, this one smaller, at the last second, and her shot flies harmlessly into the hull of the ship. But this gives her and Soren time to gain on him. I follow them, keeping pace from a distance, staying on the brick, my weapon charged and set to a low-power setting. I won't deprive Soren and Osprey the pleasure of killing him, but I won't hesitate to shoot if it means preventing him from getting away.

Osprey pulls another short arrow from her pack and nocks it in place as she and Soren round the boat to where Aulion is crouching. When he hears their footsteps approaching, he scrambles to his feet and sprints to the end of the dock. *What the hell is he doing?* I wonder a half-second before he leaps with all his might off the end.

Soren throws his knife as hard as he can. I hear a sharp *thwang* as Osprey fires off another arrow at Aulion's back. The knife and the arrow fly true. The knife hits Aulion in the small of his back, and the arrow embeds itself in his shoulder, thrumming like a musical note as he plunges into the dark water.

Suddenly all is still.

Neither Osprey nor Soren move. I run up to the dock, standing just behind them, and together the three of us walk to the end of the wood plank, where the general's body is slowly sinking under the small, gentle waves.

We stand there like that, watching the lake pull him under, the morning sun bright in our eyes as it glints over the waves. It's not long before all that's visible is a few bubbles and dark water.

"Should we try to get the acorn back?" I ask.

Osprey shakes her head. "His body will wash ashore in a few days. We'll get the pendant back then."

Soren stares at the water. After a long time, he speaks, before turning and leading us away.

"I always knew he was a coward."

Summer 5, Sector Annum 106, 8h52
Gregorian Calendar: June 25

I motion toward the main entrance of the capitol building, but my father doesn't move. Outside, thousands of voices rise and fall.

"How can I face them?" His voice is barely audible, and he stares at the door as if it opens onto a lion's den.

"You're still the chancellor of the Okarian Sector. It's your duty to address the people."

"We've failed them." He turns to me. His face contorts and his red-rimmed eyes shine with unshed tears. "I failed you. My whole life I tried to live up to my father's expectations, tried to be the father to you that I missed after he died. Now—" He stops to compose himself.

"I wish I could have met him."

"So much of who I am is because of him. He died young, but his legacy lived far longer than he did."

"I saw a picture of the two of you at The Waystation."

"The Waystation?"

"You don't remember?"

"No."

"It's Kanaan Alexander's house. There's a painting of you on the wall. You're holding your father's hand, and Brinn is sitting on Kanaan's shoulders. You're all standing in front of a newly planted live oak."

"I never knew Kanaan's place was called that," he says. "I only remember being there once or twice before my father left and then—"

"Never returned," I finish for him. "Your father died, but I still have a father." I grip his arm. "Dad, you need to go through those doors and address the crowd as the duly elected leader of this nation. We all choose our own paths. You taught me that. It's time for you to choose."

"I chose wrong."

"You have a new choice ahead of you. There are some things you can't take back. Memories that might haunt you forever. But right now none of that matters. The citizens of Okaria need you to make the right choice."

He nods, draws in a long breath, squares his shoulders, and palms open the doors.

As soon as we step outside, Okarian News Network drones swarm around us. I scan the grounds of the capital complex for signs of Remy. *Where is she?* There are too many people. Bear had organized five thousand marchers, but there are many more in the streets now. Whether curiosity seekers or concerned citizens, the ranks of the protesters and onlookers have swollen until people line the grassy knolls surrounding Assembly Hall and fill Rue Jubilation as far as the eye can see.

As soon as the drones are in position to record and broadcast the speech, my father raises a hand and a slow hush falls over the crowd.

"Fellow citizens. I see before me thousands of hardworking people from all quadrants of the Sector. You have marched on the city in peaceful protest of unjust laws and lives unfairly taken. Under my rule and those who came before me, we have deviated from the principles upon which the Okarian Sector was founded. Here, today, on Rue Jubilation, I want to assure everyone that each of you—whether you labor on our Farms or work in a factory town, whether you are a student at the Academy or a researcher at the OAC—is entitled to the full rights and privileges of citizenship. There are no exceptions." He pauses and glances toward me. "Before I walked out here, I gave the order for the Watchers to hold their fire, the SDF to stand down, and for the OAC Security Directorate to be disbanded. All law enforcement and defense forces are charged with ensuring the safety of everyone assembled here today as well as that of every citizen throughout the Sector. Again, that means no exceptions.

"Many of you have heard the leaked broadcast of my wife's—Corine Orleán's—confession. As you can imagine, this is a very difficult time for my son and me. A doctor is with her, and she is under sedation. While I cannot speak to the crimes to which she has confessed, I know she must face the consequences of her actions. The College of Deans and the College of the People will be calling for hearings, and, no doubt, criminal charges will be filed against her."

Cries rise up from the crowd, but he hushes them. Even now, it is remarkable how much sway my father holds with the people. Many, I'm sure, find it hard to believe—as I did for so long—that my parents could be capable of any crime, let alone the ones my mother confessed to on live broadcast.

"As for me," he continues, "I, too, must take responsibility. Whether by turning a blind eye, by being complicit in behaviors I knew were morally indefensible and that contravened the laws of this nation, or by violating the spirit of our founding principles, I have wronged you all and will, no doubt, also face the legal consequences of my action or inaction. That is why I can no longer serve as your chancellor."

In the history of the Okarian Sector, no chancellor has ever resigned during his or her term. The crowd stills, as if all of the oxygen has been drained from the air.

"As of this moment, I resign my position, and until such time that the Board of Directors can nominate and the Colleges can confirm someone to guide the transition to a newly elected leader, I hereby appoint my son, Valerian Augustus Orleán, to the position of interim chancellor."

"What? No!" I step backward, stunned. Even when I was leading the Seed Bank Protection Project, I had no aspiration to climb the political ladder. "You can't—"

A camera drone moves quickly to zoom in on my face, and a roar of voices rises up from the streets below: "Valerian! Valerian! Valerian!"

"Citizens!" My father raises his arms to calm the crowd. "Even while Corine and I lost our way, beguiled by the false promises of wealth and power, our son was steadfast and honorable. He stood by his friends and by his fellow citizens. At every turn, he made the difficult decisions necessary for true leadership. Even as I step aside, ashamed of my actions, I must tell you that this moment is one of the proudest of my life." He turns and gestures for me to take his place before the crowd.

I step forward with absolutely no idea what to say. The last thing I want to do is deal with the Board of Directors or the Assembly. I'm done giving speeches. I'm done being a public figure. I want to go home—wherever that might be—and hold Remy close, laugh with my friends, drink Firestone's disgusting swill. I don't want—

"Vale," my father says. "They're waiting."

I clear my throat and look out on the crowd. I see a flash of red and then another. Just like at Windy Pines. All along Rue Jubilation, I see fists raised, some swathed in red, others held high. I look back at my father. He gives me a slight nod, as if to say *get on with it.*

"Citizens of Okaria," I begin. "I pledge to uphold the Articles of Incorporation and fulfill the duties of interim chancellor until someone more experienced and more suitable can take my father's place. In the meantime, I will do my best to ensure this is a peaceful and speedy transition. To prepare for the days ahead, I will be counting on the assistance of General Kofir Bunqu and Dr. Cillian Oahu, whom many of you will remember as Director of Research of the OAC."

I'd like nothing more than to be done and get my father back inside, but I know I'm not finished yet.

"As interim chancellor, my first order is to dismantle the OAC inoculation program my mother authorized earlier today. This program, which few of you will have heard about, would have locked in through genetic alterations the physiological modifications made by the MealPaks—which were, in themselves, effectively preventing people from realizing their true potential. The parasite that has caused so many to fall ill was a modified organism that the OAC created. It was not created or disseminated by Dr. James Rhinehouse. It was distributed through the MealPaks and the disease it causes has always been curable. Watchers will be dispatched to clinics and hospitals to ensure medical personnel cease giving the inoculations that were ordered this morning and that all materials related to the inoculation program be returned to OAC headquarters immediately. Medical personnel will be working around the clock to administer the true cure which kills the parasite and relieves all symptoms. And those who have already received the injection, though we hope there will be few, will be closely monitored and cared for."

I start to wind the speech up when it hits me. As long as I'm in office, there are two more things I should do. I search the crowd for Remy's face, but I don't see her. There's no sign of Soren or Osprey, but right down front, I see Eli and Bear helping tend to the wounded.

"Given the events of this morning, I hereby rescind all previous executive orders declaring members of the Resistance traitors to the Sector. Full and unconditional amnesty is granted to all citizens who joined the Resistance, allied with them, or gave aid and comfort to them—" I think of Lyle from Windy Pines and wonder where he's being held "—and no charges shall be brought or punitive actions taken against any non-citizen Outsider living in the Sector or in the Wilds who worked with Resistance members. Further, whether in office or not, I pledge to work to eliminate the mandatory MealPak program as soon as is feasible. With help from our Outsider allies and friends in the Resistance, we will make every effort to reintroduce diverse food crops into the dietary marketplace and to allow each citizen to choose whether or not to eat foods that have been genetically modified to enhance or change physiology in any way."

With that, the protesters erupt in cheers, and scarves flutter up and down the avenue.

The nightmare is ending. I marvel at how quickly a moment can shift, how soon our lives can change. But then I think back to the long days, the sleepless nights, the walks through the woods, the puzzles, the fighting, the casualties. It only seems instantaneous because it's happening now, and the pieces on the chessboard were already in place.

Checkmate.

I hold my hands up again, and the crowd quiets. There is yet one more thing to say. I close my eyes, hoping I remember the words of one of Gabriel's poems.

"Arise, arise!

The world is alight

Morning dawns and seasons change

We gather, we harvest."

There is a long pause and then the crowd erupts, the cheering so loud I can barely hear my own voice.

I turn to my father. "Let's go." I take him by the elbow and usher him back through the doors and into Assembly Hall where two lieutenants stand guard, looking between the two of us.

"Please arrange for a squad to escort my father back to his office. Make sure he is under guard, but that he is afforded all due respect."

Despite the speeches they surely just overheard, the two soldiers look to Philip first for approval. "Vale is in charge now," my father says and bows his head, abdicating any further responsibility.

"I'll send for you as soon as I speak to the board," I tell Philip, as he's escorted down the hall.

"I'll be waiting."

I hear a pounding on the doors nearby. I glance behind me. To my astonishment, a bearded face is pressed against the glass doors to Assembly Hall. I stare. The pounding continues. After a few moments, I walk over and palm open the doors.

"Congratulations!" Miah walks in and claps me on the back. His face is haggard, but he's obviously as relieved as I am. I half expect him to have a bottle of champagne open. "The youngest chancellor ever. How do you feel?" Behind him, the smaller but much more intimidating figure of Cillian Oahu stands flanked by four Resistance fighters I vaguely recognize.

"Move." Cillian pushes past Miah and through the open doors.

Finally, I think. *Somebody who knows what they're doing.* And god knows I'm not talking about Jeremiah Sayyid.

Osprey and I stand in the doorway and watch as Jahnu helps Kenzie lower herself into a chair by the fireplace in the yard. Vale waits until she's comfortable and then adjusts a footstool and helps prop her swollen feet on it. Soren stands nearby with a tall glass of lemonade made with lemons right off a tree from the greenhouse.

"Jahnu neglected to tell me he was a ten-pound baby," Kenzie groans. "Or that twins run in his family." She takes the lemonade. "Still there are advantages to being waited on hand and foot by all these handsome men. Almost makes this whole pregnancy thing worth it." She holds the glass up like a toast.

Jahnu's face breaks out into one of his brilliant smiles and he goes to add another log to the fire. His limp is barely perceptible, and his doctor says one more operation and he'll be good as new. Since he and Kenzie have moved back to Okaria, he's taken a position as a mathematics teacher at the Academy. Kenzie says since she's gone to work in Rhinehouse's lab, he fusses over her so much, she's inclined to stay home until the babies are born. "SRI daycare will be great, but if Rhinehouse doesn't lay off, I'm going to set up a playpen in his office. Serve the old man right."

"Do those guys know women have been having babies for millennia?" Osprey says with a snort. "They treat her like she's going to break."

"You going to cast aside their ministrations if you get pregnant?"

"Are you kidding? I'll have them on rotation, so I'm never without a cadre of attentive minions."

"I don't doubt it." I hand her a bucket filled with ice. "Set this on the table."

She looks at the ice as if heartbroken. "Where's the wine?"

"Miah's unloading it from the Sarus. Vale told me his father helped them pick out several cases from the house cellar."

I follow Osprey into the yard, my arms laden with two trays overflowing with fresh fruit and sliced vegetables and dips. "How do you feel about Philip getting time off for good behavior from his Farm work?" Kenzie asks. I remember how important Kenzie's friendship was to me after Soren and I returned from the Sector prison. Our many late-night talks and her soul-warming hugs have helped me overcome and understand some of the trauma.

I look at Vale who's now headed around back to help Miah unload the Sarus. He senses my gaze, turns, and flashes a smile. "I don't know. Seems he got off light but I guess it's okay. By all accounts, Philip's been learning a lot from his time spent on the Farm rotation. Another five years, and he'll be skilled enough to take over the Ile de Orleán vineyard and winery."

"Philip Orleán wants to make wine?"

I shrug. "Seems a better vocation than politics. At any rate, I'm glad he's not in prison, for Vale's sake. Having one parent locked away is hard enough."

My thoughts darken for a moment as I stare into the flames of the big bonfire we've got going. Justice works in mysterious ways. Even with Evander and Aulion dead and gone, and Corine locked up in Sector prison, the ache I feel for all those I lost hasn't abated. The holes they leave don't ever go away. Rather, it seems, we simply expand the walls of our hearts, until it's riddled with craters in some places and yet bursting with life in others. The absences make themselves known every day. But that doesn't make the presences any less real.

"And when are we going to get to see the famous vineyard?" Osprey pulls a sweater around her shoulders and takes a chair next to Kenzie.

"You can go anytime you want. I've only been when Philip's not there. I'm not ready to see him quite yet."

"Has Vale visited his mother?" Kenzie asks.

My voice is quiet. "Yes. Only once. He offered to take Miah with him so they could both see Moriana, but Miah said no." I start rearranging the table to make room for more platters. "I think he's finally ready to move on. Saara's trying to fix him up with some doctor she works with."

"Saara, huh? She doesn't seem like the matchmaking type."

"When she's not slaying parasites or sweeping Eli off his feet, she's a regular sweetheart."

"Sweetheart? I still remember that day at the vigil. The phoenix on her back gave even me pause."

I poke Osprey with my elbow. "Come on, you could take her."

"My fighting days are behind me. Now, I'm a woman of leisure."

"Hardly," Soren interjects, pulling up another chair. "Wayfarers never relax."

"I'm relaxing now." She frowns. "Or I would be if I had a glass of wine in my hand. What's taking Miah so long?"

We're hosting our first party at the Waystation, a combination Fall Equinox celebration and homecoming for all our friends—at least all those who can make it. Some have new responsibilities; so much has happened since the day of the march, it sometimes makes my head spin.

Vale held the post of interim chancellor for less than a week. He'd nominated Dr. Oahu to take his place, but because of her history with the Board, several members were reluctant to consider her. That didn't last long after she and other Resistance members from the capital—including Kenzie's and Jahnu's parents—told their stories before members of the Security Committees from both the Colleges of the Deans and of the People. My dad was called to testify, and Eli spent hours retelling his story as the investigation into the SRI massacre was reopened. Even Rhinehouse testified, albeit reluctantly. He's back to his cranky old self, telling the legislators he had lives to save and didn't have time for politics. "They've got enough old bones to pick over," he'd growled. "They don't need mine."

And of course Soren and I testified about our time as prisoners. We were all questioned for weeks. It was exhausting. Bear was grilled on his role at Round Barn and on hijacking Sector trains and organizing an illegal march. But with Linnea's prodding, now back at work at the ONN, Bear became a media sensation and she had reporters following him around for weeks, even going with him and Rose to visit Luis, who was on his way to a full recovery. Now, Bear can't keep up with his fan mail. He's one we'll miss today since he's with Zeke and Reika, still working on supply lines to move produce throughout the Sector. Linnea testified at length about the virus she infected Eli with. Charges were considered against her but eventually dropped when she volunteered to work on the urban farms as Sector service. Bear thinks Linnea's aiming to run ONN someday. Maybe even merge the sports network with the news network. Some things never change, and Linnea's ambition is one of them.

"Hey!" Firestone shouts, rolling a barrel around the corner of the house. "Valerian, get your lazy ass over here. I've got somethin' for you." Soren shakes his head dramatically and puts a finger to his temple, pretending to pull the trigger. Firestone stares daggers at him. "Don't you give me that, you ingrate. You think you're too good for my homebrew?"

"No, Mr. Firestone, your honor. Certainly not."

"Good, 'cause this isn't even made with my recipe." Another man, distinguished looking with silver at the temples, rounds the corner pushing a second barrel. "Meet Jamison Fitzpatrick. Co-founder of the Firestone Fitzpatrick Brewing and Aeroship Design Company."

"Fitz!" Vale's eyes go wide. He's carrying a case of wine in his arms and gestures toward Firestone with an elbow. "How the hell did you get mixed up with this miscreant?"

"Hello, Vale. I only associate with miscreants—everyone else is too damn boring. By the way, we could use some seed money if you can see your way to investing in our little venture."

"See why I like him?" Firestone laughs. "He's a man who is willing to get right to the point."

Vale fakes a businessman's tone: "Give me your sales pitch."

Jamison and Firestone exchange a glance, then Jamison says, "I don't know about no sales pitch, but our wise advisors Elijah Tawfiq and Jeremiah Sayyid have assured us that we will be rich men in under a year's time. They say they know people with deep pockets. I'm assuming that's you."

Vale shakes his head. "Let me taste what's in that barrel first."

"Eli should be arriving soon with the Phoenix in tow. May have a few other friends with them—I'm assuming that's okay with our hosts." Firestone rolls the barrel to a stop at the edge of the food table and starts fussing with the pour spout.

Osprey perks up, bringing her empty glass over to the barrel. "Well, shall I begin? Someone's got to taste test, after all."

And so the party begins. After an hour of drinking, the final guests arrive fashionably, yet uncharacteristically, late, their arrival marked by the elegant *whoosh* of a sleek airship setting down on the water by the dock.

I hear the distinctive bass voice of Kofir Bunqu—"After you"—and see Soo-Sun and Chan-Yu emerge and step down onto the dock. They head straight to the food table where they unload some boxes and bags brought in from Okaria.

Last time I saw Onion and Chan-Yu, both were quiet, self-confident men whose faces hid more than a hint of sadness. There are no traces of sadness now, and it's clear that their friendship is far more intimate than either of them led us to believe.

"We're so glad you're here." I have to stand on tiptoes to kiss each one on the cheek.

"We couldn't celebrate the Equinox without you," Vale adds.

My father's resonant voice breaks through the various conversations as he stands. "Now that we're all here, everyone get something to drink—Jahnu, get Kenzie some more lemonade." He waits as glasses are filled, and then everyone gathers around him. With his back to the fire and the evening sun shimmering through the trees, he looks every bit the wise poet that he is. He raises his glass. "To old friends and new, and on behalf of Remy, Vale, Eli, and me, welcome to the Waystation."

"Now, I know you're hungry, but I hope you will forgive a writer for a bit of speechifying. I've been working these past months on a poem for this gathering, but I must admit, I came up short. I'm still getting used to not having my muse by my side, but looking out at each of you, I am inspired anew." We hold our glasses up, ready to drink, but he continues. "Since I couldn't find the appropriate words, Eli threatened to wrest my duties from me and make the host's toast so we could all just get on with it. But no luck, I'm afraid."

Eli looks around at the group and shrugs his shoulders as if to say, *I tried.* "You're not planning to recite the *Illiad* or some other epic poem you've memorized," Eli says, and my father—our father—arches a dark brow at him.

"I'm going to recite a line from another Sector poet, a line that has touched me deeply. Remy told me about it, and although it is short, I believe it symbolizes what we've all been fighting for: a yearning for truth and honesty in our dealings with each other and with our environment. And so, with no further ado …" He raises his glass and tips it toward Bunqu. We all turn toward the general as my father says, "Listen to the forest floor."

A sheepish smile spreads across Bunqu's face, and then he turns, eyes wide with alarm, as Chan-Yu begins to recite the full poem:

"Listen to the forest floor
Smell the flowers blooming near
Taste the rivers running clear
Touch the wind in the trees
See the starlight burning bright
Breathe in, breathe out, the beauty of the earth."

Bunqu laughs. "I knew I never should have shown you that doggerel. I'm going to have to lock up my plasma from now on."

Chan-Yu shakes his head. "I can pick any lock you've got, my friend."

The general then turns toward me and shakes his finger. "And you, Remy Alexander, are forbidden from ever again reciting any of my poetry to your father."

"Listen to the forest floor!" Eli raises his glass high, and finally, we all drink.

"Too bad Rhinehouse couldn't make it," Vale whispers, wrapping his arm around my waist, as everyone heads toward the table. Jahnu and my father help Kenzie up out of her chair, and Miah holds an arm out for one of Saara's friends, as if he's an Old World courtier.

"I'm not surprised, but I'm sure Soren is disappointed."

Vale chuckles. "I think he sees plenty of the old man. Rhinehouse has him and Osprey running all over the Wilds collecting botanical samples. Maybe they'll be the next Kanaan and Gold. Exploring far beyond the bounds of our little world."

"Would you like to go exploring?" I look up at him.

He pauses and looks out into the distance. "Maybe someday. Right now, I'm just happy to be home."

Acknowledgements

We'd like to thank all our readers. There is nothing more exhilarating for an author than discovering people you don't even know have fallen in love with the characters and the story that you've worked so hard to bring to life. Thanks to every one of our friends and fellow authors who have read early drafts, or who have helped us understand the science we explore, or who have given us an encouraging word. With three co-authors, we each have particular people we'd like to thank.

From Amira—To the brilliant friends, talented authors, and wonderful people who answered questions my questions, gave us ideas, and supported me on this strange and wild journey, with particular thanks to Kristen Scheitler-Ring, Alexander Augustyn, Prashant Parmar, Lori Buchanan, Jason Finkes, Daryl Rothman, Jess West, Nillu Nasser Stelter, Jonathan Paul, and many more. A special shout-out to the fir trees of Oregon, the green rolling hills of California, and the sweet blue water of the west coast for keeping me grounded and inspired as we brought these books to life.

From Elena— I want to thank the sun, moon, and stars for always reminding me what's truly important. Much appreciation to friends who supported me on this sometimes arduous and many times enlightening journey of writing books. Special thanks to my sister and co-author Amira who pushed me through to the end and who daily inspires me with her passion and perseverance.

From Kristy—Thanks to my mom and my two sisters, to Jason for putting up with me, to my steadfast friends who believed in me, and to my amazing daughters for helping me bring Remy and Vale to life, and for going along with me on the most gratifying adventure in *my* life.

About the Author(s)

K. Makansi is the pen name for the mother-daughter writing trio of:

Kristina Blank Makansi

Born and raised in Southern Illinois, Kristina has a B.A. in Government from University of Texas at Austin and an M.A.T. from the College of New Jersey. She is founder and publisher of Blank Slate Press, an award-winning imprint, now part of Amphorae Publishing Group, and also helps self-published authors on the path to publication through Blank Slate Communications. She has published *Oracles of Delphi*, an historical mystery set in ancient Greece.

Amira K. Makansi

Amira is a wanderer of foot and spirit. After earning her bachelor's degree in History from the University of Chicago, she traveled across America and France to learn the trade of winemaking. While traveling, she found her passion for writing through her journal and her blog, The Z-Axis. She is never far from her notebook or journal, and nearly always has a glass of wine or beer in hand. When she's not writing, she can be found with purple hands in the wine cellar, or out walking among the grapevines or live oak forests of the Central Coast in California. Amira has big projects in the pipeline after Seeds, so stay up to date and find her online at https://artz3.wordpress.com/.

Elena K. Makansi

Elena graduated from Oberlin College where she concentrated on food justice and food system politics. She won several writing and poetry awards and scholarships and attended the Iowa Young Writers' Studio and the Washington University Summer Writers Institute as a teenager. Elena works as an editor and a cover designer for Blank Slate Communications. As a vegan, she is interested in intersectional food justice politics and animal rights—and in seeking the nirvana of the perfect avocado. Visit her website at elenamakansi.com.